Help Us! Great Warrior™

WHASAHAAH?!
SNORT

BOOM! BOX™

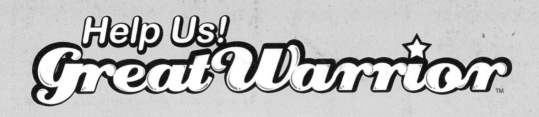

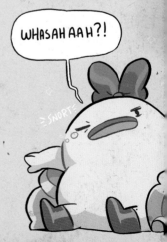

BOOM! BOX™

HELP US! GREAT WARRIOR, March 2016. Published by
BOOM! Box, a division of Boom Entertainment, Inc. HELP US!
GREAT WARRIOR is ™ & © 2016 Madeleine Flores. Originally
published in single magazine form as HELP US! GREAT
WARRIOR No. 1-6. ™ & © 2015 Madeleine Flores. All rights
reserved. BOOM! Box™ and the BOOM! Box logo are trademarks
of Boom Entertainment, Inc., registered in various countries
and categories. All characters, events, and institutions depicted
herein are fictional. Any similarity between any of the names,
characters, persons, events, and/or institutions in this publication
to actual names, characters, and persons, whether living or dead,
events, and/or institutions is unintended and purely coincidental.
BOOM! Box does not read or accept unsolicited submissions of
ideas, stories, or artwork.

A catalog record of this book is available from OCLC and from
the BOOM! Studios website, www.boom-studios.com, on the
Librarians Page.

BOOM! Studios, 5670 Wilshire Boulevard, Suite 450, Los
Angeles, CA 90036-5679. Printed in China. First Printing.

ISBN: 978-1-60886-802-5, eISBN: 978-1-61398-473-4

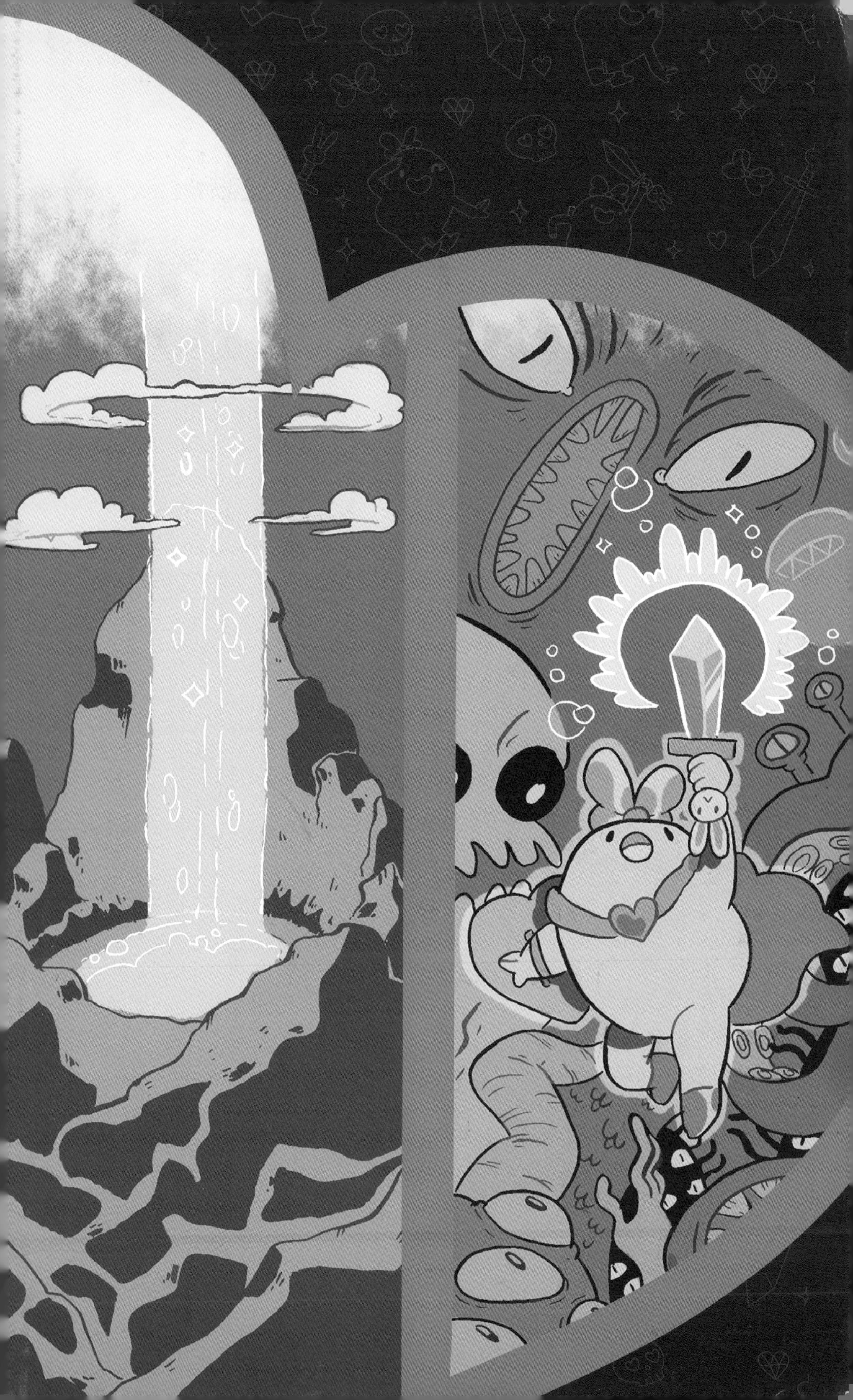

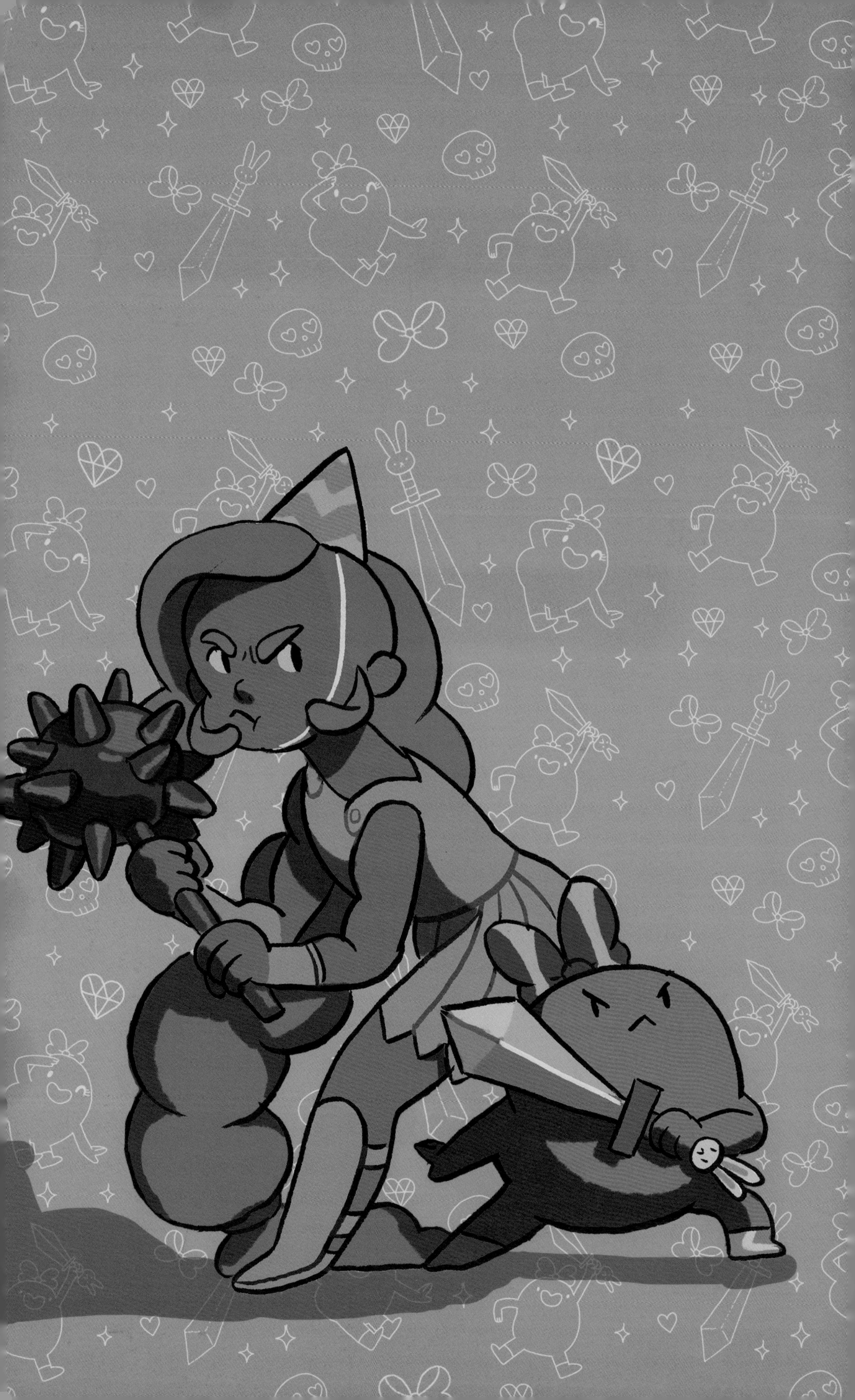

Created by MADELEINE FLORES

Written & Illustrated by
MADELEINE FLORES

Colors by
TRILLIAN GUNN

Cover by
MADELEINE FLORES

Designer
MICHELLE ANKLEY

Editor
SHANNON WATTERS

Special thanks to
Jack Qu'emi Gutierrez
and Zach Marcus

Chapter
One

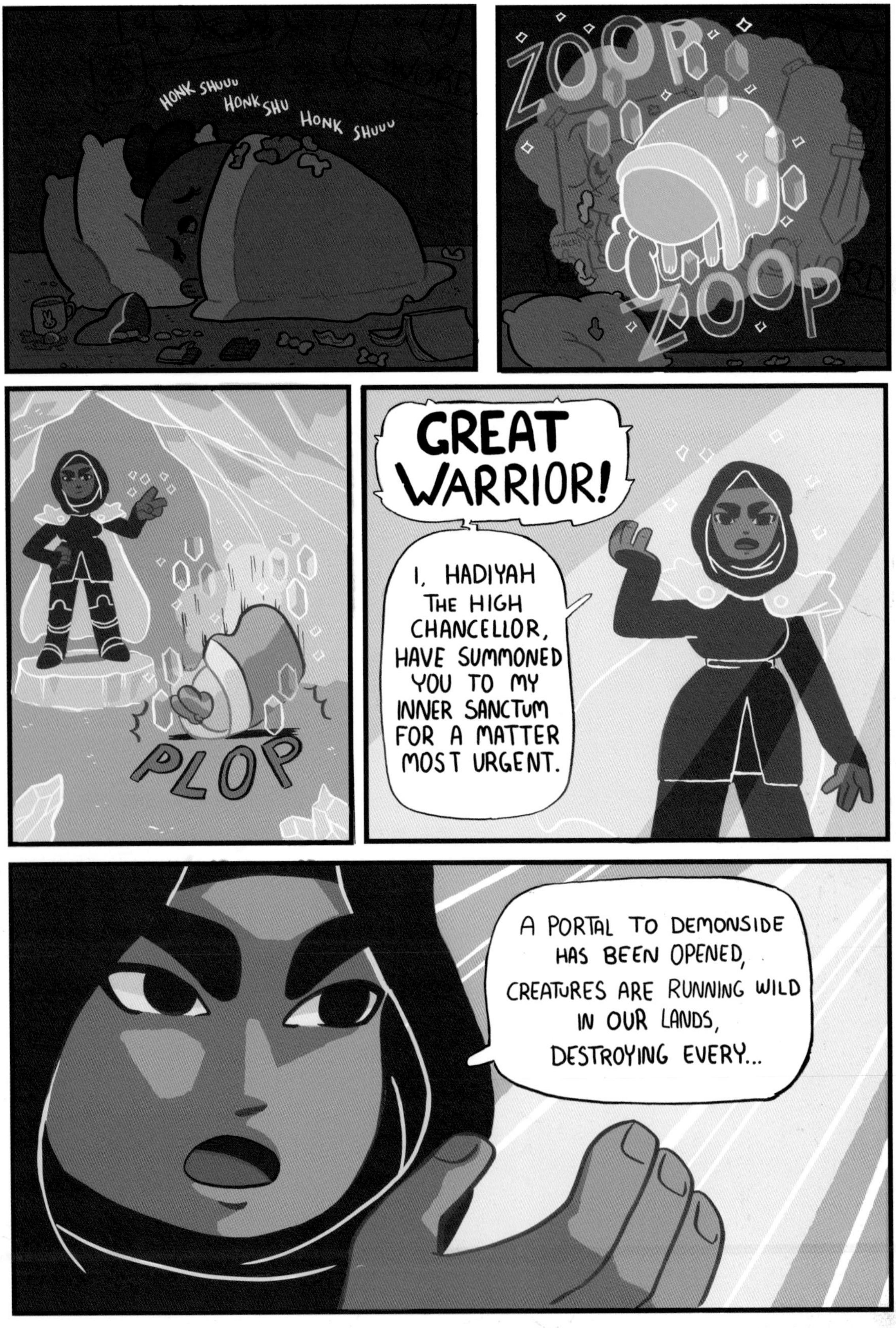
HONK SHUUU
HONK SHU
HONK SHUUU
ZOOP
ZOOP
PLOP
GREAT WARRIOR!
I, HADIYAH THE HIGH CHANCELLOR, HAVE SUMMONED YOU TO MY INNER SANCTUM FOR A MATTER MOST URGENT.
A PORTAL TO DEMONSIDE HAS BEEN OPENED, CREATURES ARE RUNNING WILD IN OUR LANDS, DESTROYING EVERY...

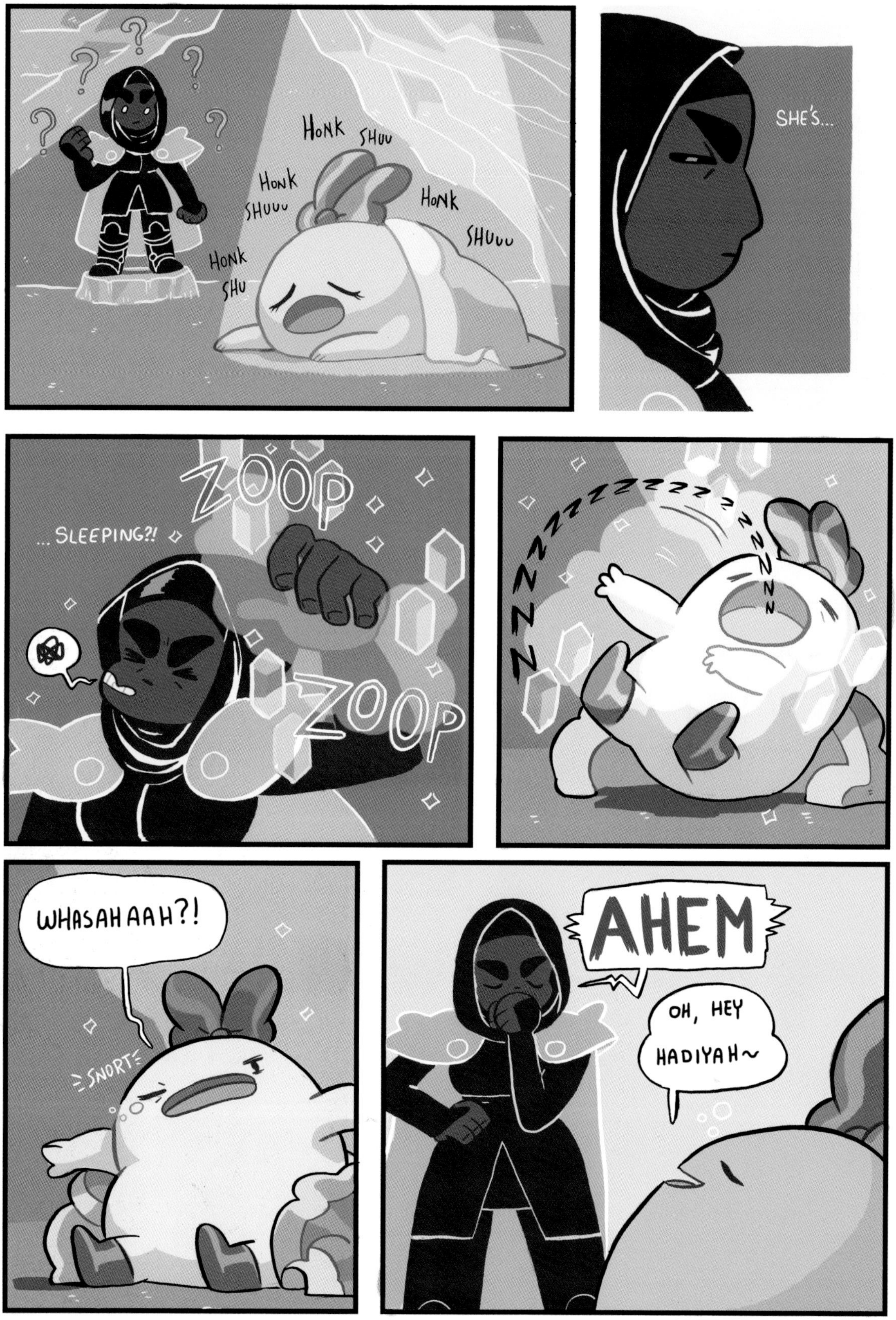
HONK
SHUU
HONK
SHUUU
HONK
SHUUU
HONK
SHU
SHE'S...
...SLEEPING?!
ZOOP
ZOOP
WHASAHAAH?!
SNORT
AHEM
OH, HEY HADIYAH~

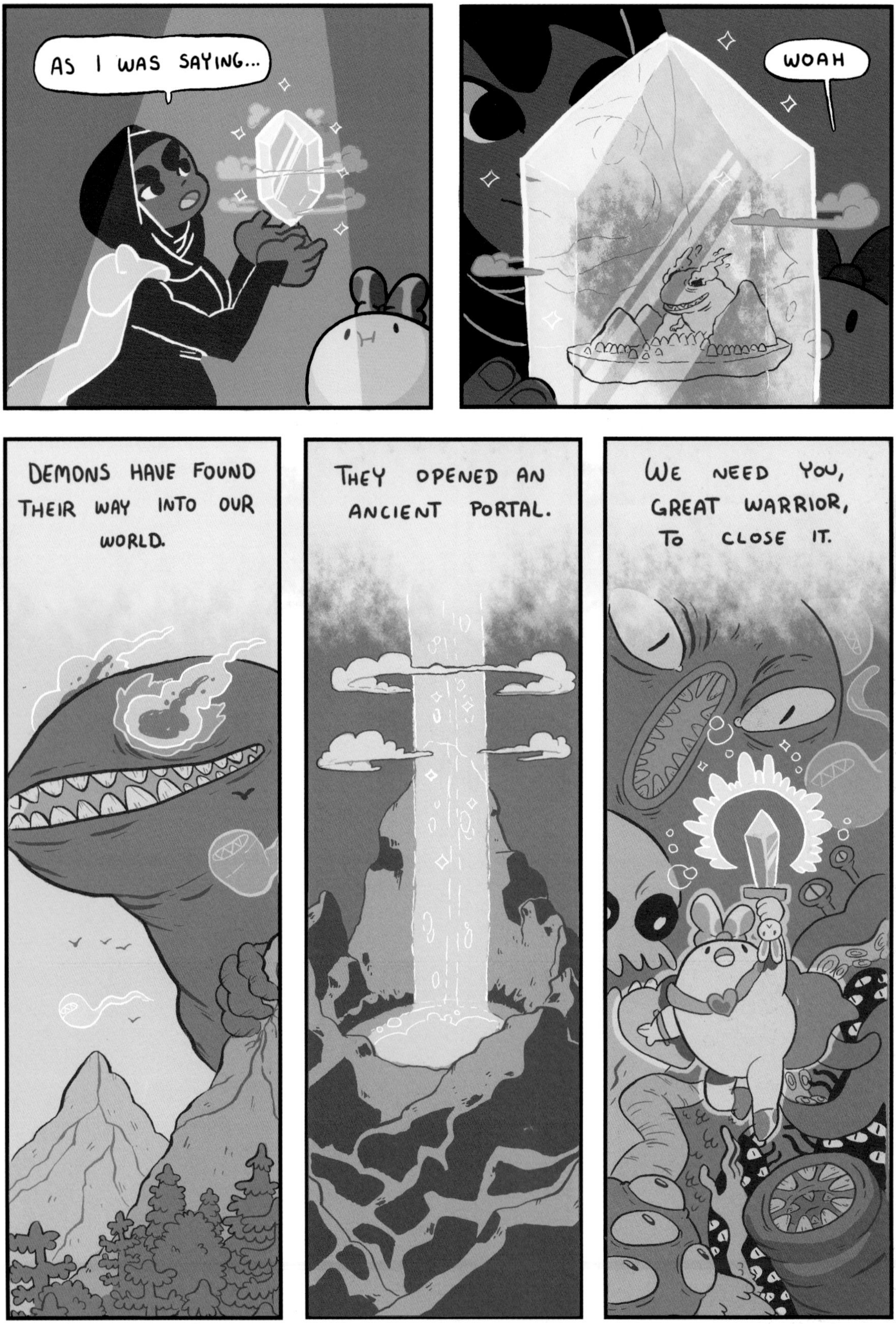
AS I WAS SAYING...
WOAH
DEMONS HAVE FOUND THEIR WAY INTO OUR WORLD.
THEY OPENED AN ANCIENT PORTAL.
WE NEED YOU, GREAT WARRIOR, TO CLOSE IT.

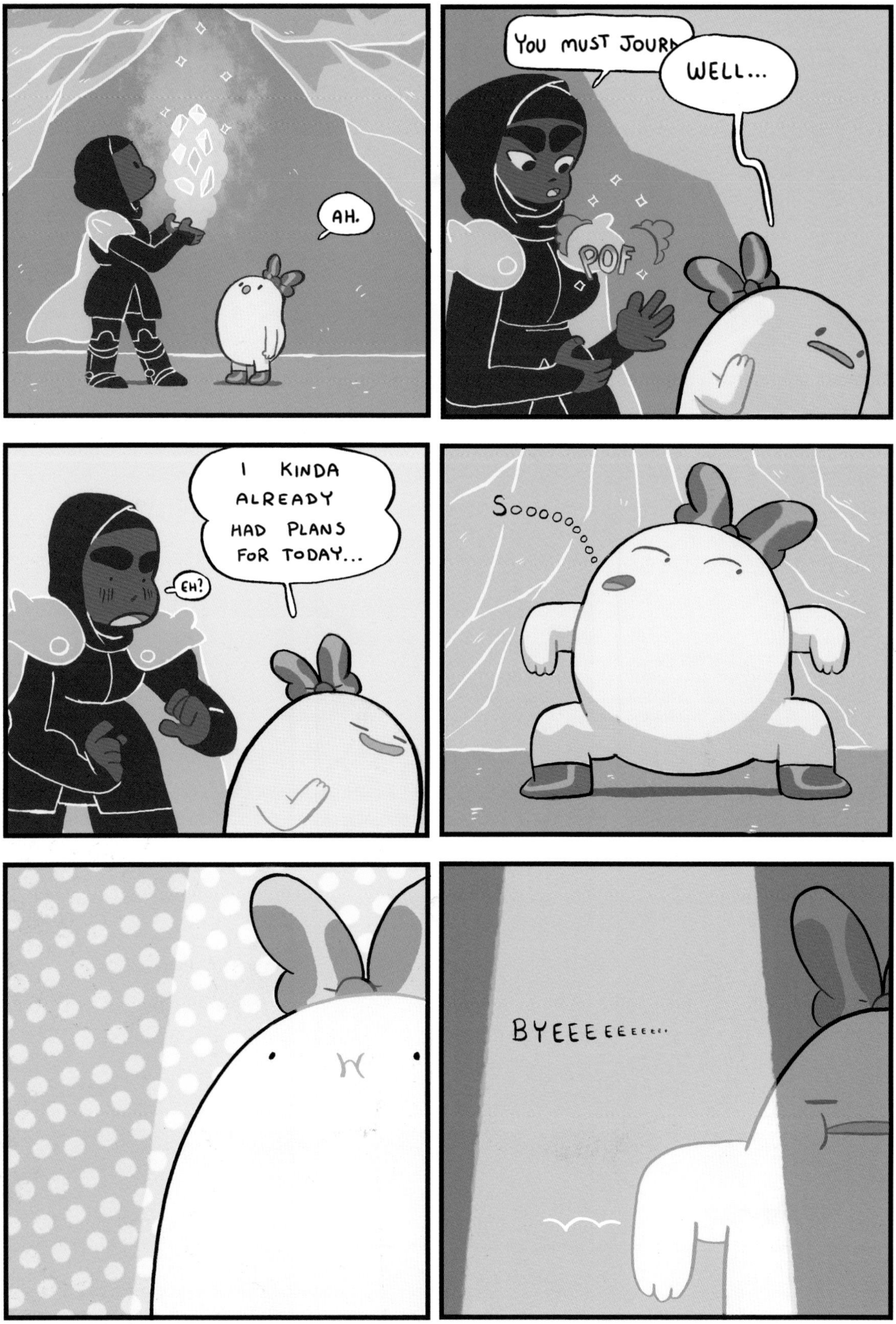
AH.
YOU MUST JOURN
WELL...
POF
I KINDA ALREADY HAD PLANS FOR TODAY...
EH?
SOOOOOOOOO
BYEEEEEEEE...

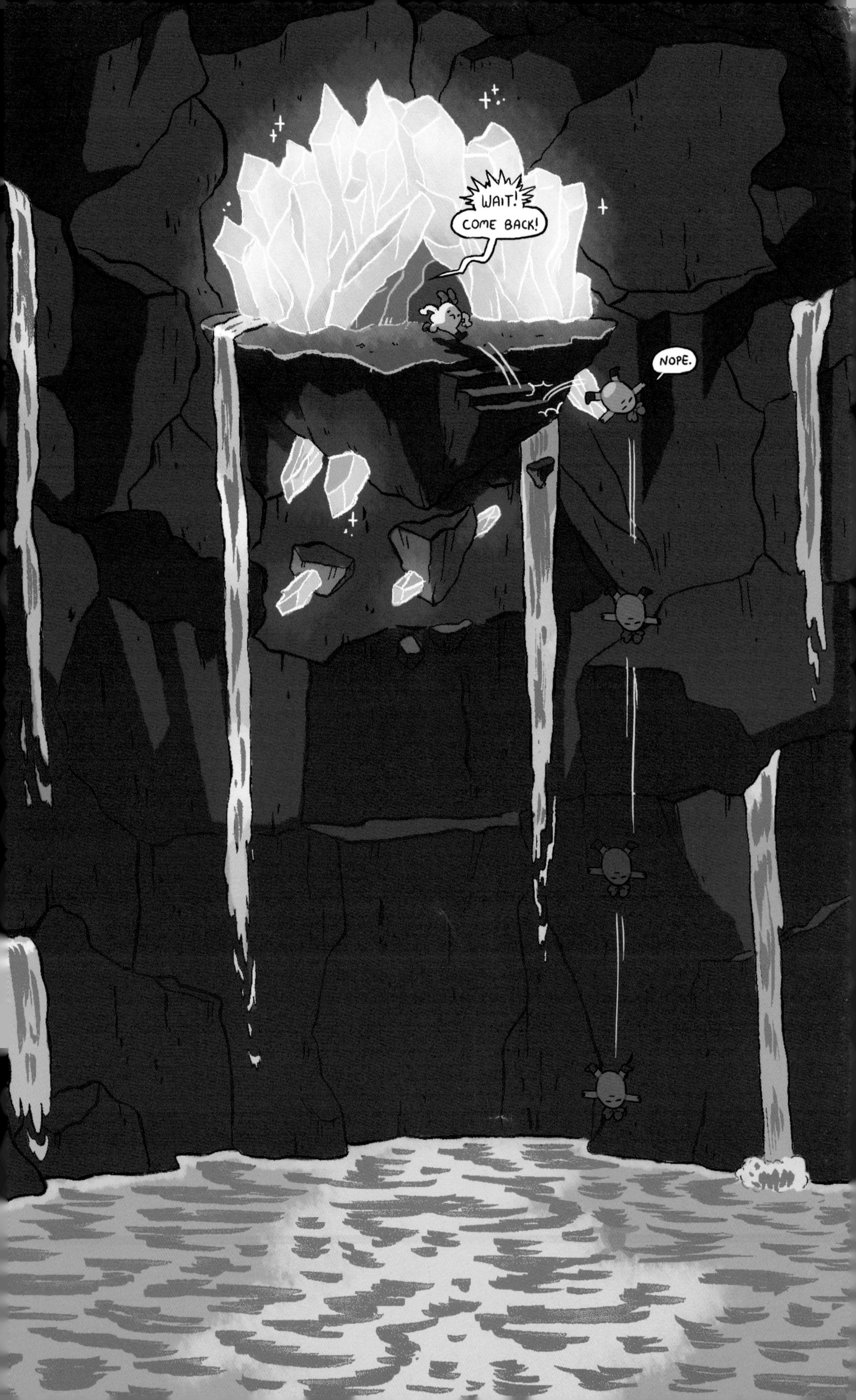
WAIT!
COME BACK!
NOPE.

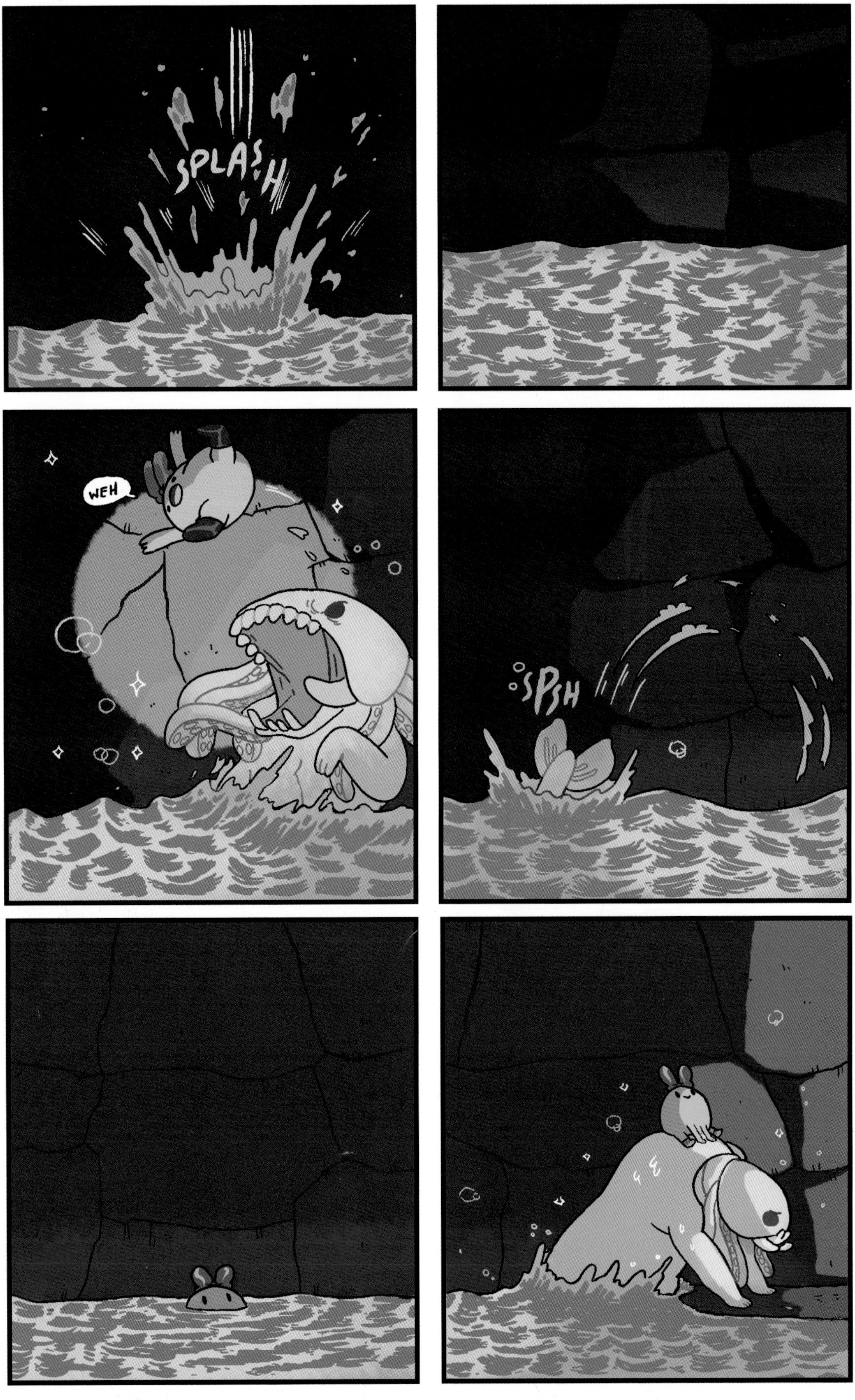
SPLASH
WEH
SPSH

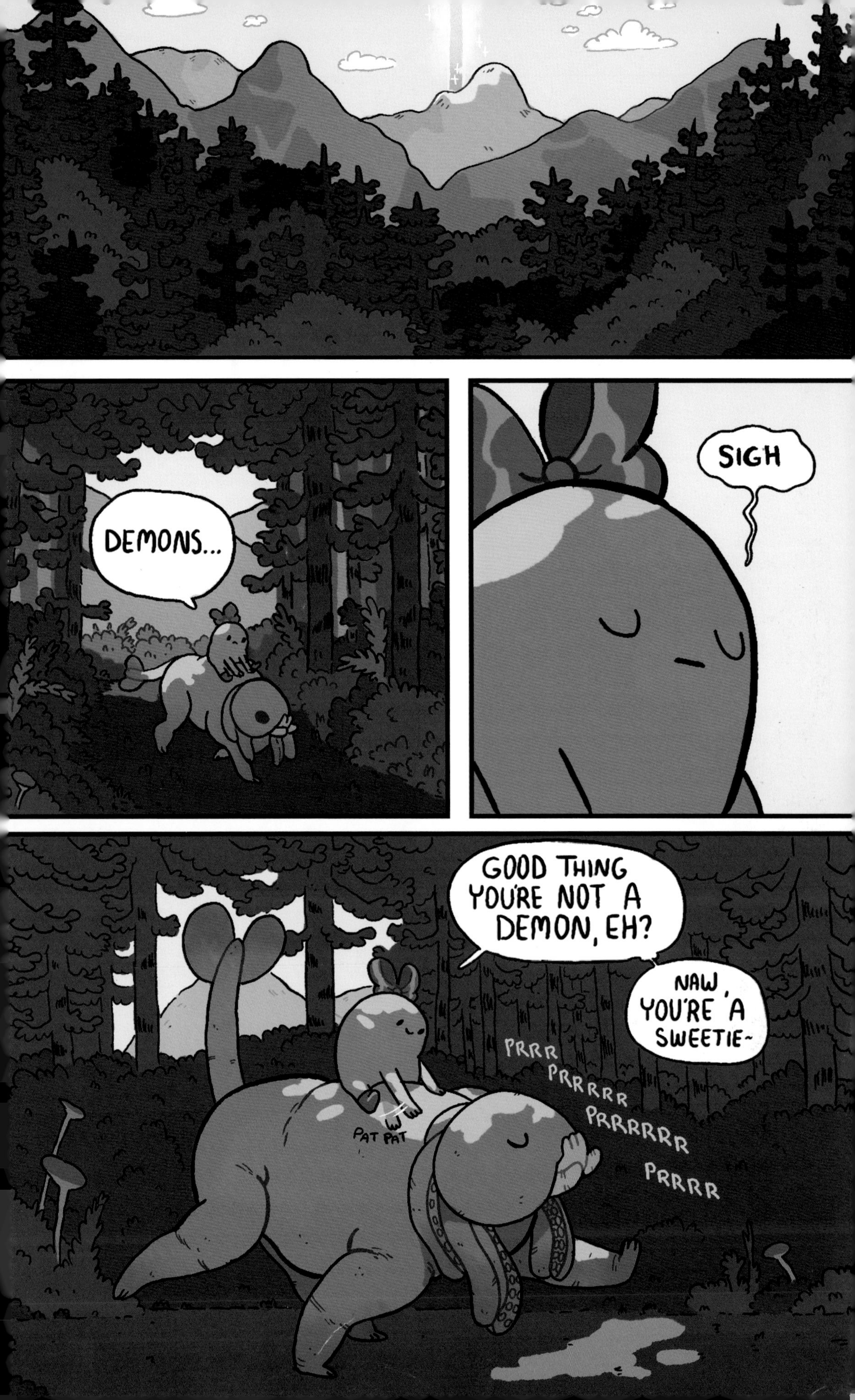
DEMONS...
SIGH
GOOD THING YOU'RE NOT A DEMON, EH?
NAW, YOU'RE A SWEETIE~
PAT PAT
PRRR
PRRRRR
PRRRRRRR
PRRRR

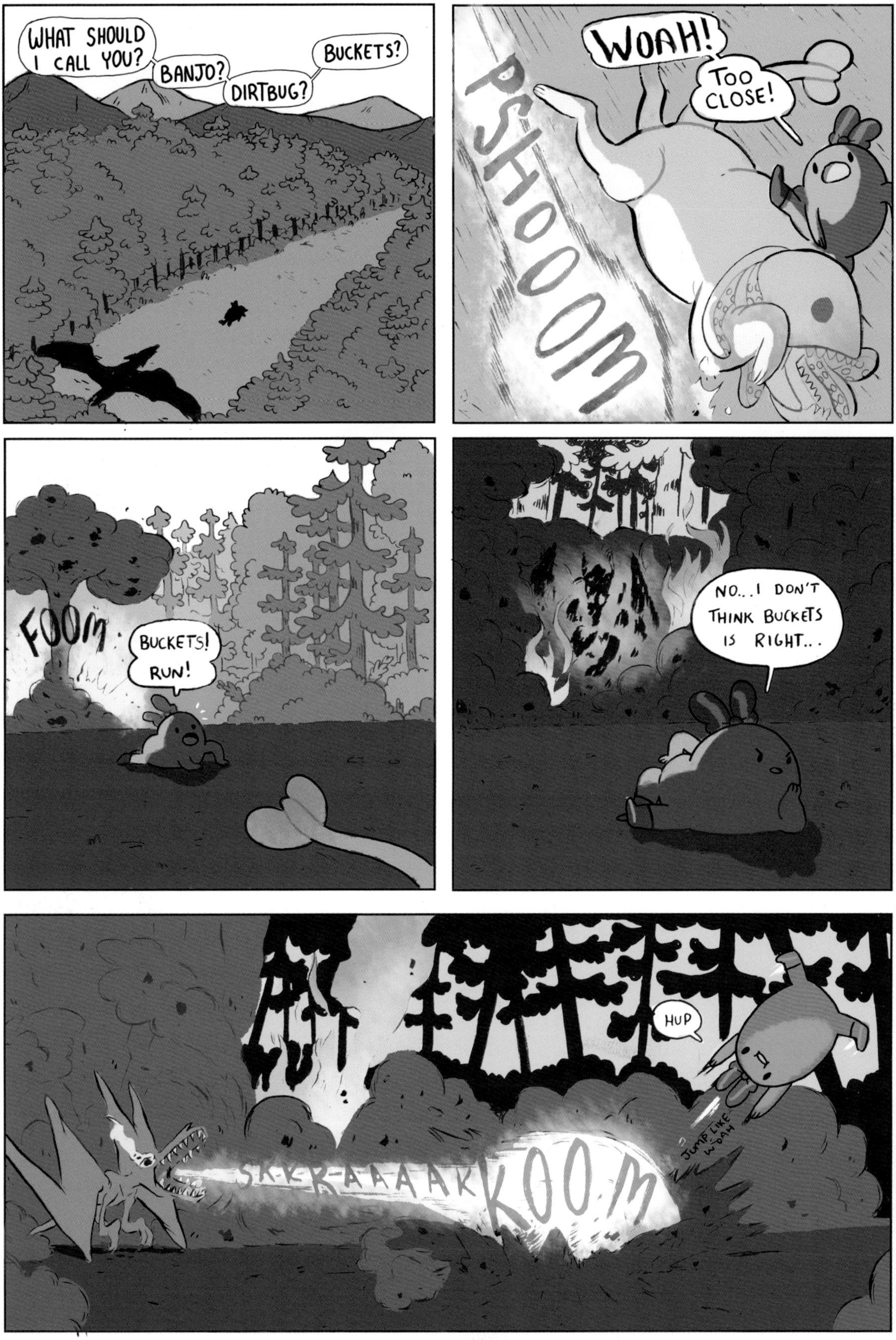
WHAT SHOULD I CALL YOU?
BANJO?
DIRTBUG?
BUCKETS?
WOAH!
TOO CLOSE!
PSHOOOOM
FOOM
BUCKETS! RUN!
NO...I DON'T THINK BUCKETS IS RIGHT...
HUP
JUMP LIKE WOAH
SKKRAAAAAK
KOOM

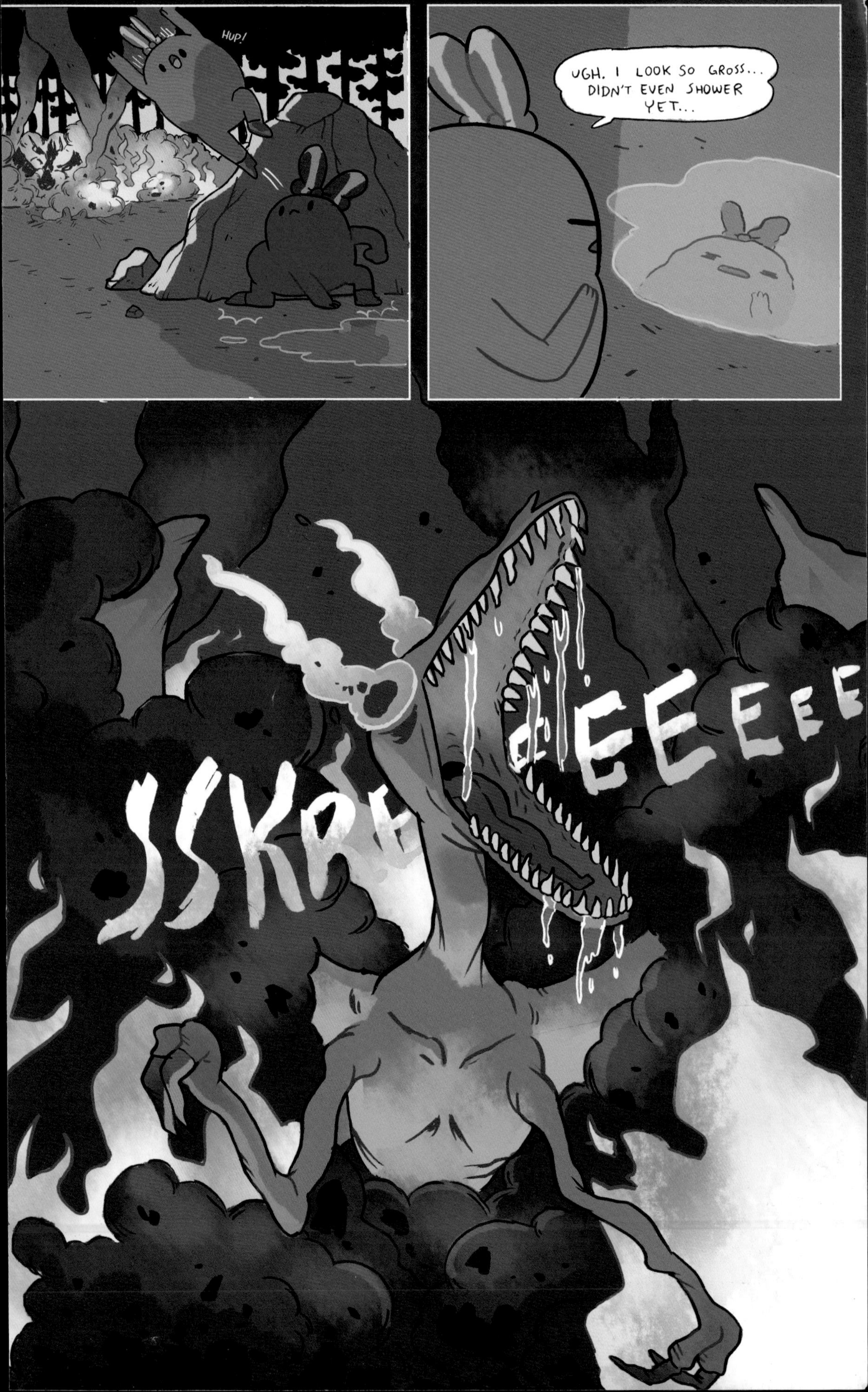
HUP!
UGH. I LOOK SO GROSS... DIDN'T EVEN SHOWER YET...
SSKRE
EEEEEE

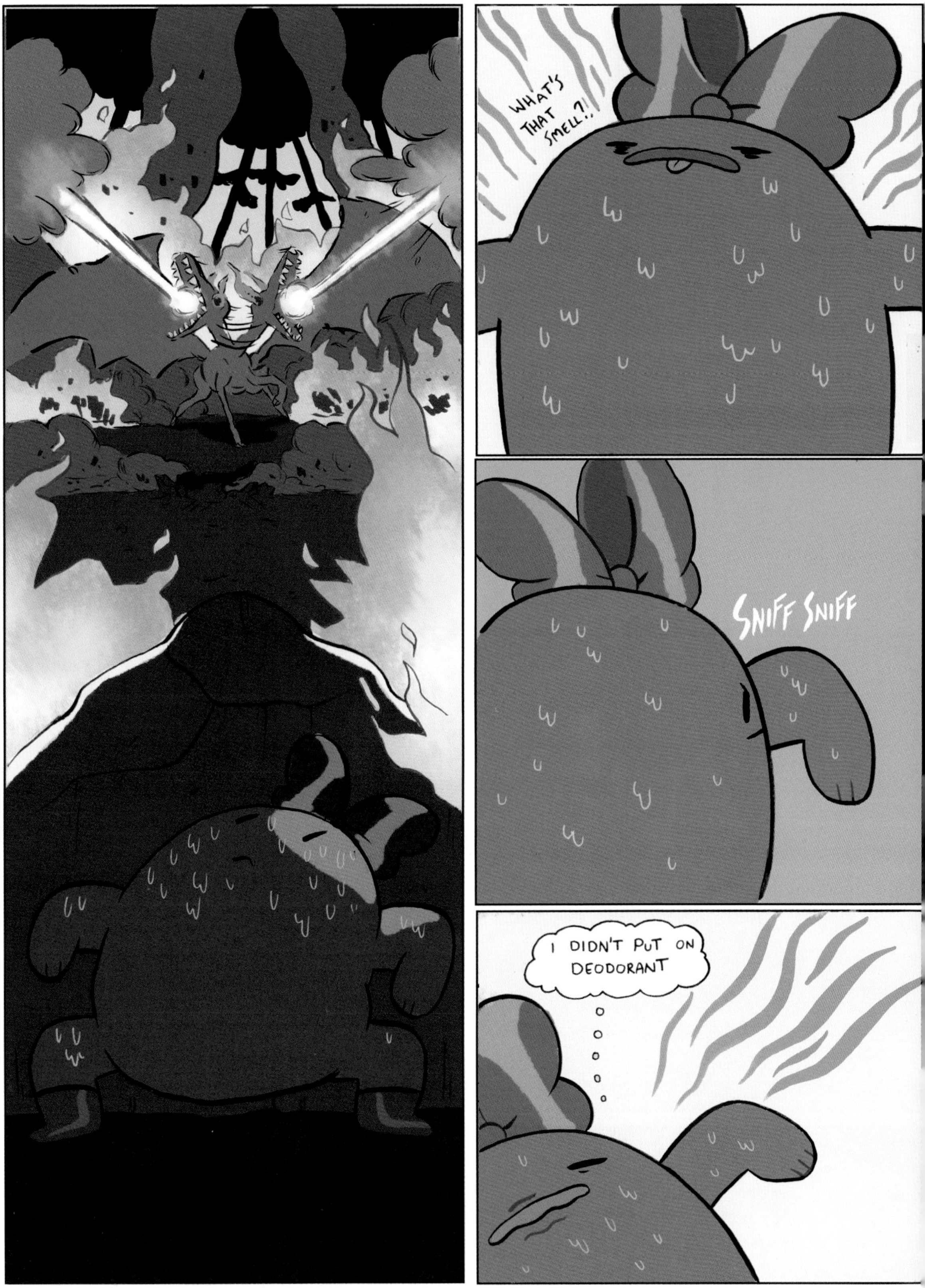
WHAT'S THAT SMELL?!
SNIFF SNIFF
I DIDN'T PUT ON DEODORANT

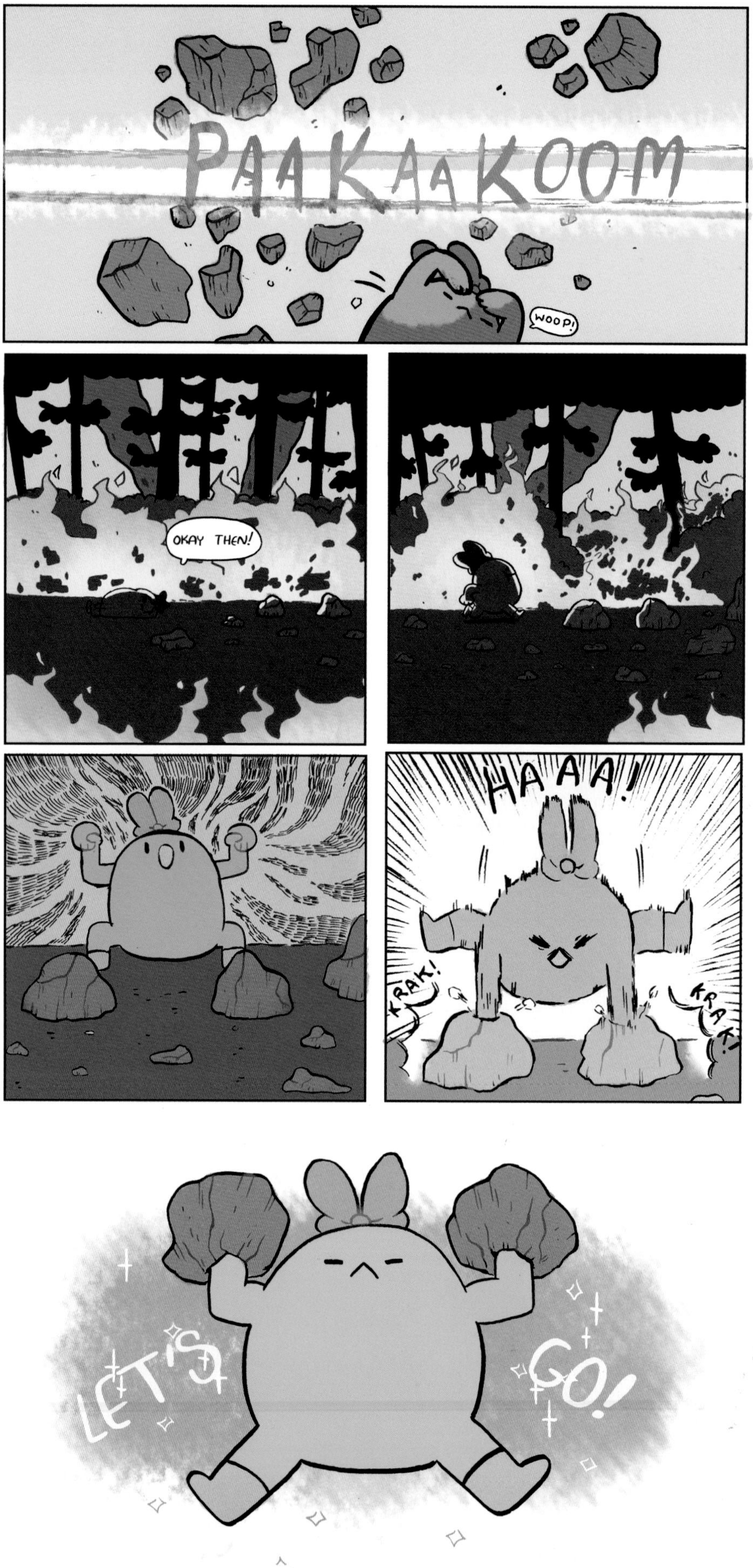
PAAKAAKOOM
WOOP!
OKAY THEN!
HAAAA!
KRAK!
KRAK!
LET'S GO!

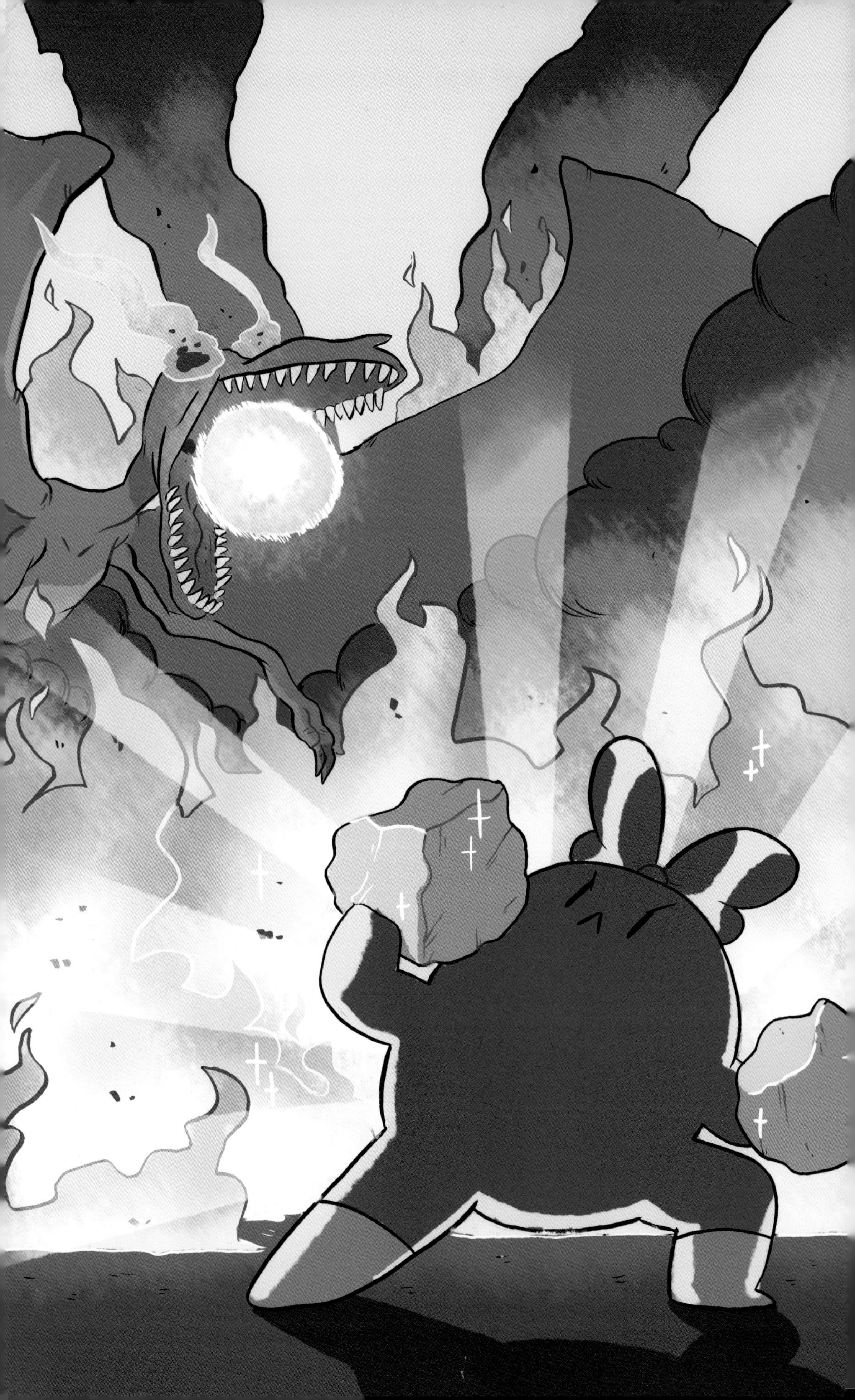

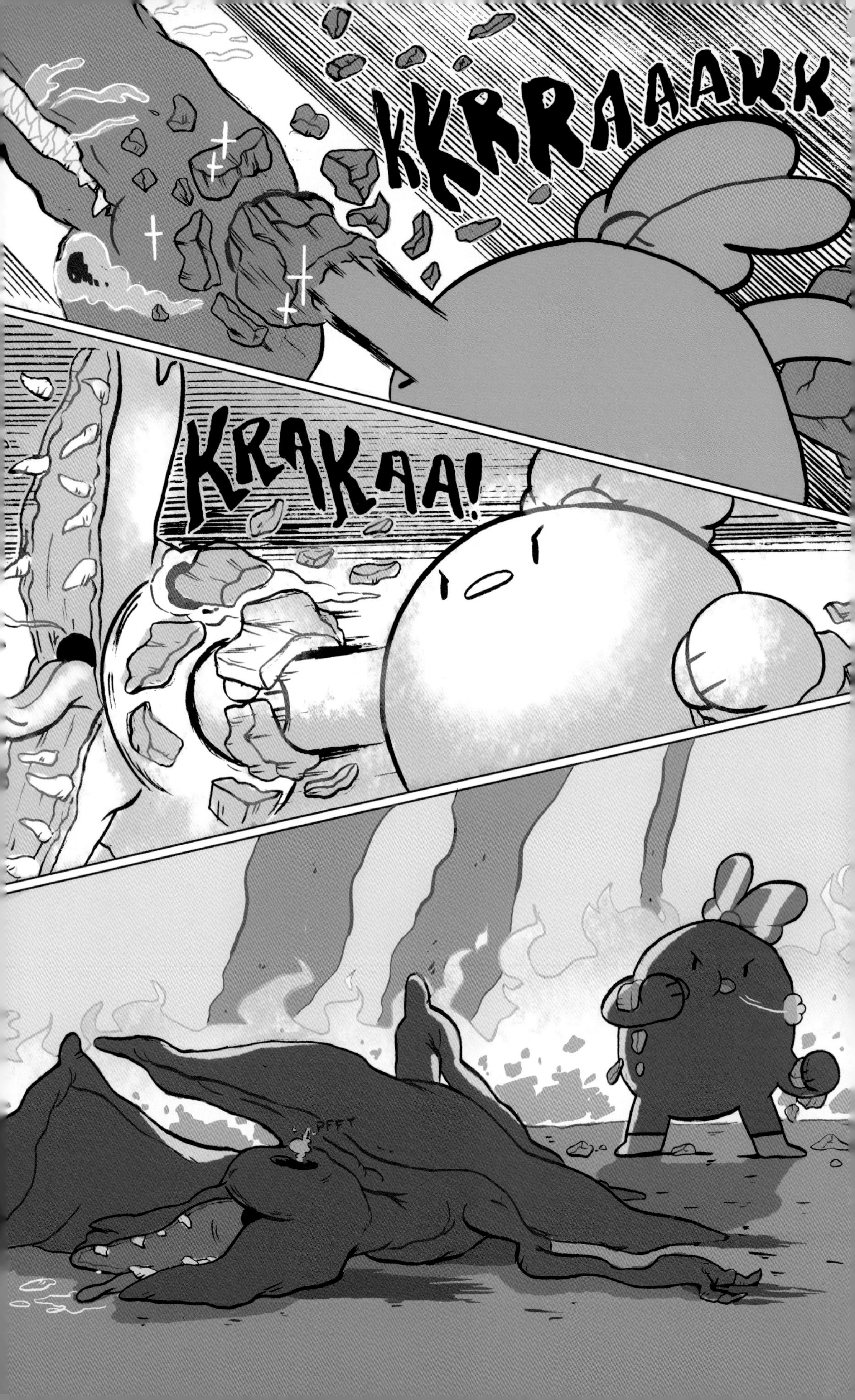
KKRRAAAKK
KRAKAA!
PFFT

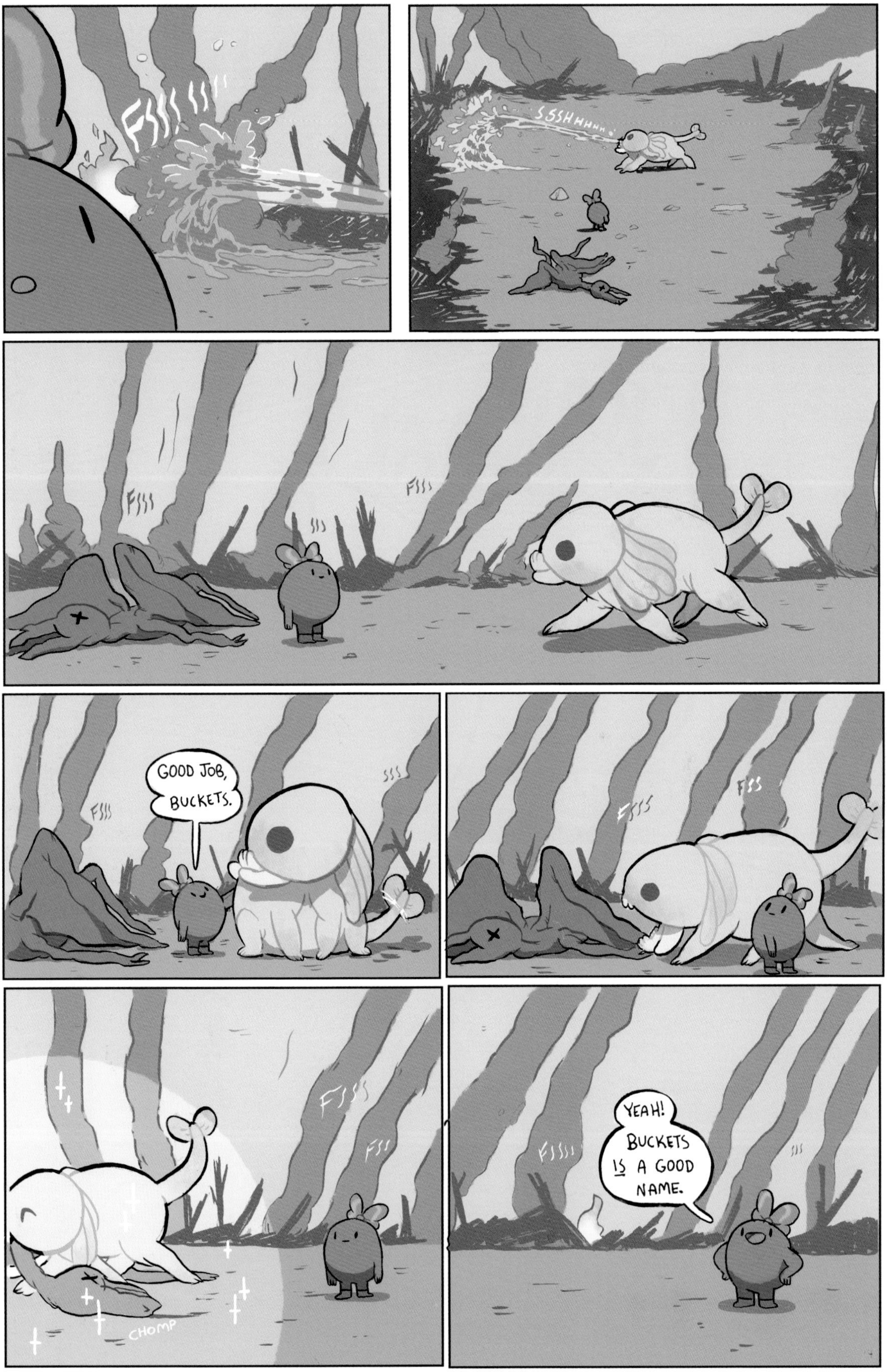
FSSSSSS
SSSHHHHHH
FSSS
FSSS
GOOD JOB, BUCKETS.
FSSS
FSSS
FSSS
FSSS
FSSS
CHOMP
FSSSS
YEAH! BUCKETS IS A GOOD NAME.

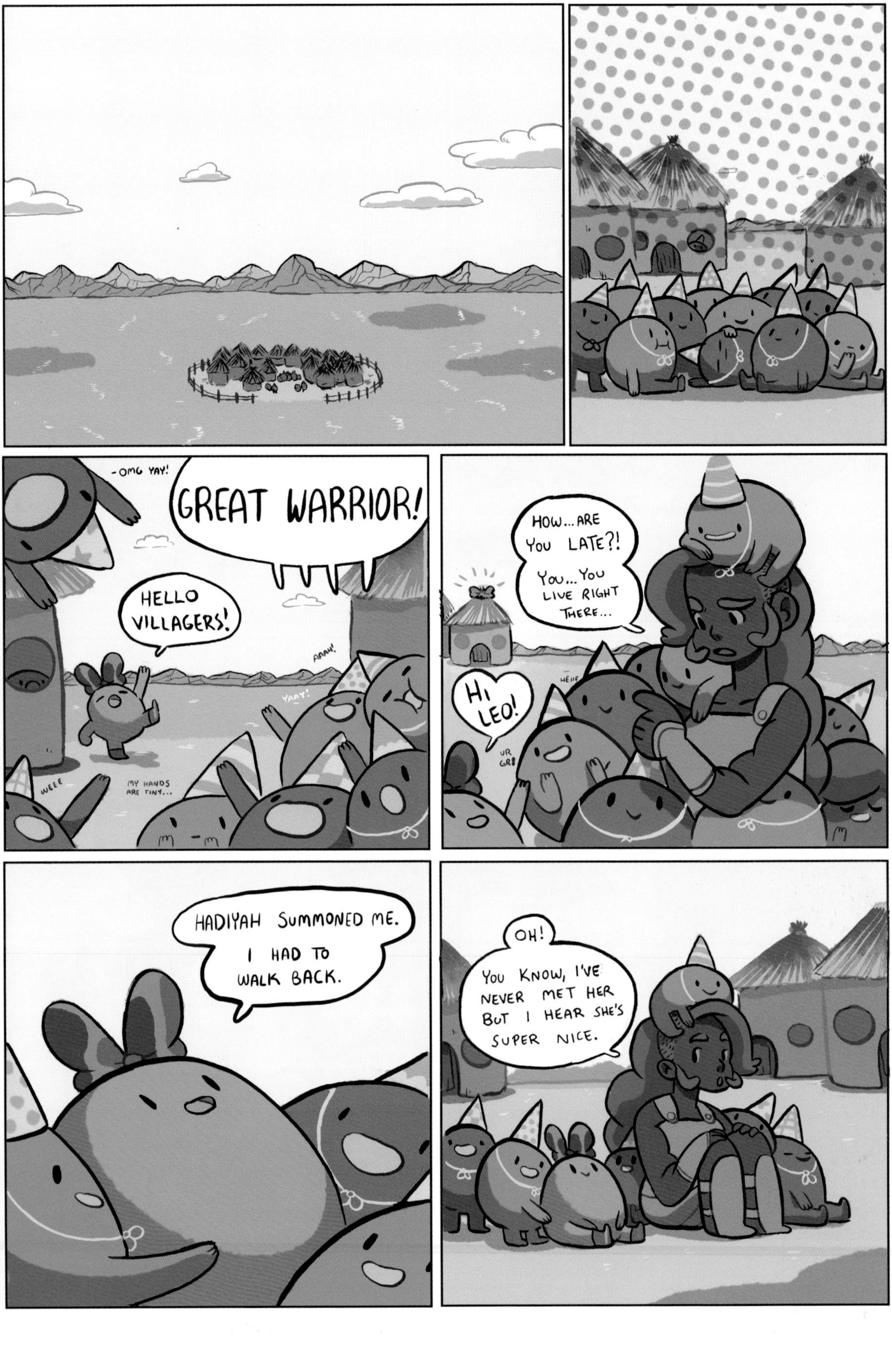

-OMG YAY!
GREAT WARRIOR!
HELLO VILLAGERS!
AAAH!
YAAY!
WEEE
MY HANDS ARE TINY...
HOW... ARE YOU LATE?!
YOU... YOU LIVE RIGHT THERE...
HEHE
HI LEO!
UR GR8
HADIYAH SUMMONED ME.
I HAD TO WALK BACK.
OH!
YOU KNOW, I'VE NEVER MET HER BUT I HEAR SHE'S SUPER NICE.

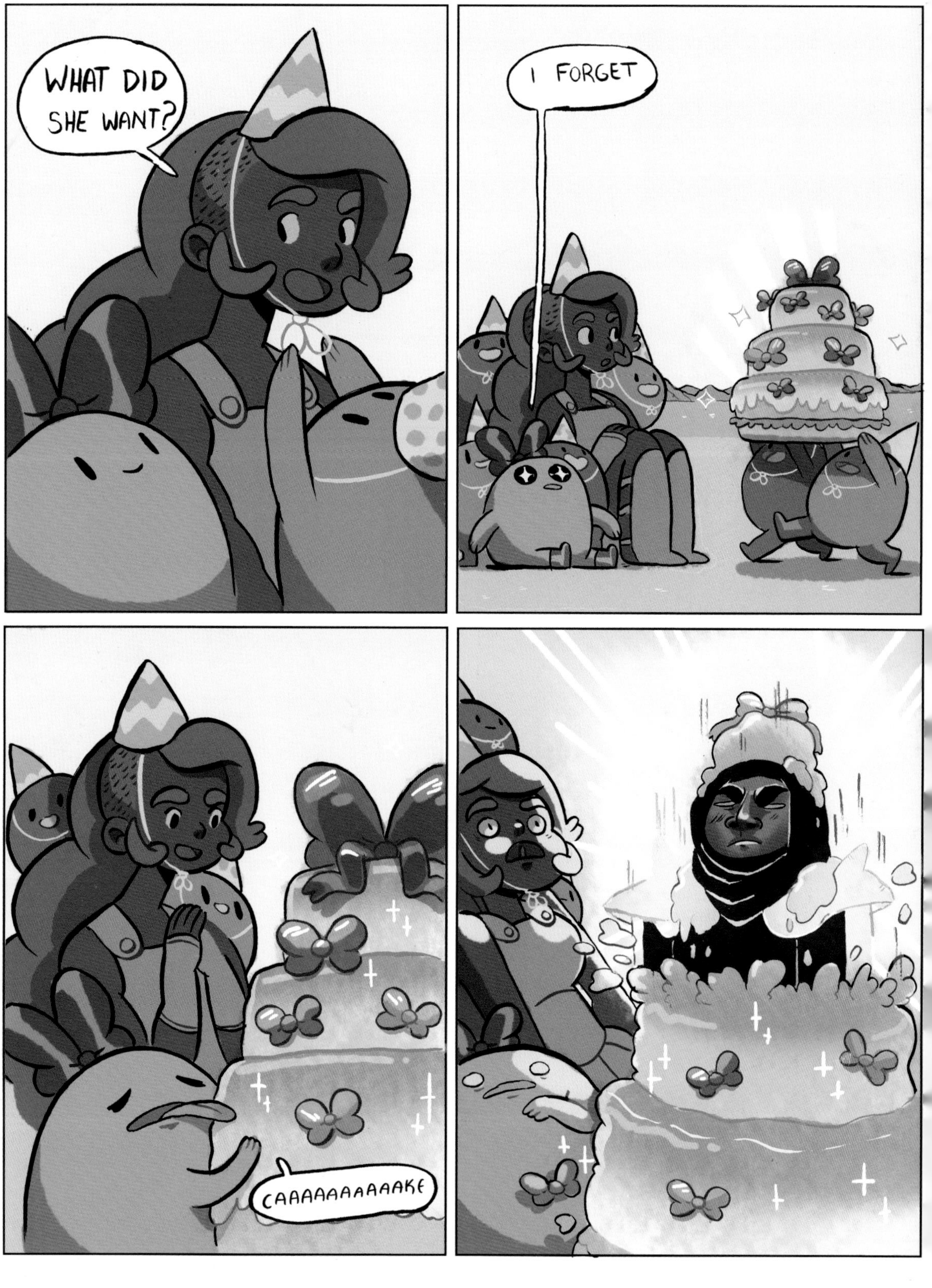
WHAT DID SHE WANT?
I FORGET
CAAAAAAAAAAKE

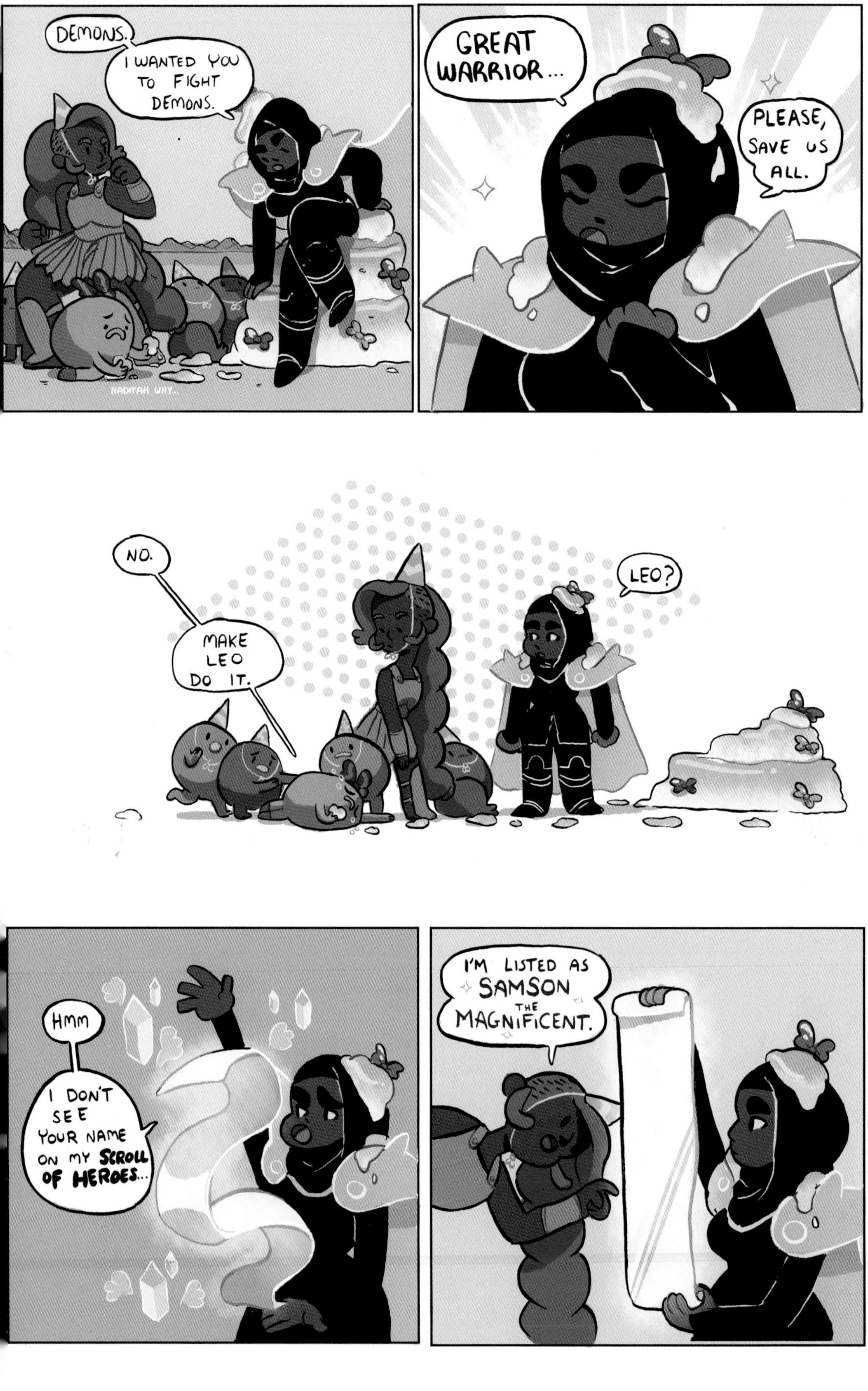
DEMONS.
I WANTED YOU TO FIGHT DEMONS.
HADIYAH WHY...
GREAT WARRIOR...
PLEASE, SAVE US ALL.
NO.
MAKE LEO DO IT.
LEO?
Hmm
I DON'T SEE YOUR NAME ON MY SCROLL OF HEROES...
I'M LISTED AS SAMSON THE MAGNIFICENT.

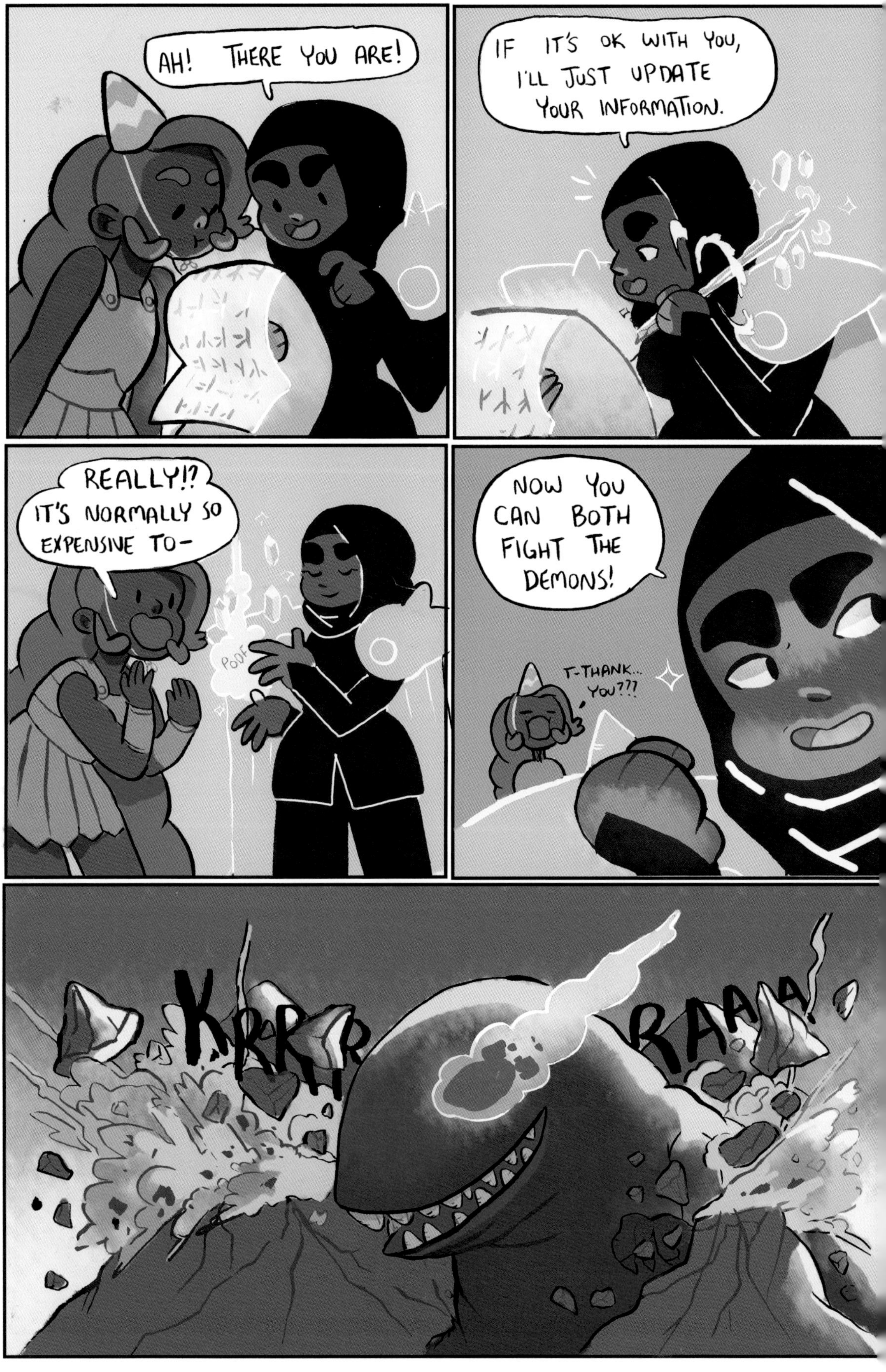
AH! THERE YOU ARE!
IF IT'S OK WITH YOU, I'LL JUST UPDATE YOUR INFORMATION.
REALLY!? IT'S NORMALLY SO EXPENSIVE TO-
POOF
NOW YOU CAN BOTH FIGHT THE DEMONS!
T-THANK... YOU???
KRRRR
RAAA!

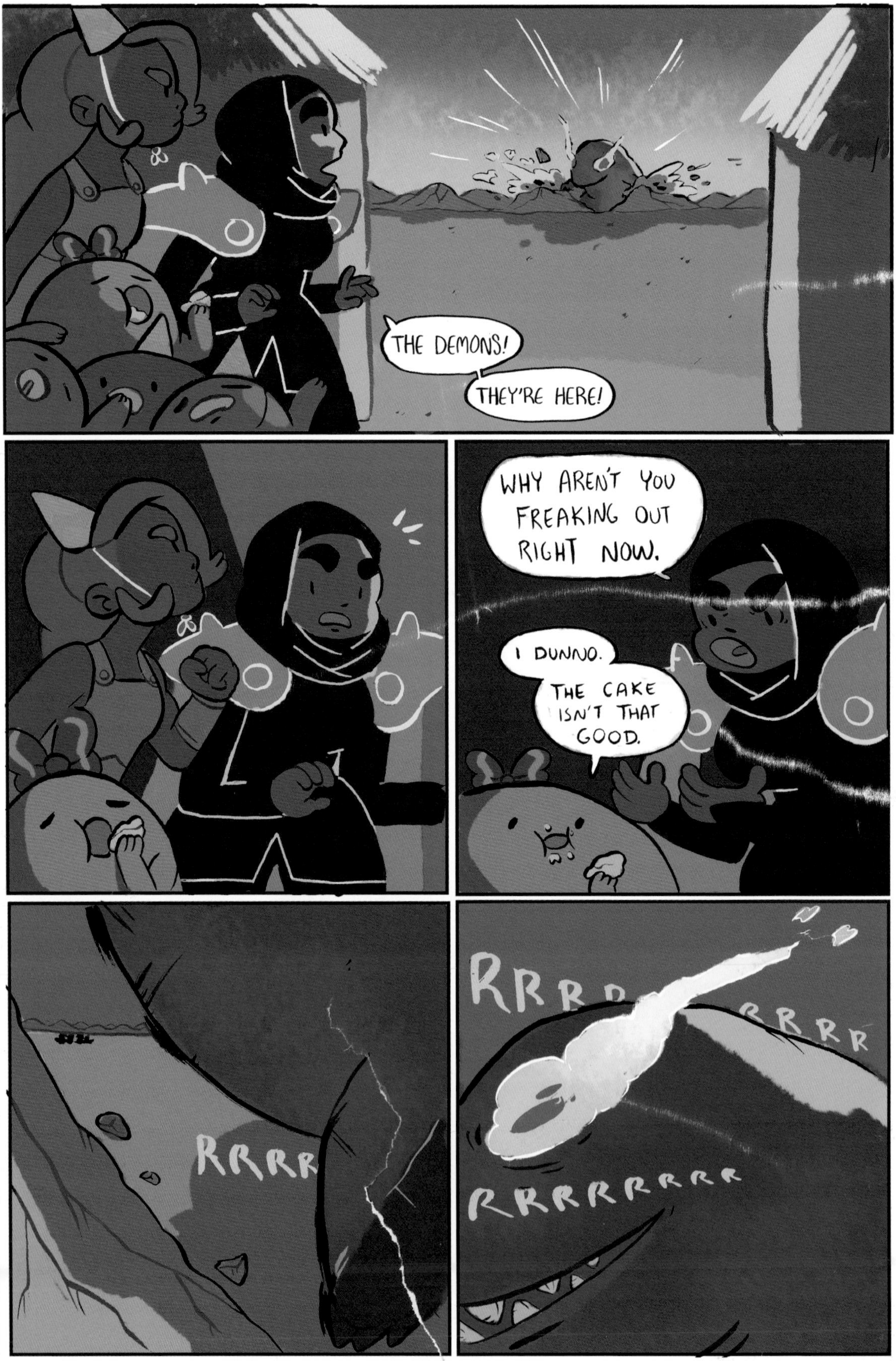
THE DEMONS!
THEY'RE HERE!
WHY AREN'T YOU FREAKING OUT RIGHT NOW.
I DUNNO.
THE CAKE ISN'T THAT GOOD.
RRRR
RRRRRRRR
RRRRRRRRR

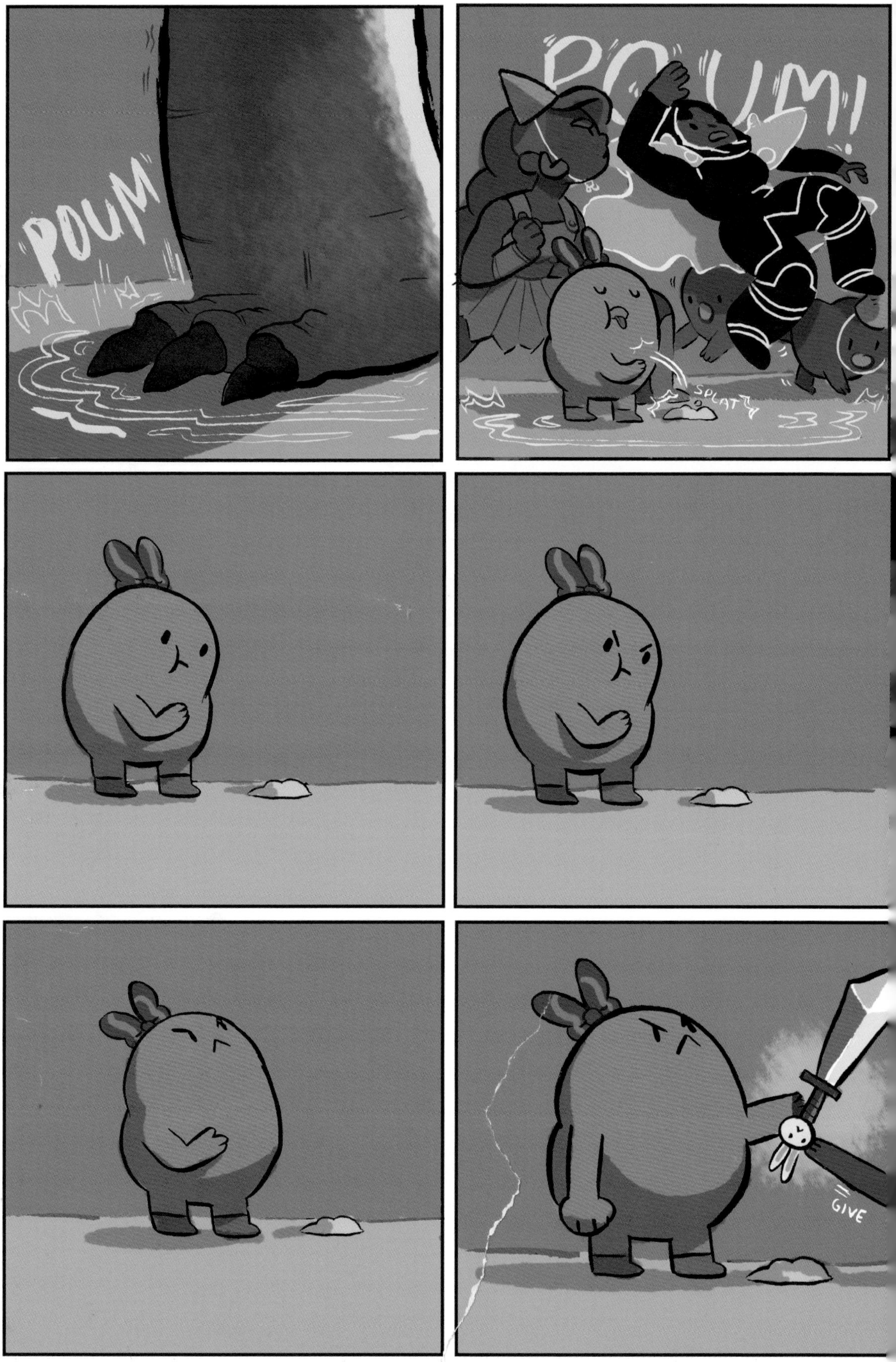
POUM
POUM!
SPLAT
GIVE

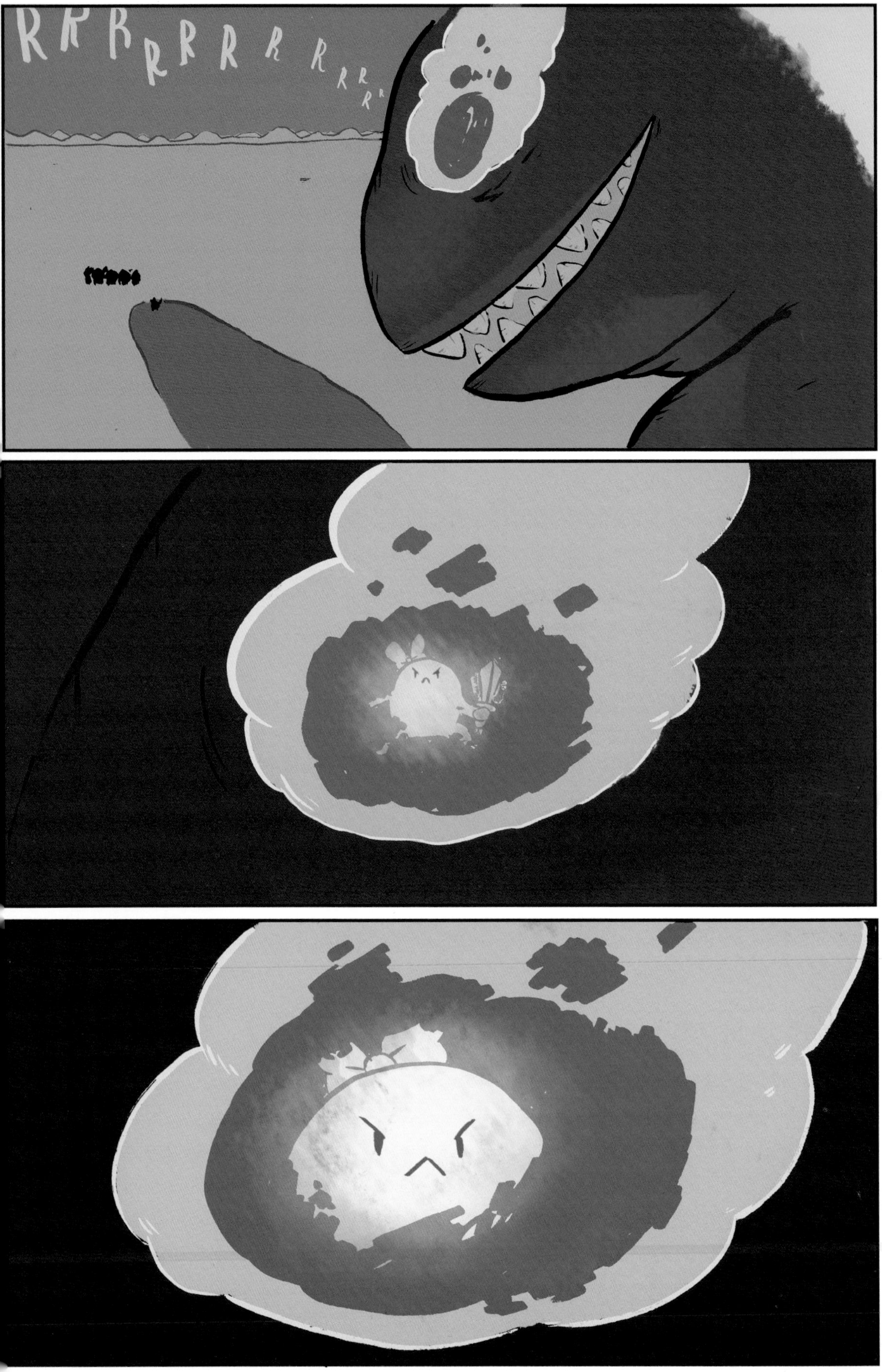
RRRRRRRRRRRRRR

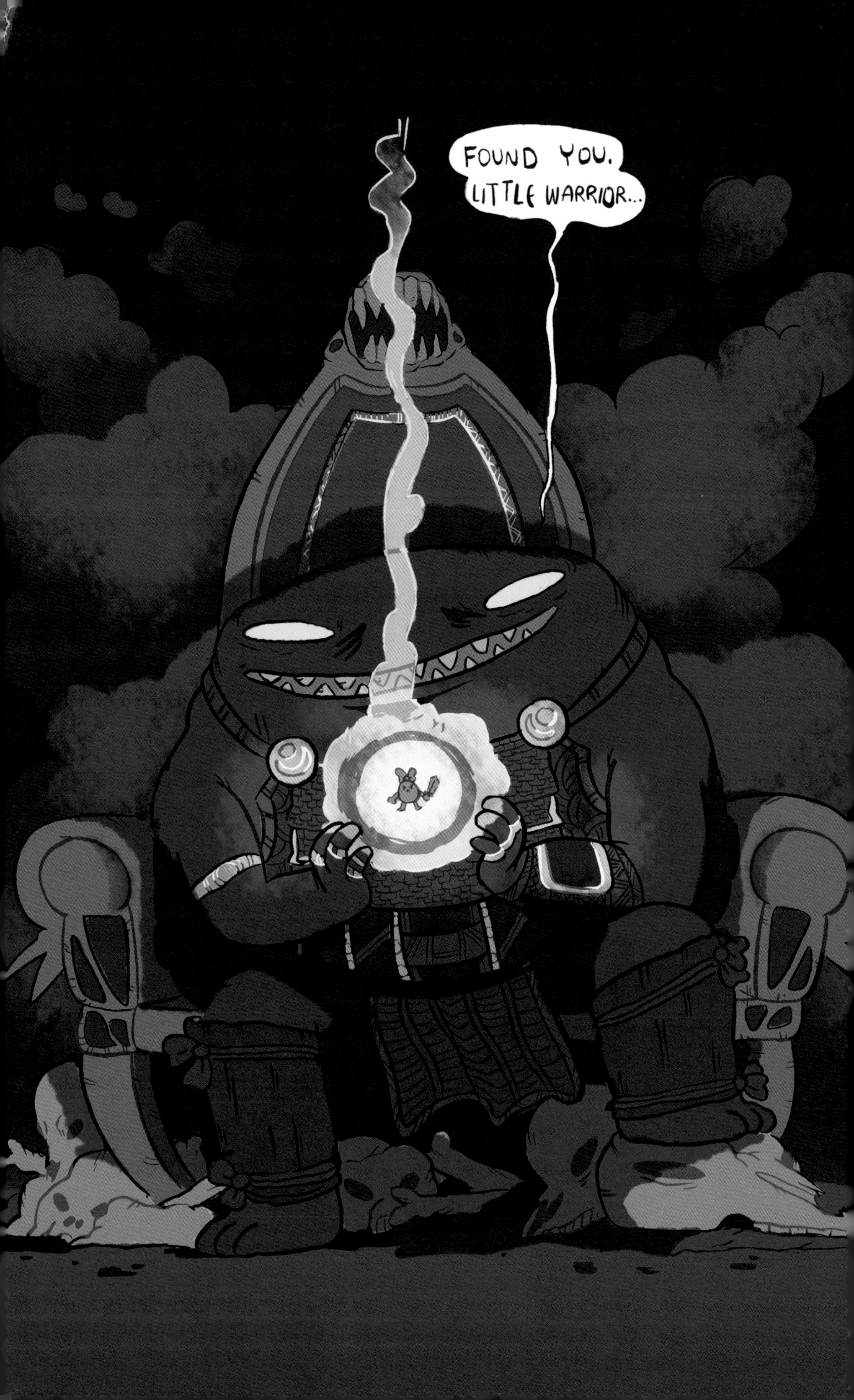
FOUND YOU, LITTLE WARRIOR...

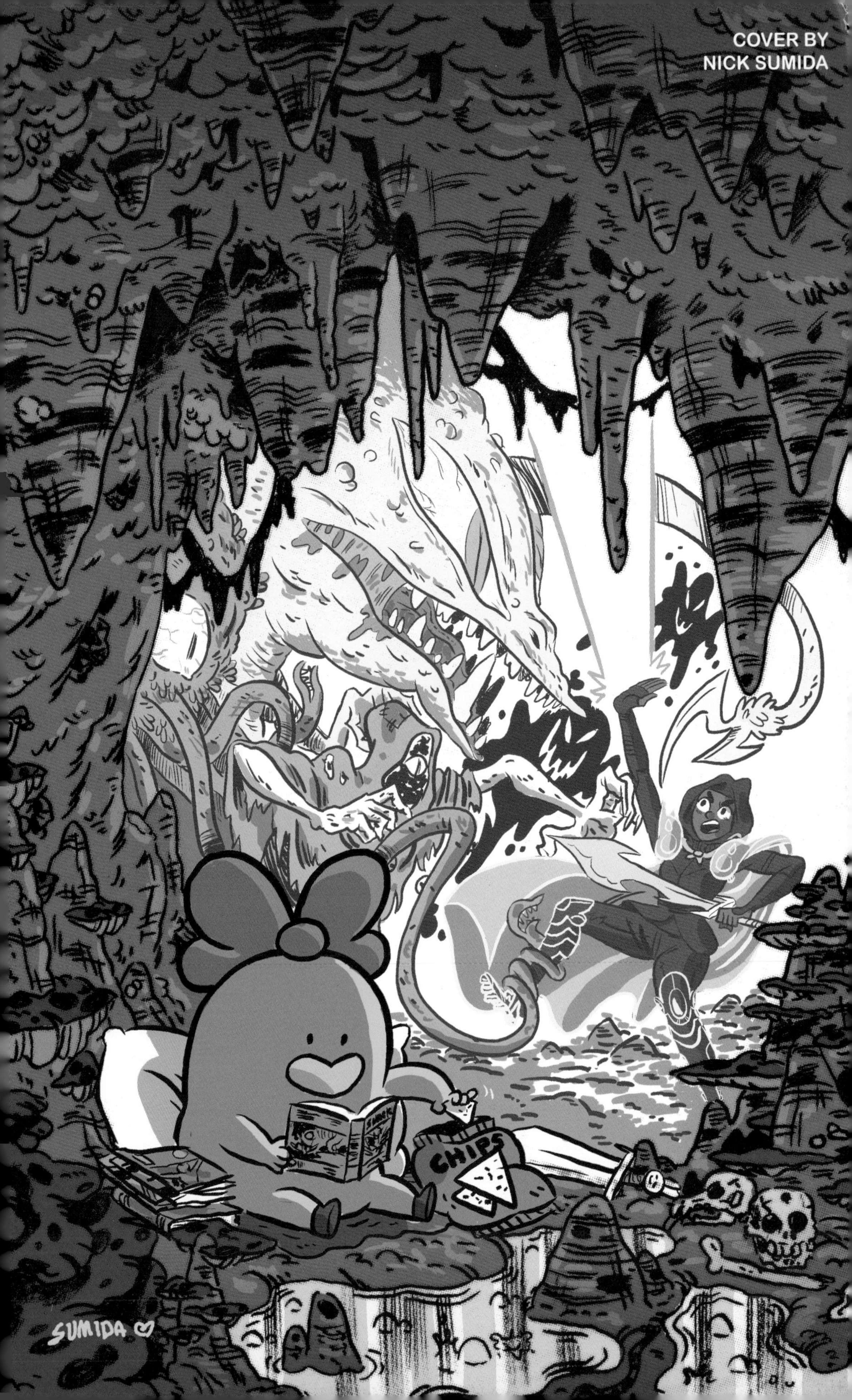
CHIPS
SUMIDA

COVER BY
NICK SUMIDA

Chapter
Two

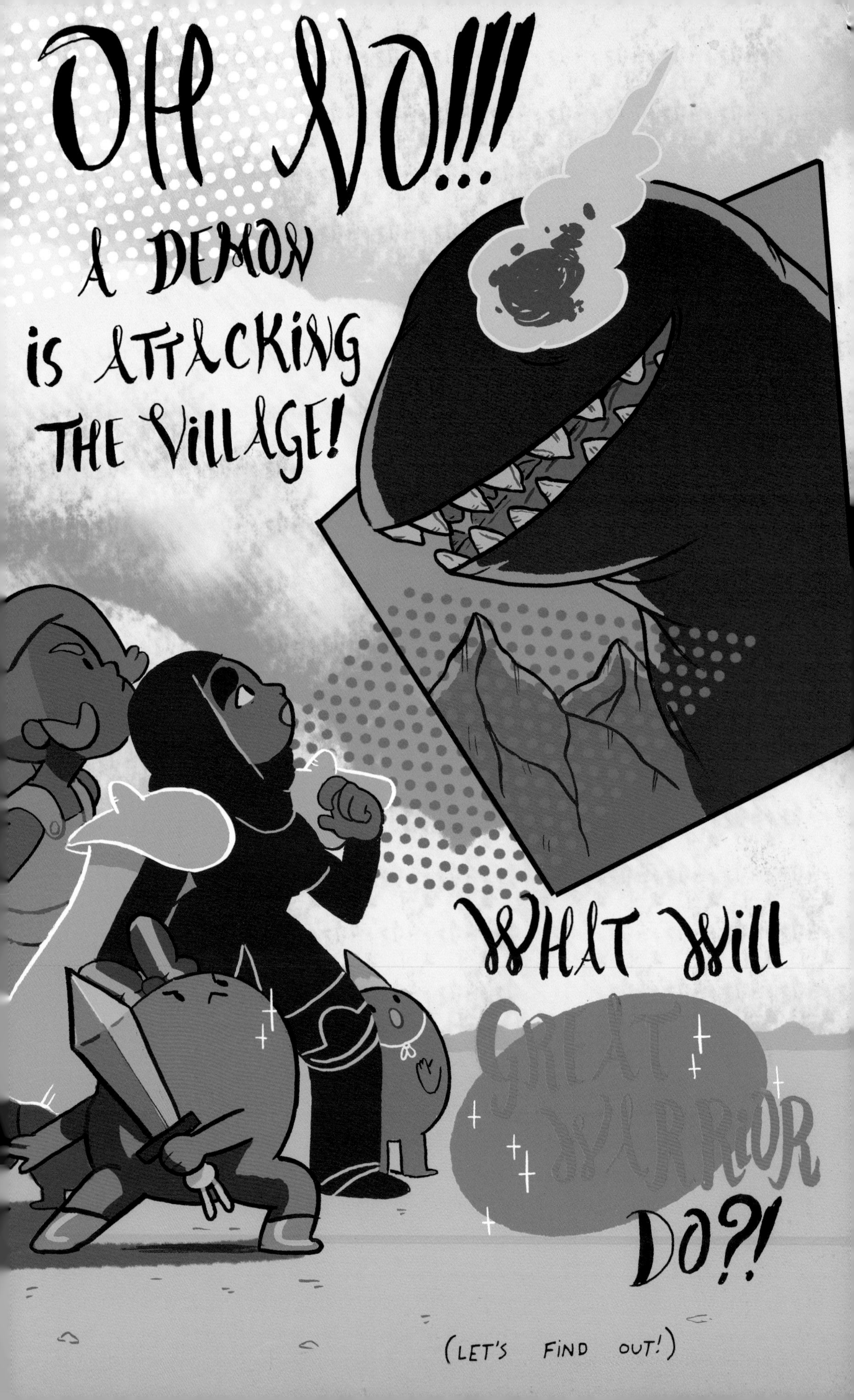
OH NO!!!
A DEMON IS ATTACKING THE VILLAGE!
WHAT WILL GREAT WARRIOR DO?!
(LET'S FIND OUT!)

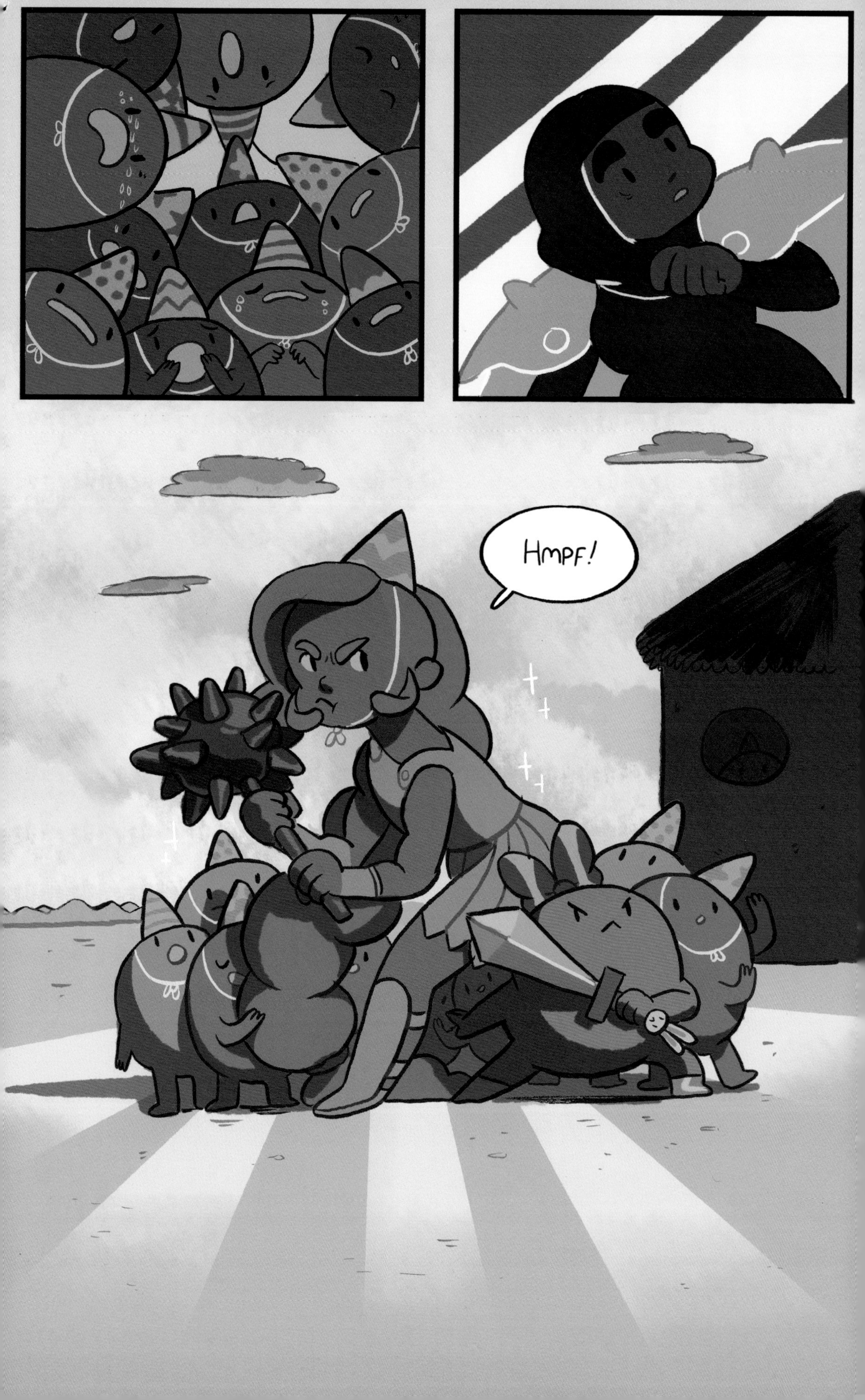
Hmpf!

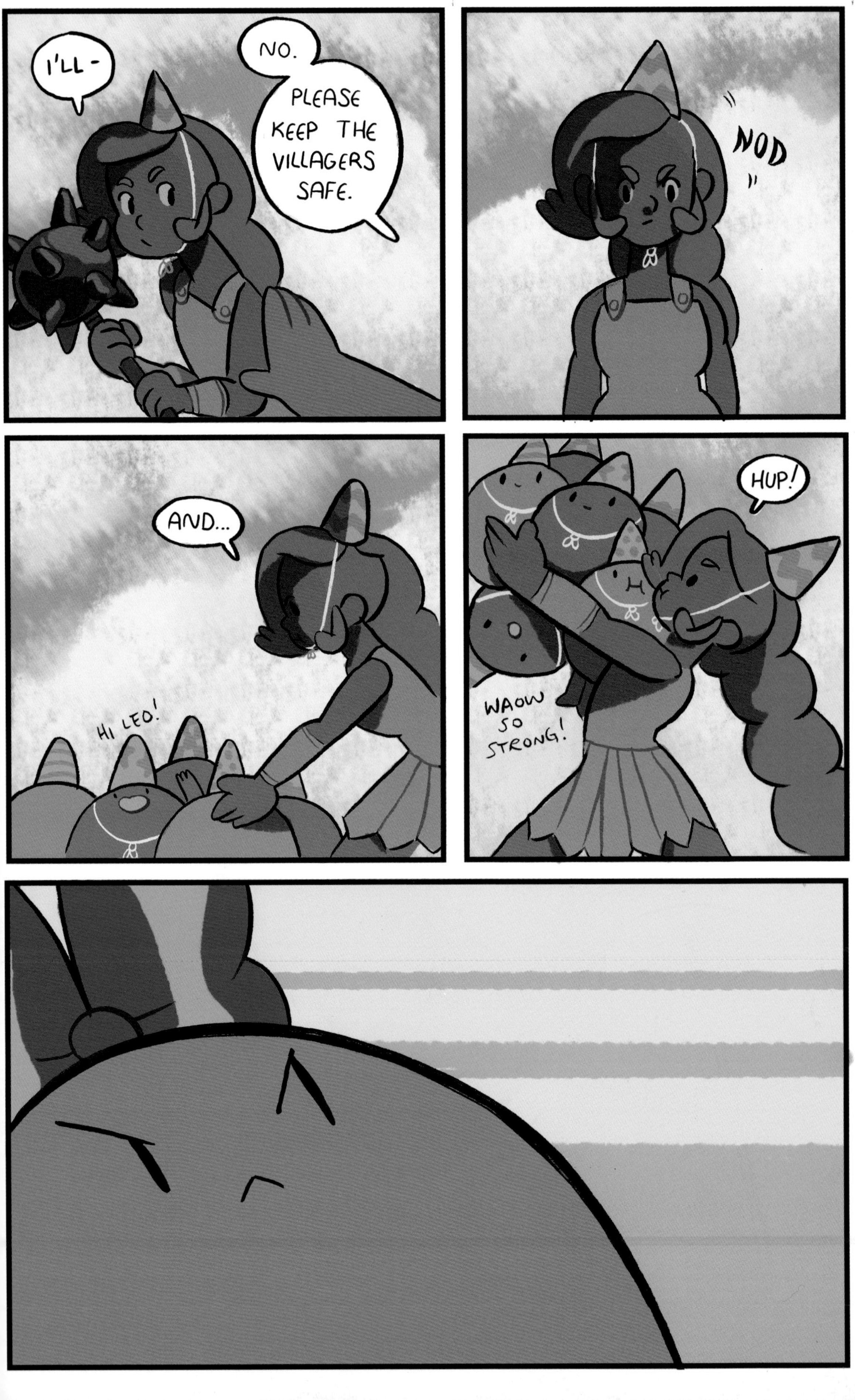

I'LL-
NO.
PLEASE KEEP THE VILLAGERS SAFE.
NOD
AND...
HI LEO!
HUP!
WAOW SO STRONG!

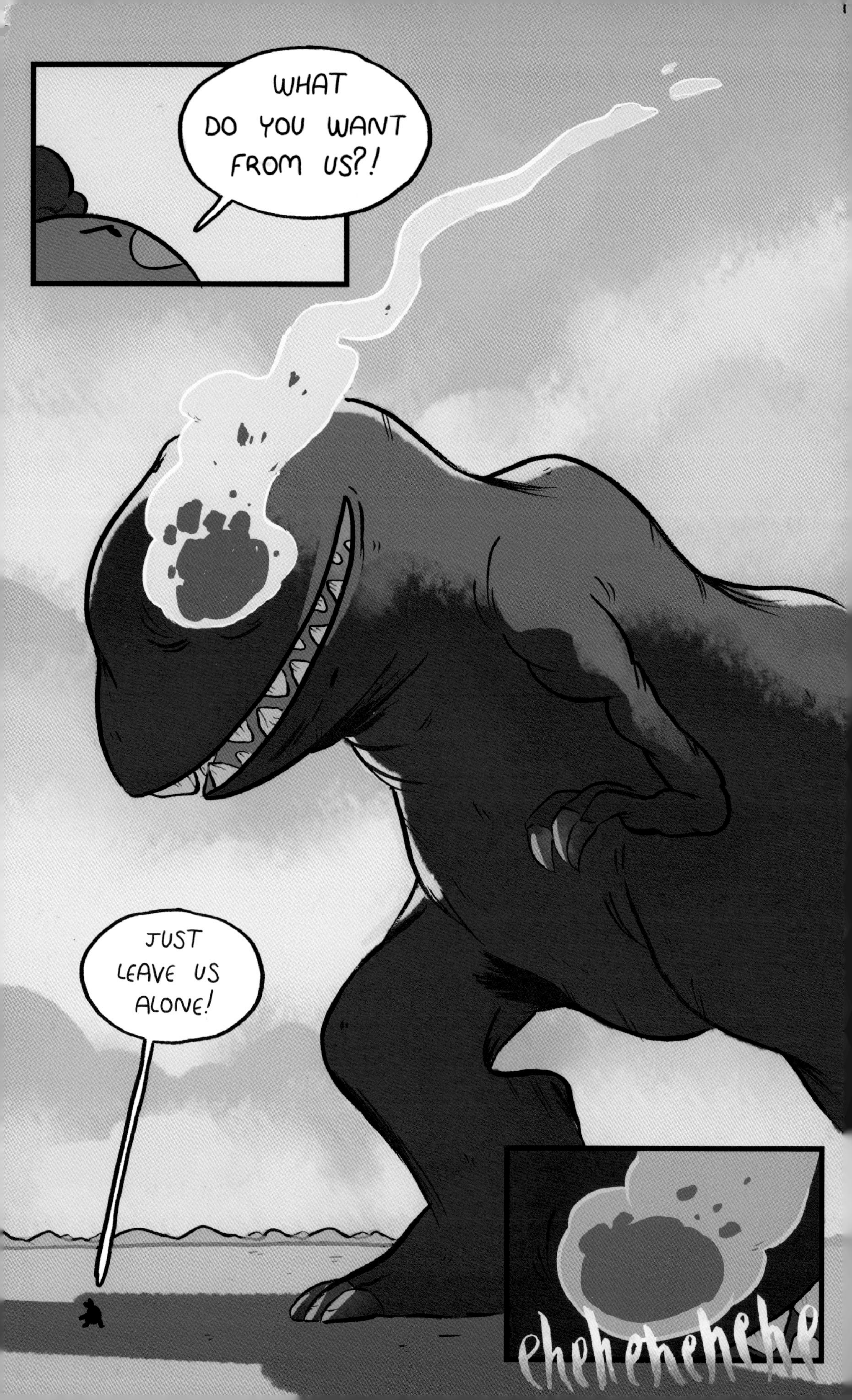
WHAT DO YOU WANT FROM US?!
JUST LEAVE US ALONE!
ehehehehehe

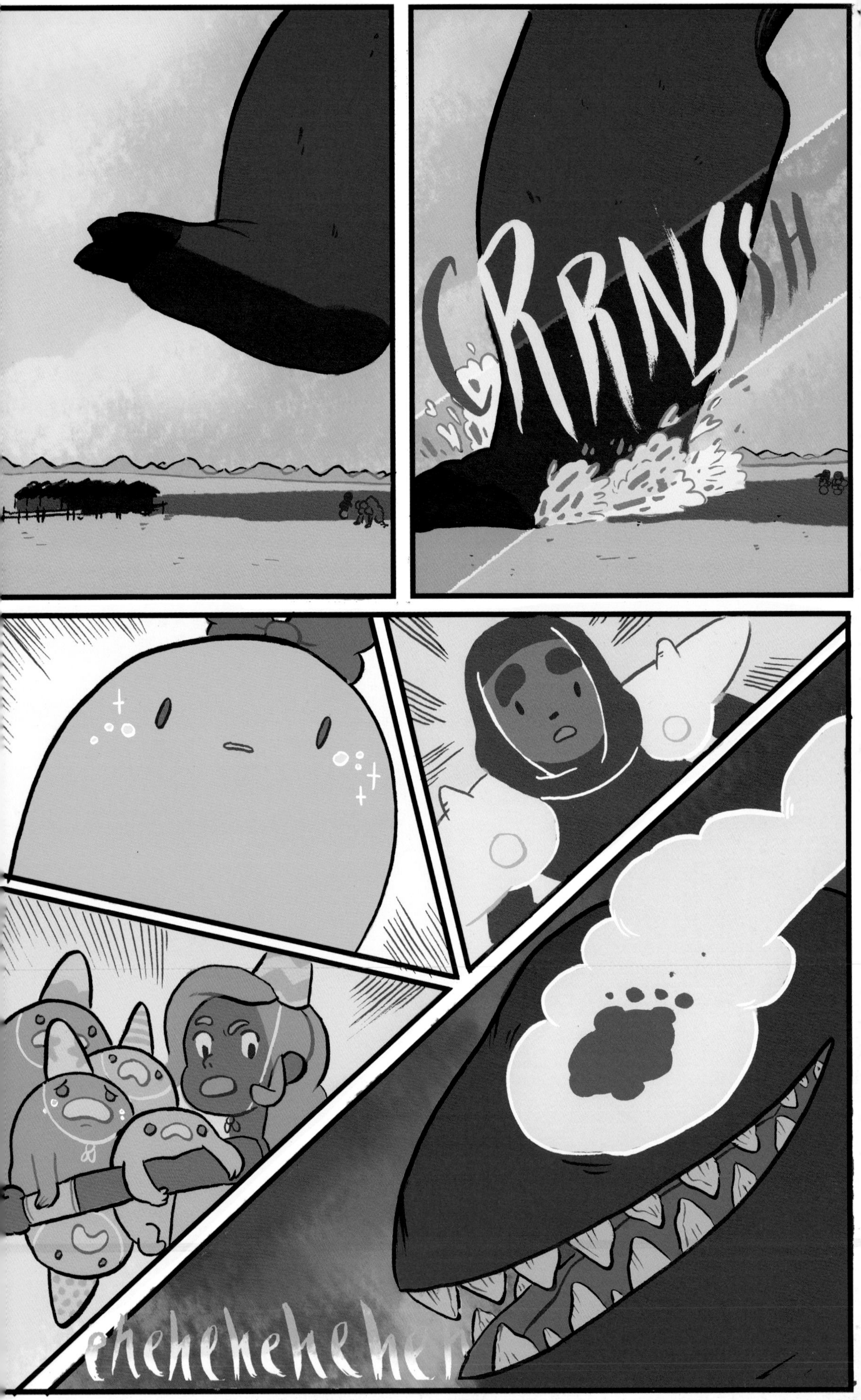
CRRNSSH
ehehehehehehe

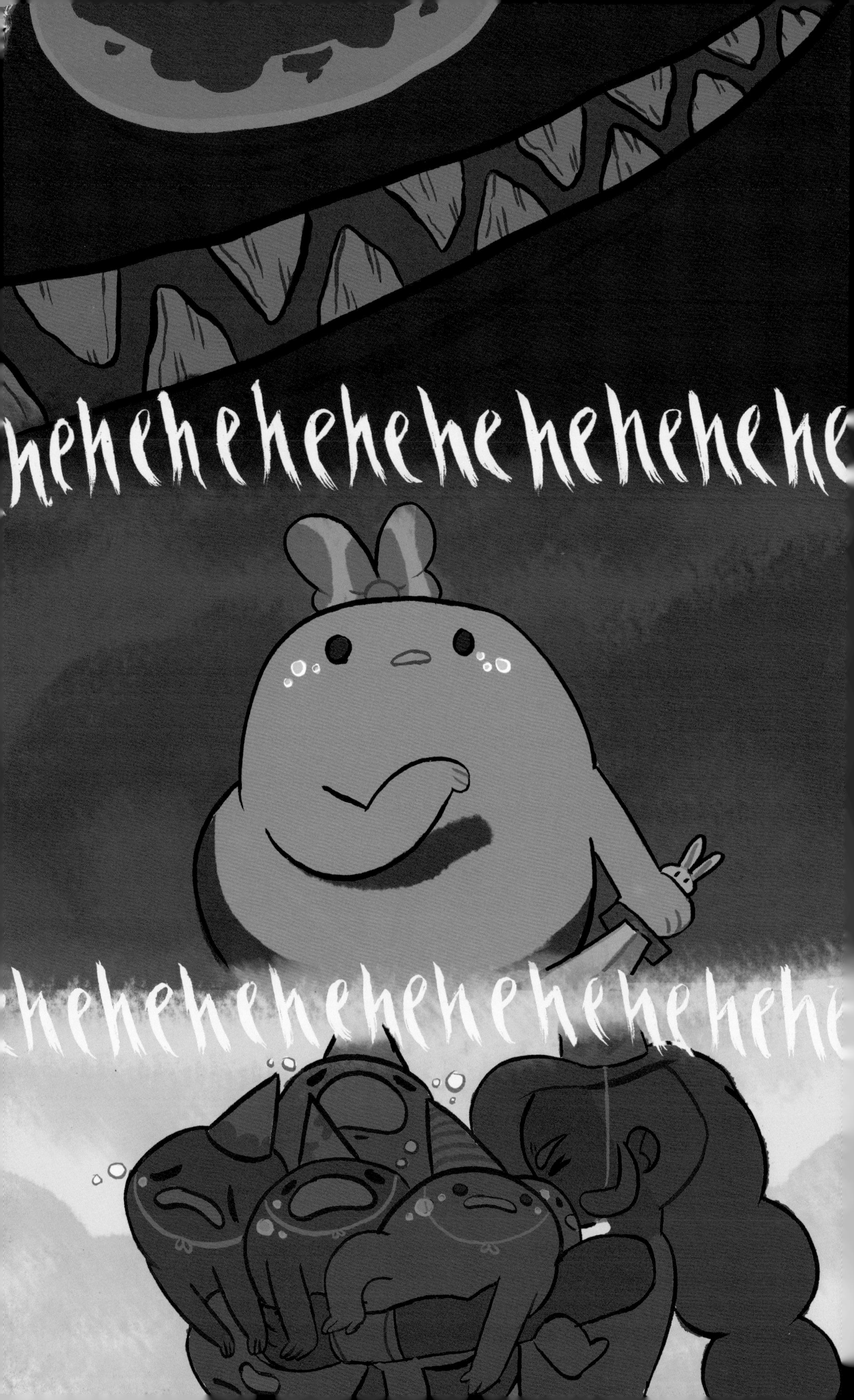
hehehehehehehehehe
hehehehehehehehehe

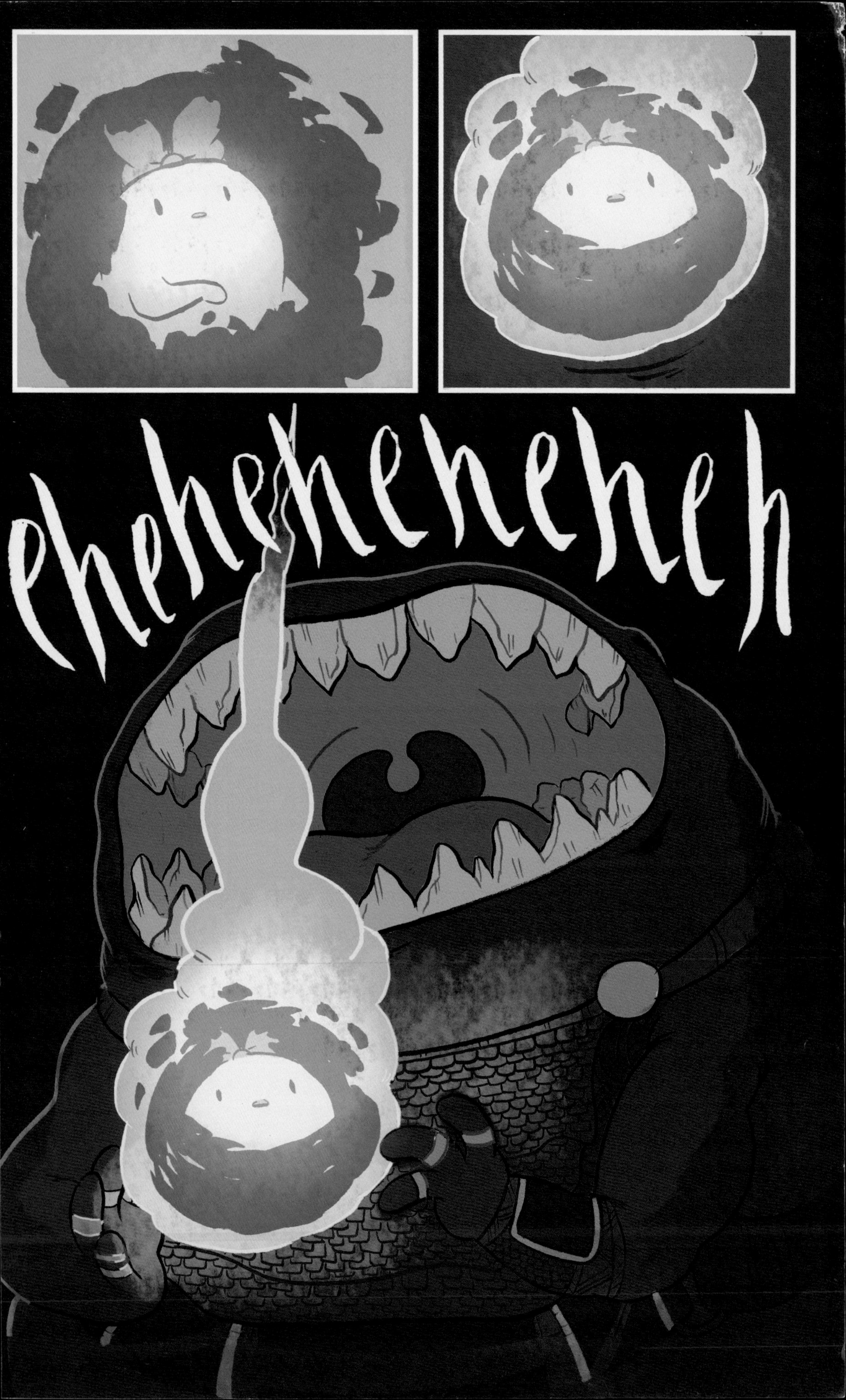
ehehehehehehe h

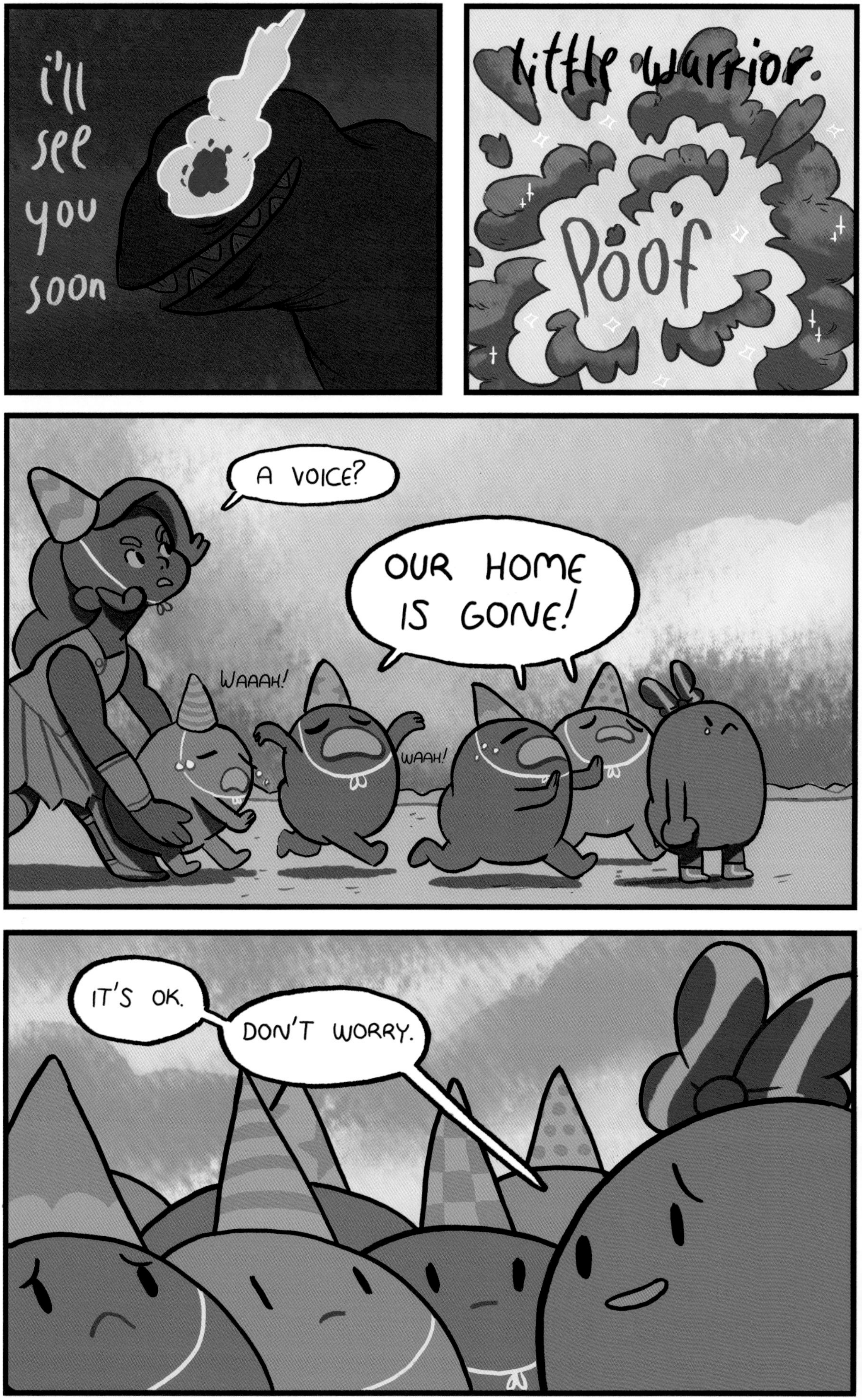
i'll see you soon
little warrior.
POOF
A VOICE?
OUR HOME IS GONE!
WAAAH!
WAAH!
IT'S OK.
DON'T WORRY.

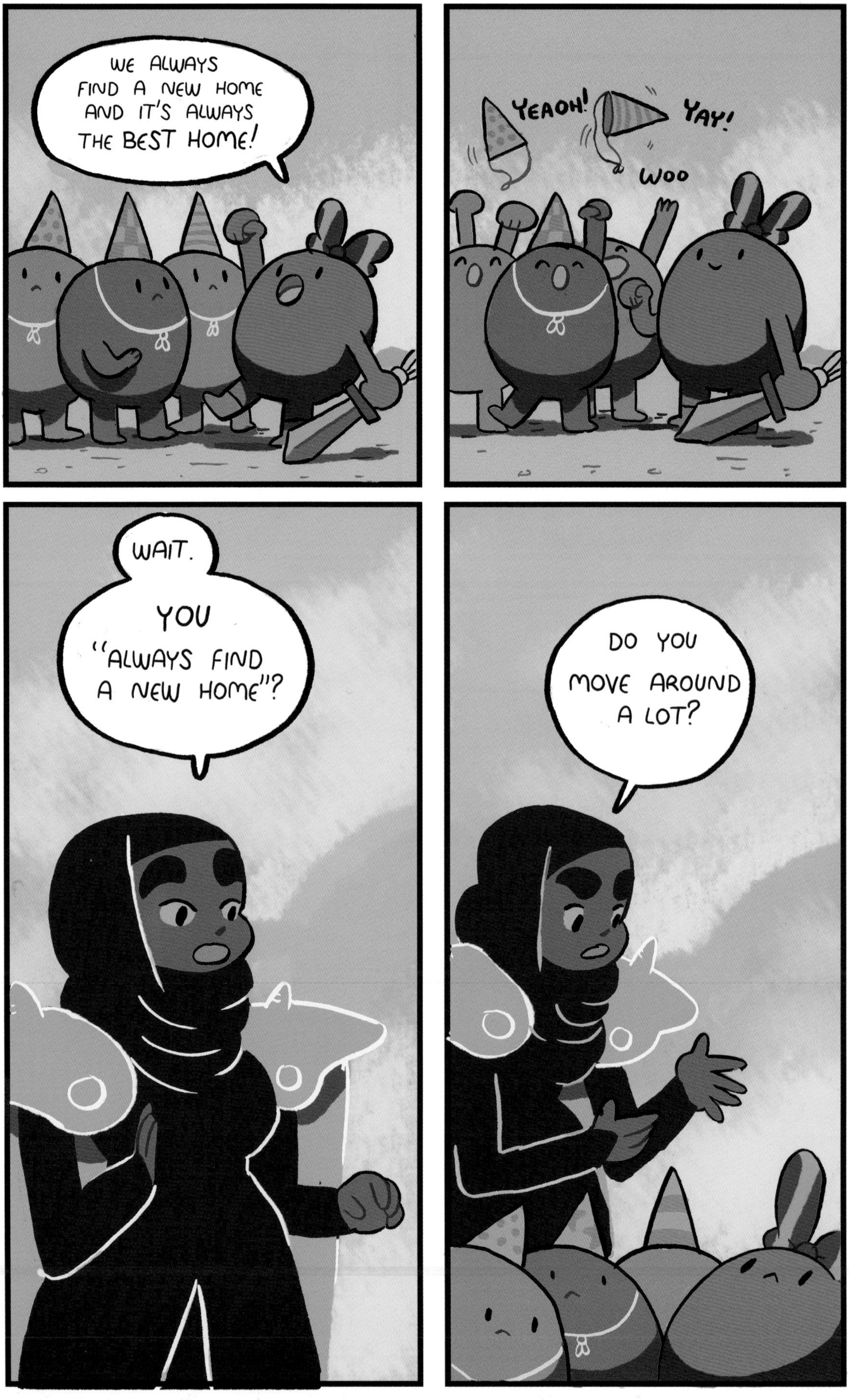
WE ALWAYS FIND A NEW HOME AND IT'S ALWAYS THE BEST HOME!
YEAOH!
YAY!
WOO
WAIT.
YOU "ALWAYS FIND A NEW HOME"?
DO YOU MOVE AROUND A LOT?

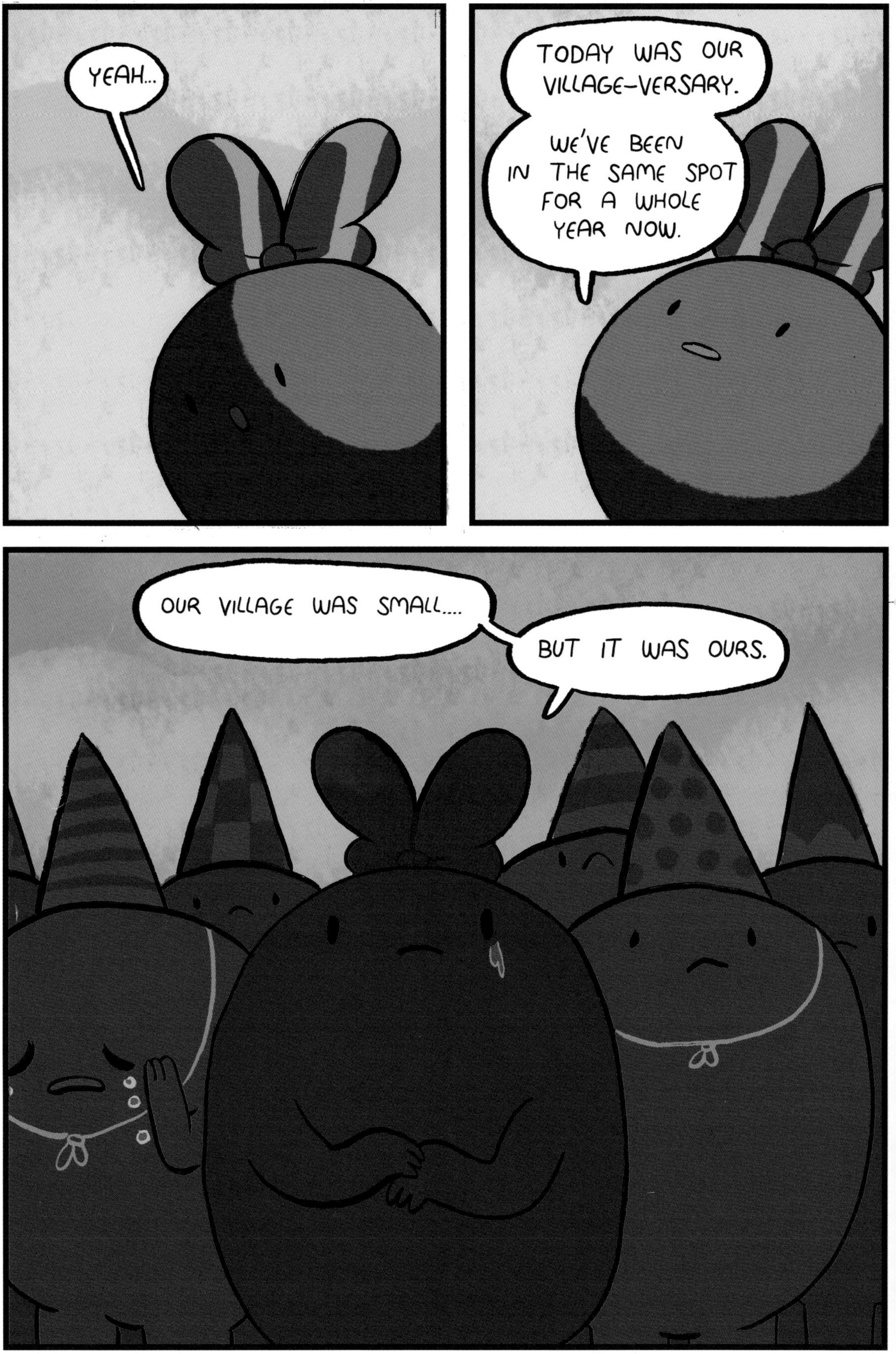
YEAH...
TODAY WAS OUR VILLAGE-VERSARY.
WE'VE BEEN IN THE SAME SPOT FOR A WHOLE YEAR NOW.
OUR VILLAGE WAS SMALL....
BUT IT WAS OURS.

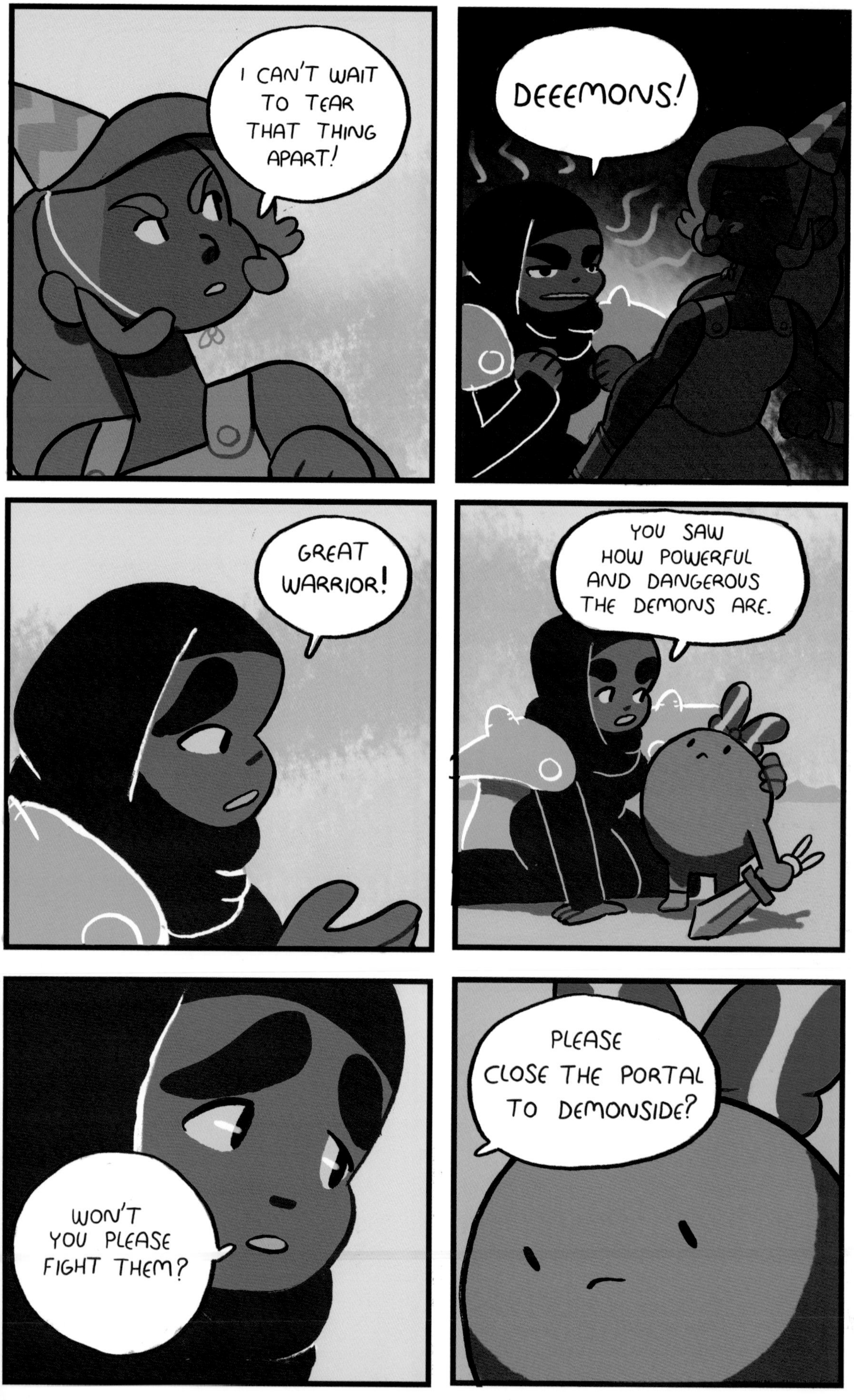
I CAN'T WAIT TO TEAR THAT THING APART!
DEEEMONS!
GREAT WARRIOR!
YOU SAW HOW POWERFUL AND DANGEROUS THE DEMONS ARE.
WON'T YOU PLEASE FIGHT THEM?
PLEASE CLOSE THE PORTAL TO DEMONSIDE?

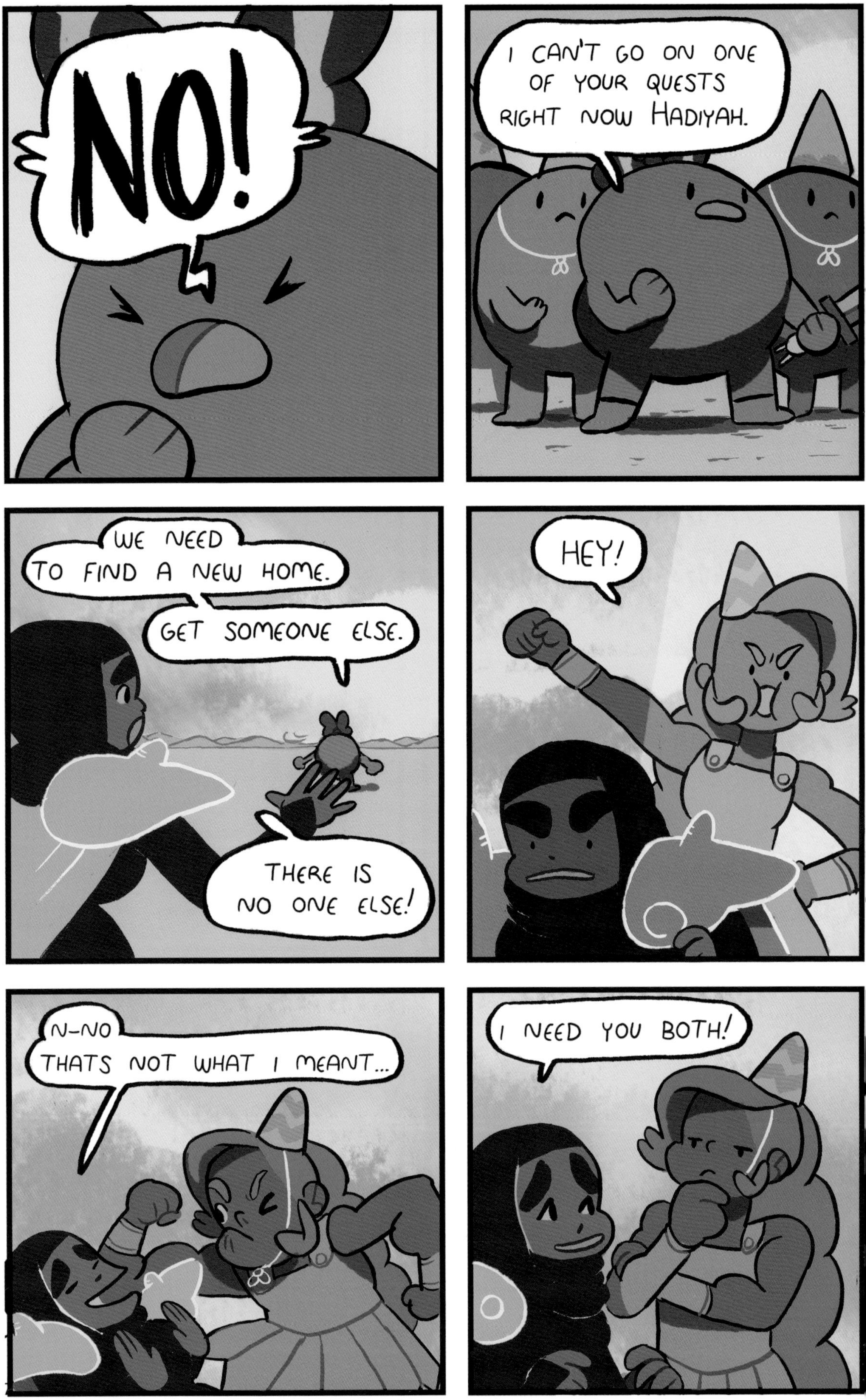
NO!
I CAN'T GO ON ONE OF YOUR QUESTS RIGHT NOW HADIYAH.
WE NEED TO FIND A NEW HOME.
GET SOMEONE ELSE.
THERE IS NO ONE ELSE!
HEY!
N-NO
THATS NOT WHAT I MEANT...
I NEED YOU BOTH!

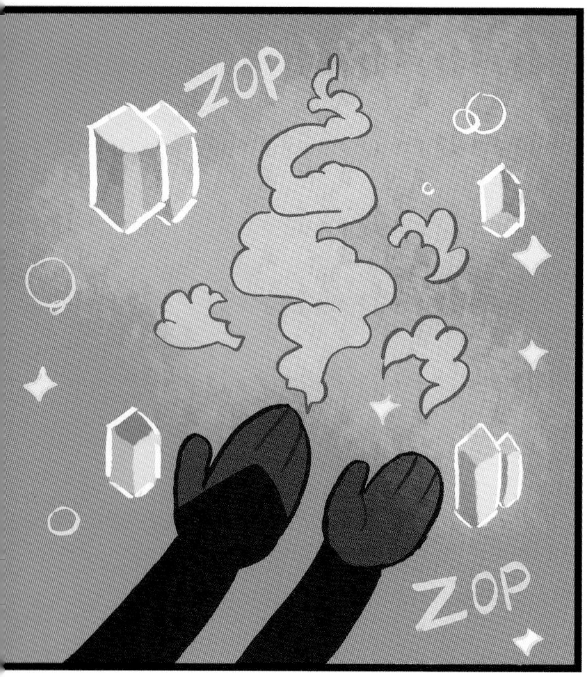
ZOP
ZOP

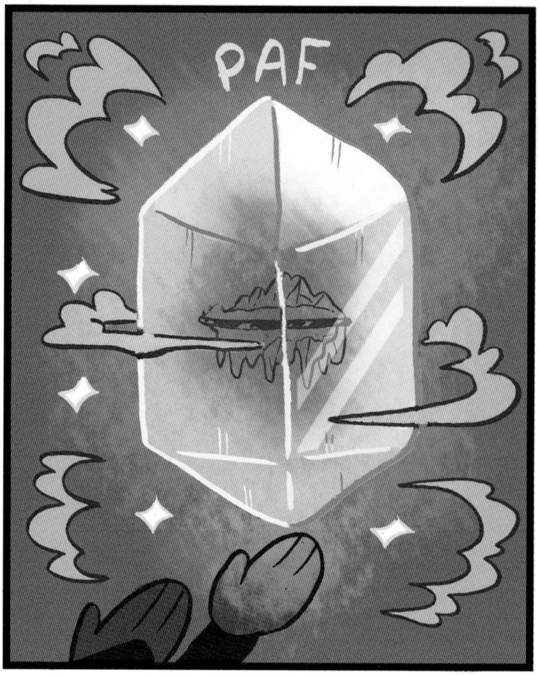
PAF

THOUSANDS OF YEARS AGO,

THERE WERE TWO LANDS.

ONE, RULED BY JUSTICE AND SUN AND LIFE.

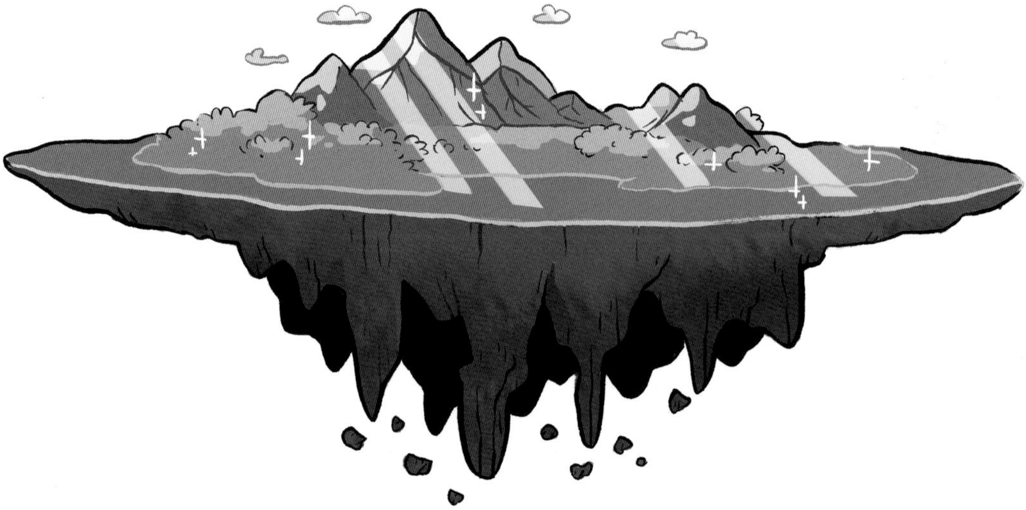

THE OTHER,

RULED BY WICKEDNESS AND DARKNESS AND WAR.

DEMONS INVADED THE LANDS OF JUSTICE

AND DESTROYED EVERYTHING GOOD.

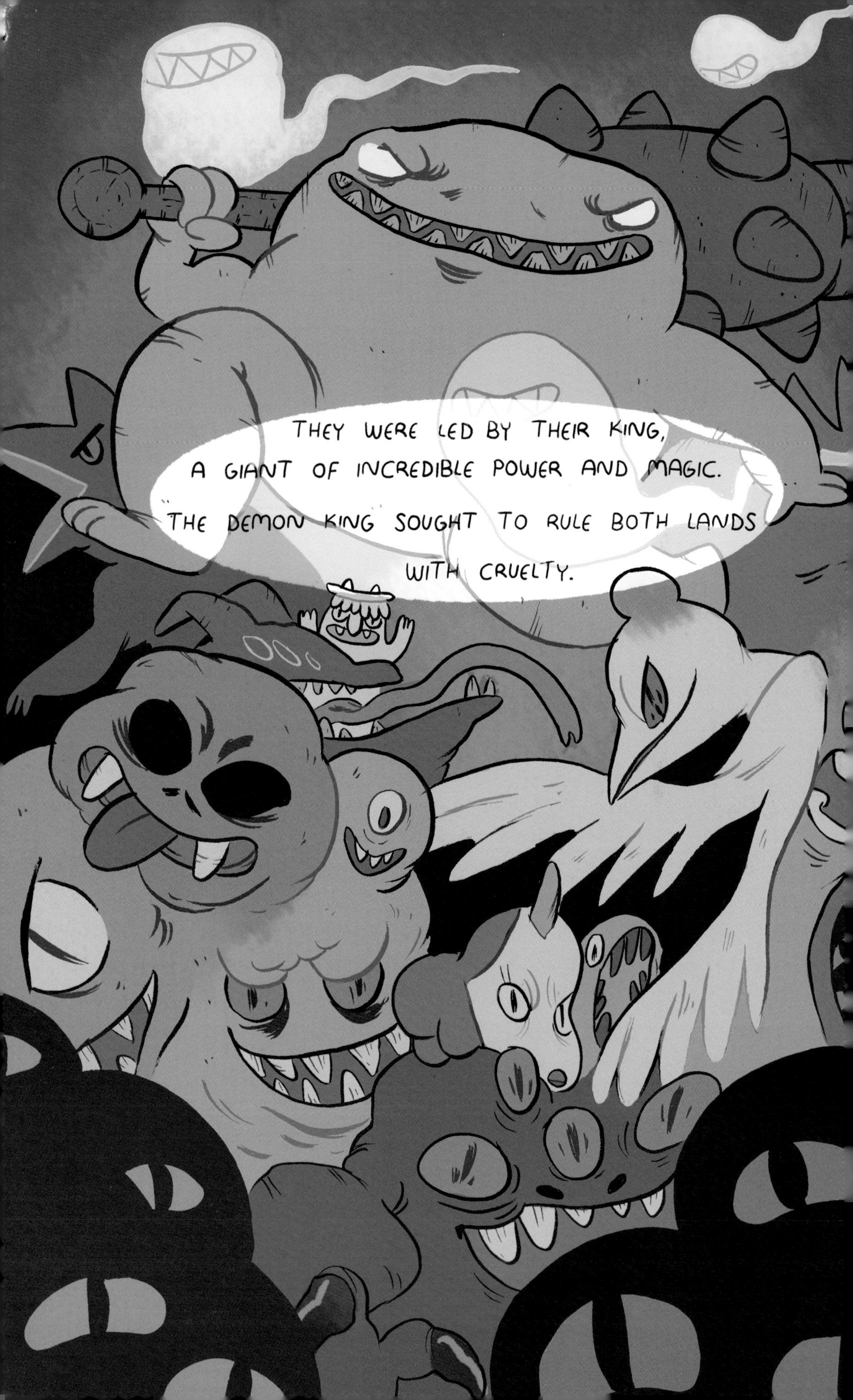
THEY WERE LED BY THEIR KING,
A GIANT OF INCREDIBLE POWER AND MAGIC.
"THE DEMON KING" SOUGHT TO RULE BOTH LANDS
WITH CRUELTY.

HOWEVER, A BRAVE HERO
WAS ABLE TO SOMEHOW
SEPARATE THE TWO LANDS.

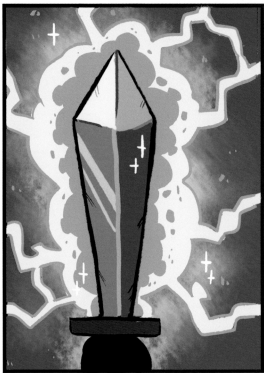

SEALING EACH BEHIND TWO SEPARATE PORTALS.

THEY BECAME PARALLEL WORLDS.

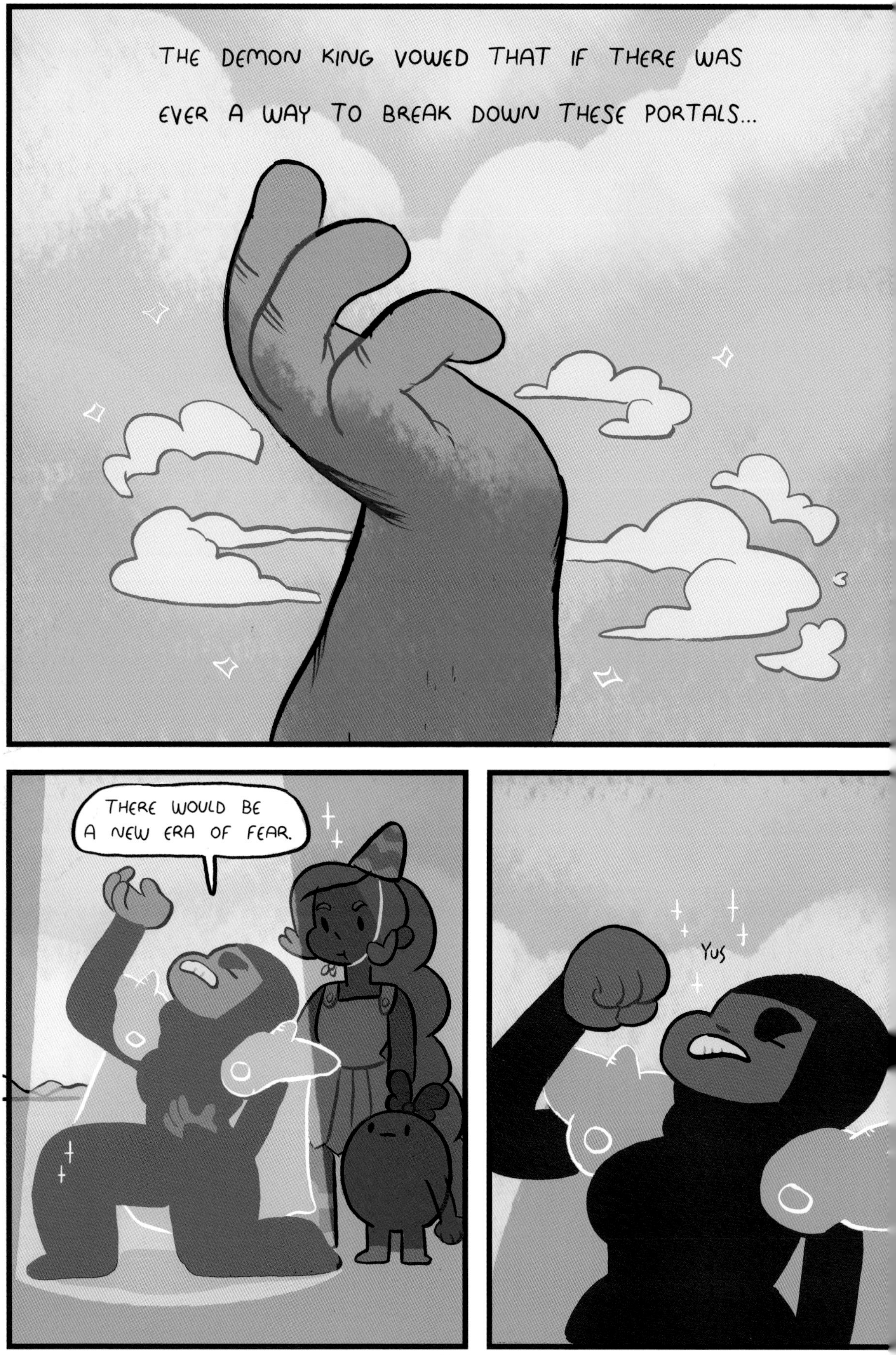
THE DEMON KING VOWED THAT IF THERE WAS EVER A WAY TO BREAK DOWN THESE PORTALS...
THERE WOULD BE A NEW ERA OF FEAR.
YUS

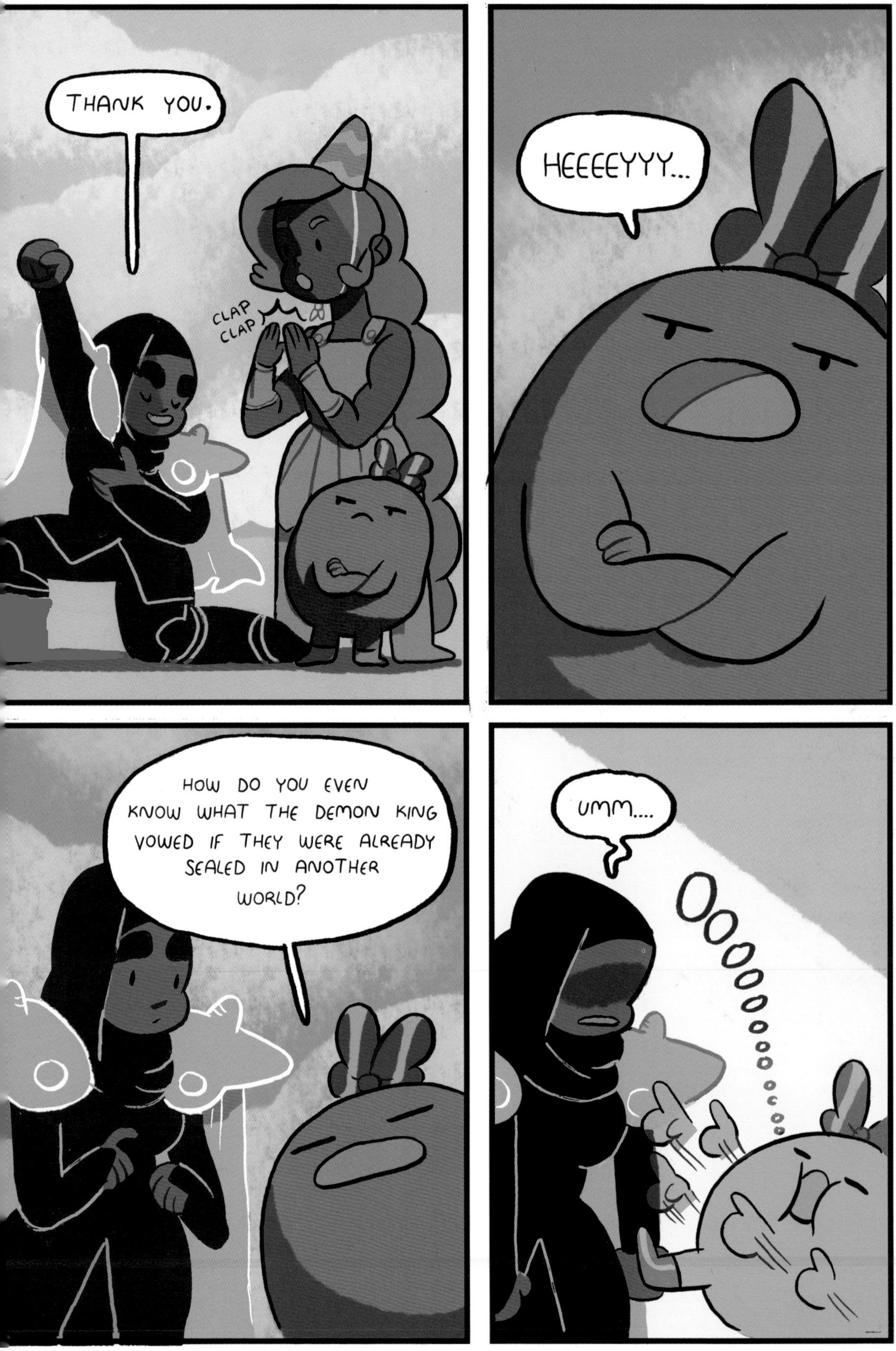
THANK YOU.
CLAP CLAP
HEEEEYYY...
HOW DO YOU EVEN KNOW WHAT THE DEMON KING VOWED IF THEY WERE ALREADY SEALED IN ANOTHER WORLD?
UMM....
OOOOOOOOOOOOO

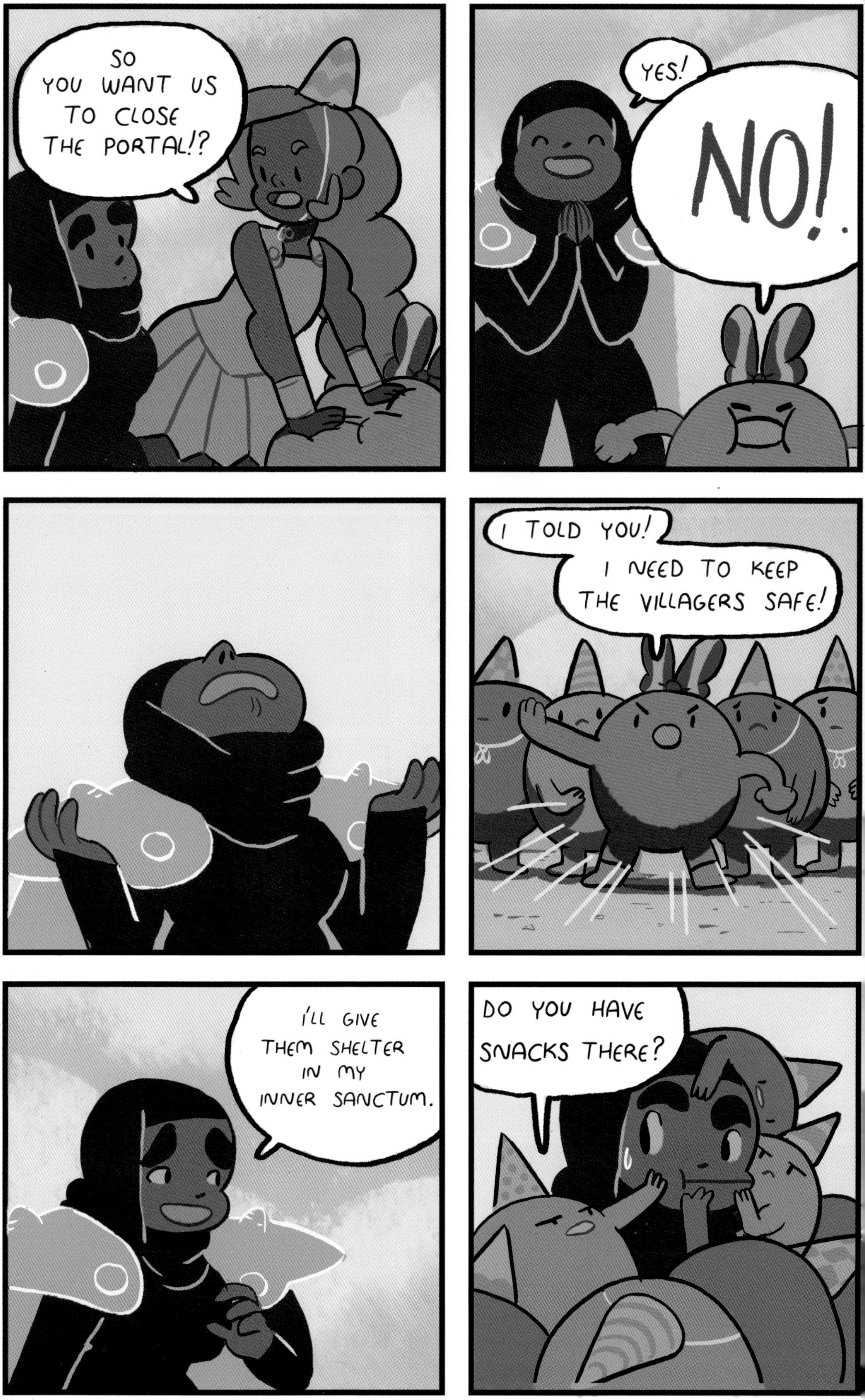
SO YOU WANT US TO CLOSE THE PORTAL!?
YES!
NO!
I TOLD YOU!
I NEED TO KEEP THE VILLAGERS SAFE!
I'LL GIVE THEM SHELTER IN MY INNER SANCTUM.
DO YOU HAVE SNACKS THERE?

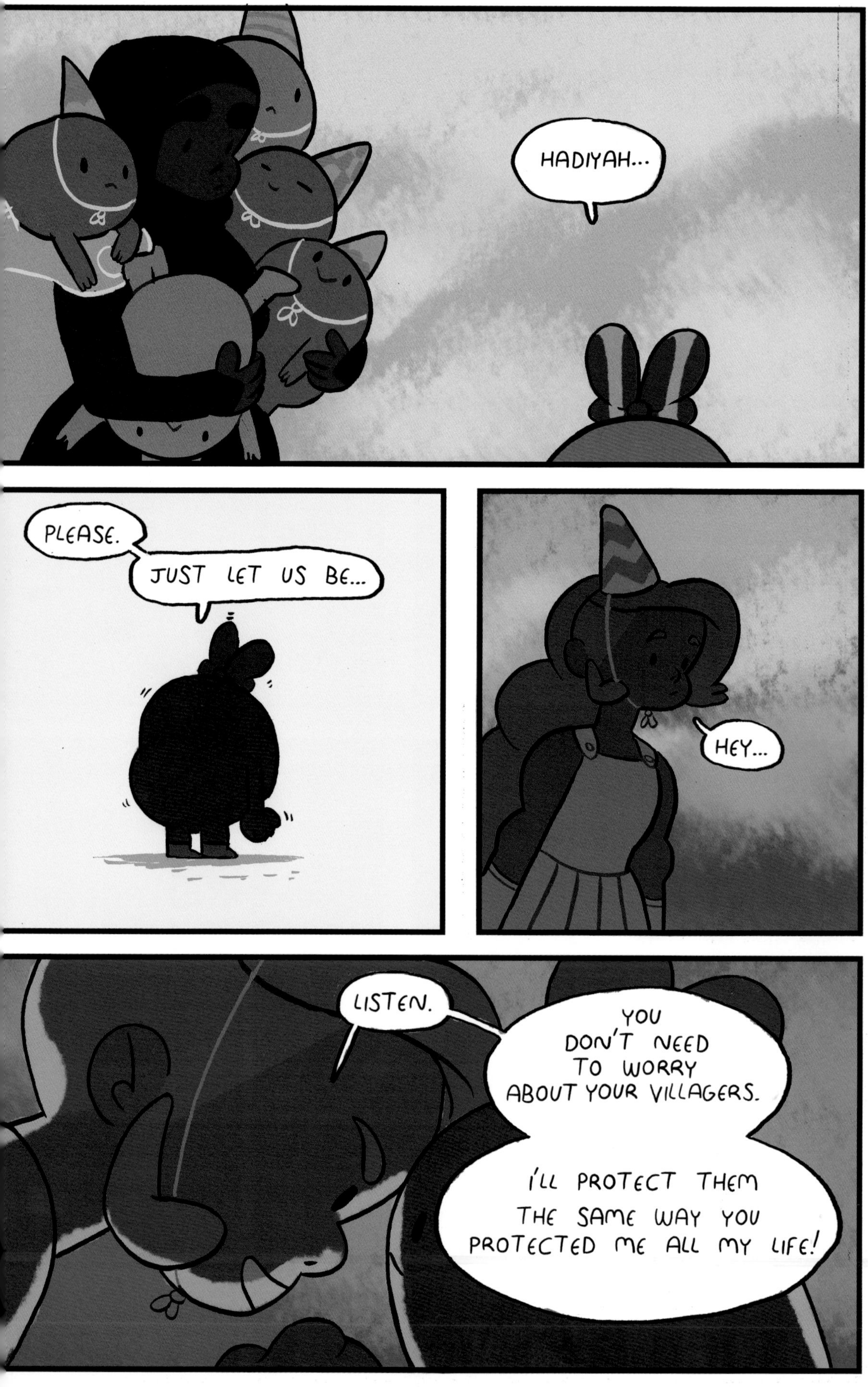
HADIYAH...
PLEASE.
JUST LET US BE...
HEY...
LISTEN.
YOU DON'T NEED TO WORRY ABOUT YOUR VILLAGERS.
I'LL PROTECT THEM THE SAME WAY YOU PROTECTED ME ALL MY LIFE!

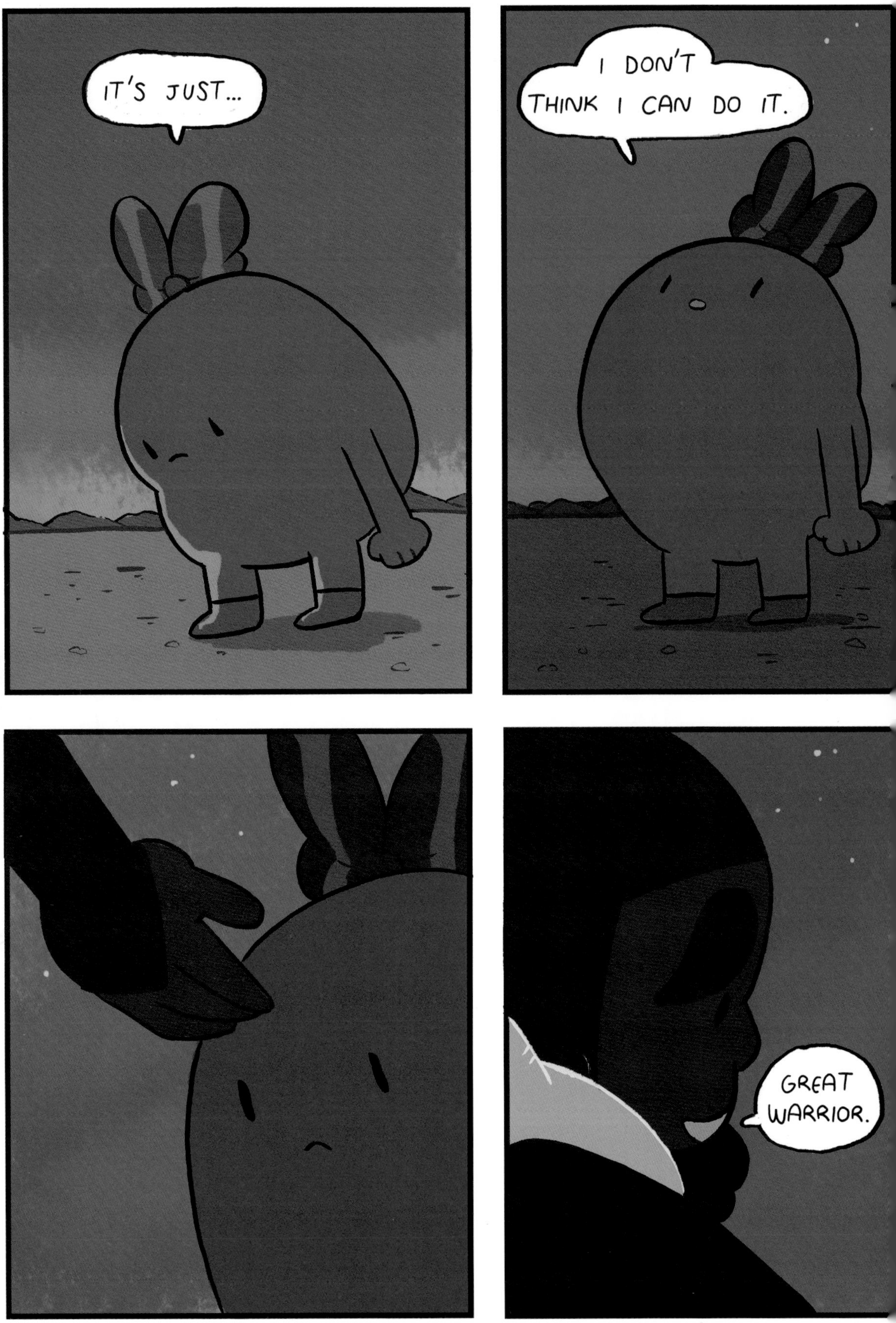
IT'S JUST...
I DON'T THINK I CAN DO IT.
GREAT WARRIOR.

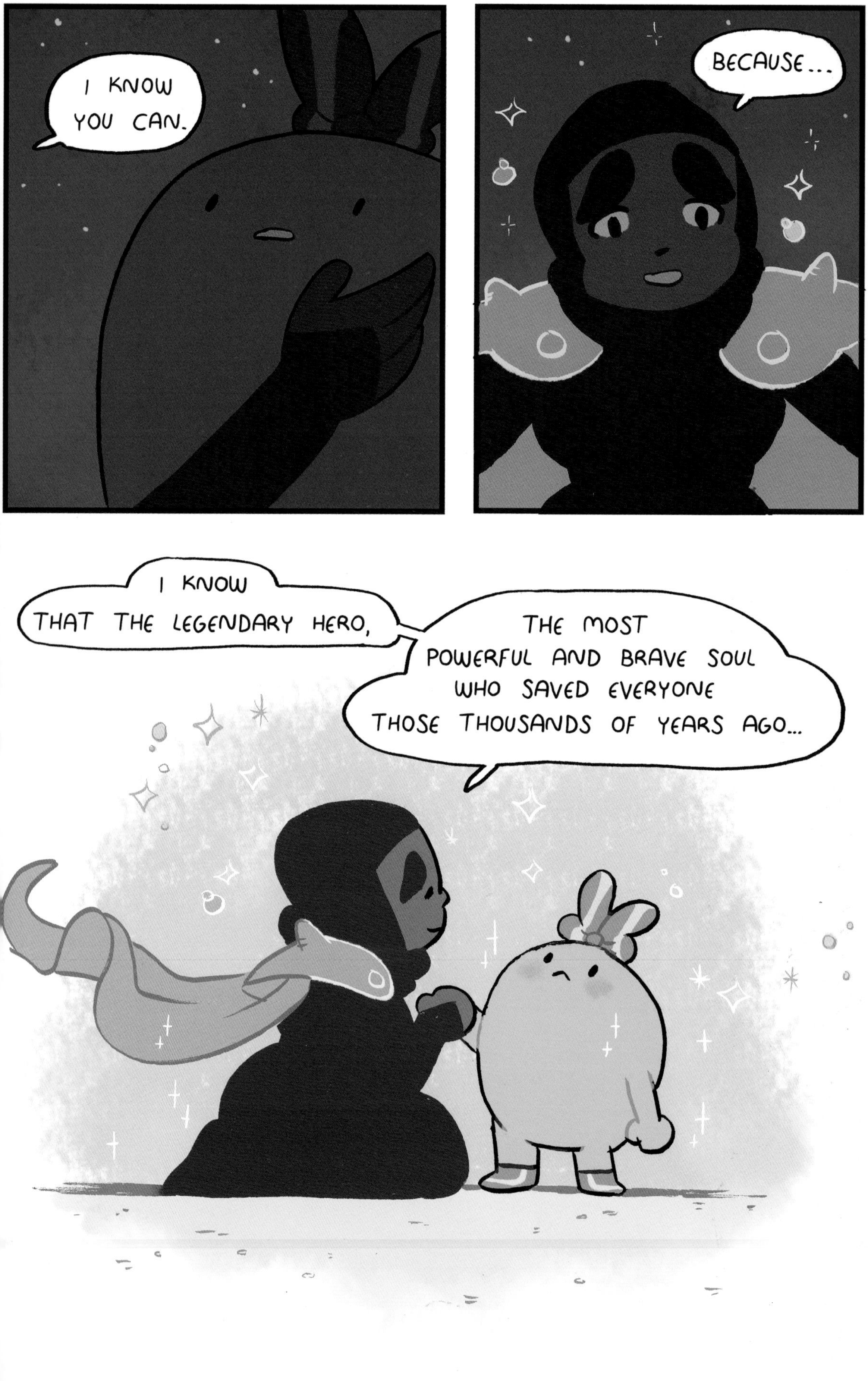
I KNOW YOU CAN.
BECAUSE...
I KNOW THAT THE LEGENDARY HERO,
THE MOST POWERFUL AND BRAVE SOUL WHO SAVED EVERYONE THOSE THOUSANDS OF YEARS AGO...

...WAS YOU.

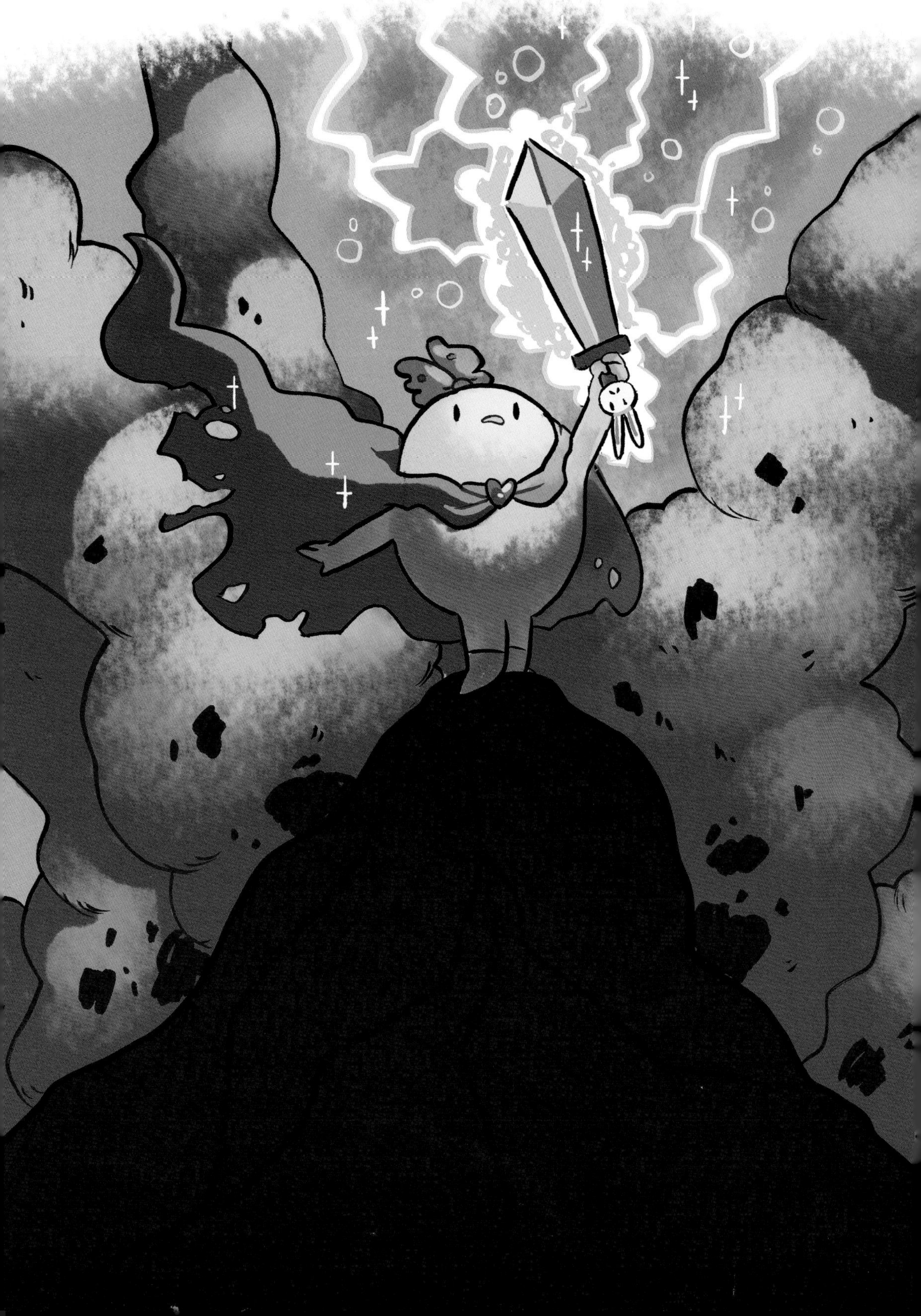

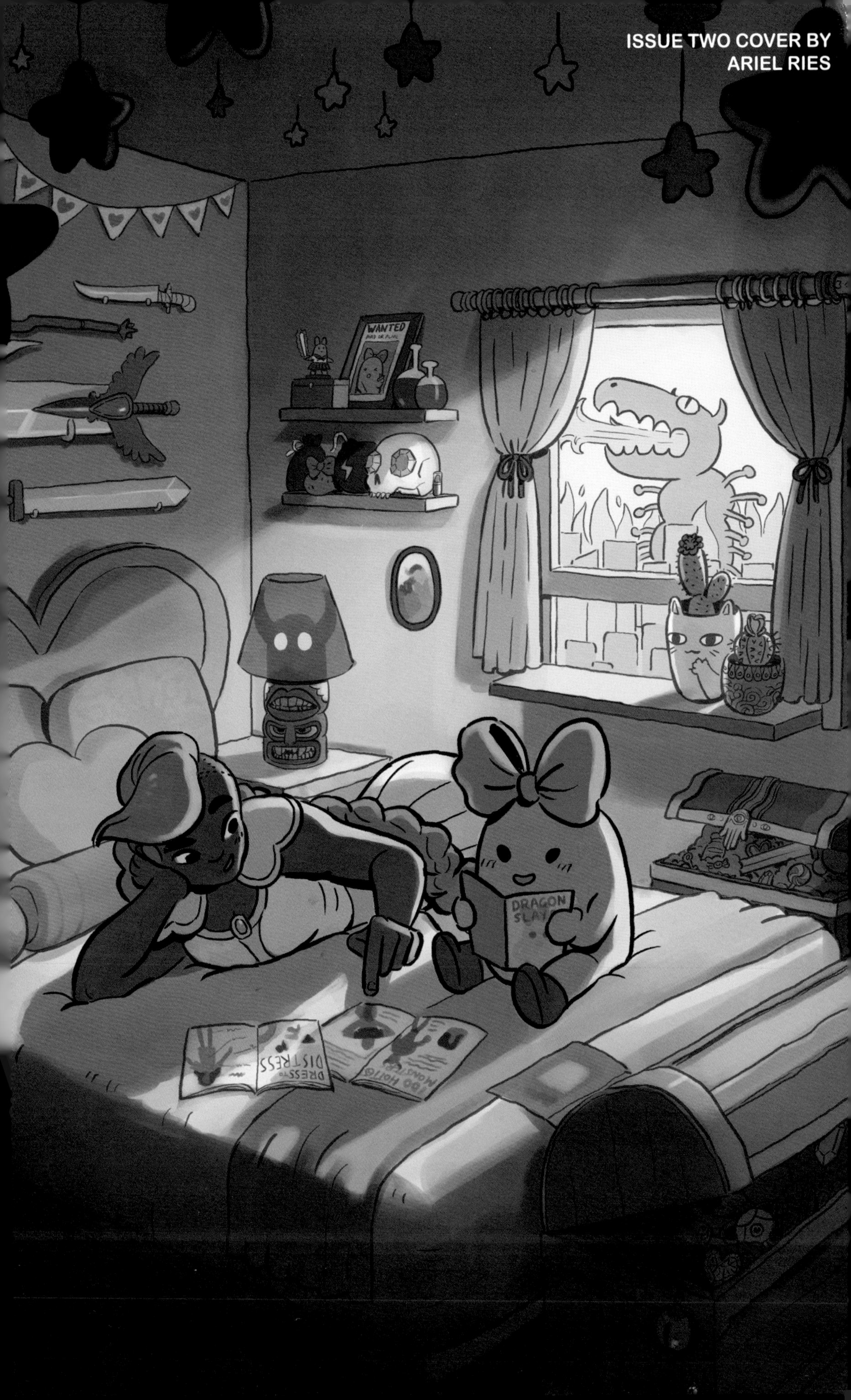
WANTED
DRESS to DISTRESS

ISSUE TWO COVER BY
ARIEL RIES

Chapter
Three

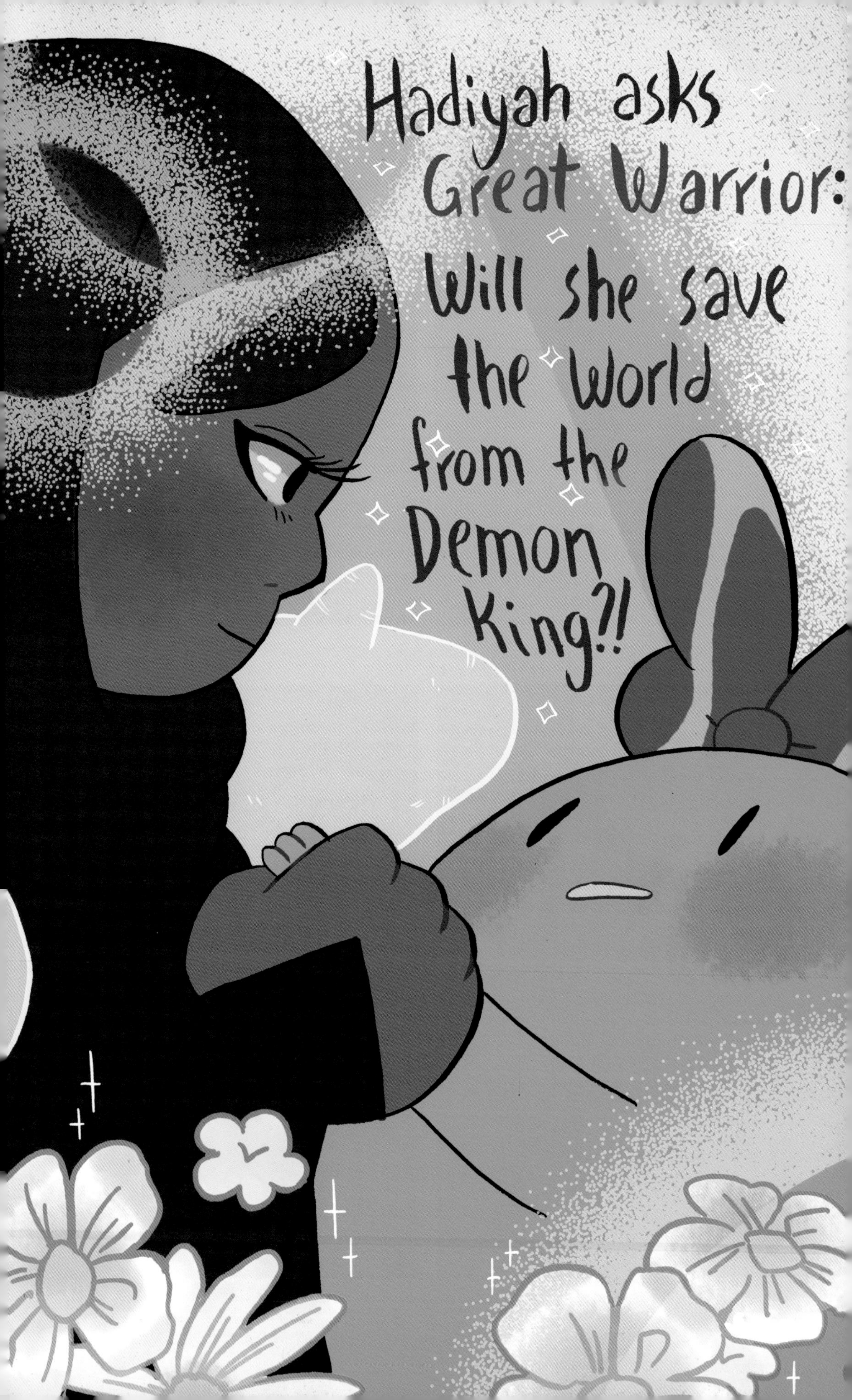
Hadiyah asks Great Warrior: Will she save the World from the Demon King?!

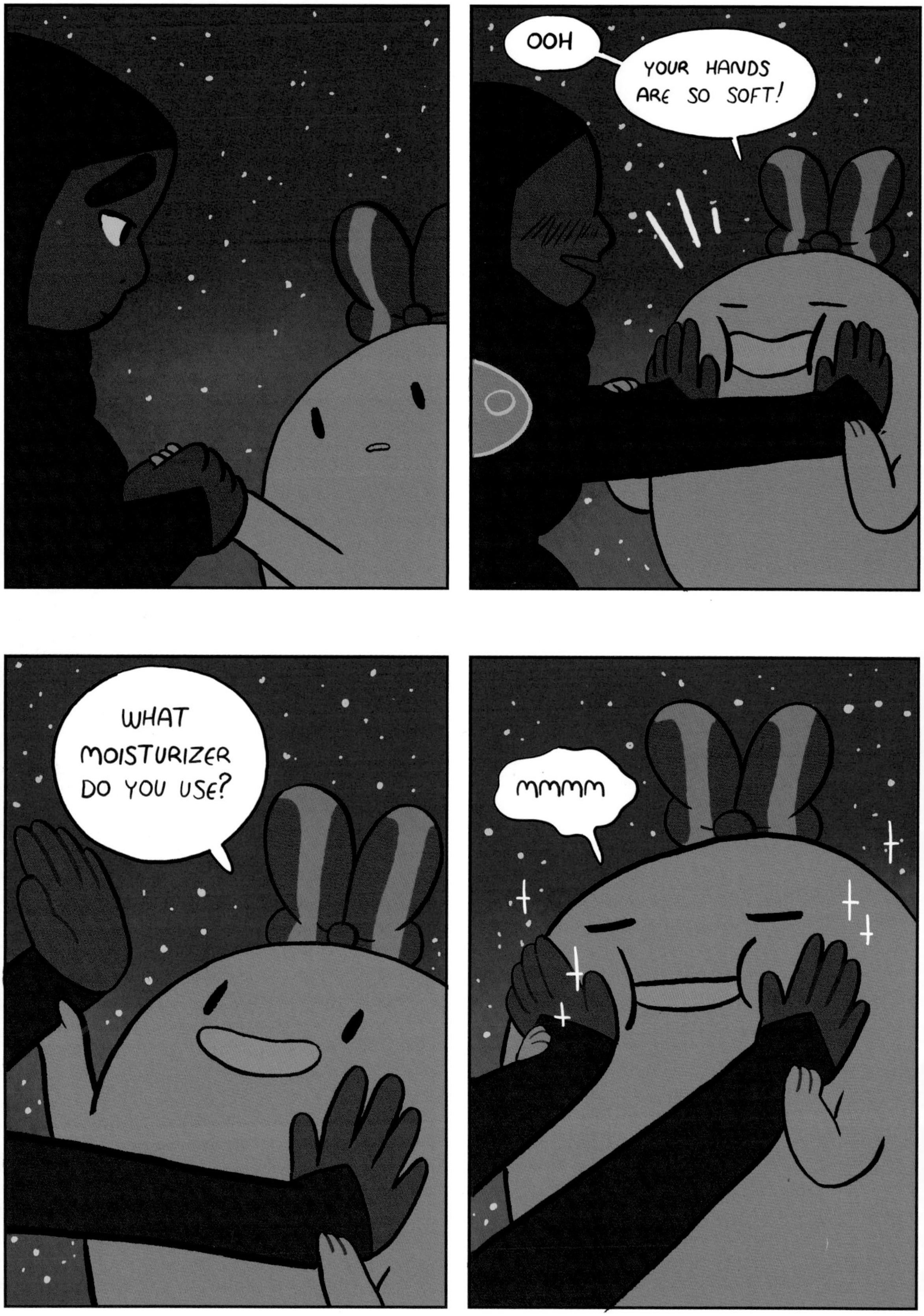
OOH
YOUR HANDS ARE SO SOFT!
WHAT MOISTURIZER DO YOU USE?
mmmm

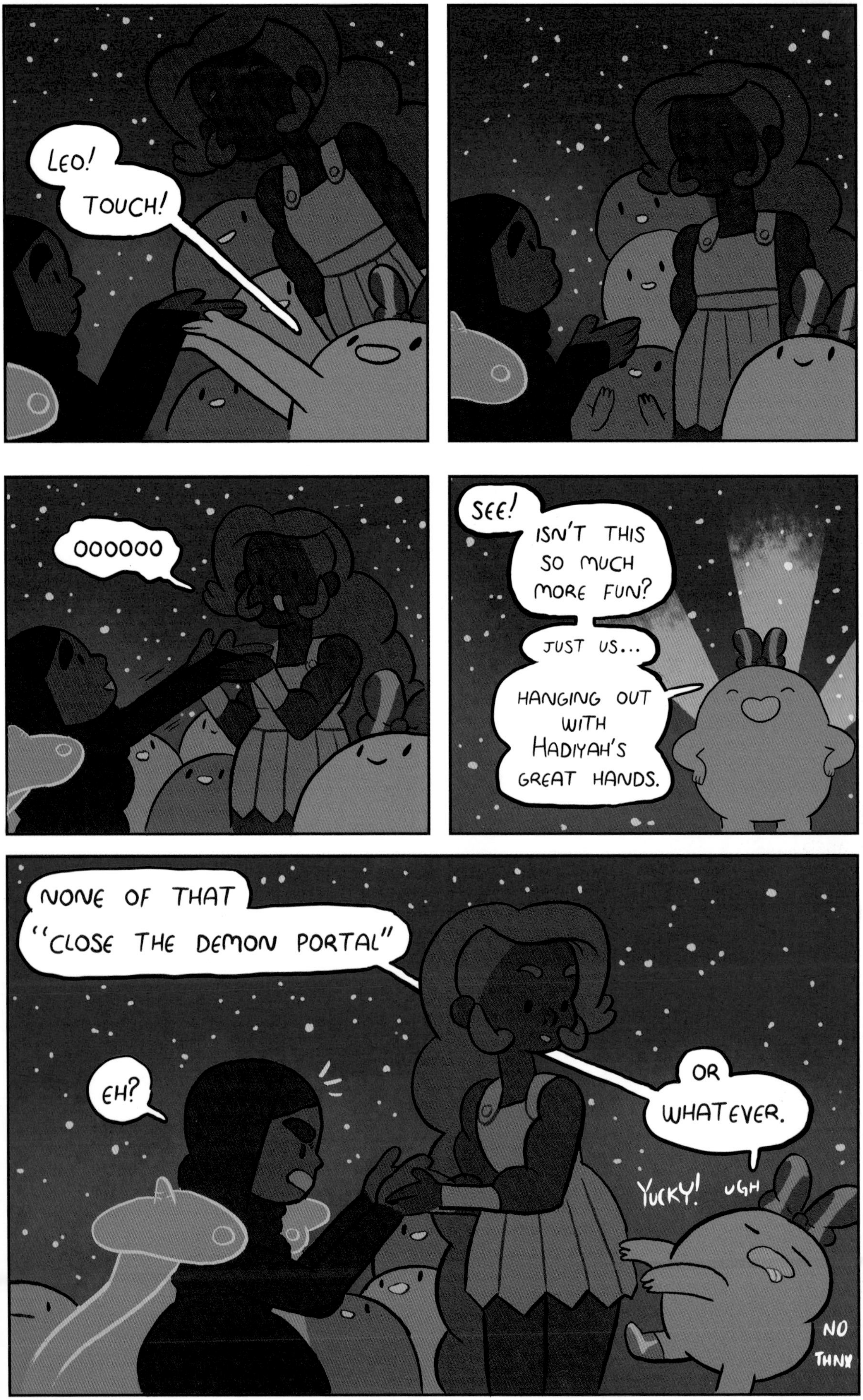
LEO!
TOUCH!
OOOOOO
SEE!
ISN'T THIS SO MUCH MORE FUN?
JUST US...
HANGING OUT WITH HADIYAH'S GREAT HANDS.
NONE OF THAT "CLOSE THE DEMON PORTAL"
OR WHATEVER.
EH?
YUCKY!
UGH
NO THNX

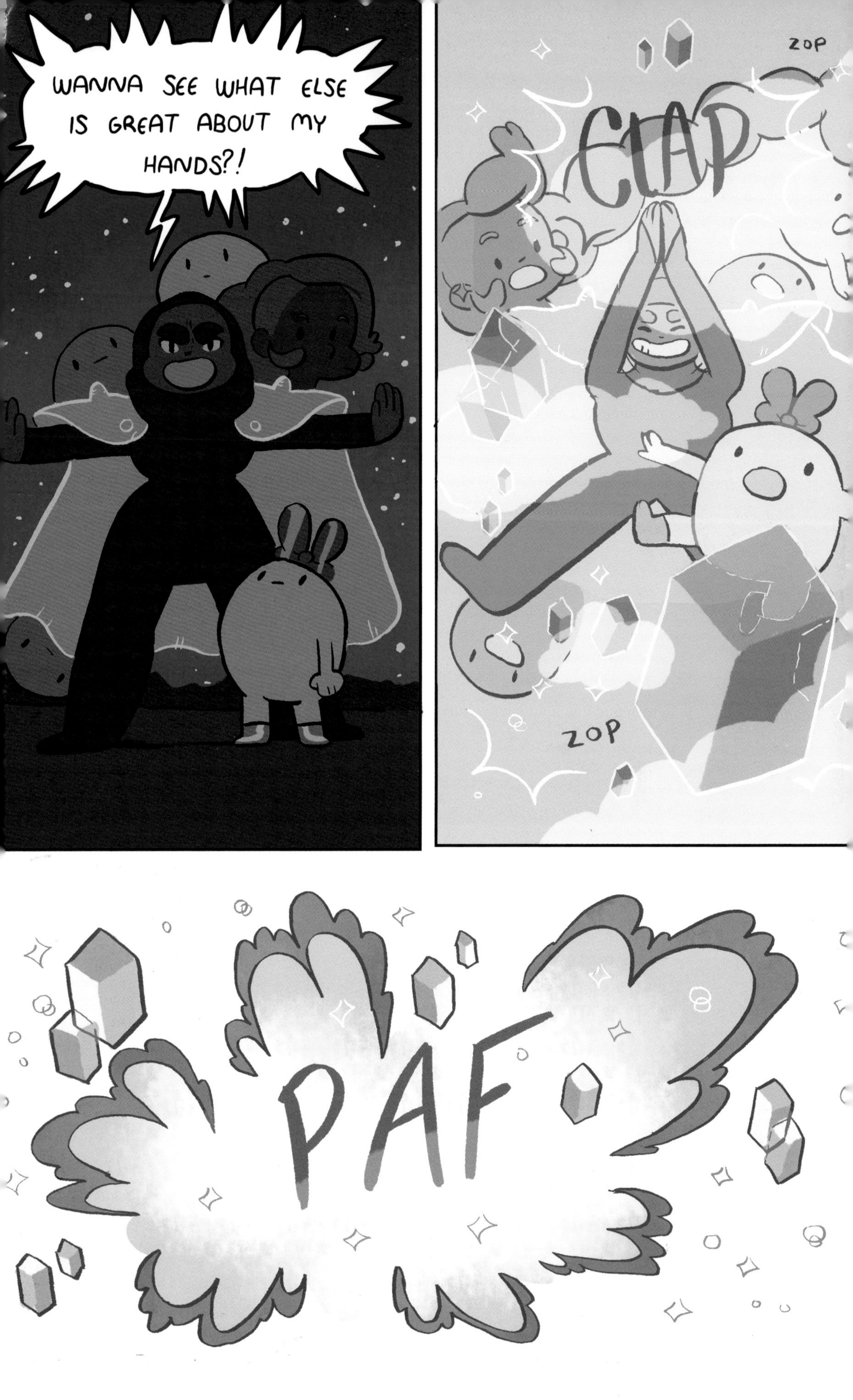
WANNA SEE WHAT ELSE IS GREAT ABOUT MY HANDS?!
ZOP
CLAP
ZOP
PAF

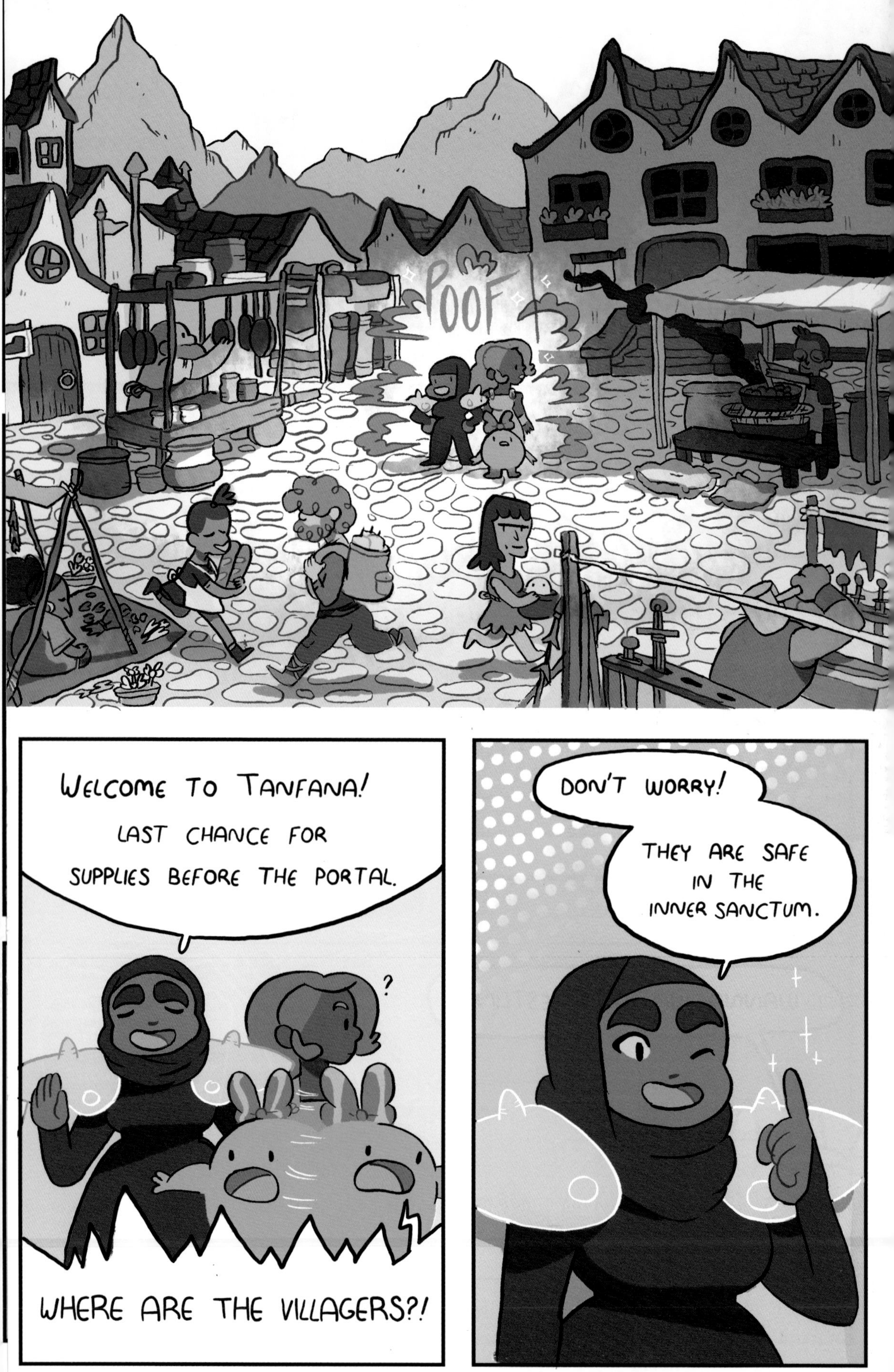
POOF
WELCOME TO TANFANA! LAST CHANCE FOR SUPPLIES BEFORE THE PORTAL.
?
WHERE ARE THE VILLAGERS?!
DON'T WORRY! THEY ARE SAFE IN THE INNER SANCTUM.

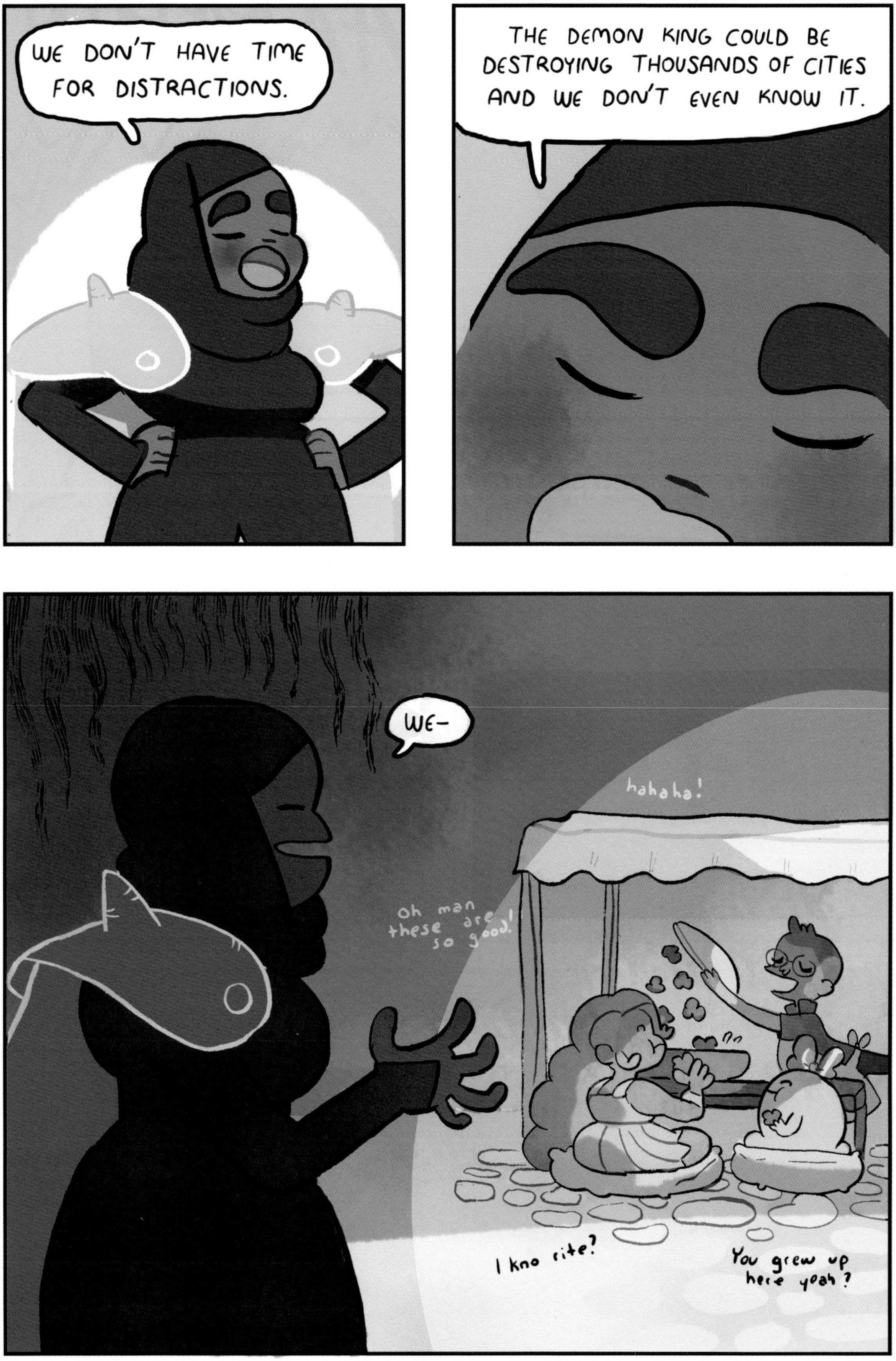
WE DON'T HAVE TIME FOR DISTRACTIONS.
THE DEMON KING COULD BE DESTROYING THOUSANDS OF CITIES AND WE DON'T EVEN KNOW IT.
WE-
hahaha!
oh man these are so good!
I kno rite?
You grew up here yeah?

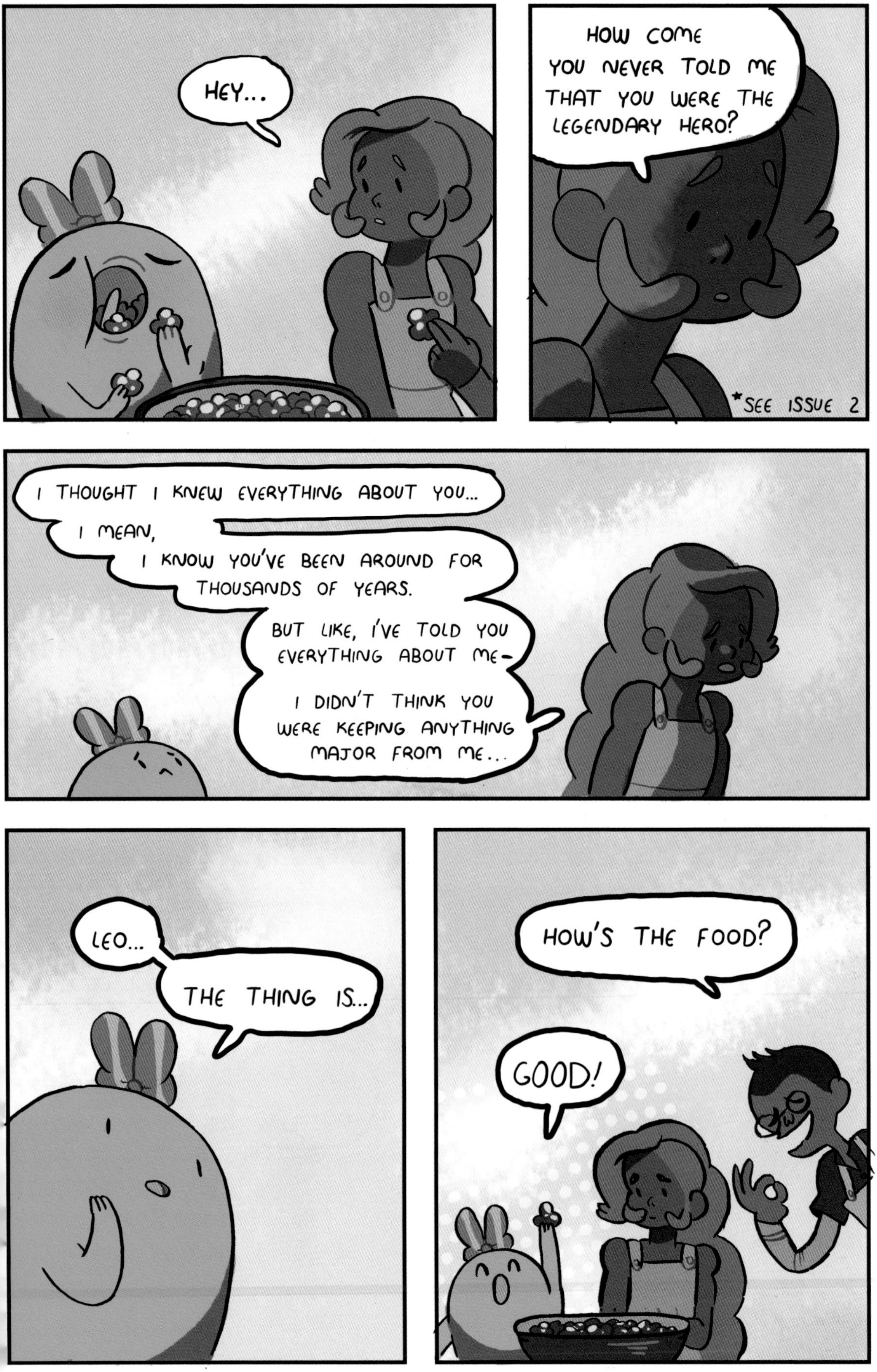
HEY...
HOW COME YOU NEVER TOLD ME THAT YOU WERE THE LEGENDARY HERO?
*SEE ISSUE 2
I THOUGHT I KNEW EVERYTHING ABOUT YOU...
I MEAN,
I KNOW YOU'VE BEEN AROUND FOR THOUSANDS OF YEARS.
BUT LIKE, I'VE TOLD YOU EVERYTHING ABOUT ME-
I DIDN'T THINK YOU WERE KEEPING ANYTHING MAJOR FROM ME...
LEO...
THE THING IS...
HOW'S THE FOOD?
GOOD!

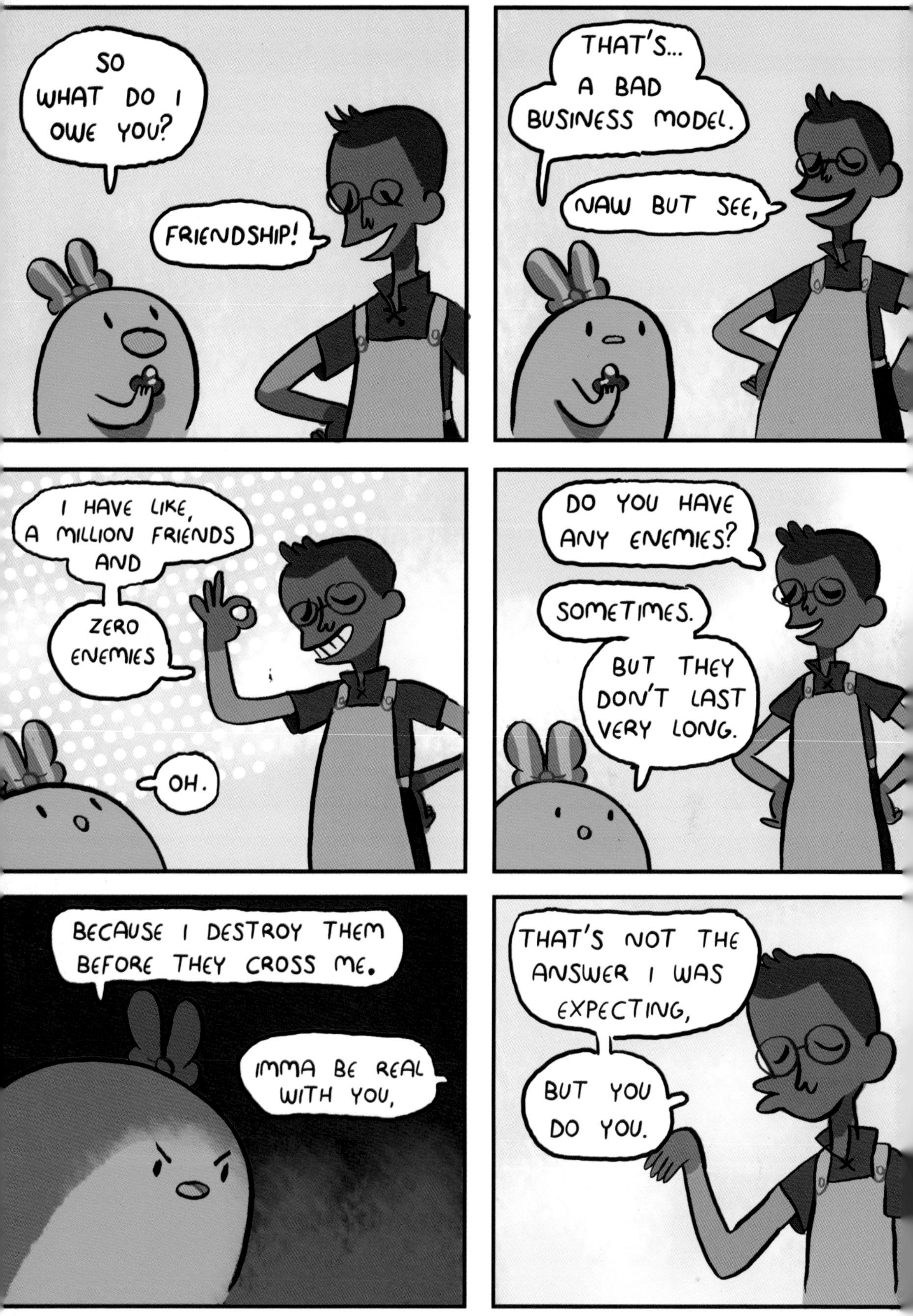
SO WHAT DO I OWE YOU?
FRIENDSHIP!
THAT'S... A BAD BUSINESS MODEL.
NAW BUT SEE,
I HAVE LIKE, A MILLION FRIENDS AND
ZERO ENEMIES
OH.
DO YOU HAVE ANY ENEMIES?
SOMETIMES.
BUT THEY DON'T LAST VERY LONG.
BECAUSE I DESTROY THEM BEFORE THEY CROSS ME.
IMMA BE REAL WITH YOU,
THAT'S NOT THE ANSWER I WAS EXPECTING,
BUT YOU DO YOU.

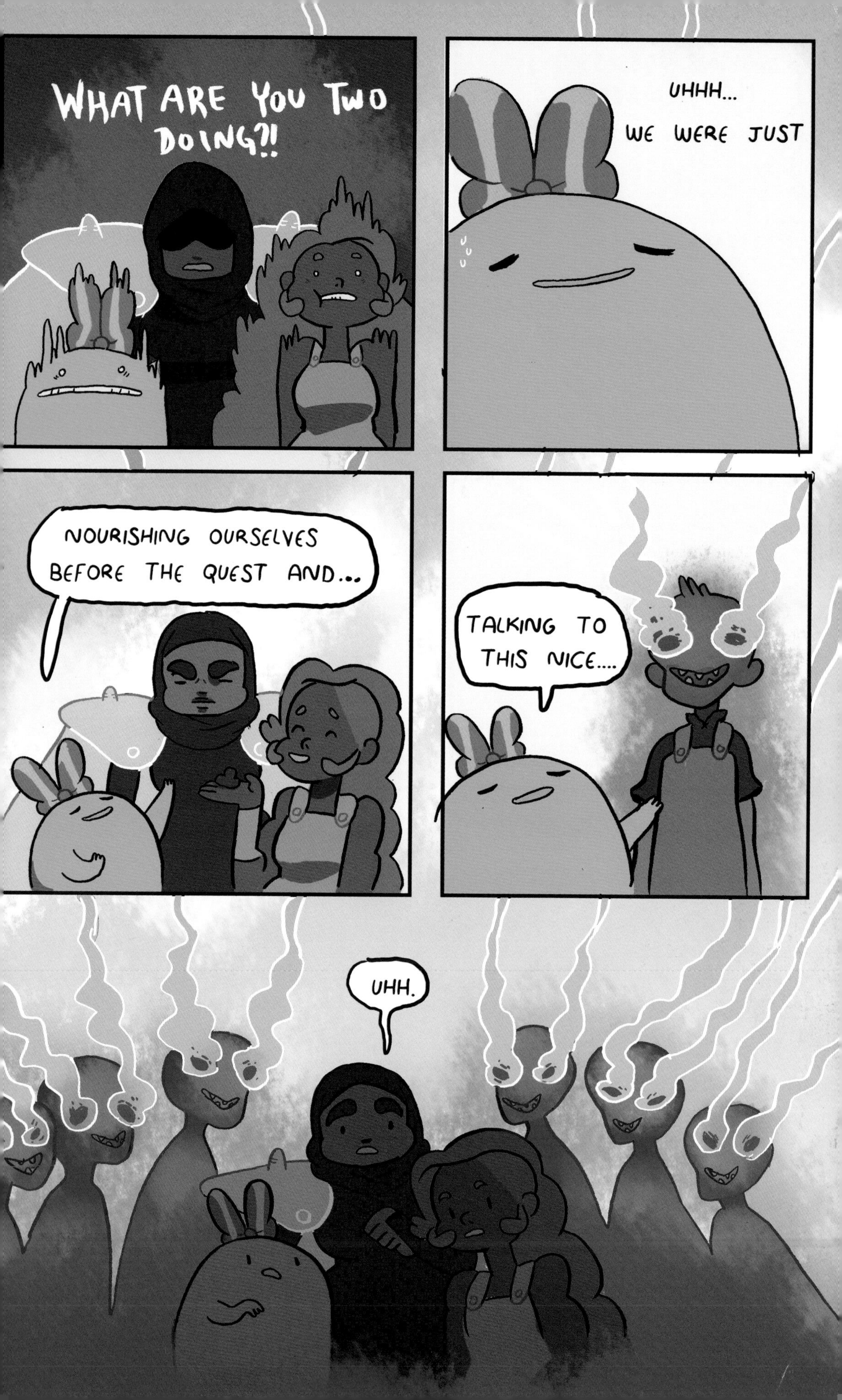
WHAT ARE YOU TWO DOING?!
UHHH...
WE WERE JUST
NOURISHING OURSELVES BEFORE THE QUEST AND...
TALKING TO THIS NICE....
UHH.

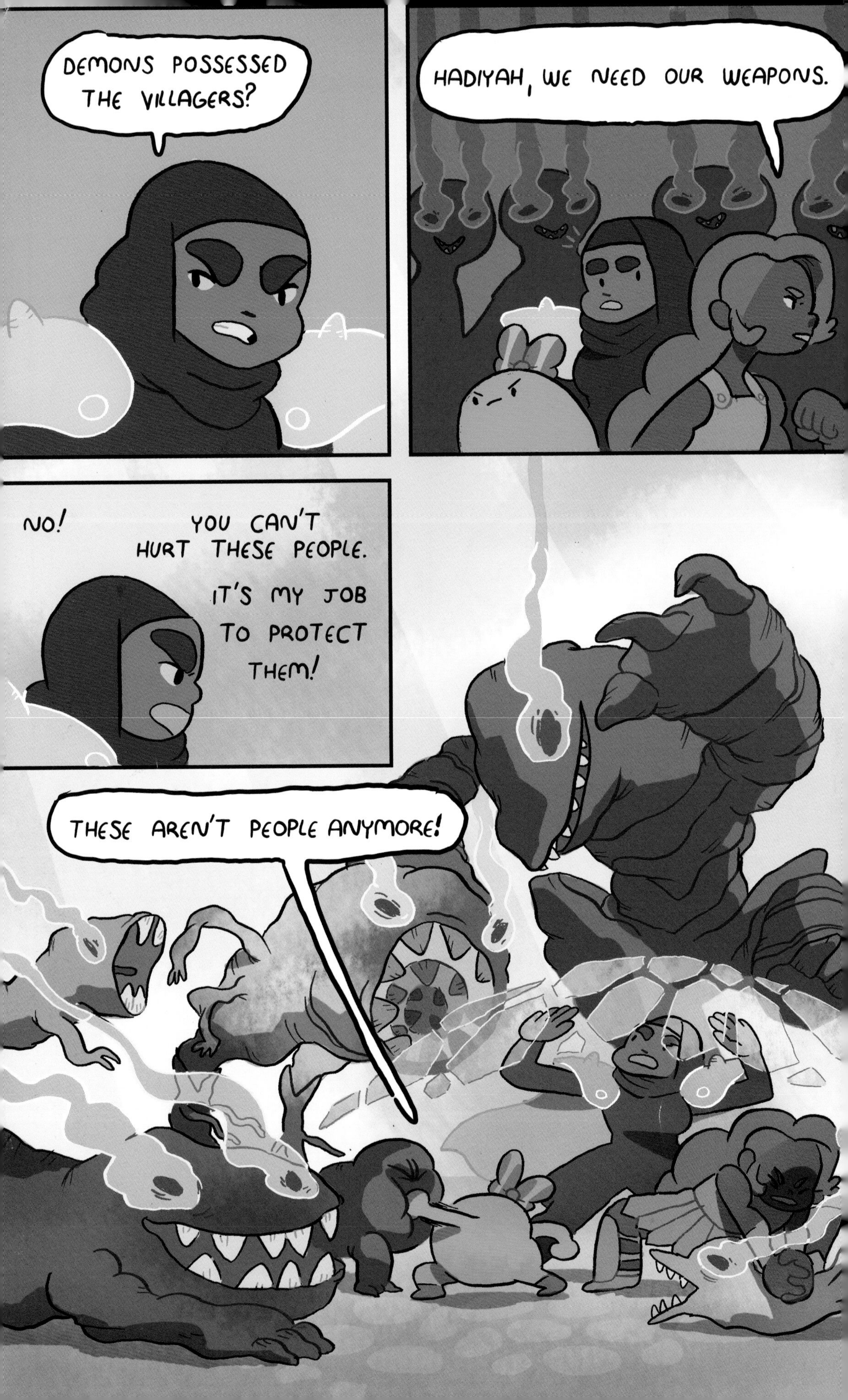
DEMONS POSSESSED THE VILLAGERS?
HADIYAH, WE NEED OUR WEAPONS.
NO!
YOU CAN'T HURT THESE PEOPLE.
IT'S MY JOB TO PROTECT THEM!
THESE AREN'T PEOPLE ANYMORE!

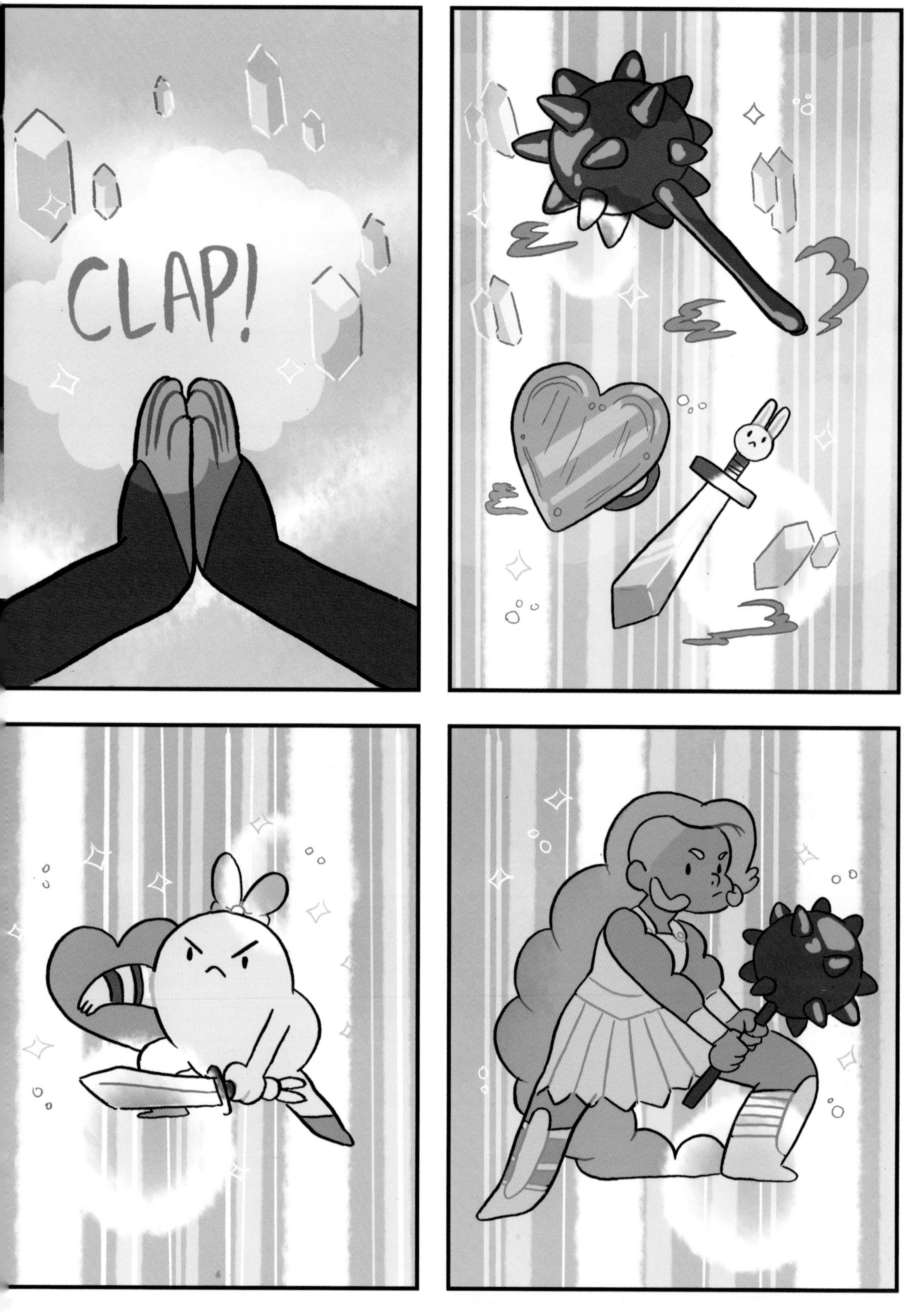
CLAP!

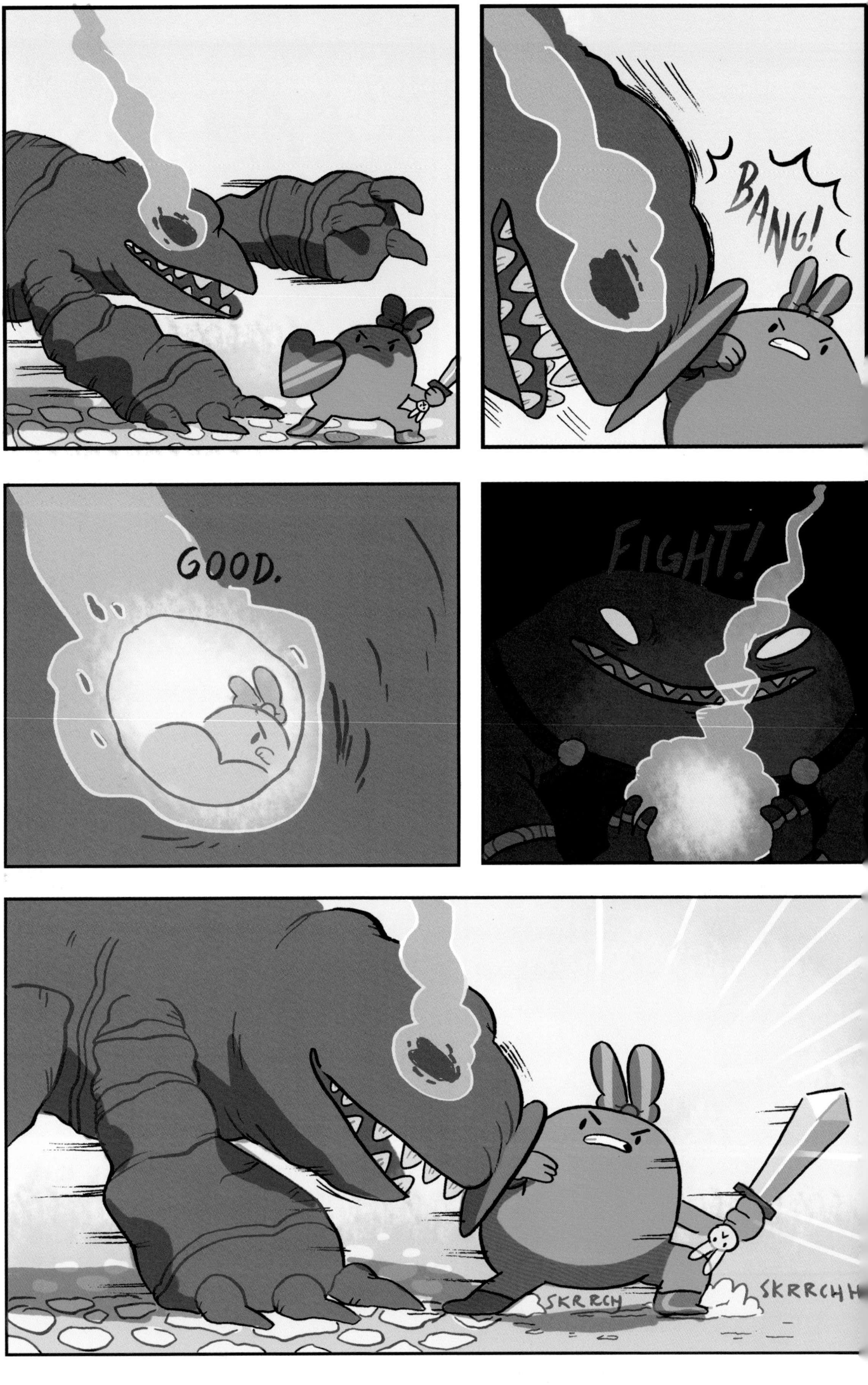
BANG!
GOOD.
FIGHT!
SKRRCH
SKRRCHH

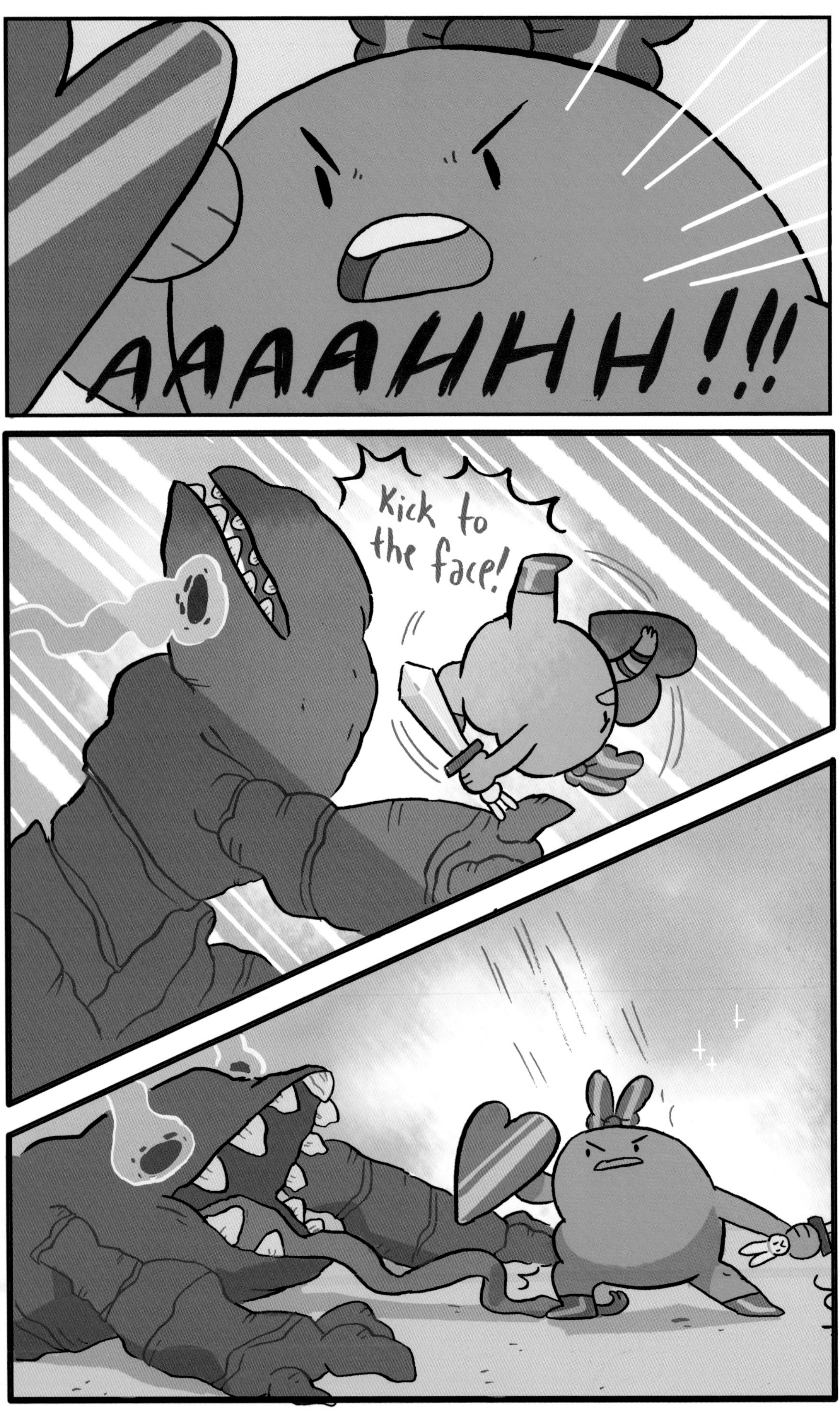
AAAAAHHH!!!
Kick to the face!

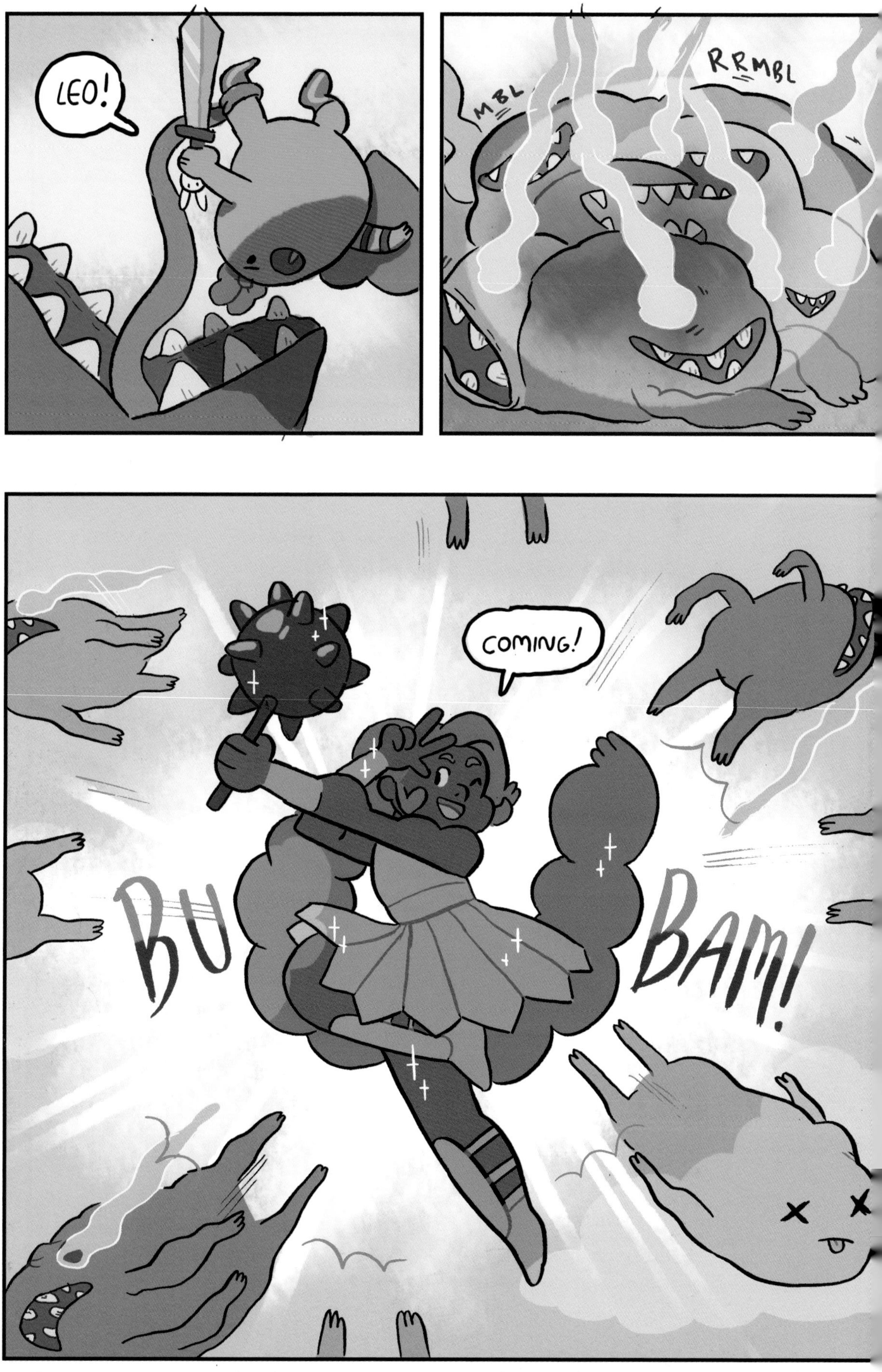
LEO!
MBL
RRMBL
COMING!
BU
BAM!

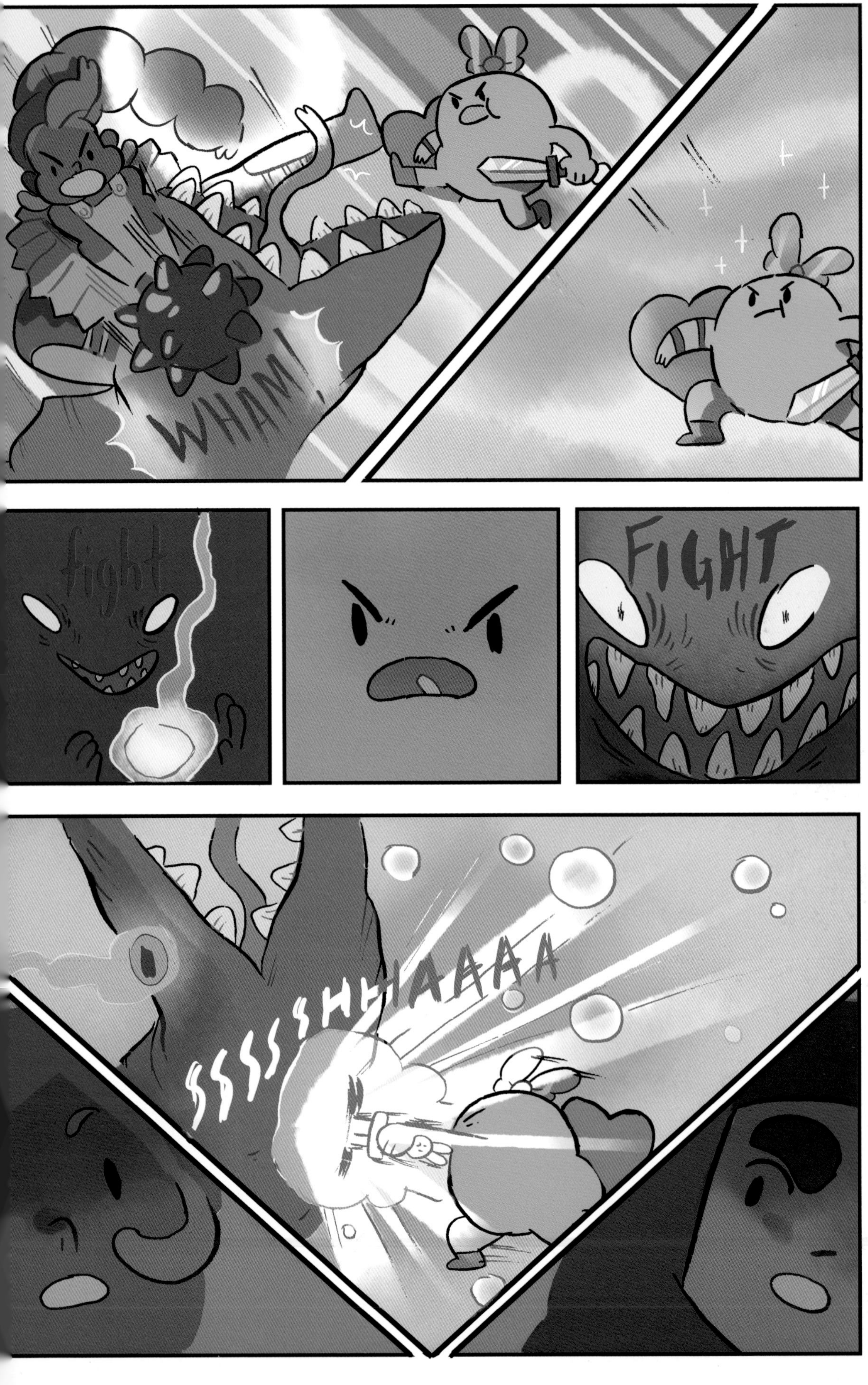
WHAM!
fight
FIGHT
SSSSSHHHAAAAA

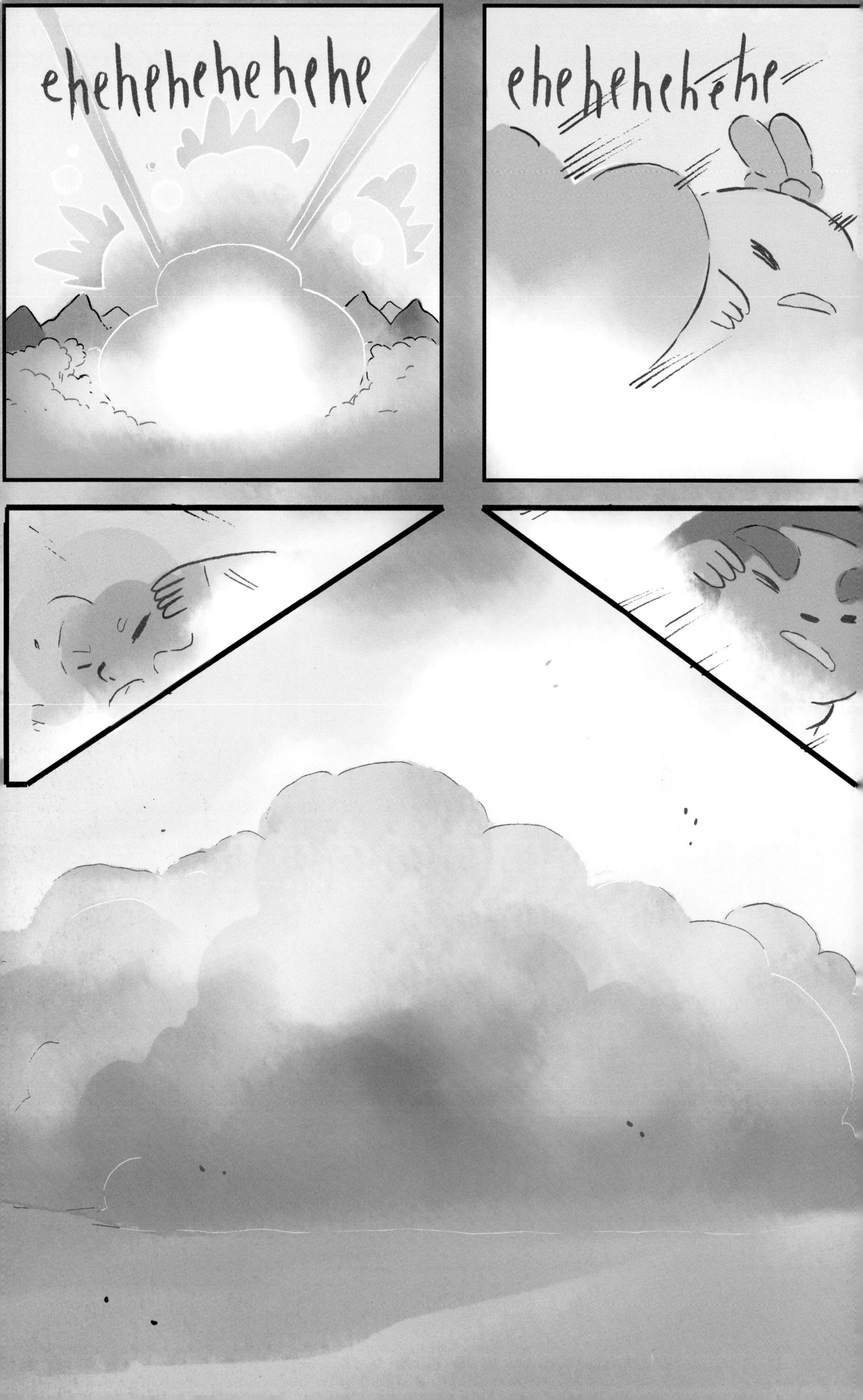
ehehehehehehe
ehehehehehe

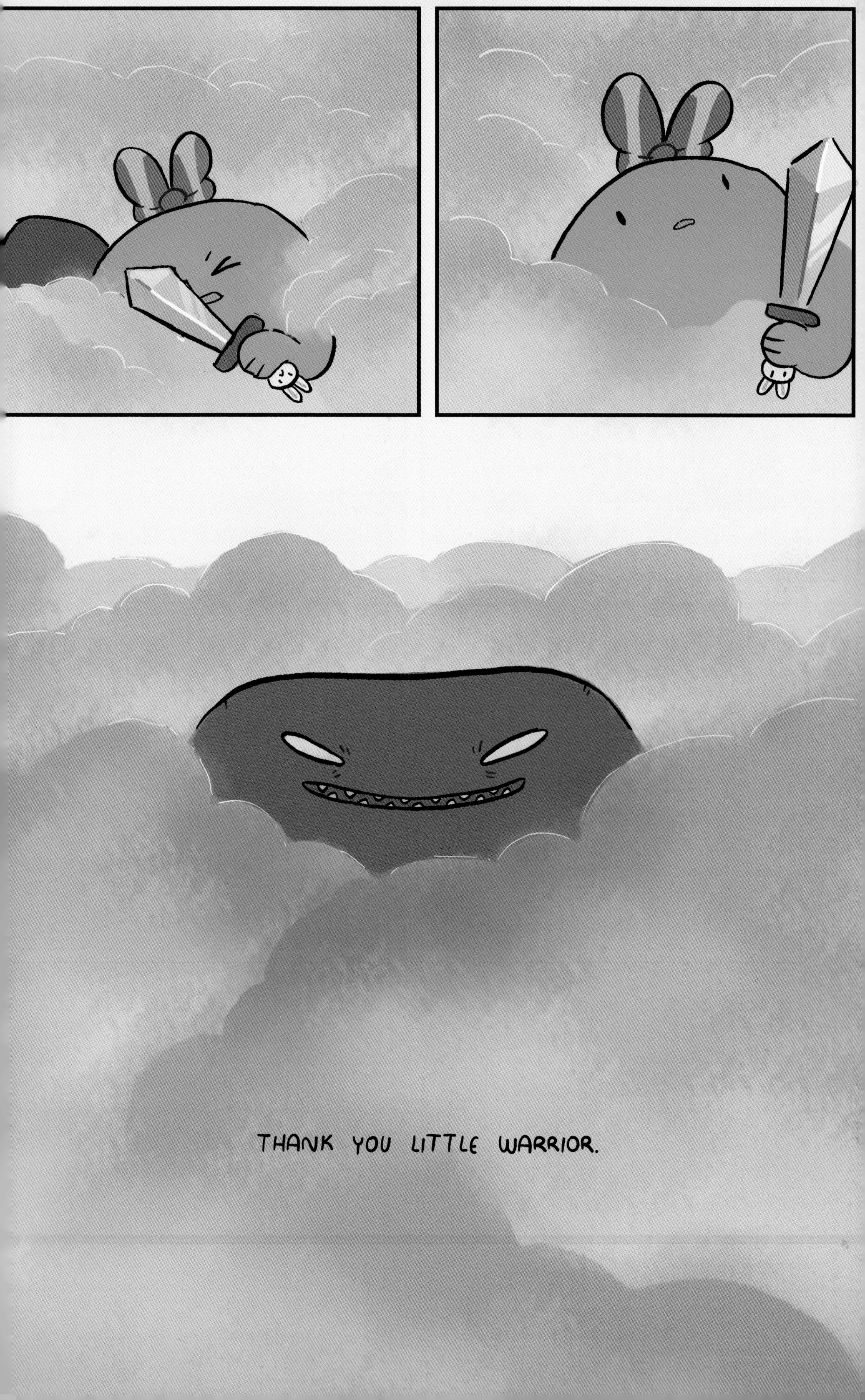
THANK YOU LITTLE WARRIOR.

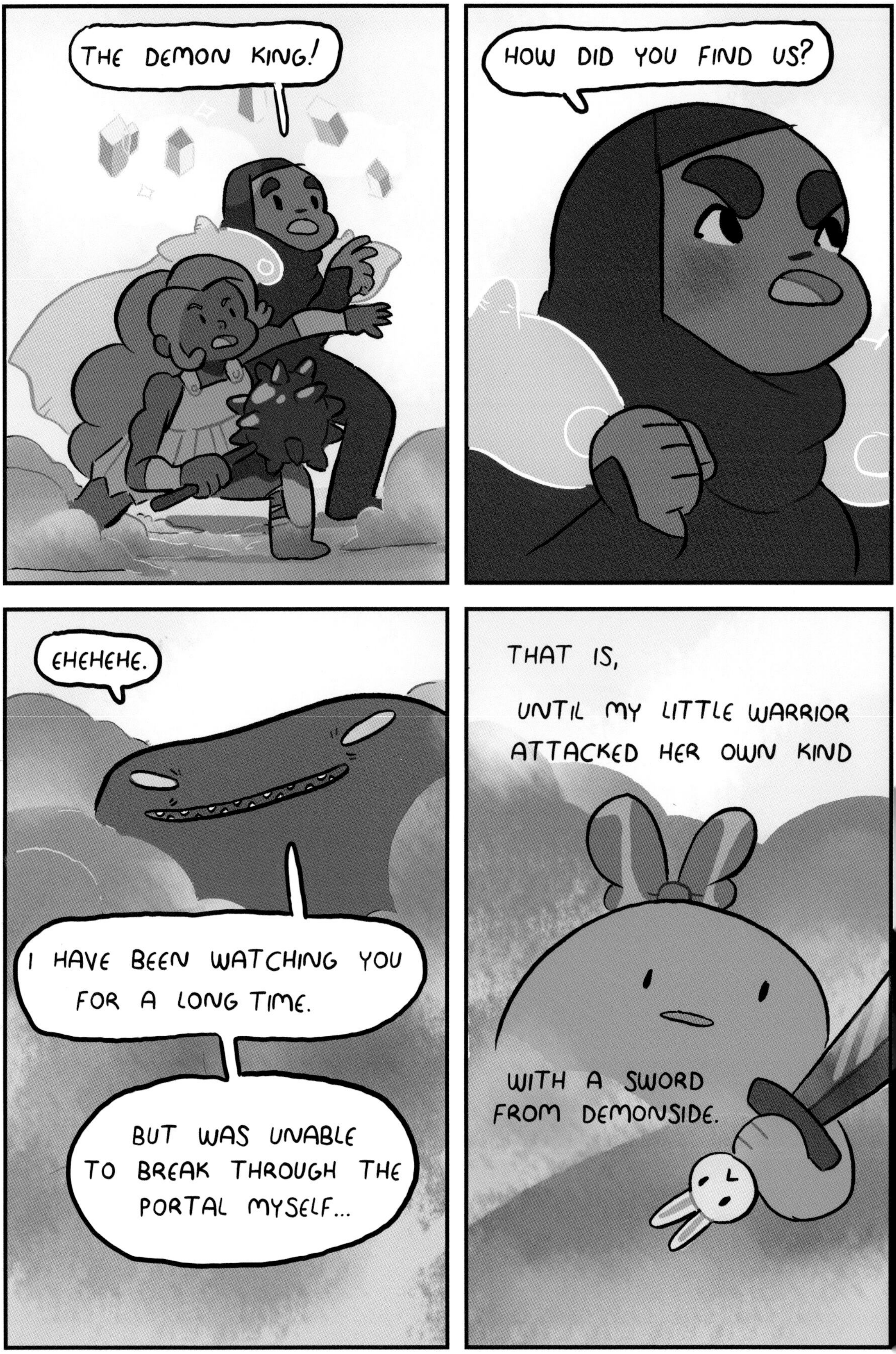
THE DEMON KING!
HOW DID YOU FIND US?
EHEHEHE.
I HAVE BEEN WATCHING YOU FOR A LONG TIME.
BUT WAS UNABLE TO BREAK THROUGH THE PORTAL MYSELF...
THAT IS,
UNTIL MY LITTLE WARRIOR ATTACKED HER OWN KIND
WITH A SWORD FROM DEMONSIDE.

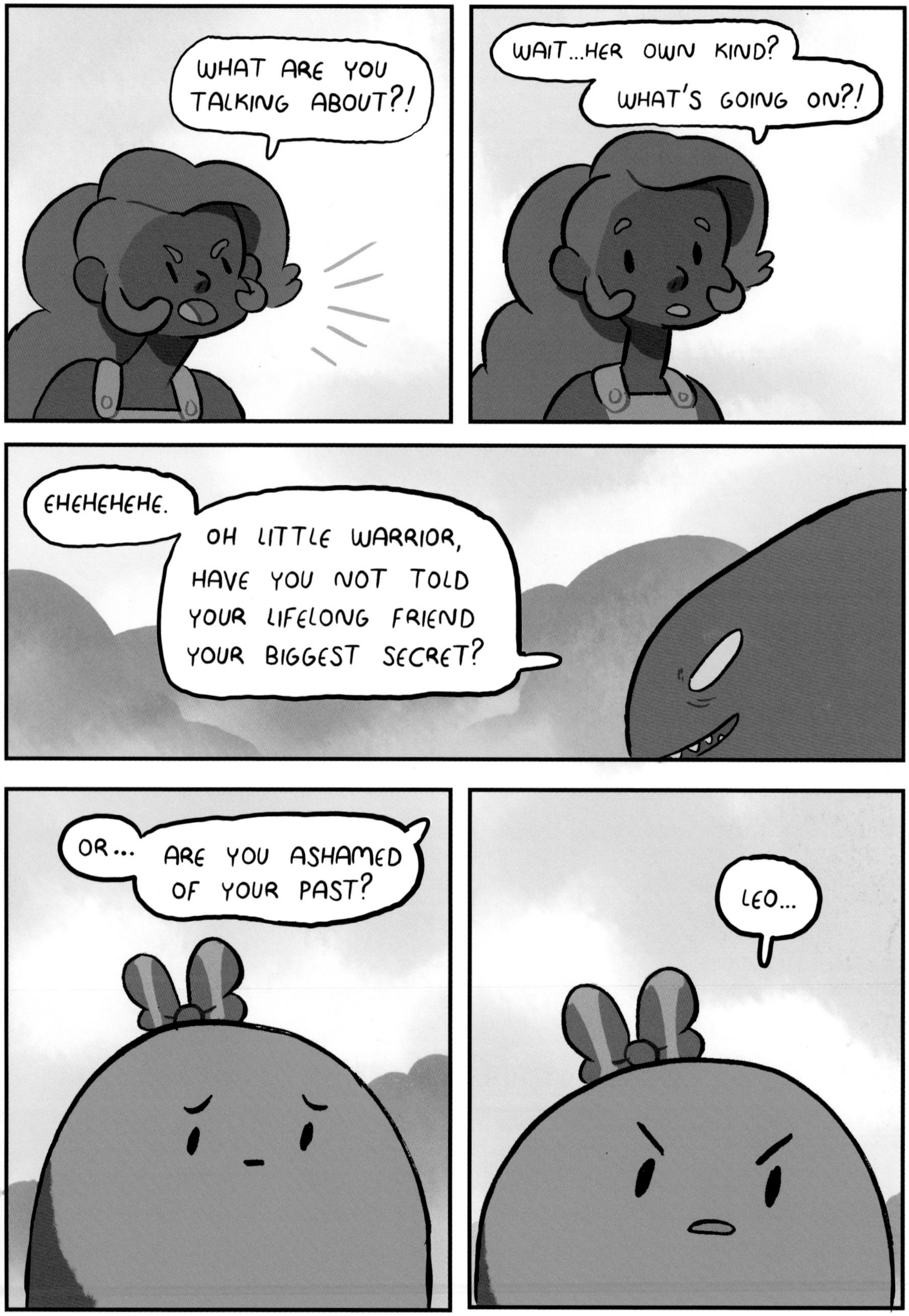
WHAT ARE YOU TALKING ABOUT?!
WAIT...HER OWN KIND?
WHAT'S GOING ON?!
EHEHEHEHE.
OH LITTLE WARRIOR, HAVE YOU NOT TOLD YOUR LIFELONG FRIEND YOUR BIGGEST SECRET?
OR...
ARE YOU ASHAMED OF YOUR PAST?
LEO...

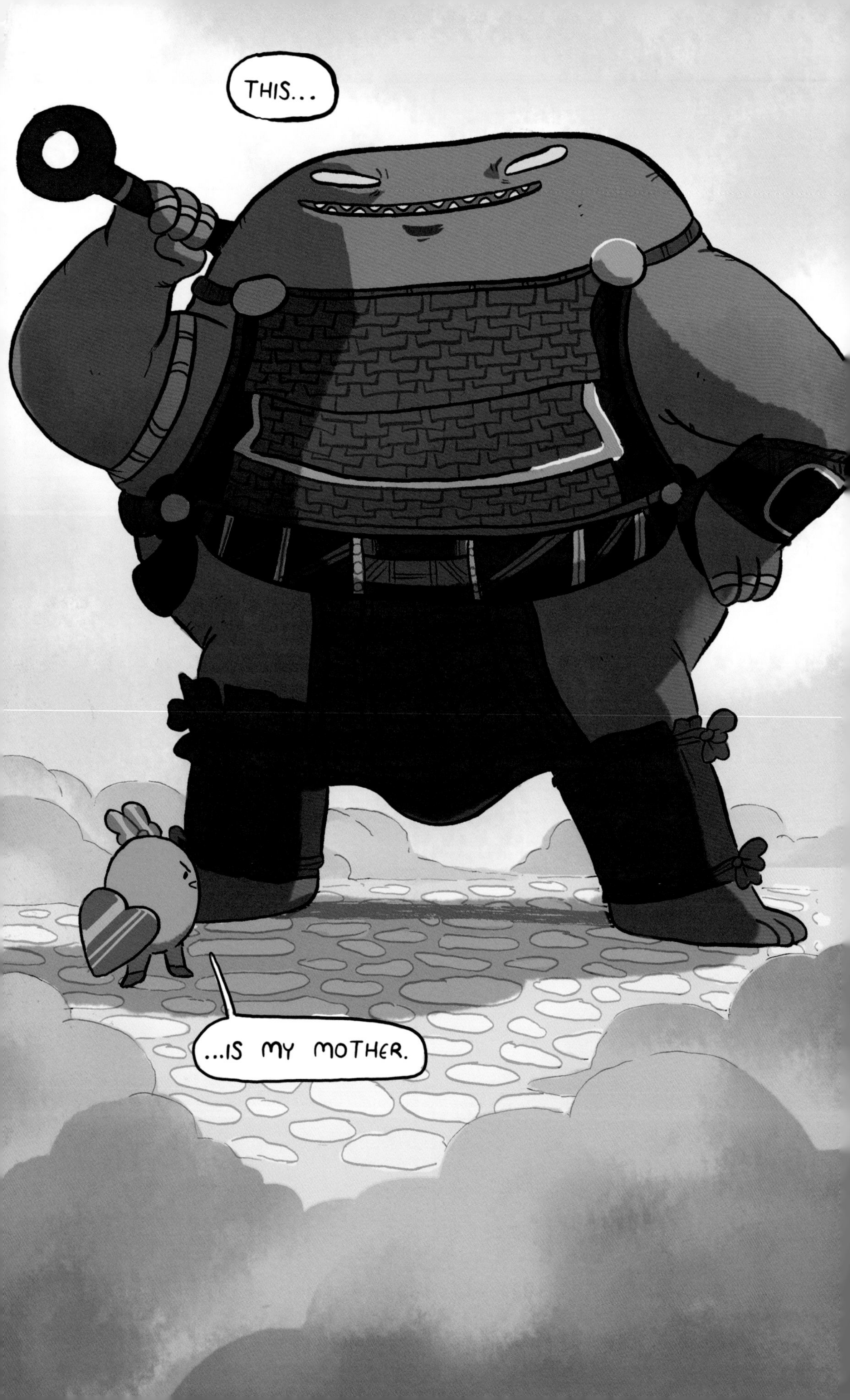
THIS...
...IS MY MOTHER.

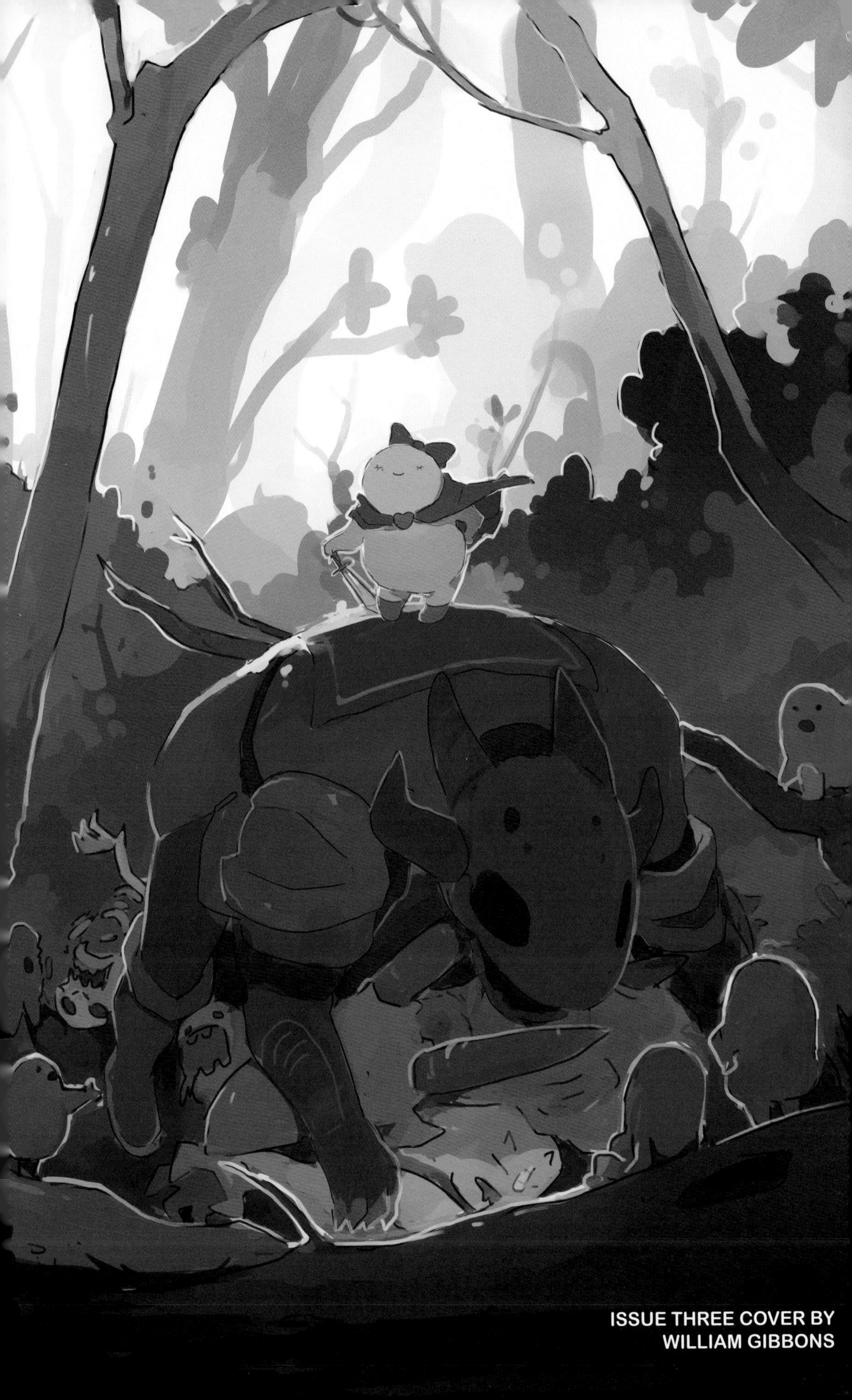

ISSUE THREE COVER BY
WILLIAM GIBBONS

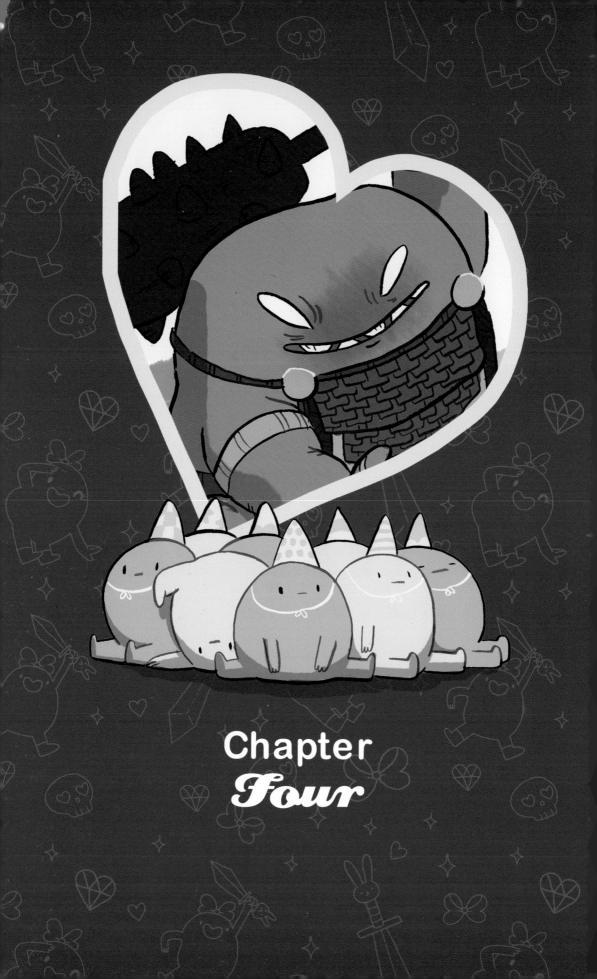

Chapter
Four

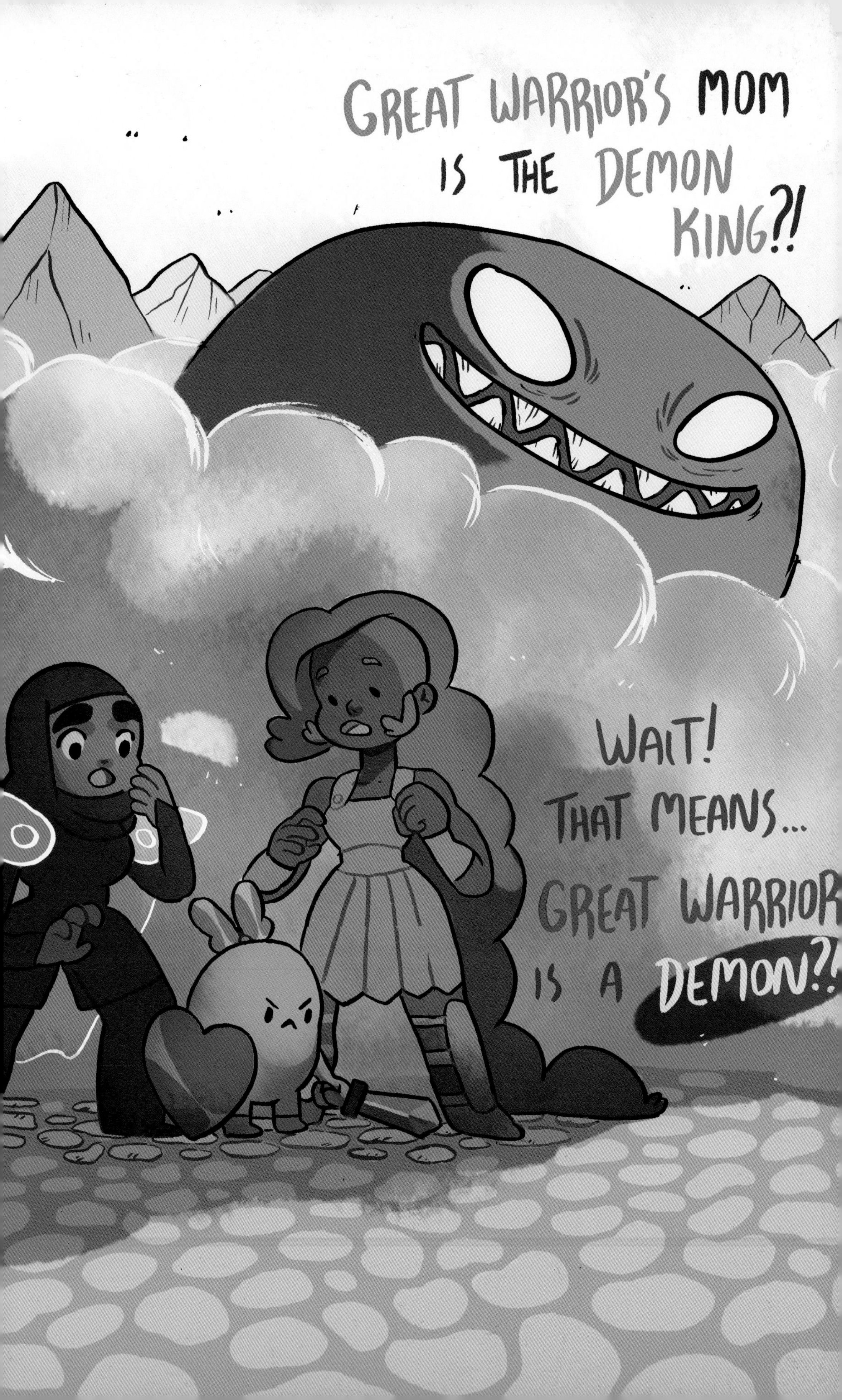

GREAT WARRIOR'S MOM IS THE DEMON KING?!
WAIT! THAT MEANS... GREAT WARRIOR IS A DEMON?!

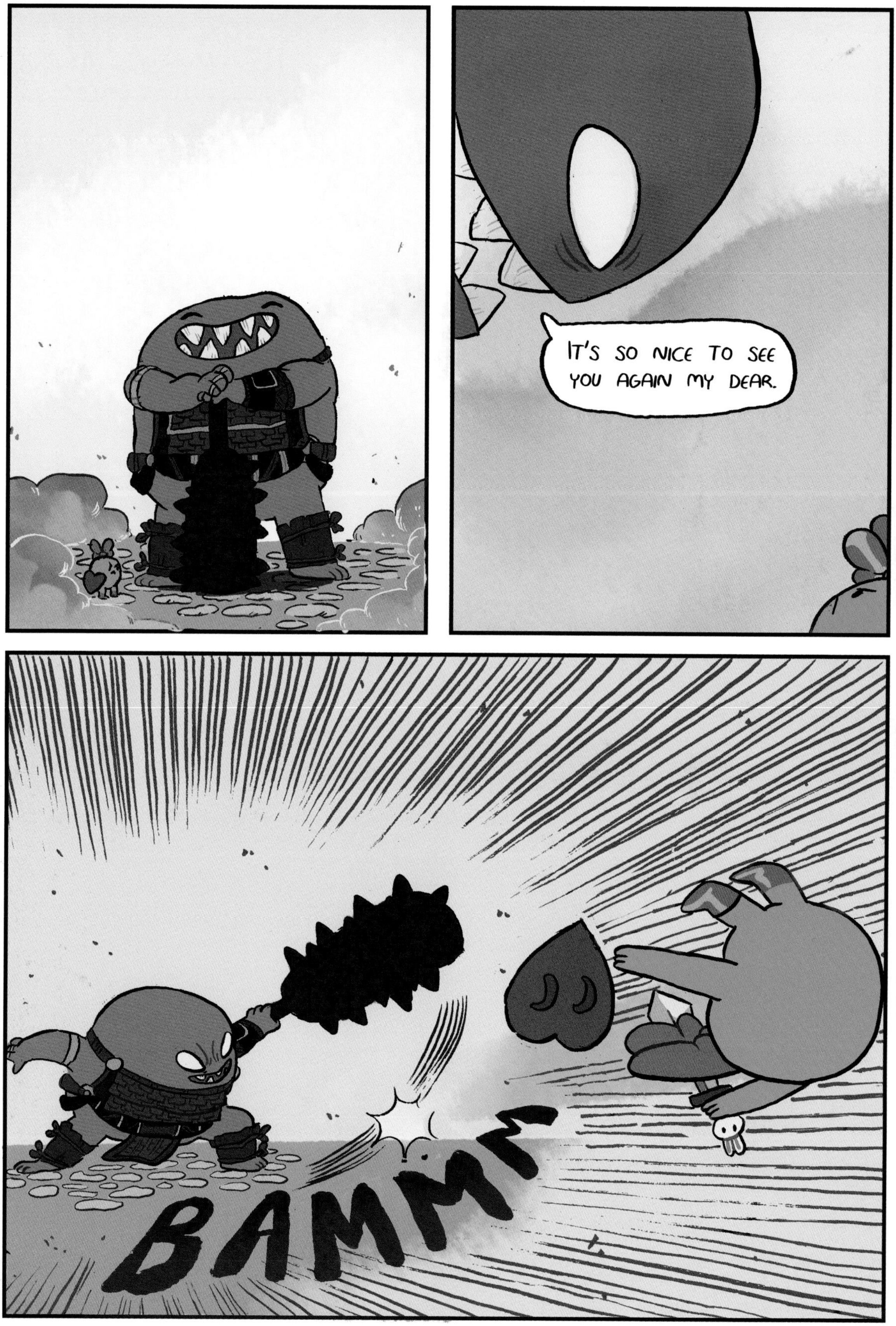
IT'S SO NICE TO SEE YOU AGAIN MY DEAR.
BAMM!

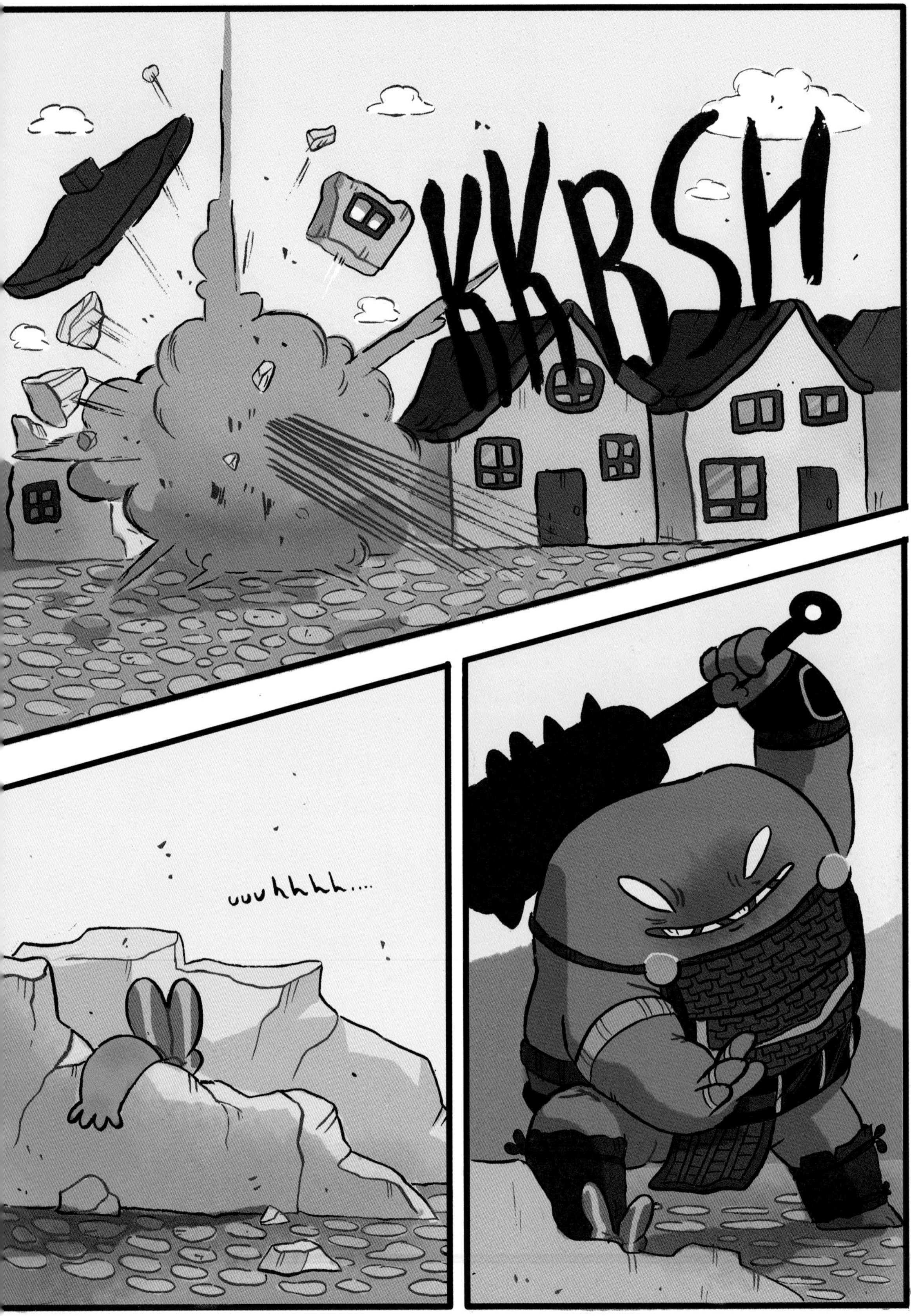
KKBSH
uuuhhhh....

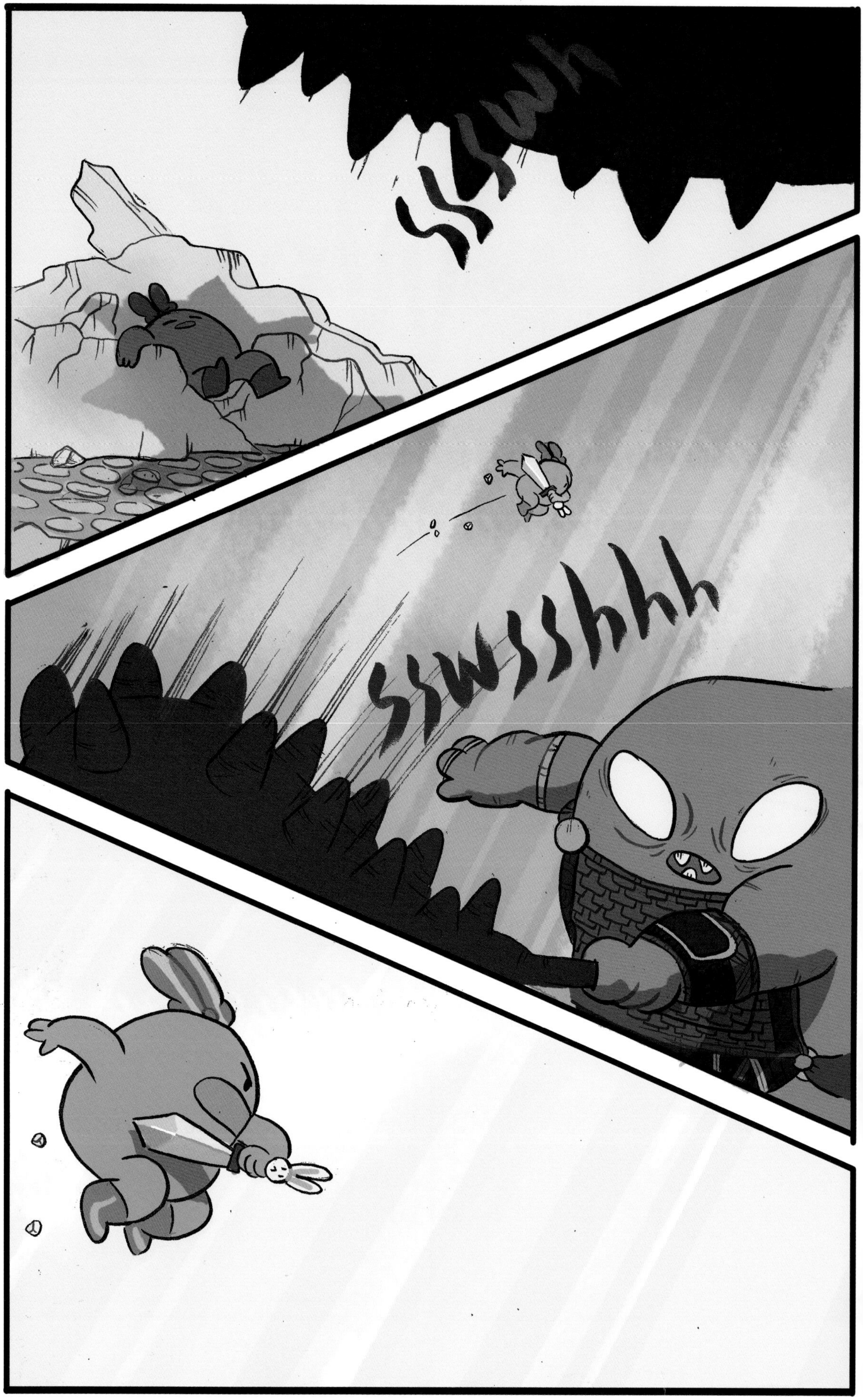
sswwh
sswsshhh

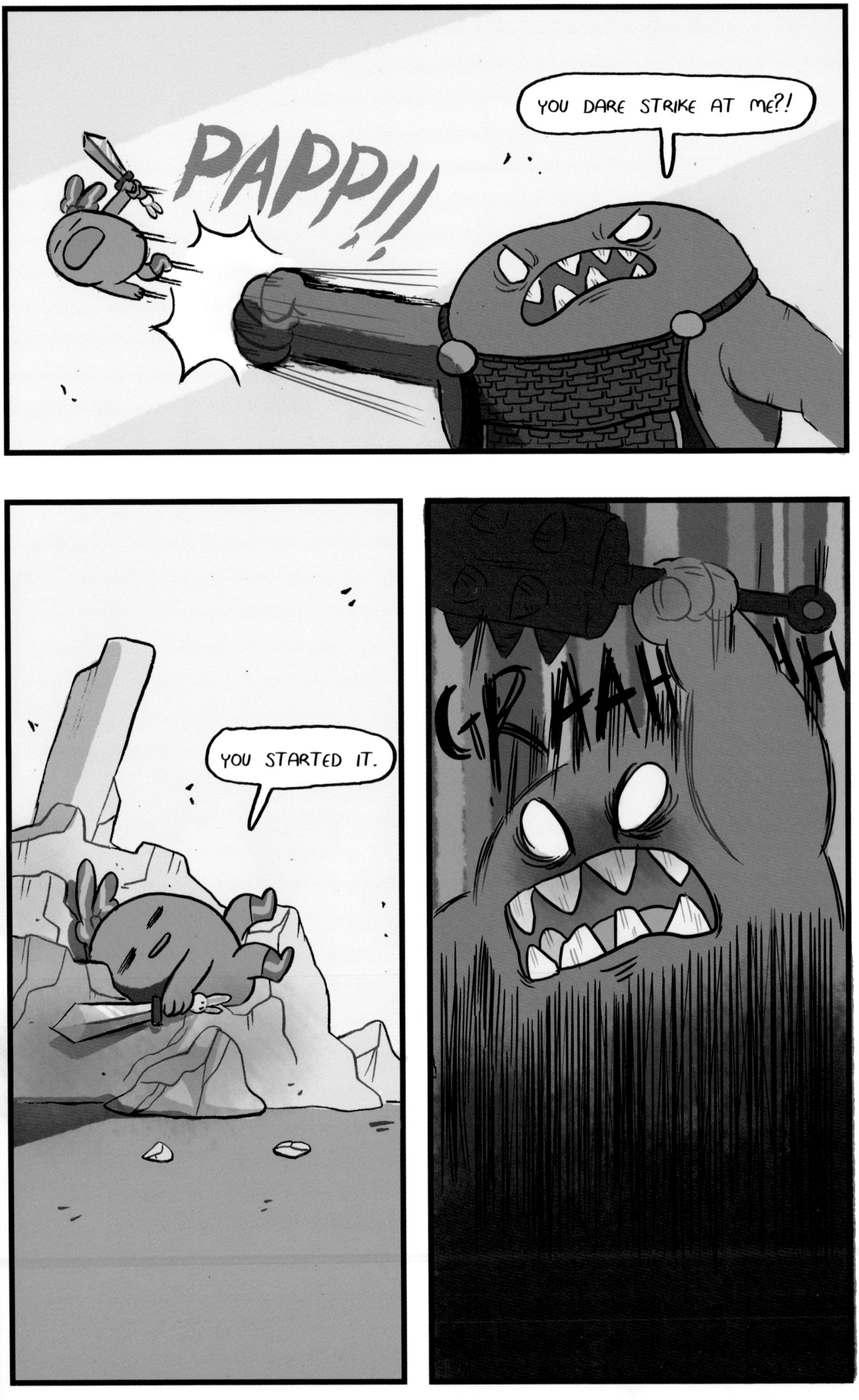
PAPP!!
YOU DARE STRIKE AT ME?!
YOU STARTED IT.
GRAAHH

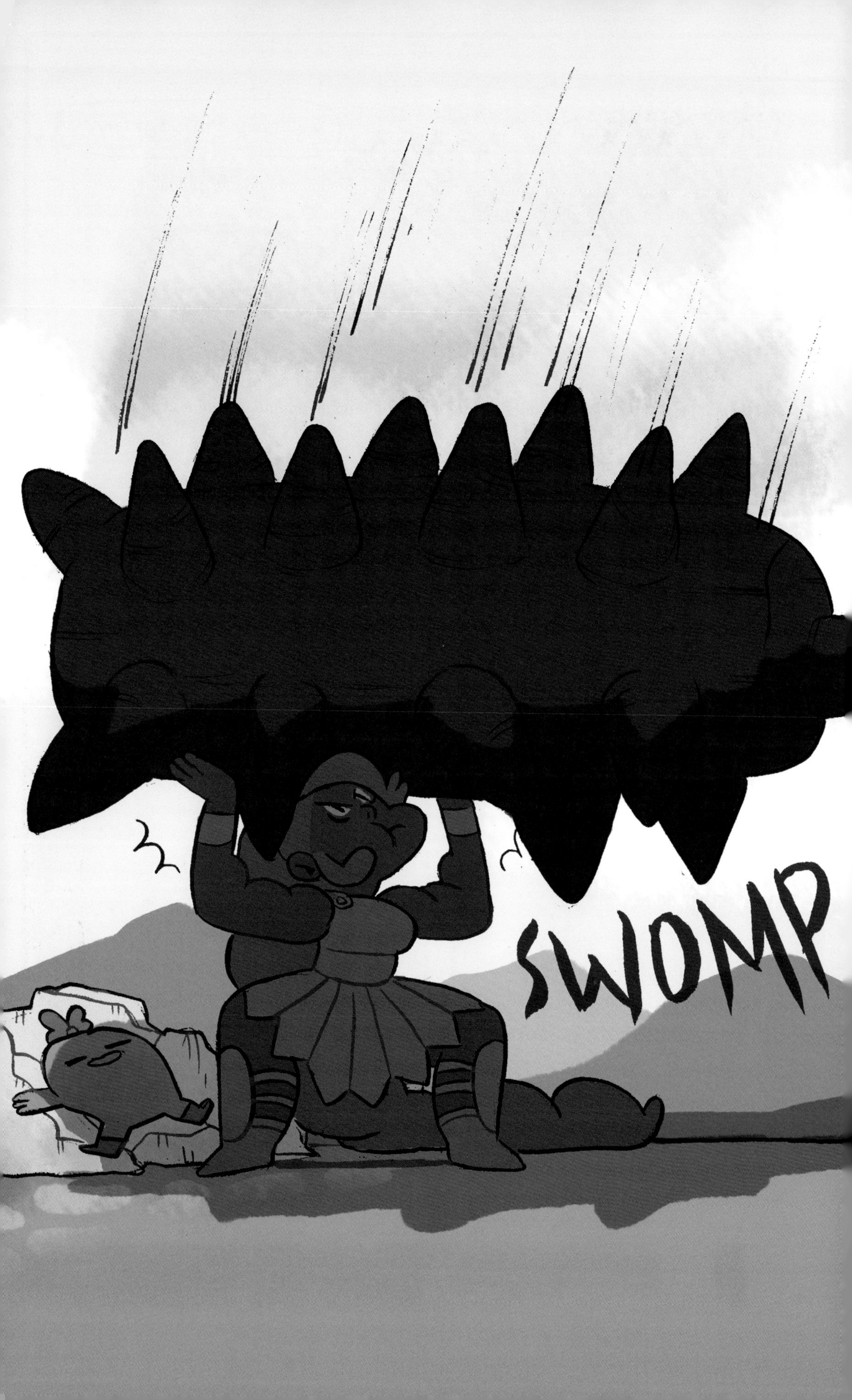
SWOMP

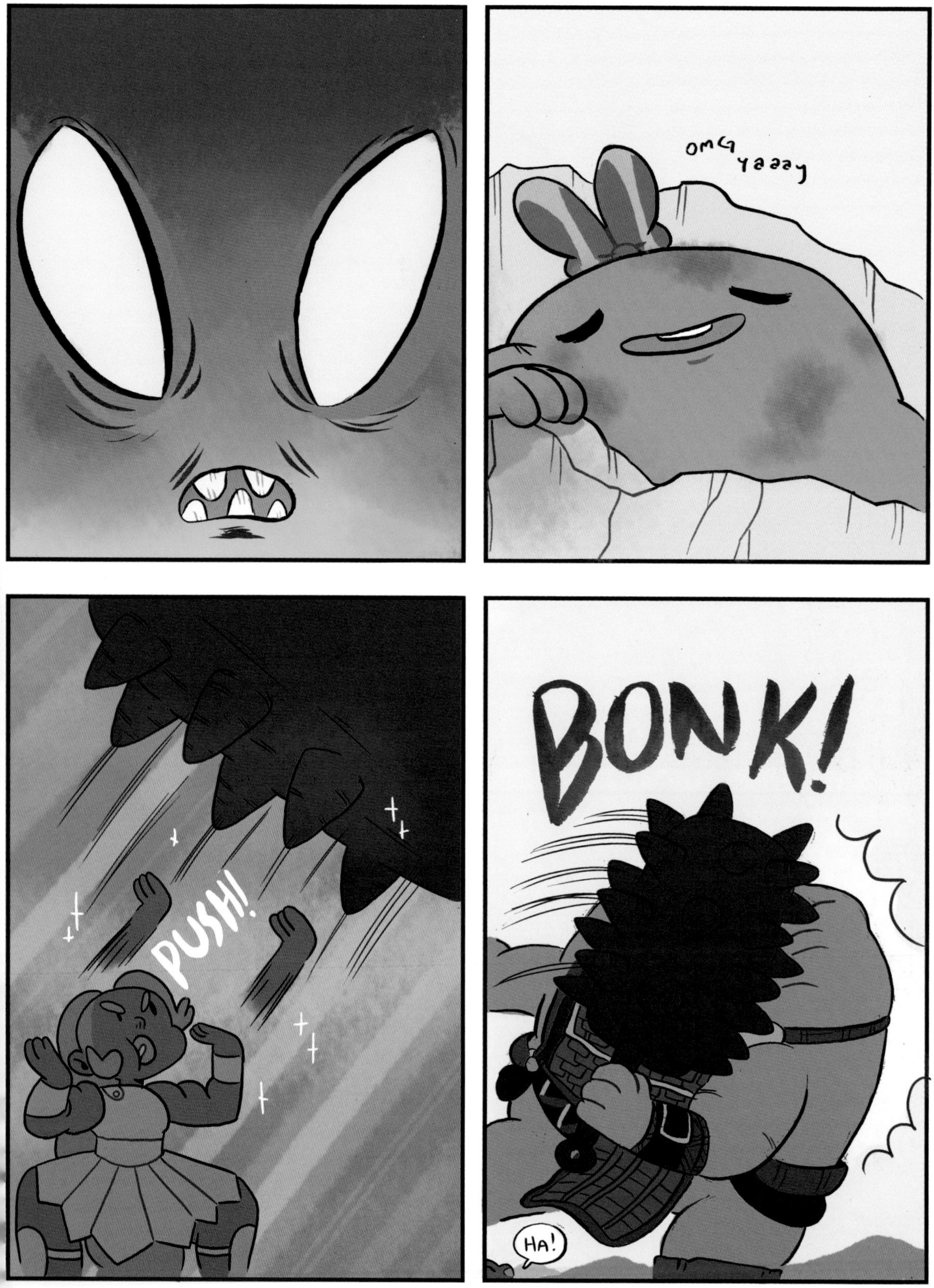
OMG yaaay
PUSH!
BONK!
HA!

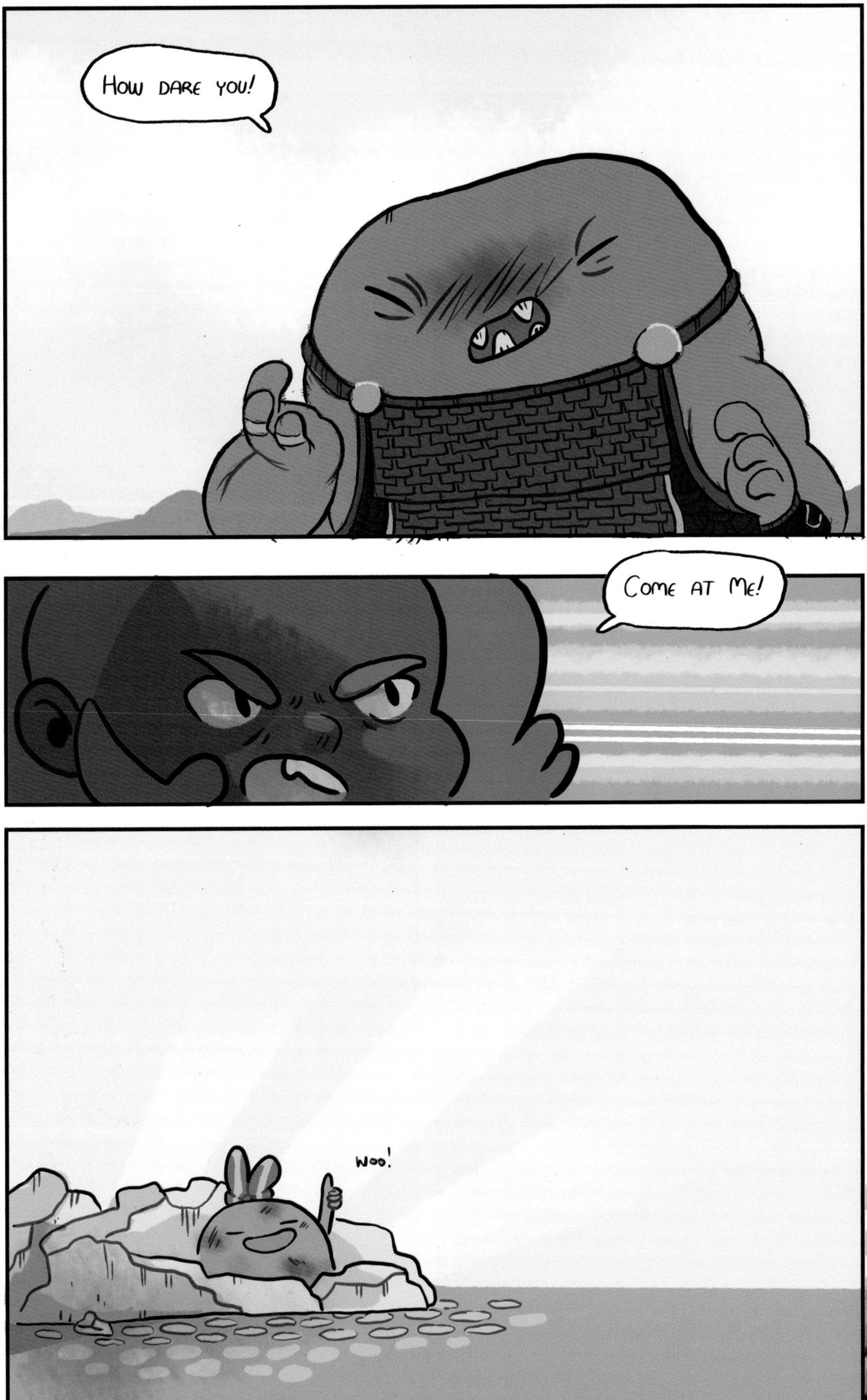
HOW DARE YOU!
COME AT ME!
WOO!

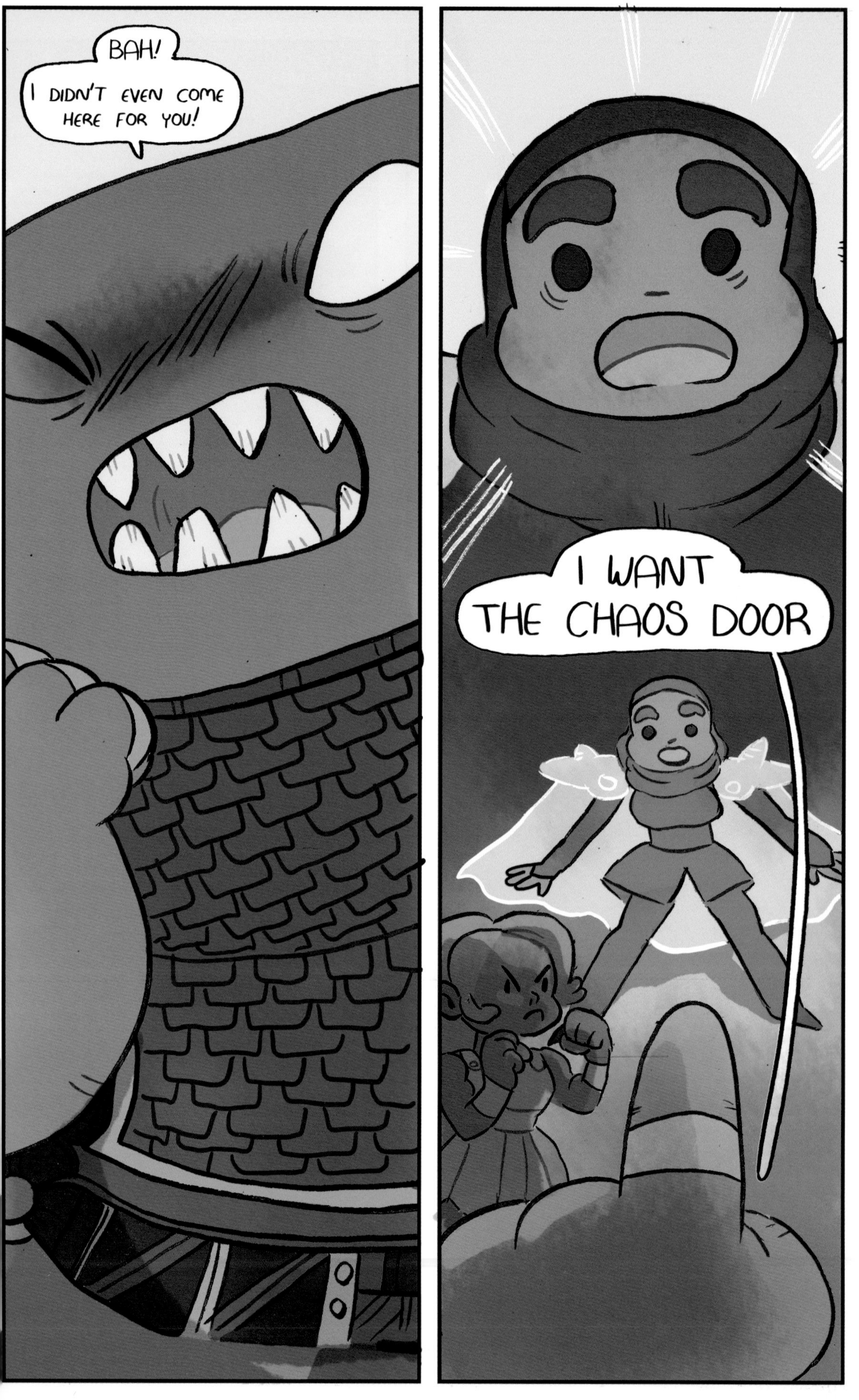
BAH!
I DIDN'T EVEN COME HERE FOR YOU!
I WANT THE CHAOS DOOR

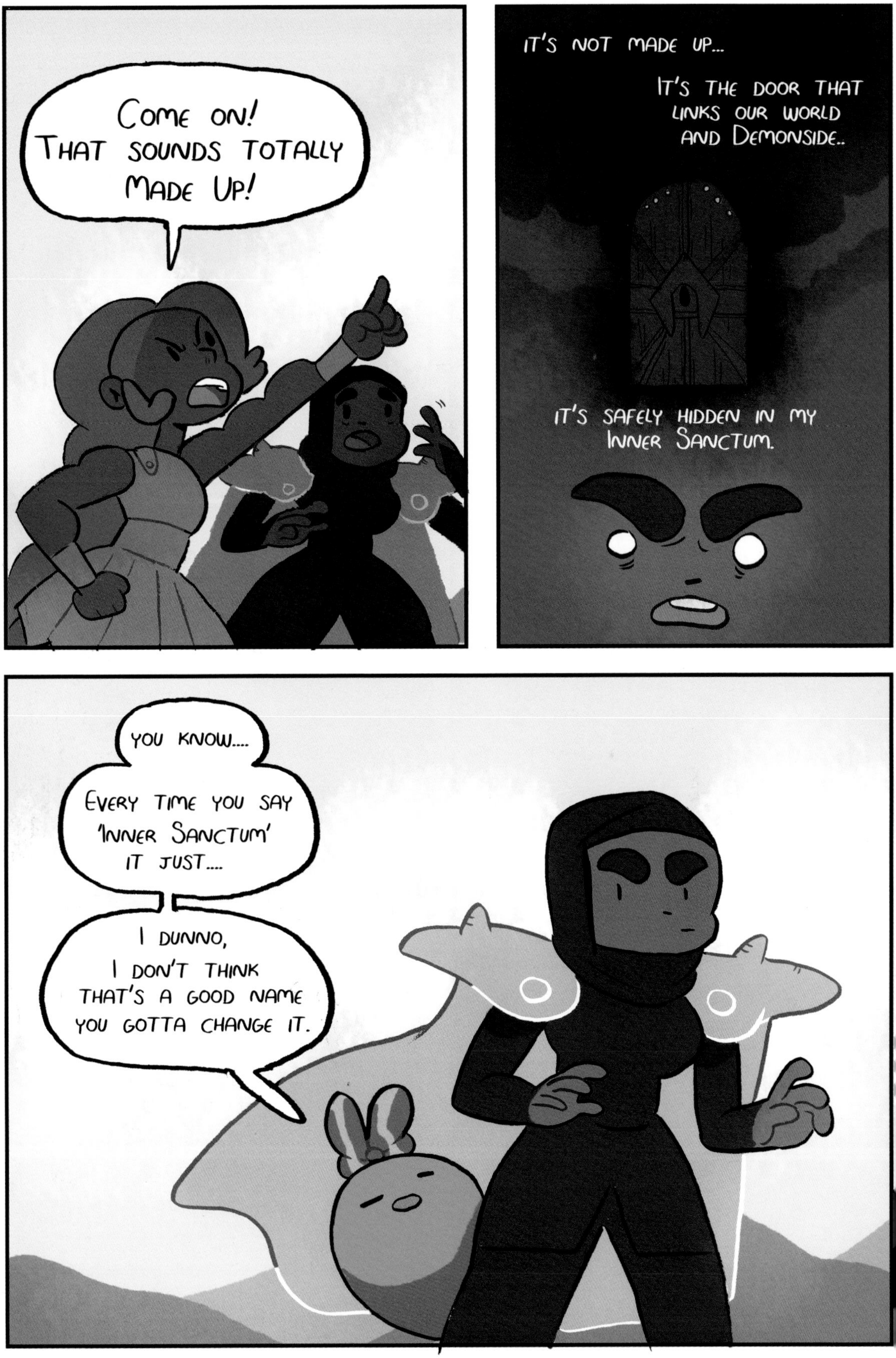
COME ON! THAT SOUNDS TOTALLY MADE UP!
IT'S NOT MADE UP...
IT'S THE DOOR THAT LINKS OUR WORLD AND DEMONSIDE..
IT'S SAFELY HIDDEN IN MY INNER SANCTUM.
YOU KNOW....
EVERY TIME YOU SAY 'INNER SANCTUM' IT JUST....
I DUNNO, I DON'T THINK THAT'S A GOOD NAME YOU GOTTA CHANGE IT.

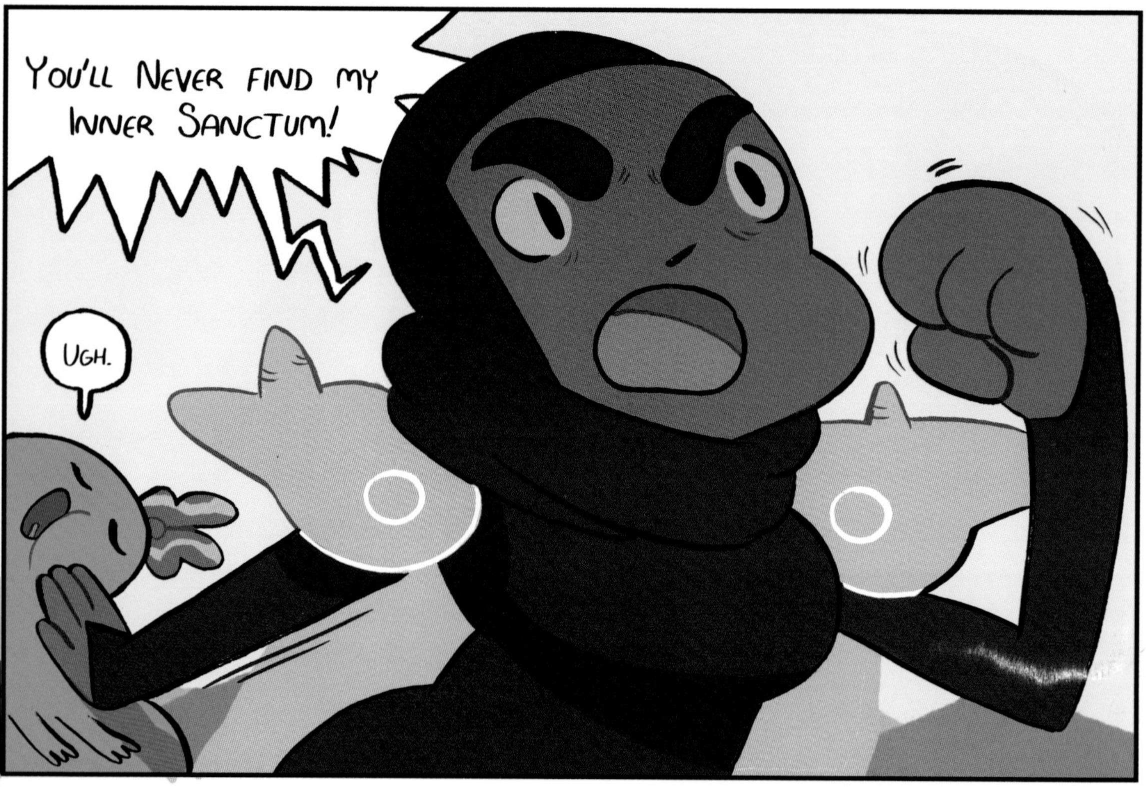
You'll Never find my Inner Sanctum!
Ugh.

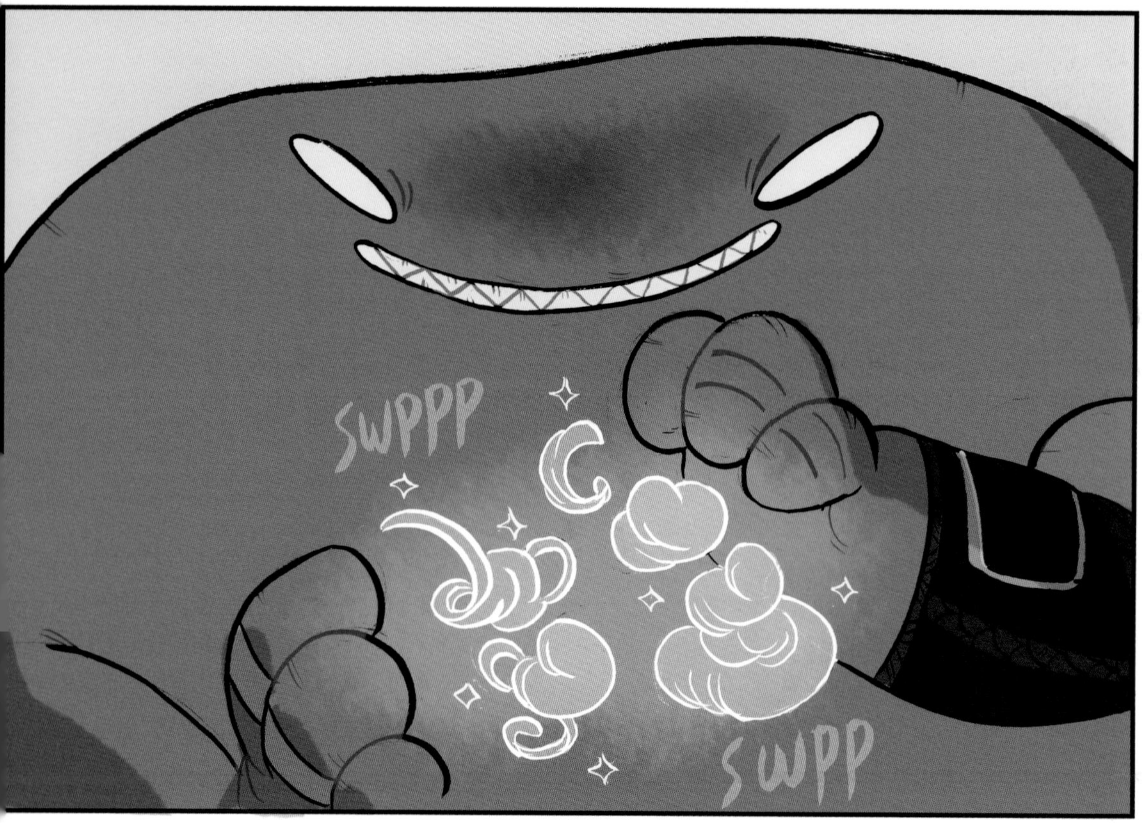
SWPPP
SWPP

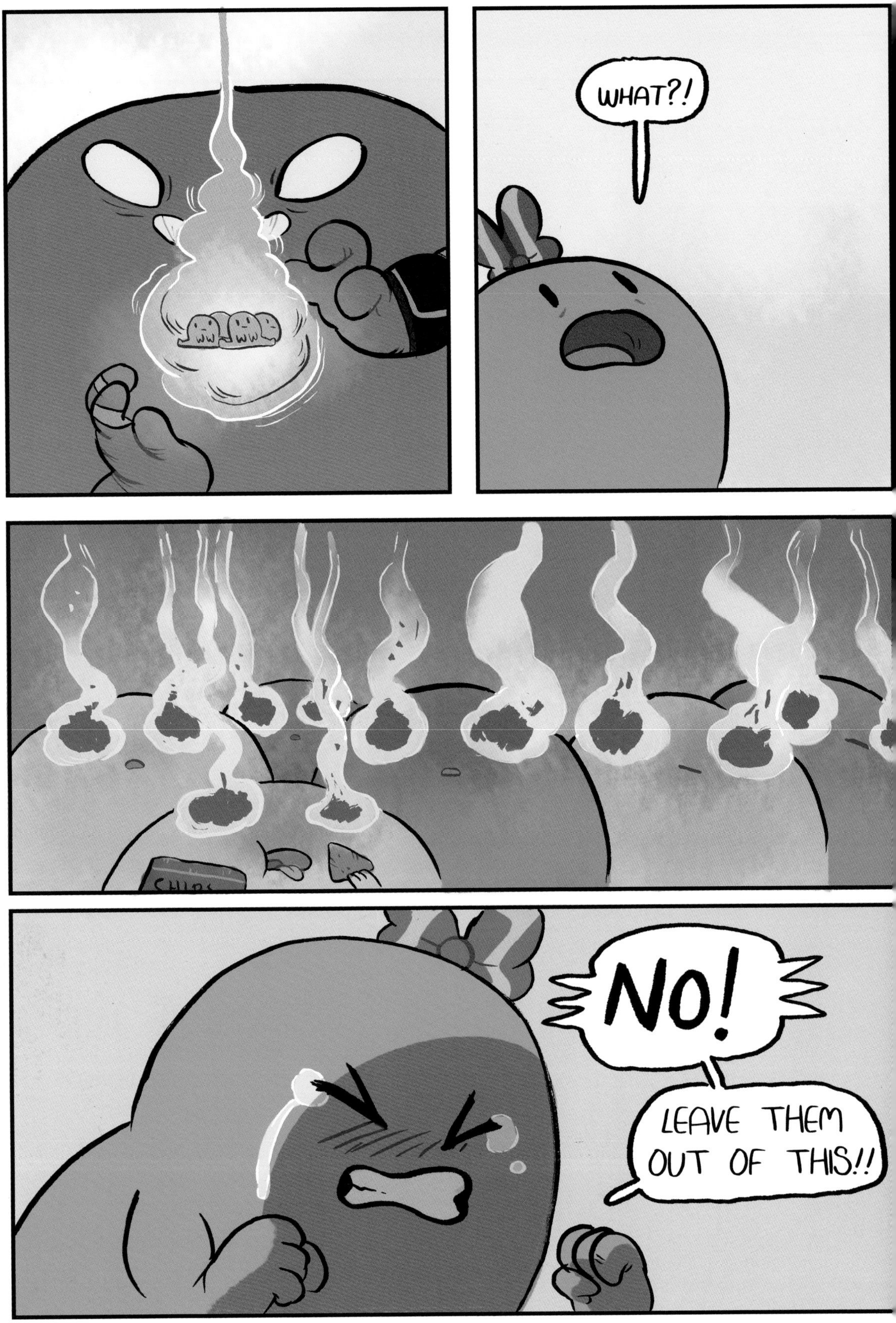
WHAT?!
NO!
LEAVE THEM OUT OF THIS!!

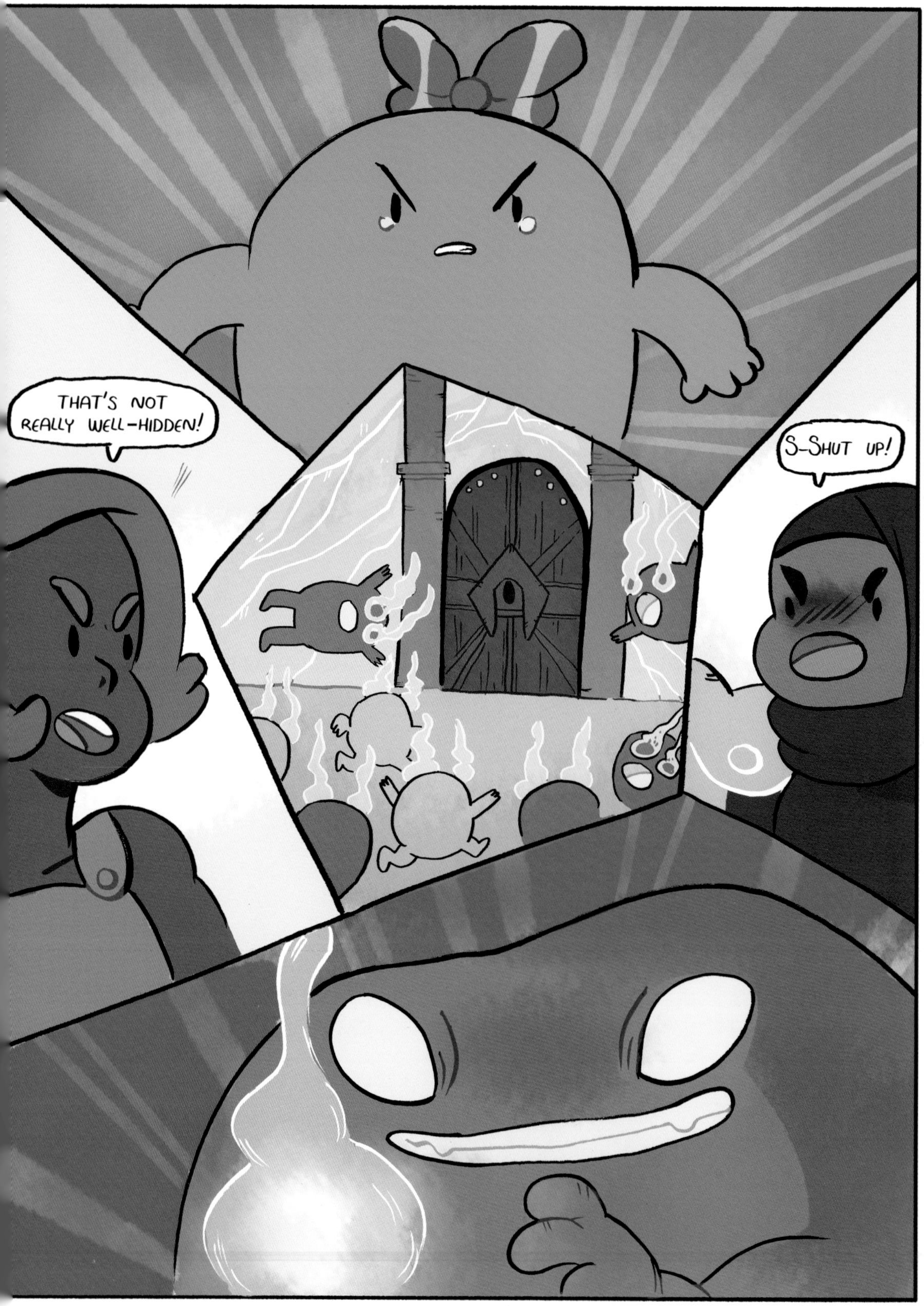
THAT'S NOT REALLY WELL-HIDDEN!
S-SHUT UP!

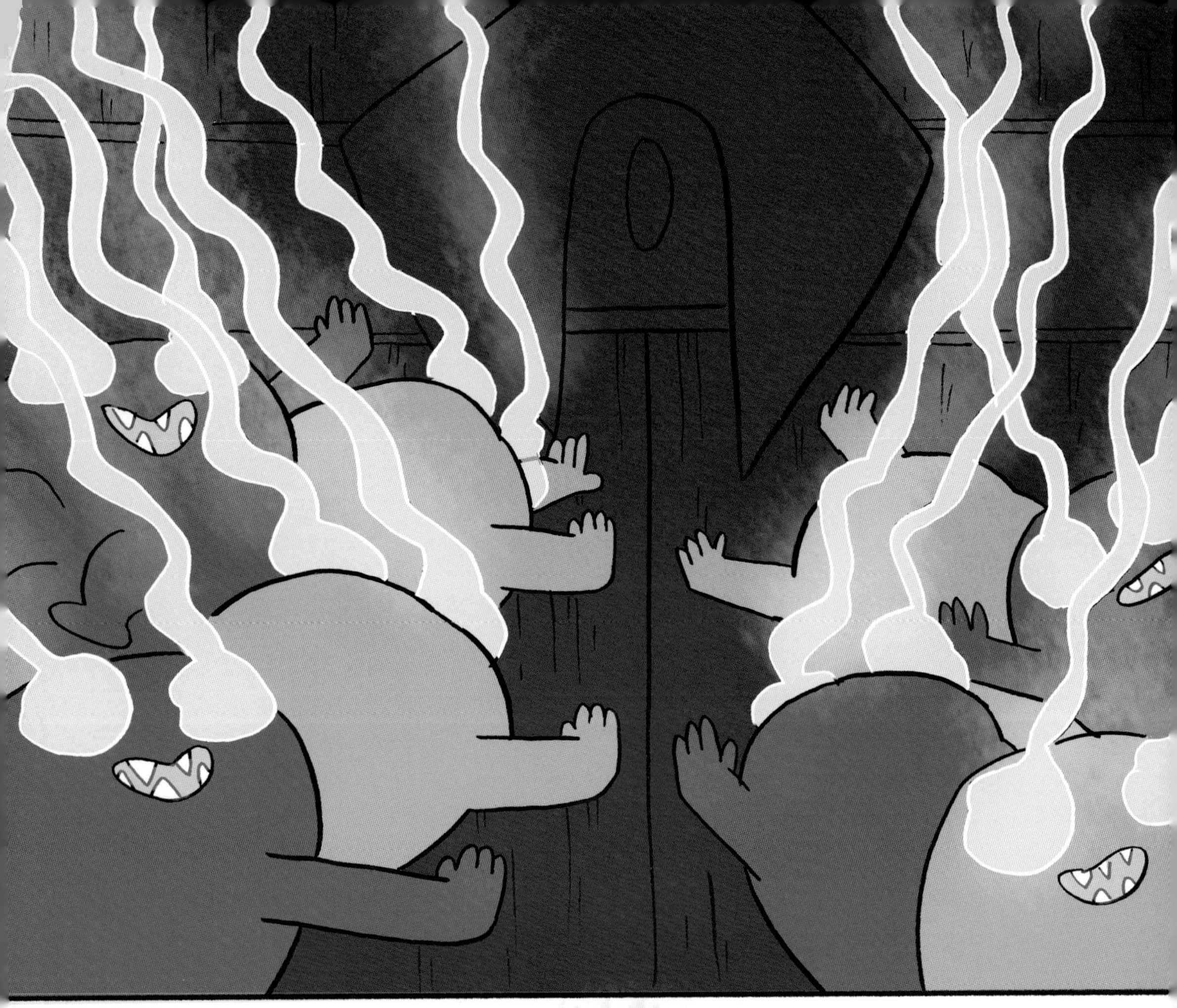
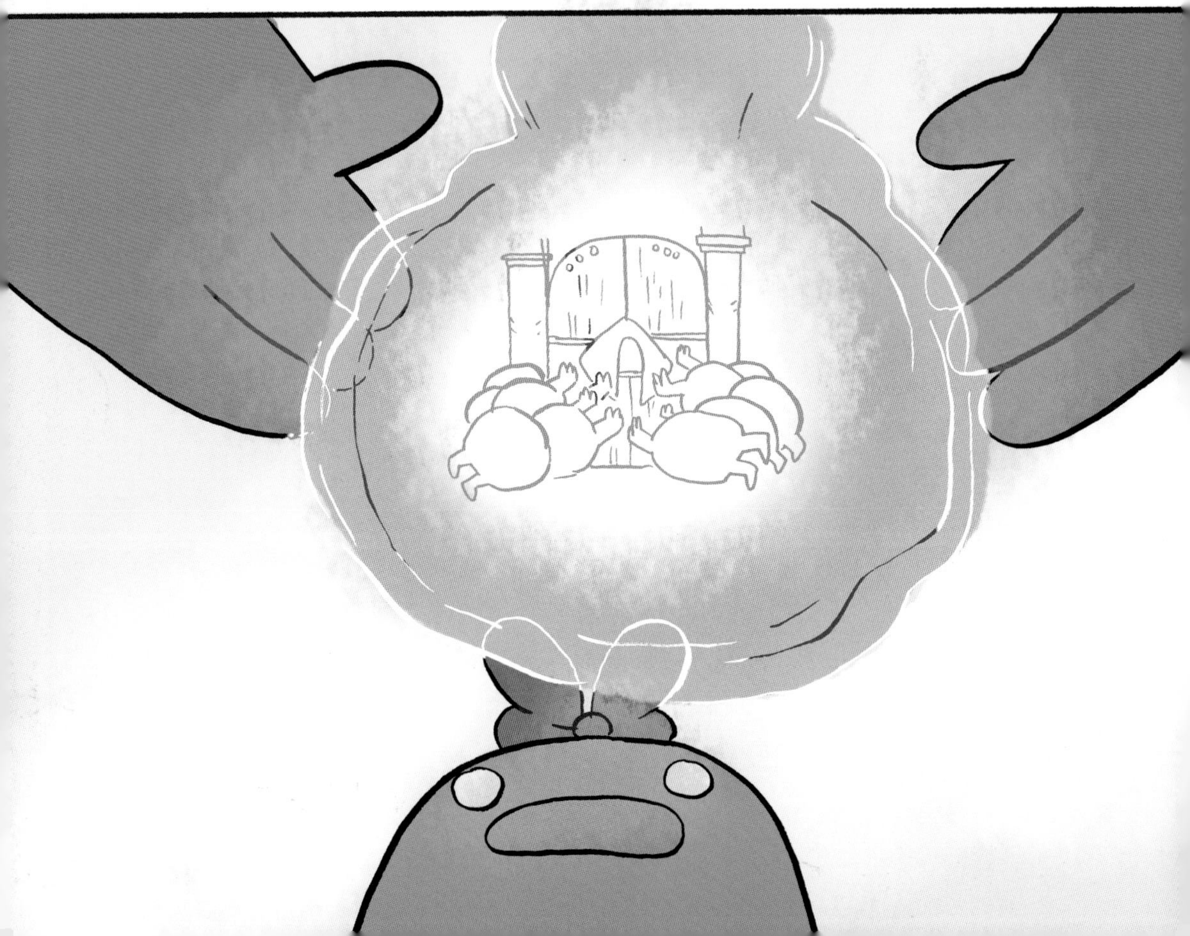

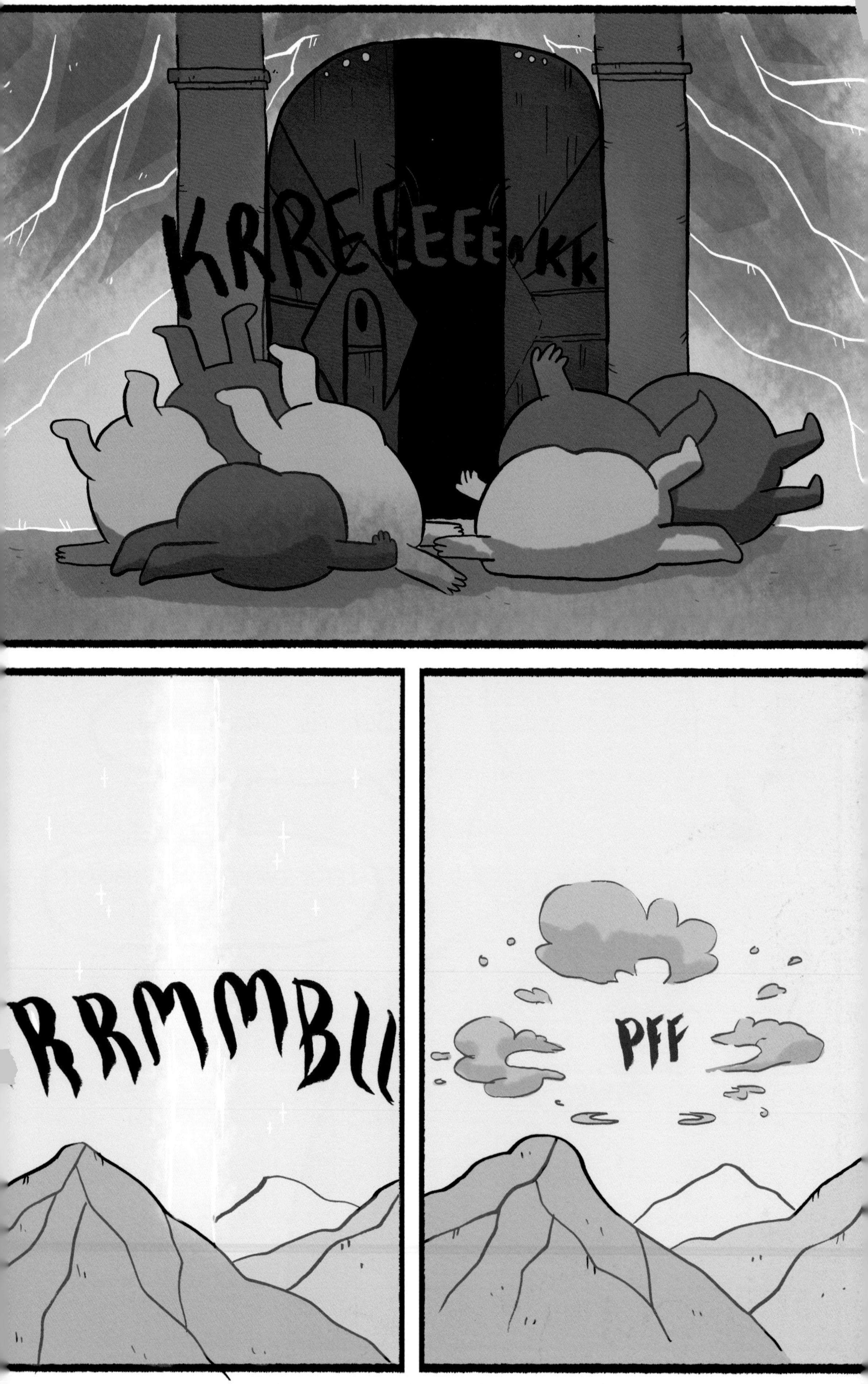
KRREEEEEkk
RRMMBLL
PFF

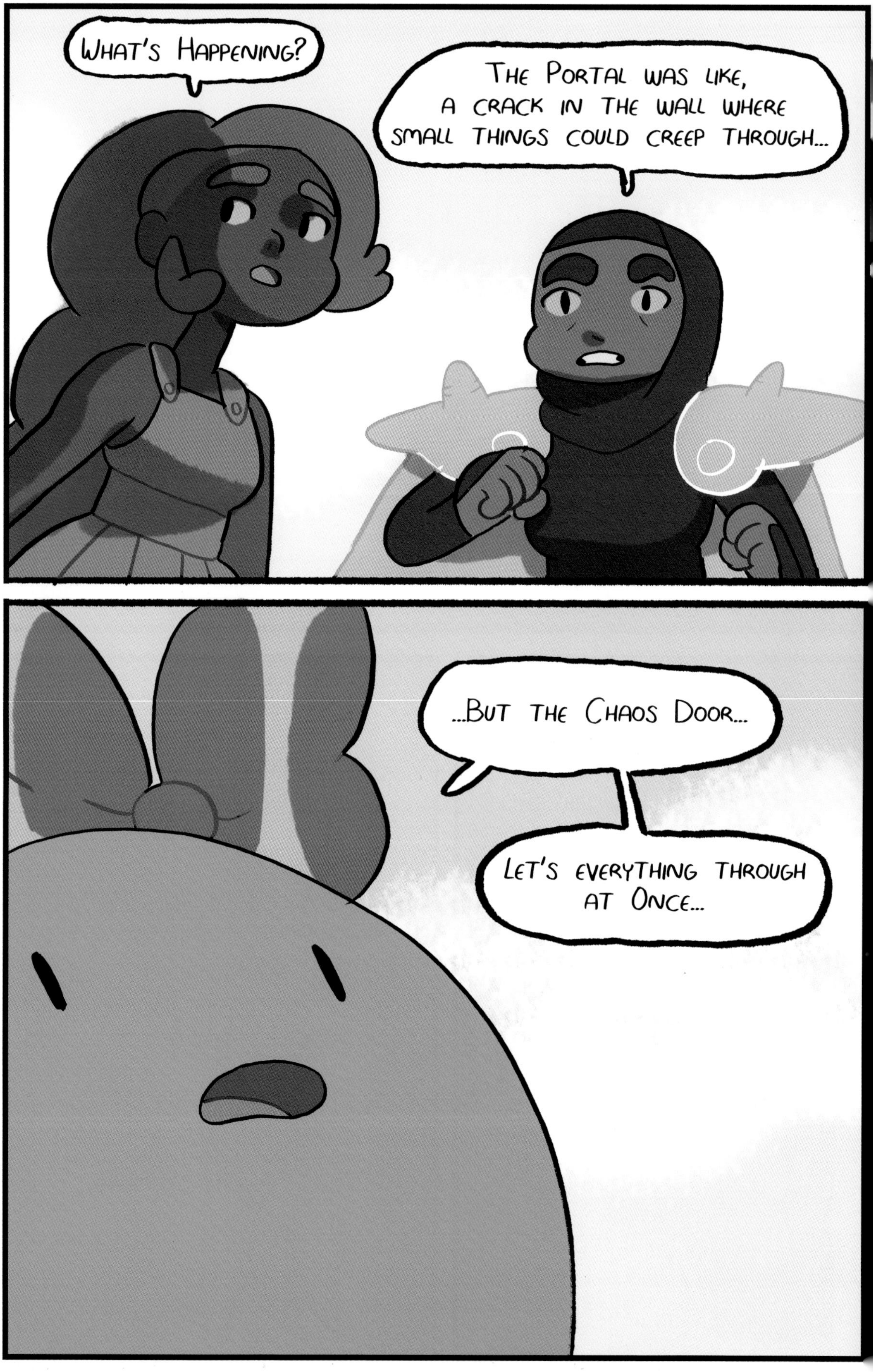
WHAT'S HAPPENING?
THE PORTAL WAS LIKE, A CRACK IN THE WALL WHERE SMALL THINGS COULD CREEP THROUGH...
...BUT THE CHAOS DOOR...
LET'S EVERYTHING THROUGH AT ONCE...

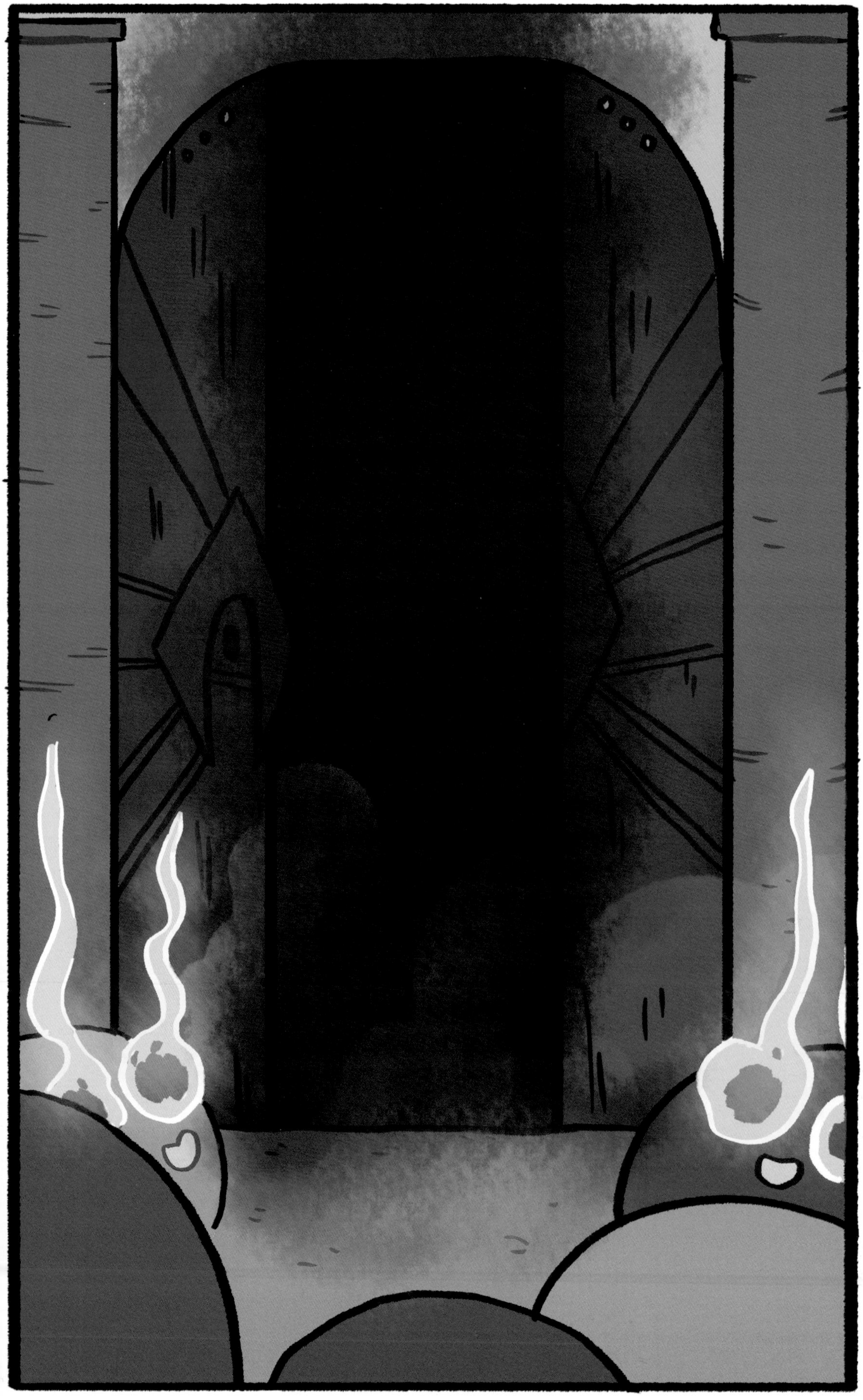

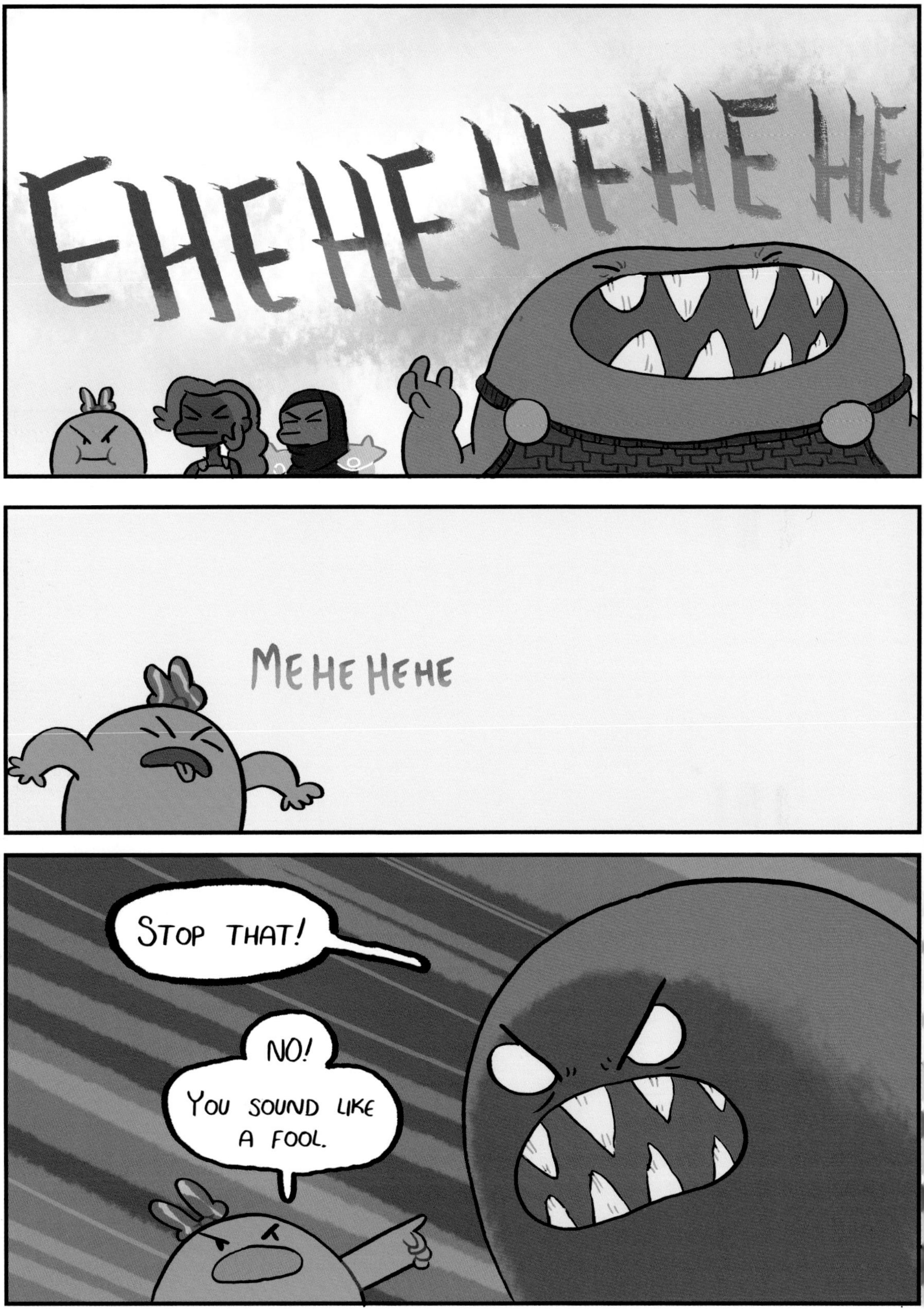
EHEHEHEHEHEHE
MEHEHEHE
STOP THAT!
NO!
YOU SOUND LIKE A FOOL.

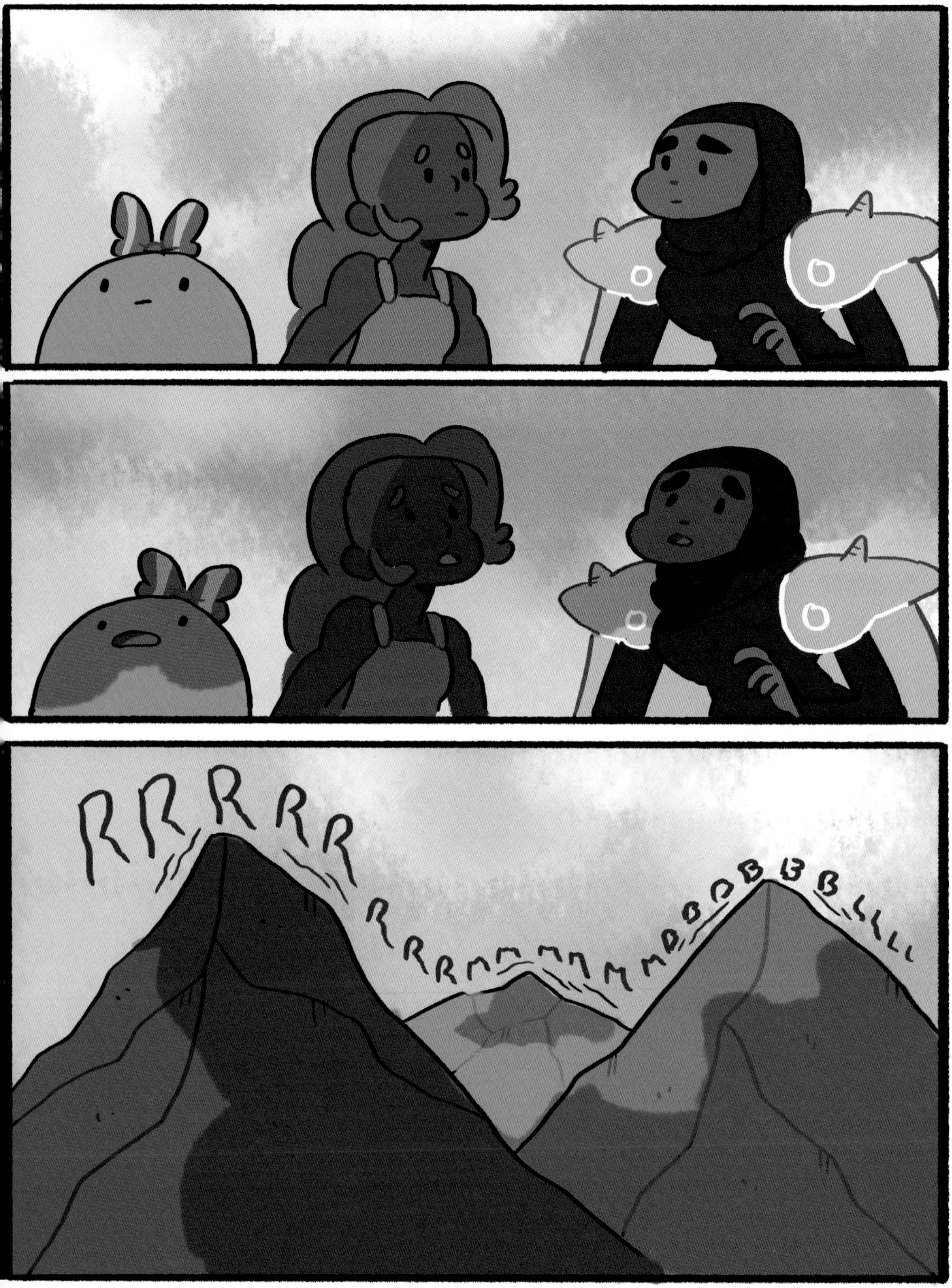
RRRRRRRRmmmmmmBBBBBBLLLL

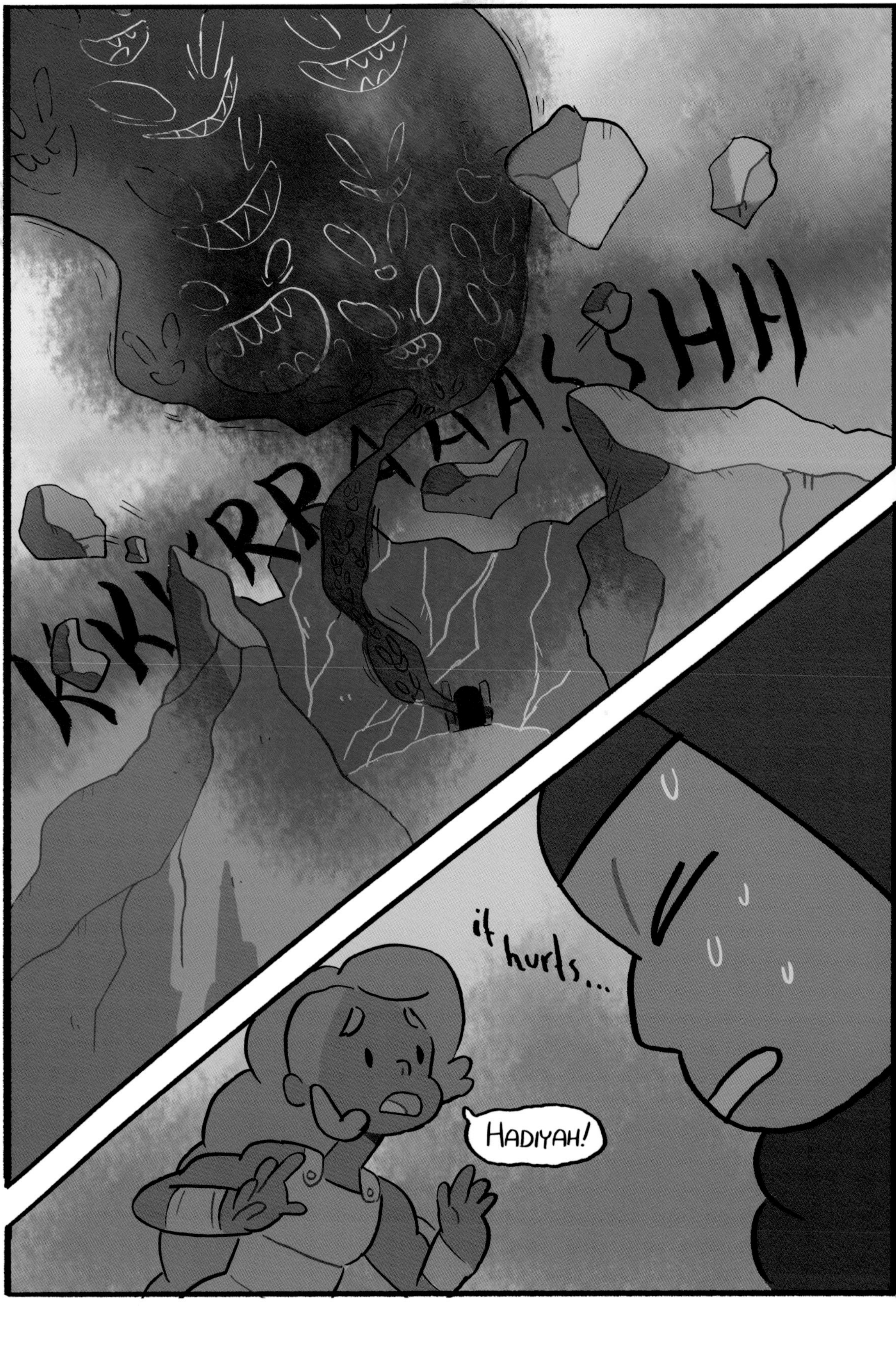
KKKRRAAAASHH
it hurts...
HADIYAH!

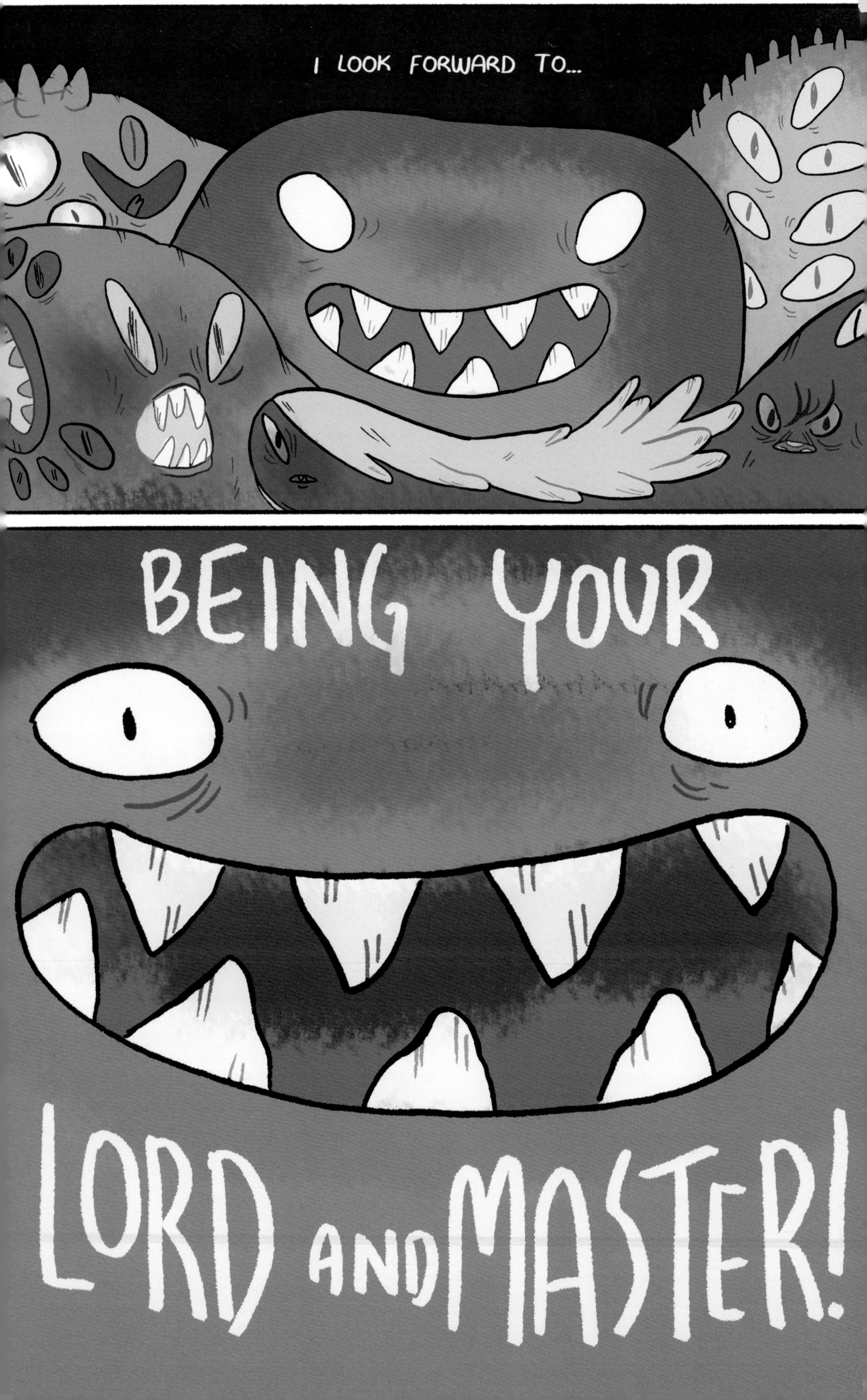
I LOOK FORWARD TO...
BEING YOUR
LORD AND MASTER!

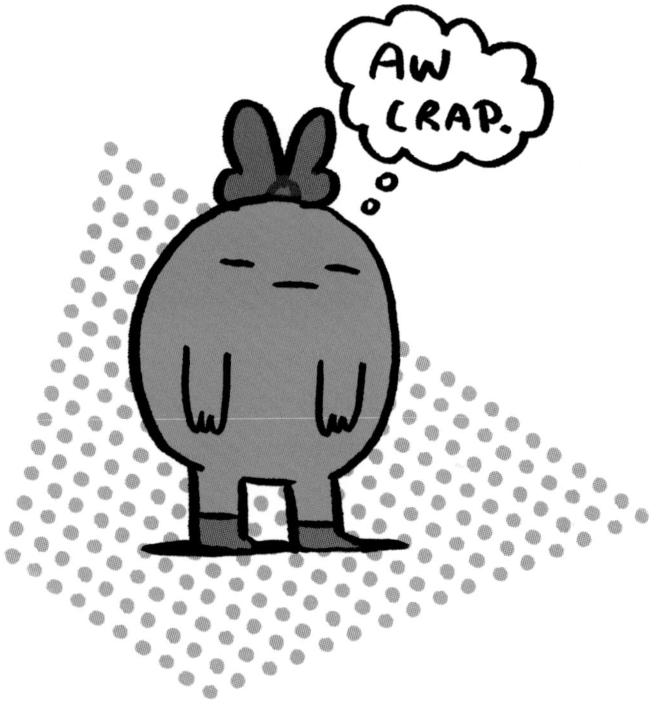
AW
CRAP.

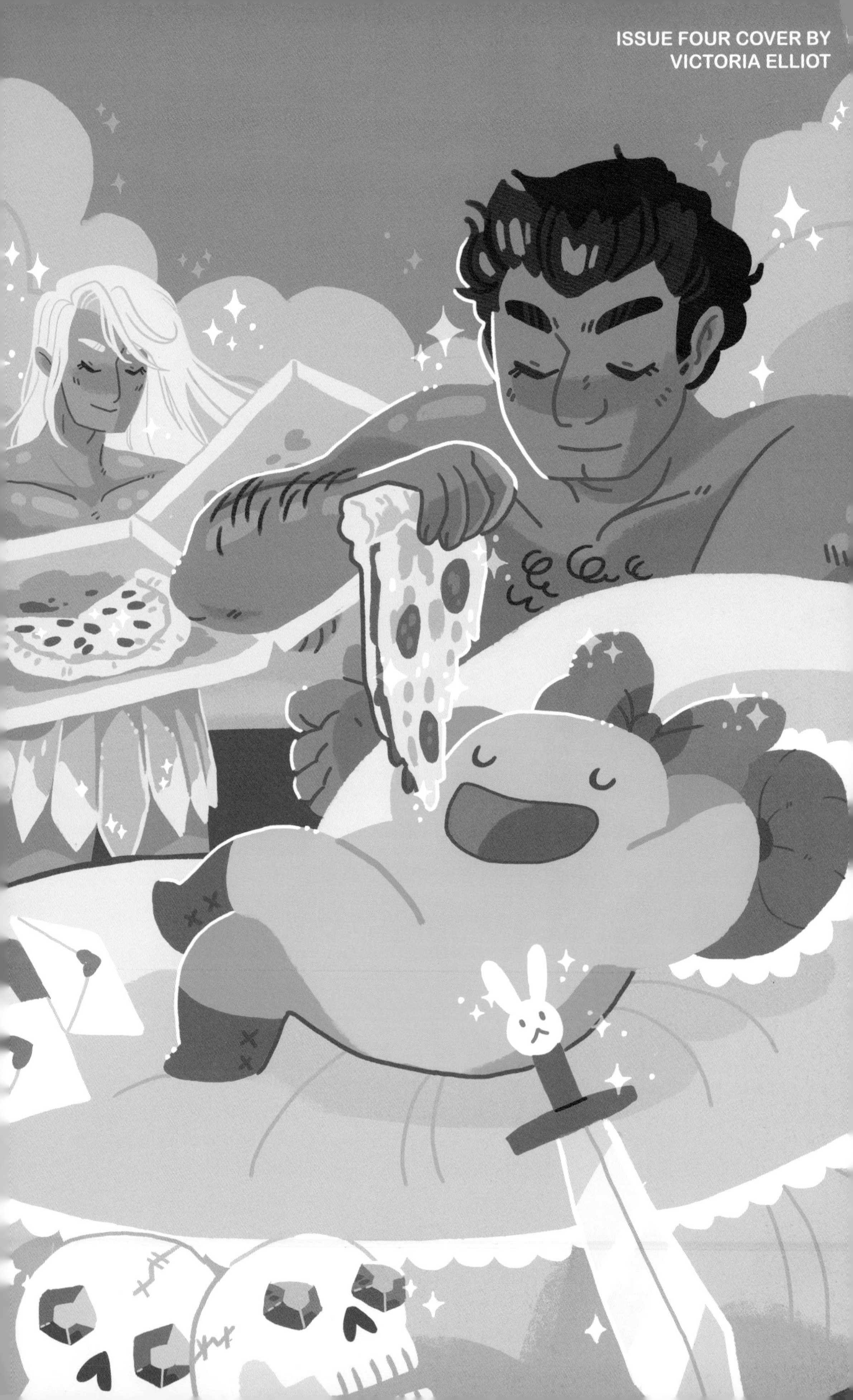

ISSUE FOUR COVER BY
VICTORIA ELLIOT

Chapter
Five

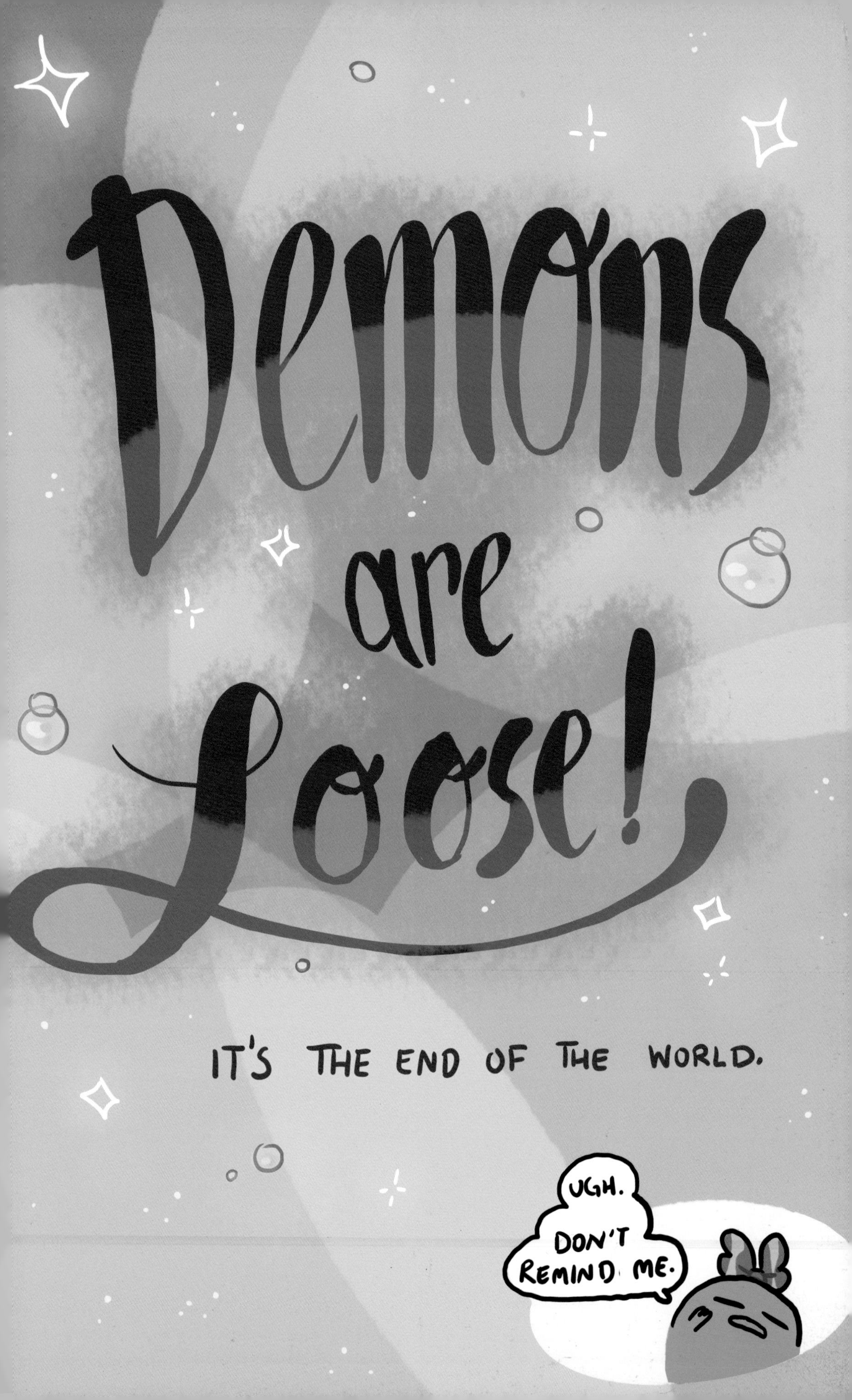
Demons are Loose!
IT'S THE END OF THE WORLD.
UGH.
DON'T REMIND ME.

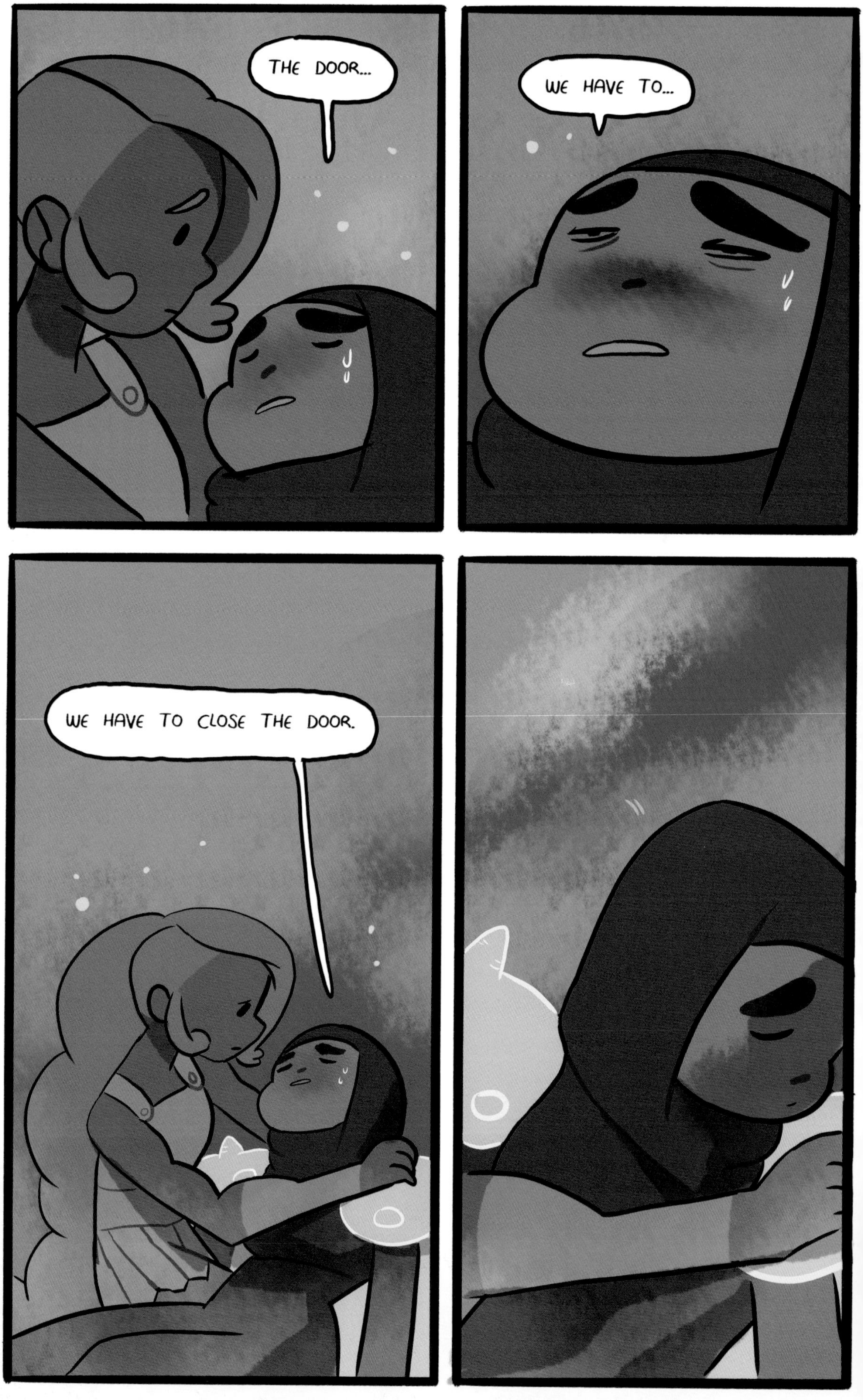
THE DOOR...
WE HAVE TO...
WE HAVE TO CLOSE THE DOOR.

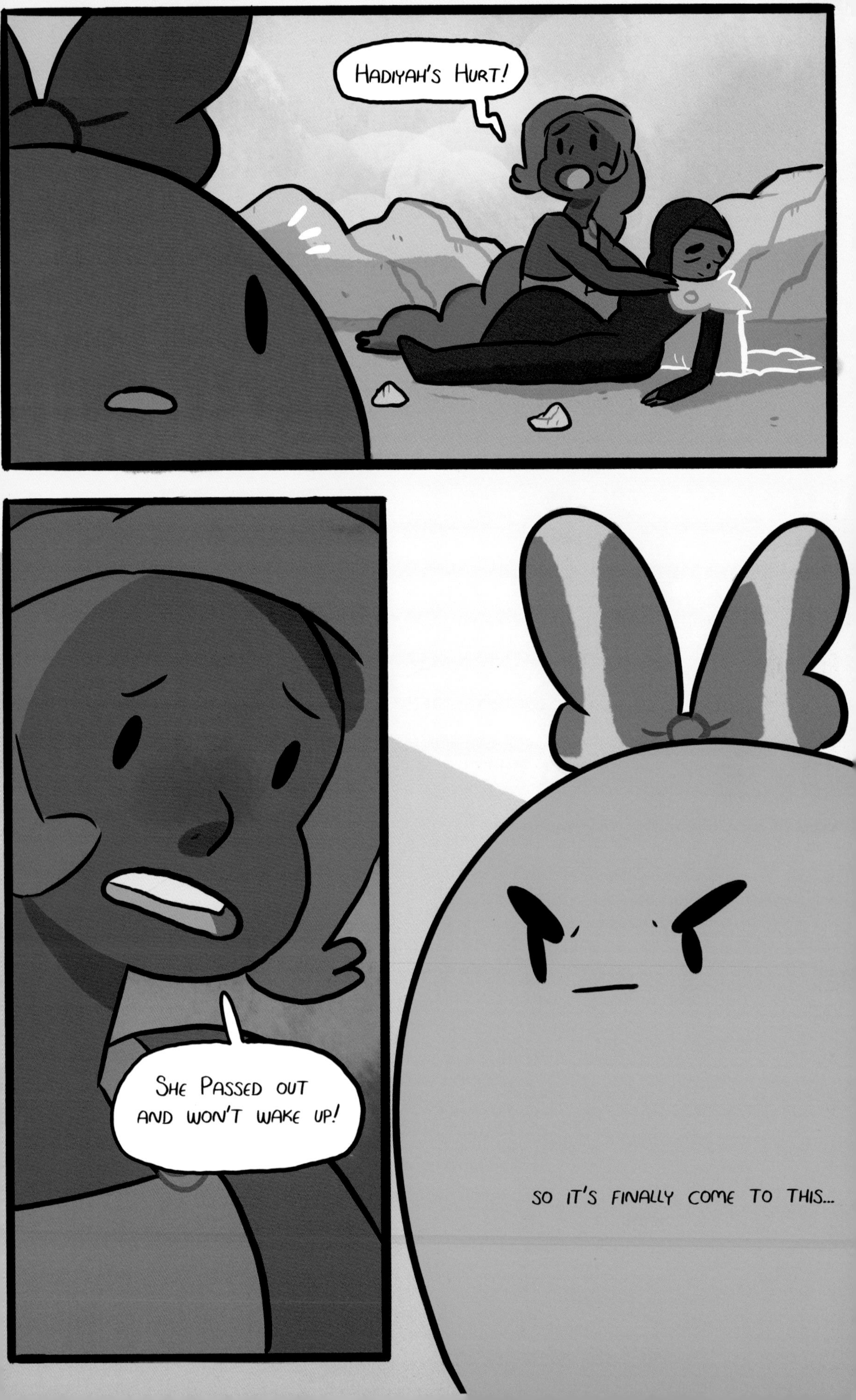
Hadiyah's Hurt!
She Passed out and won't wake up!
so it's finally come to this...

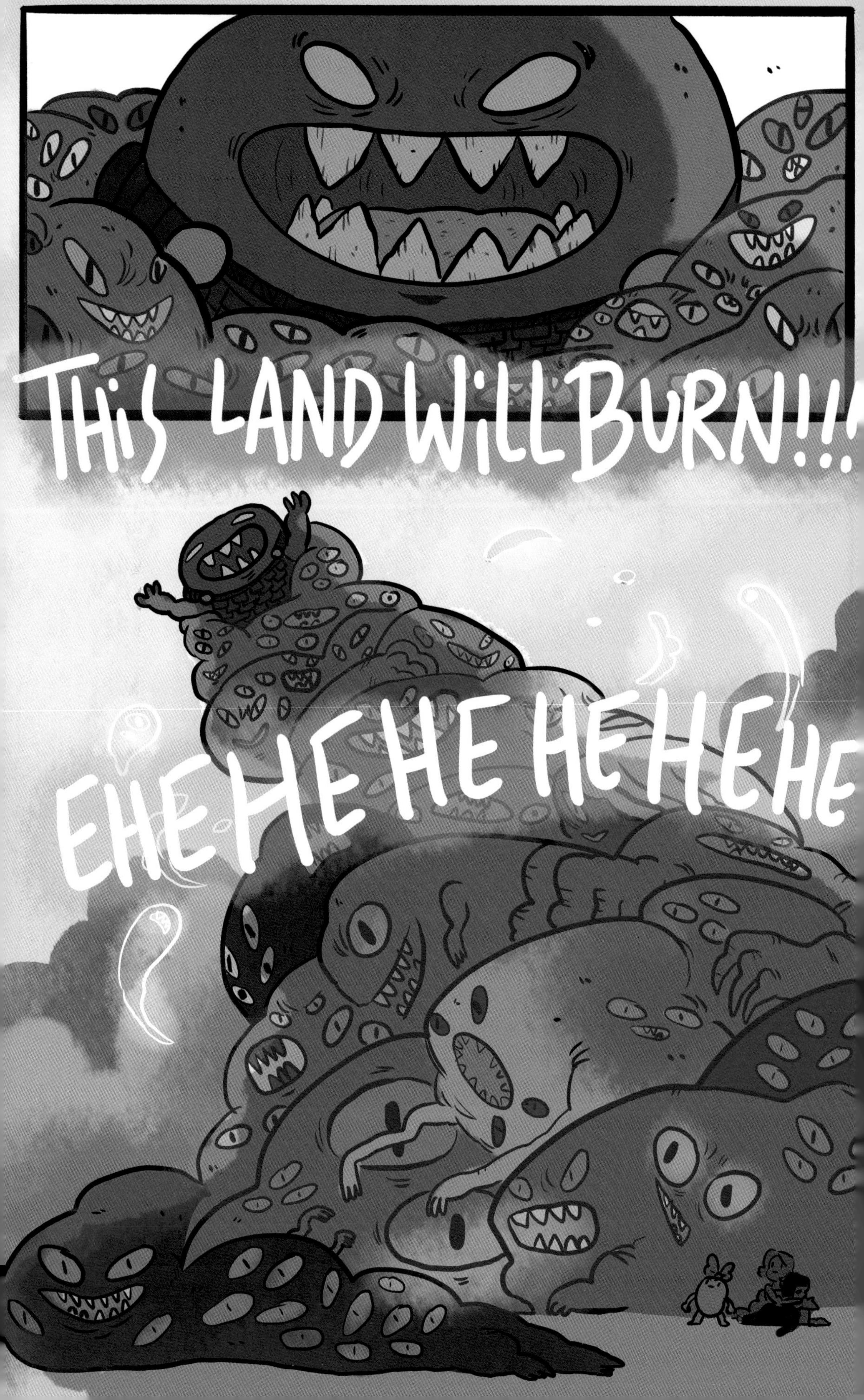
THIS LAND WILL BURN!!!
EHEHEHEHEHEHE

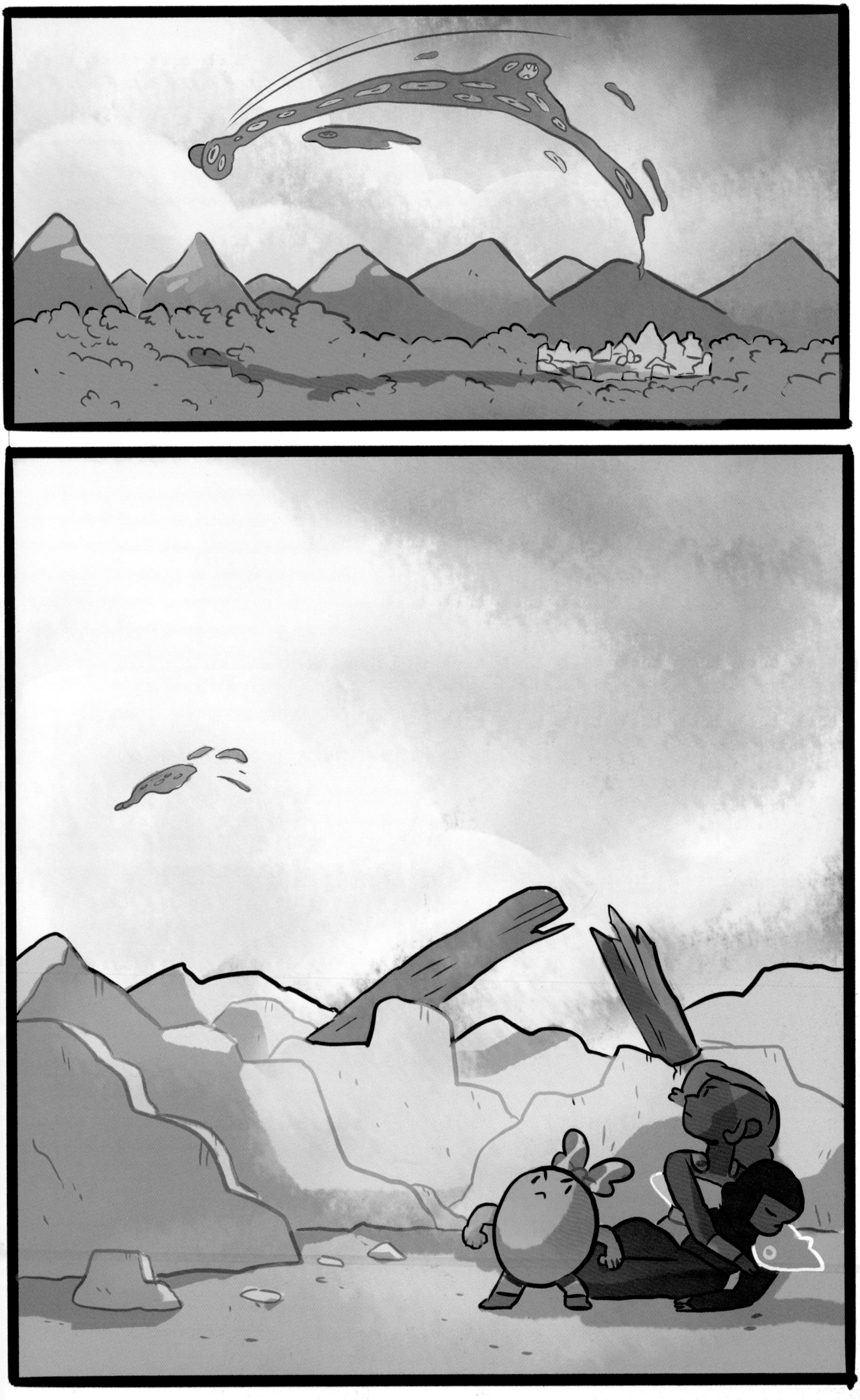

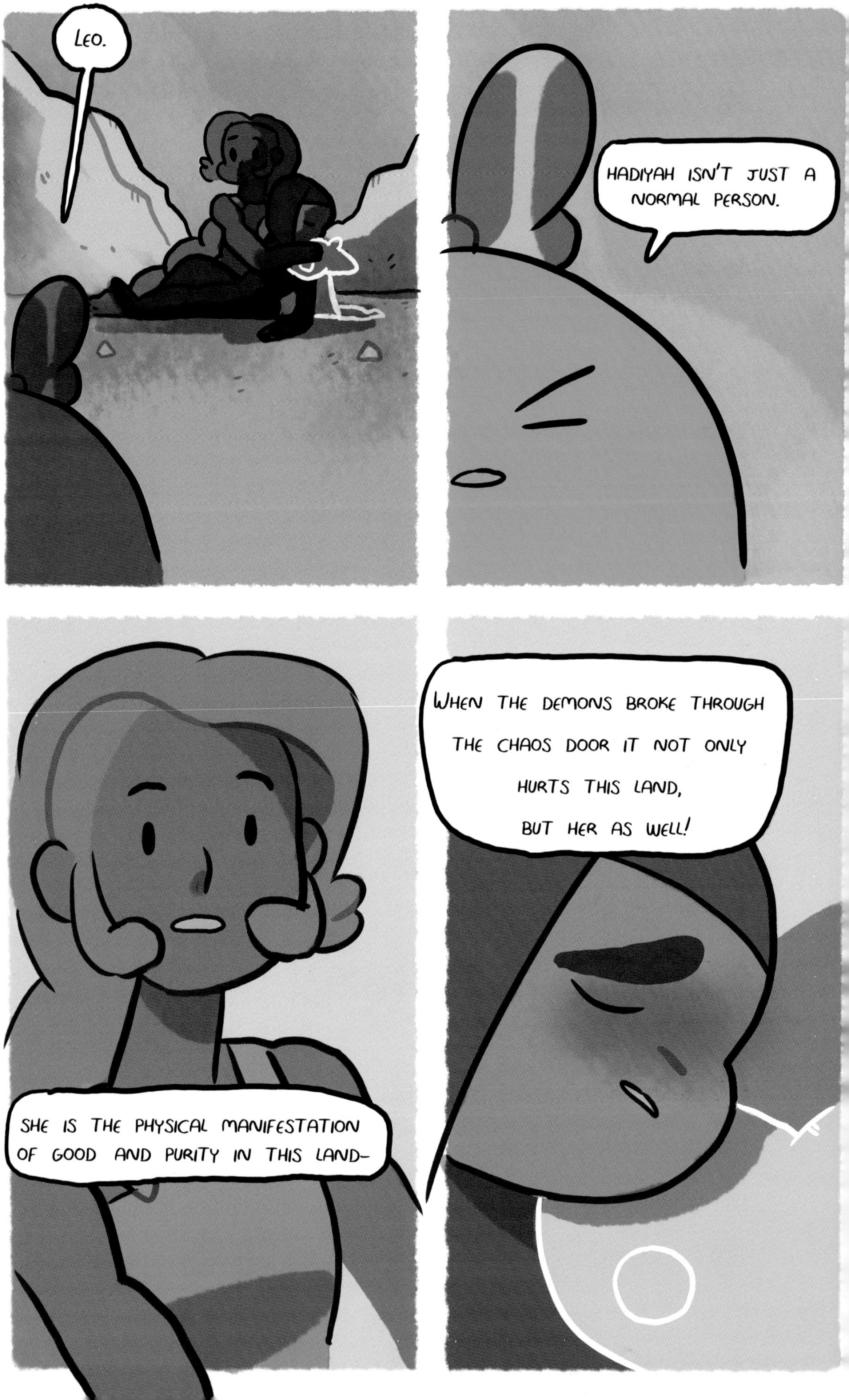
LEO.
HADIYAH ISN'T JUST A NORMAL PERSON.
SHE IS THE PHYSICAL MANIFESTATION OF GOOD AND PURITY IN THIS LAND-
WHEN THE DEMONS BROKE THROUGH THE CHAOS DOOR IT NOT ONLY HURTS THIS LAND,
BUT HER AS WELL!

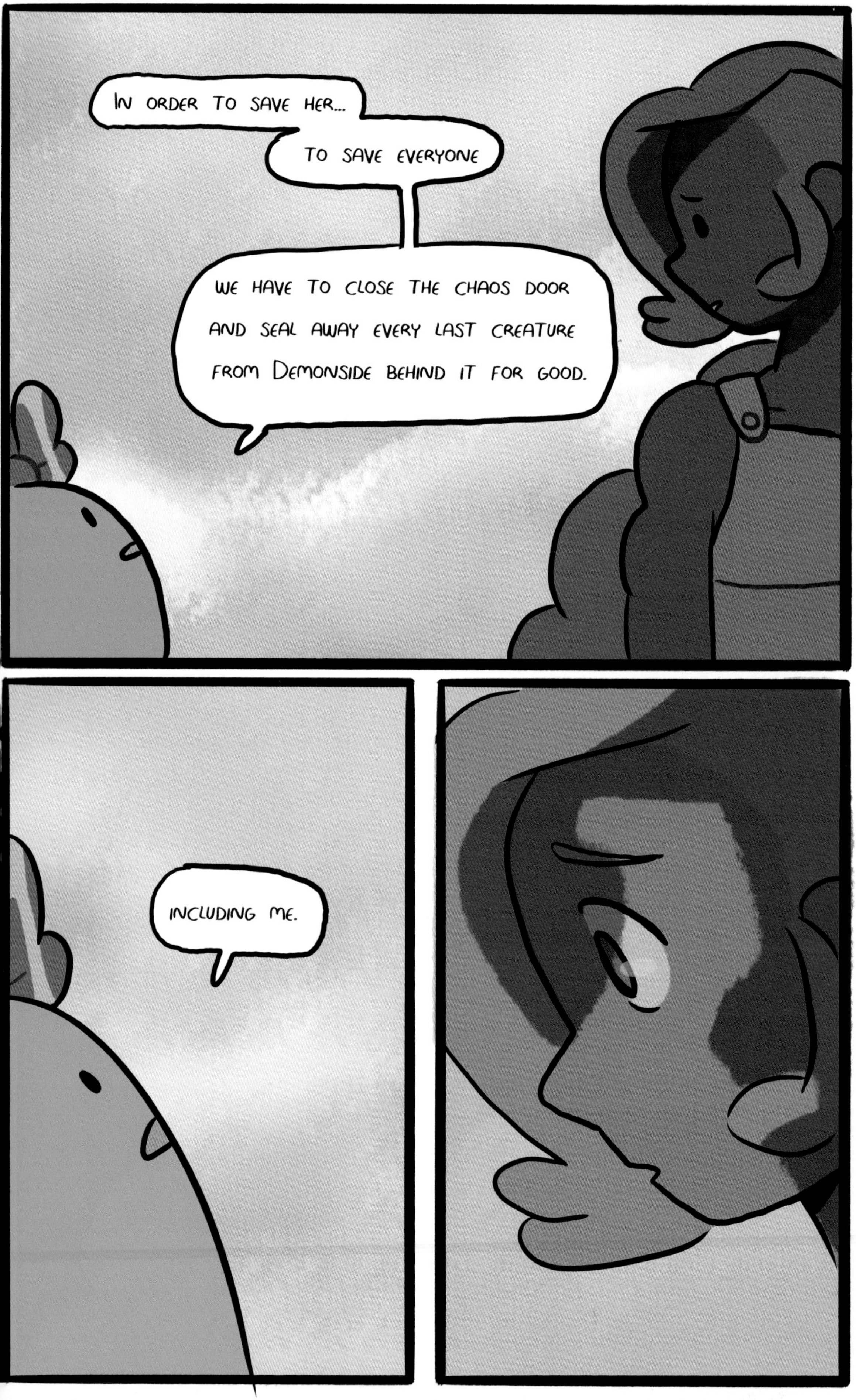
IN ORDER TO SAVE HER...
TO SAVE EVERYONE
WE HAVE TO CLOSE THE CHAOS DOOR AND SEAL AWAY EVERY LAST CREATURE FROM DEMONSIDE BEHIND IT FOR GOOD.
INCLUDING ME.

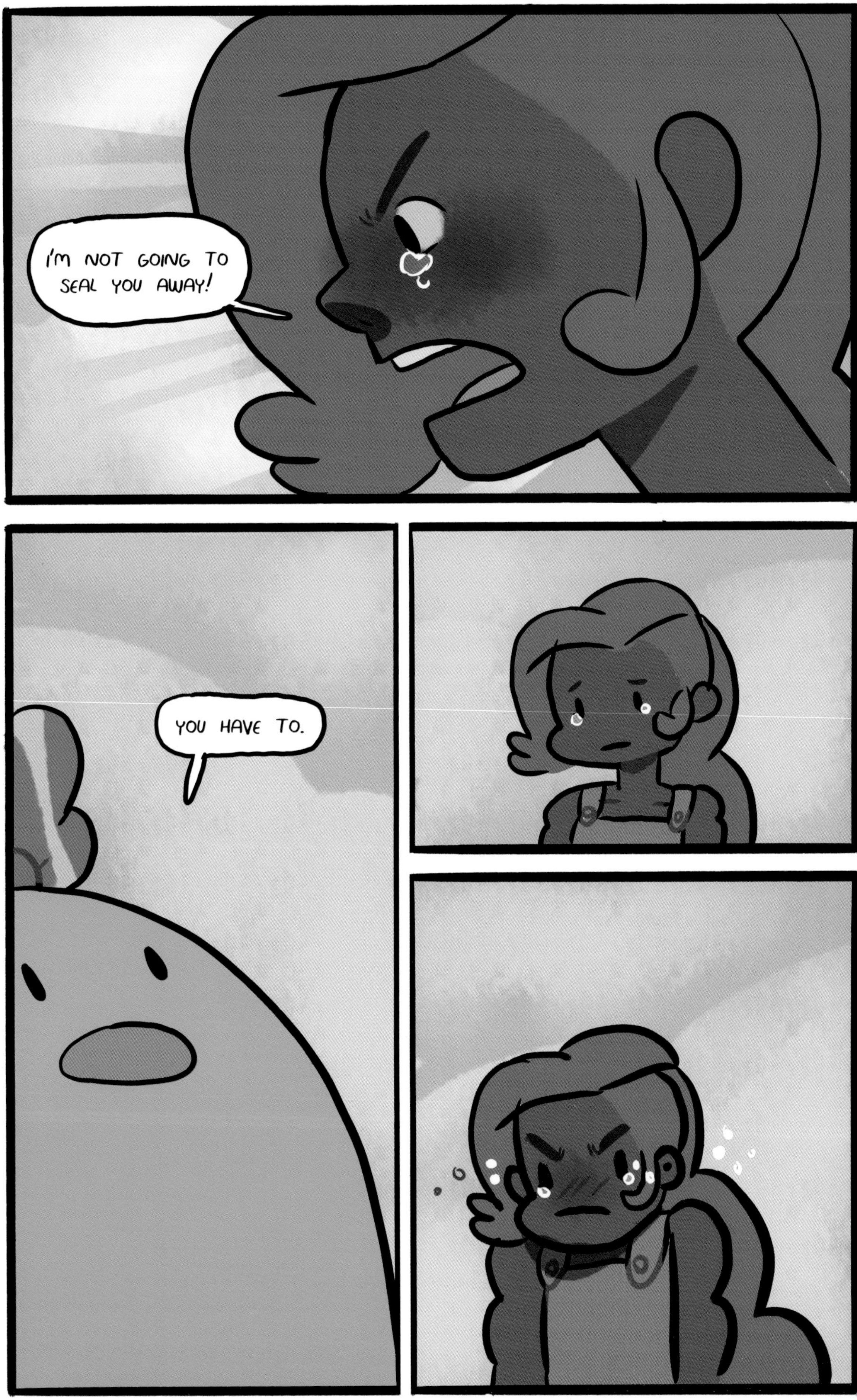
I'M NOT GOING TO SEAL YOU AWAY!
YOU HAVE TO.

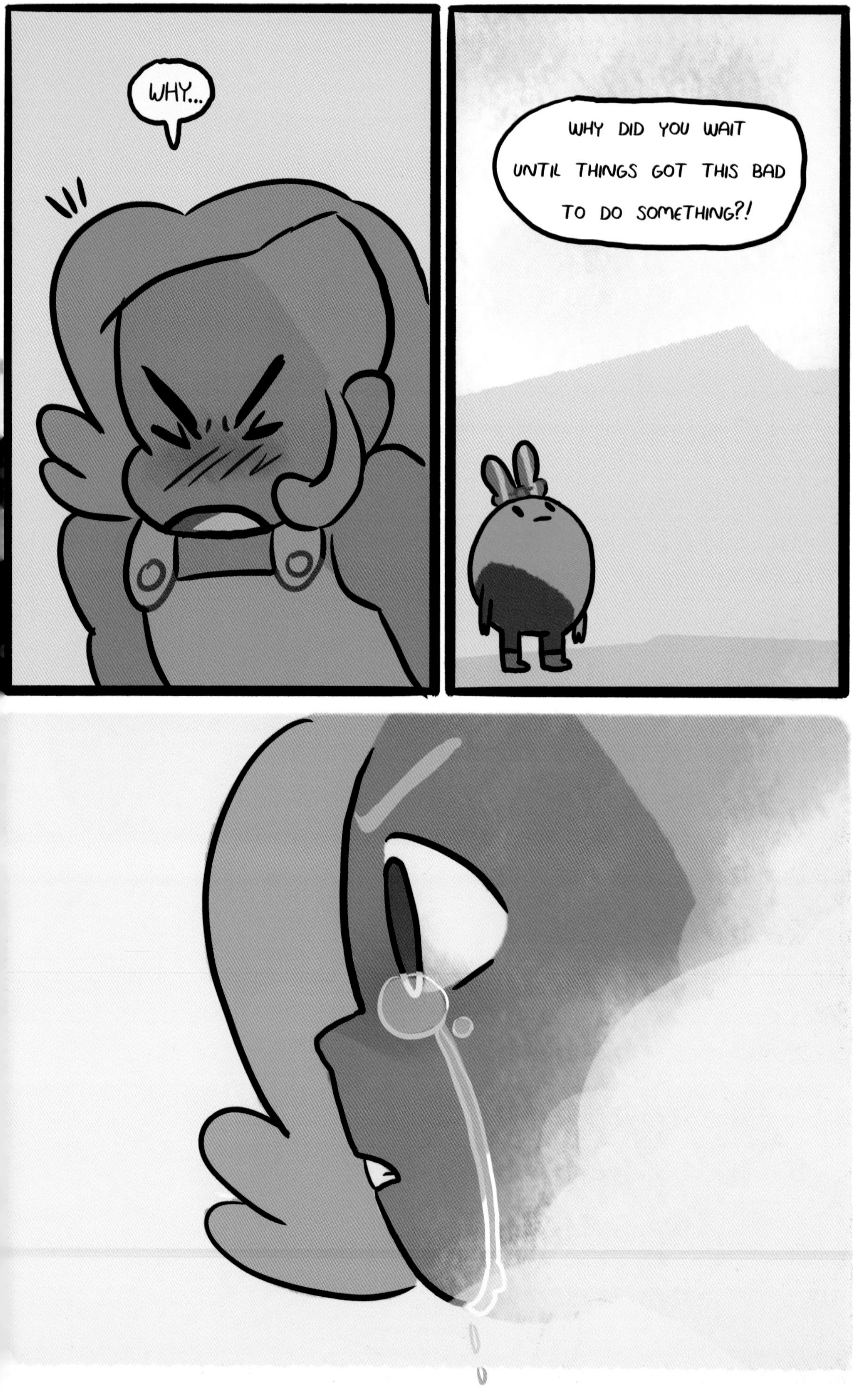
WHY...
WHY DID YOU WAIT UNTIL THINGS GOT THIS BAD TO DO SOMETHING?!

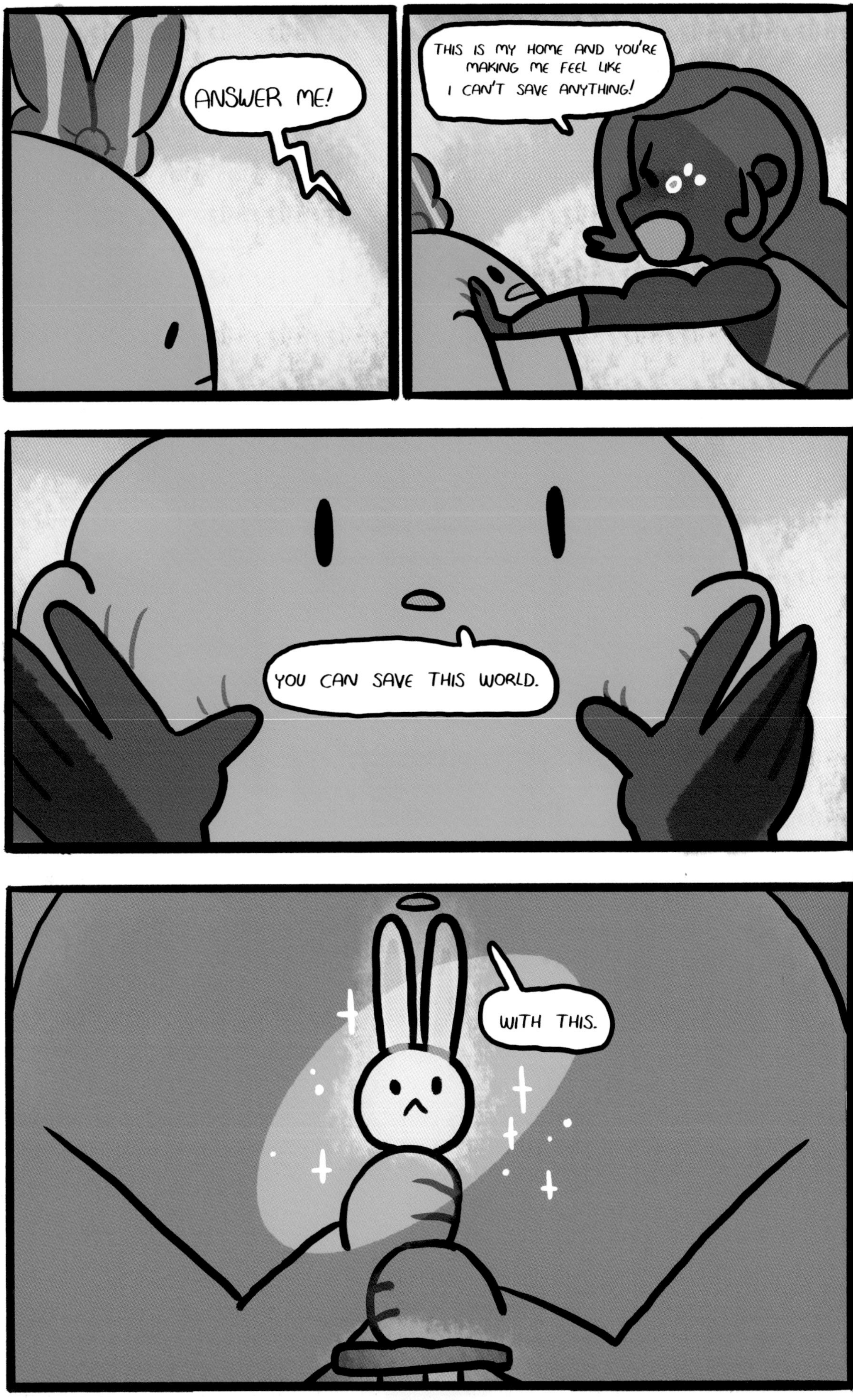
ANSWER ME!
THIS IS MY HOME AND YOU'RE MAKING ME FEEL LIKE I CAN'T SAVE ANYTHING!
YOU CAN SAVE THIS WORLD.
WITH THIS.

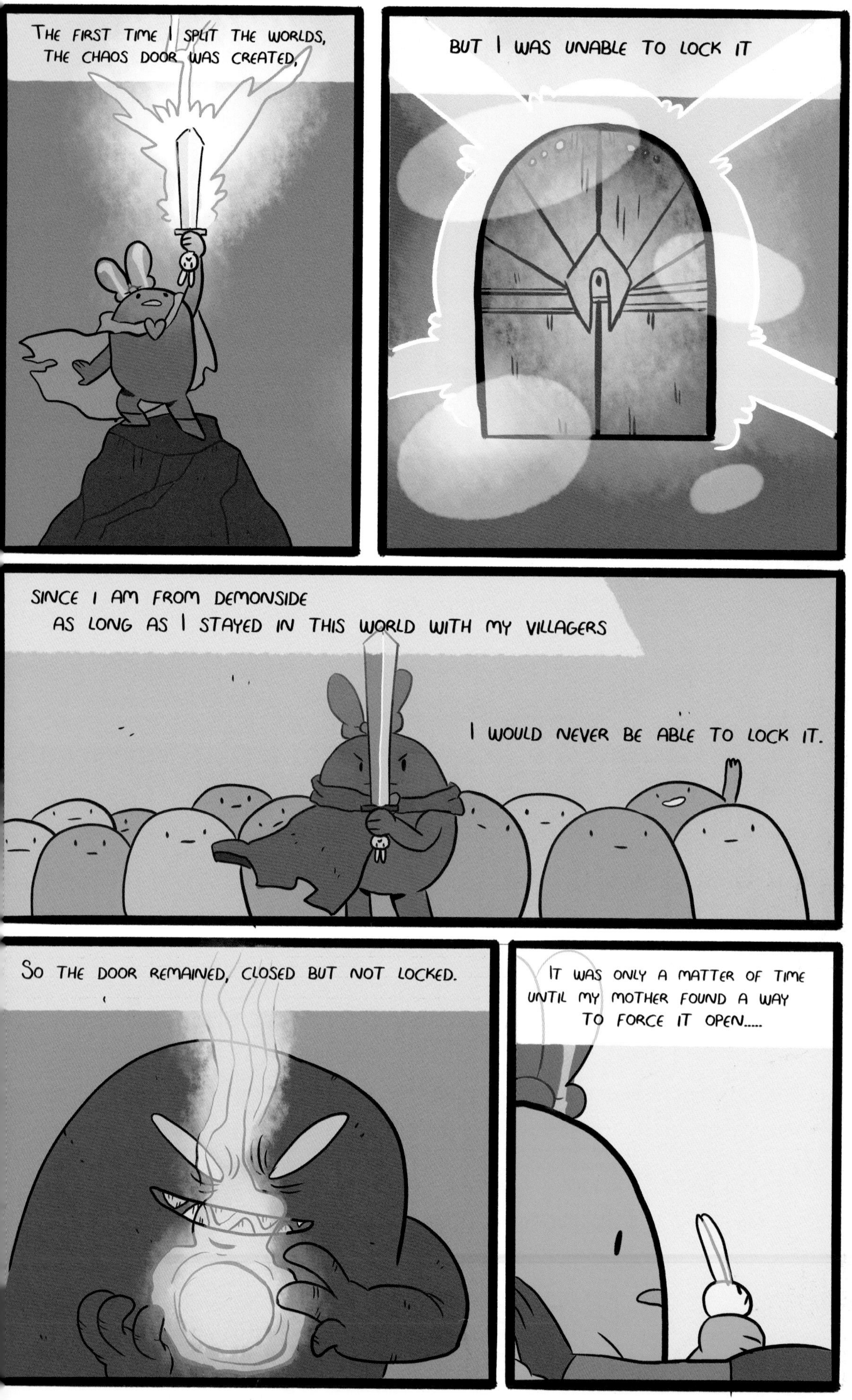
THE FIRST TIME I SPLIT THE WORLDS, THE CHAOS DOOR WAS CREATED,
BUT I WAS UNABLE TO LOCK IT
SINCE I AM FROM DEMONSIDE AS LONG AS I STAYED IN THIS WORLD WITH MY VILLAGERS
I WOULD NEVER BE ABLE TO LOCK IT.
SO THE DOOR REMAINED, CLOSED BUT NOT LOCKED.
IT WAS ONLY A MATTER OF TIME UNTIL MY MOTHER FOUND A WAY TO FORCE IT OPEN.....

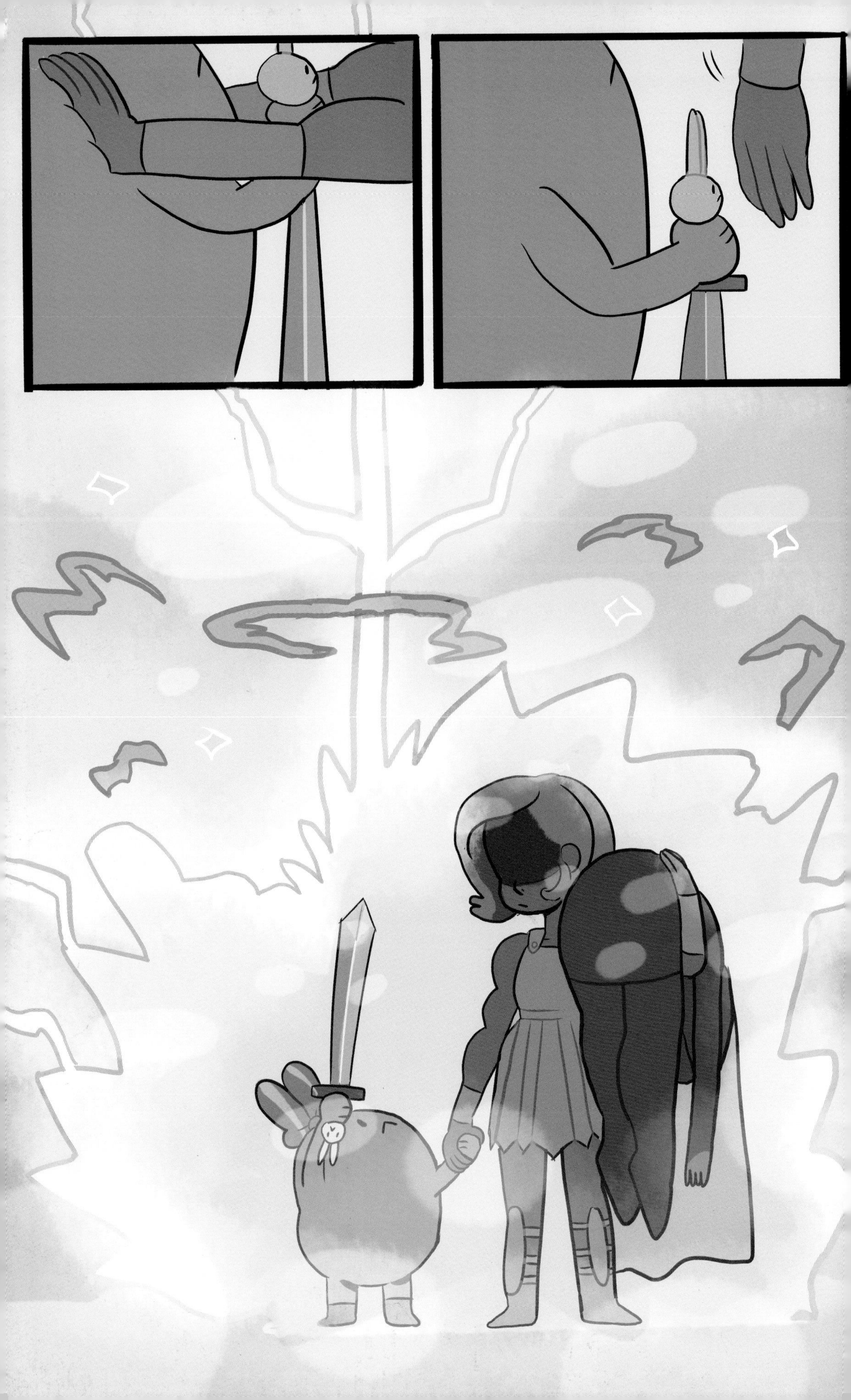

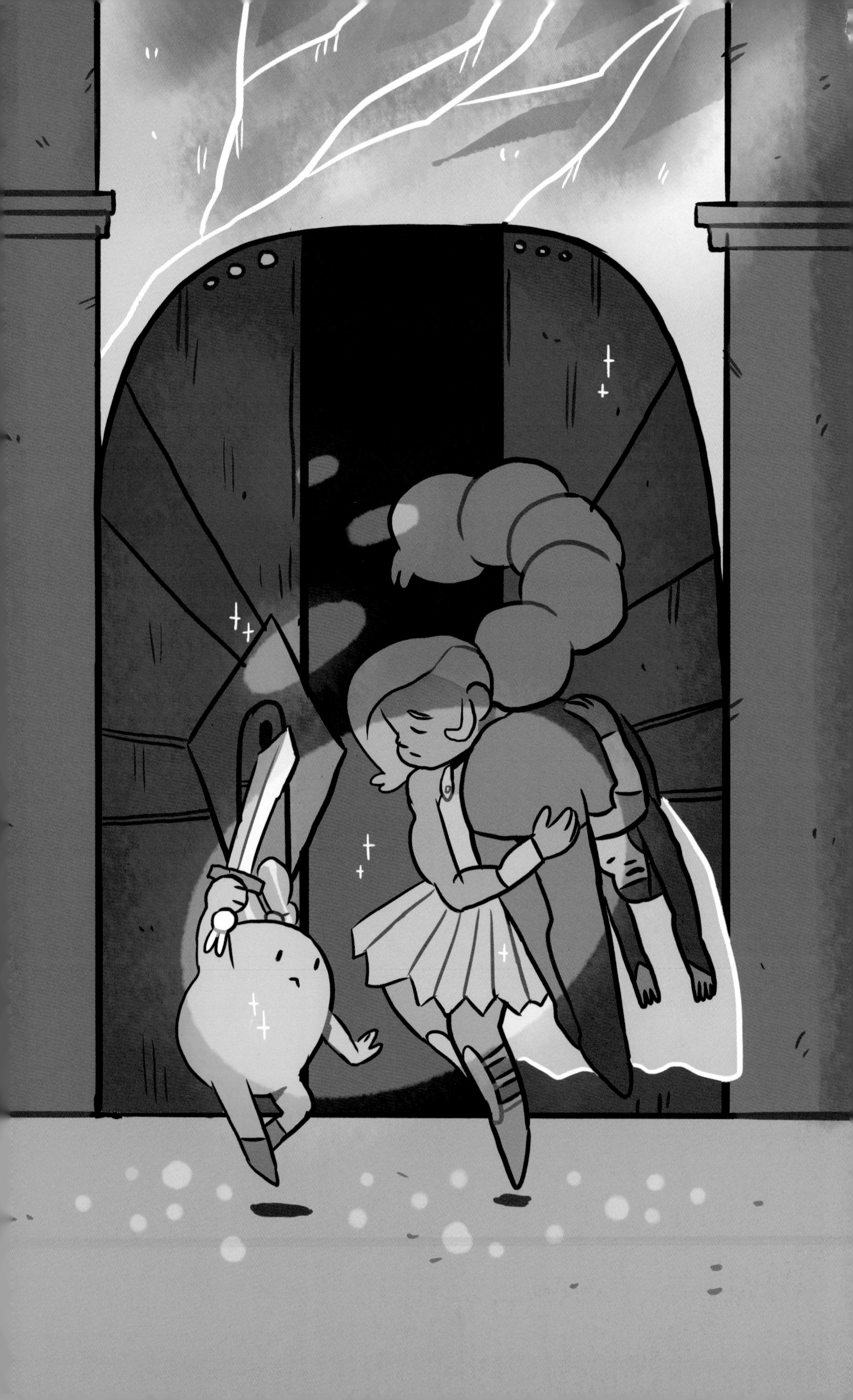

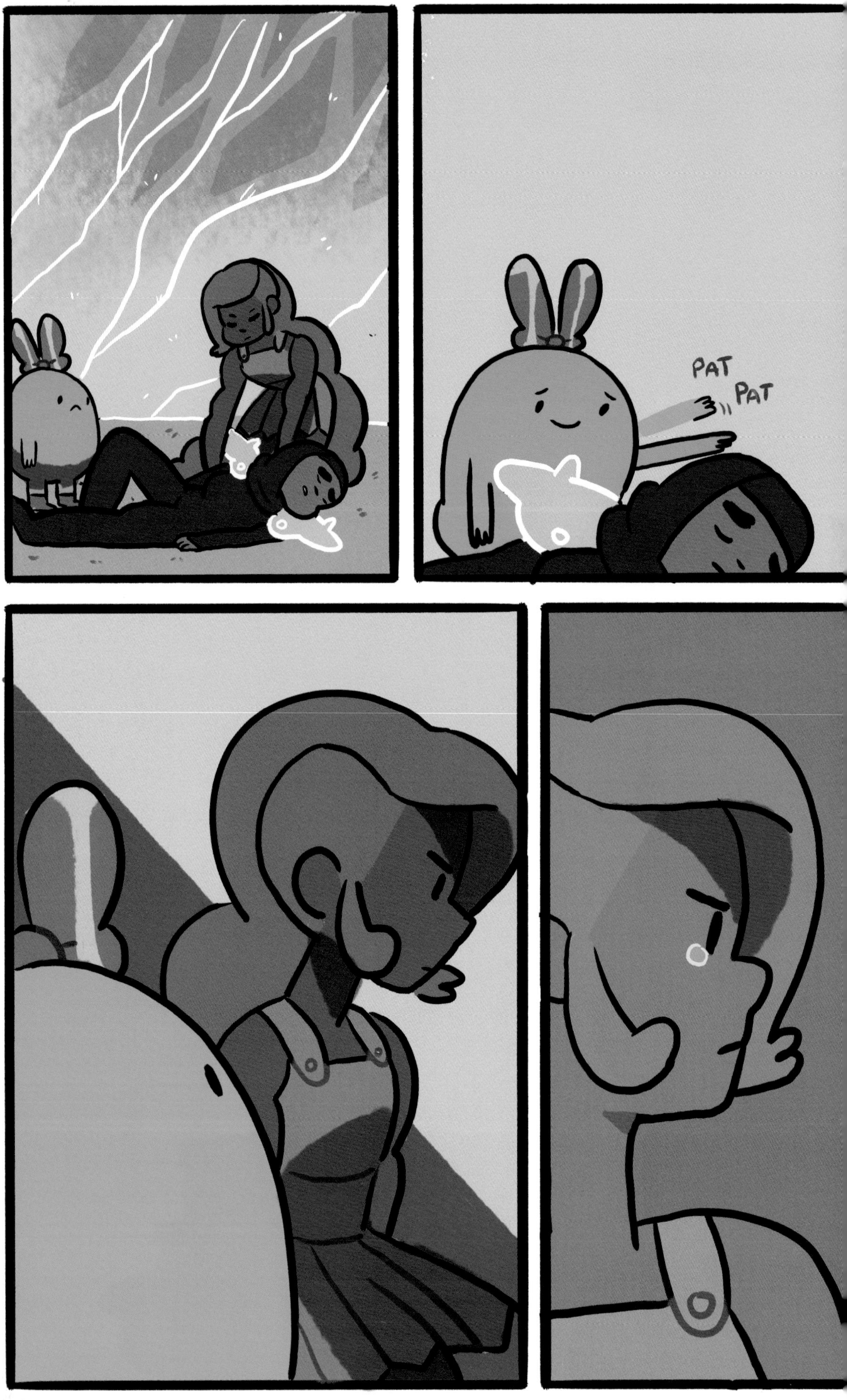
PAT
PAT

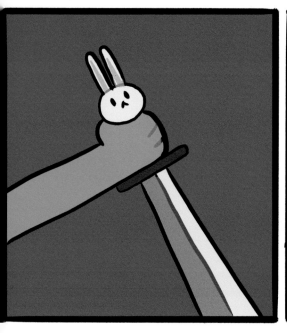

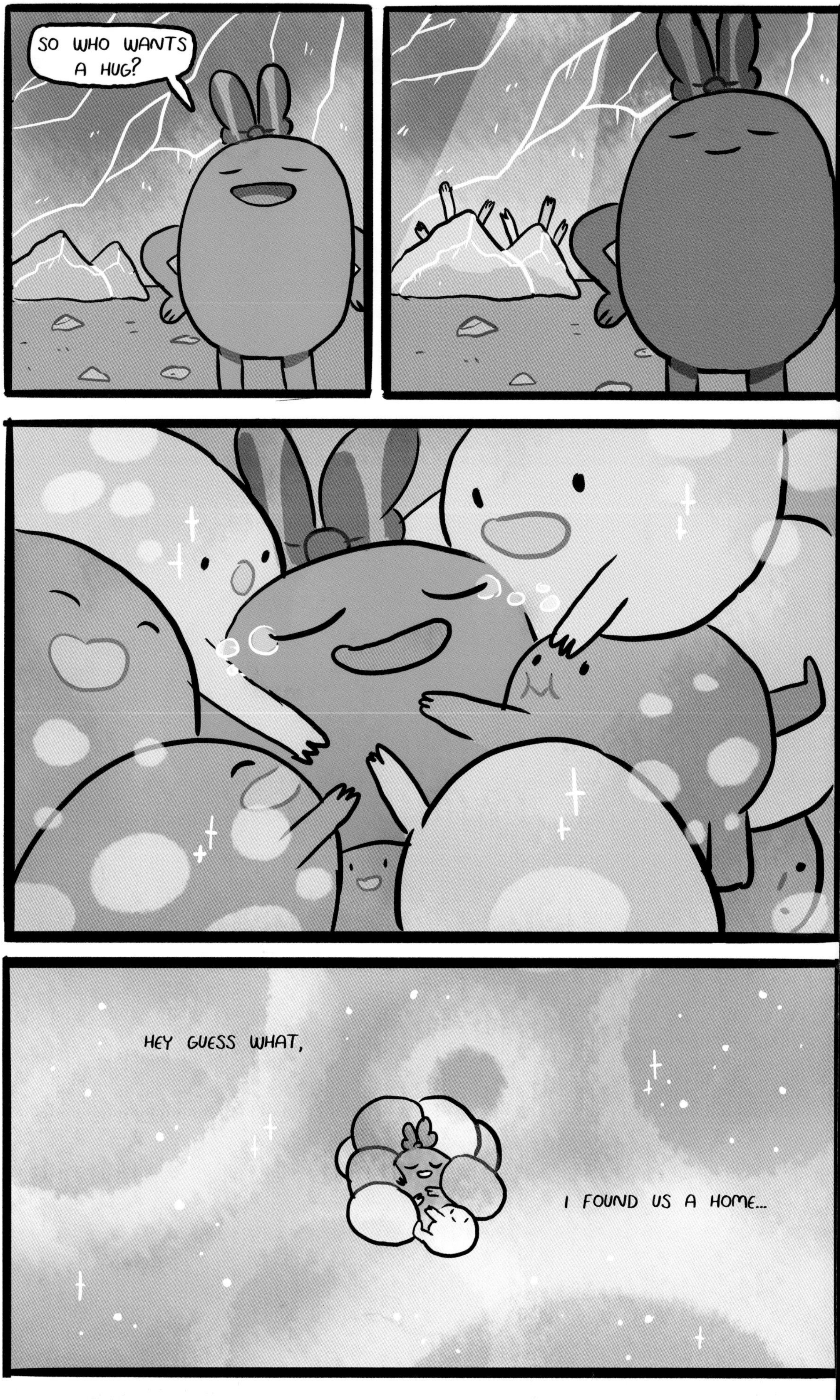
SO WHO WANTS A HUG?
HEY GUESS WHAT,
I FOUND US A HOME...

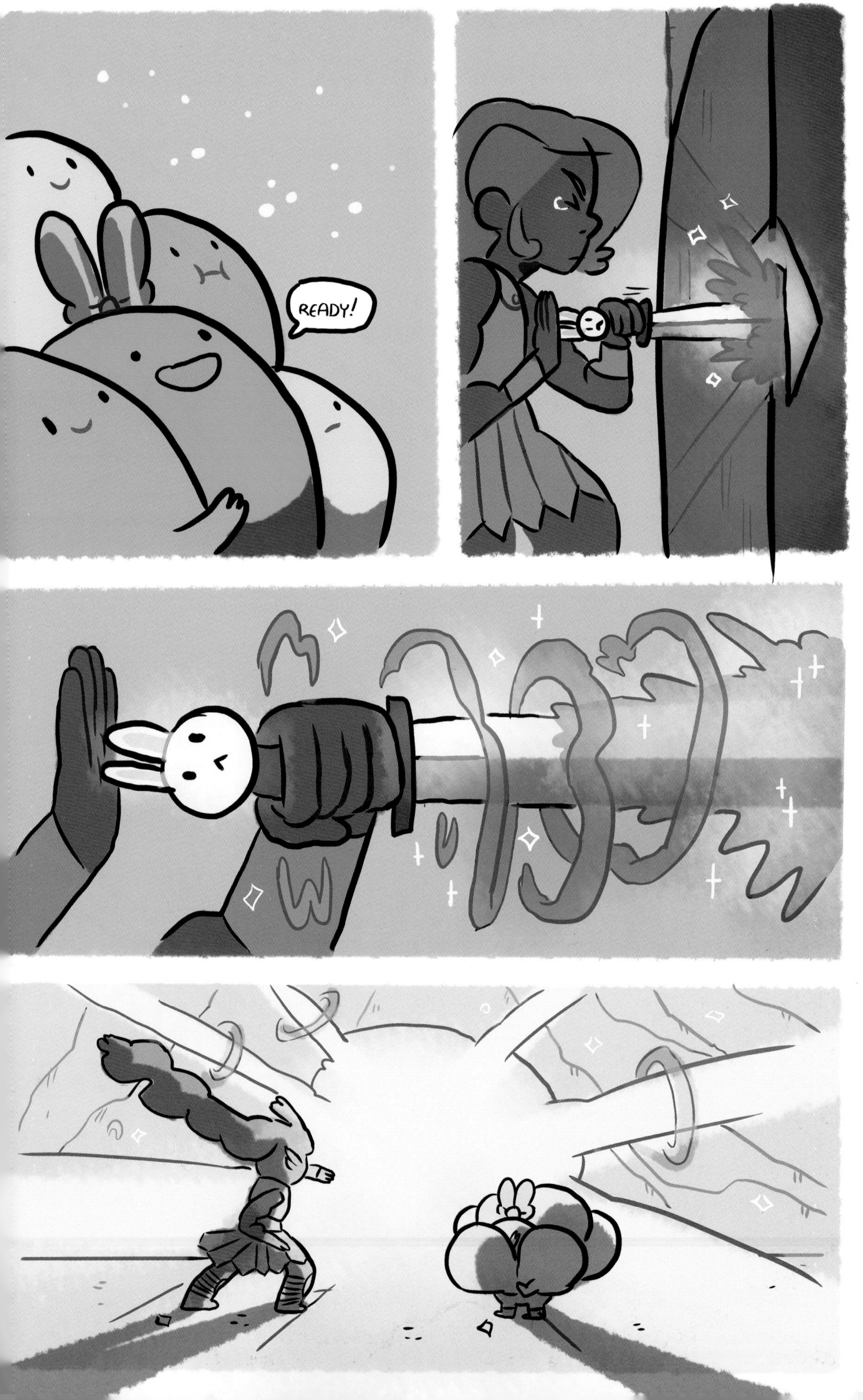
READY!

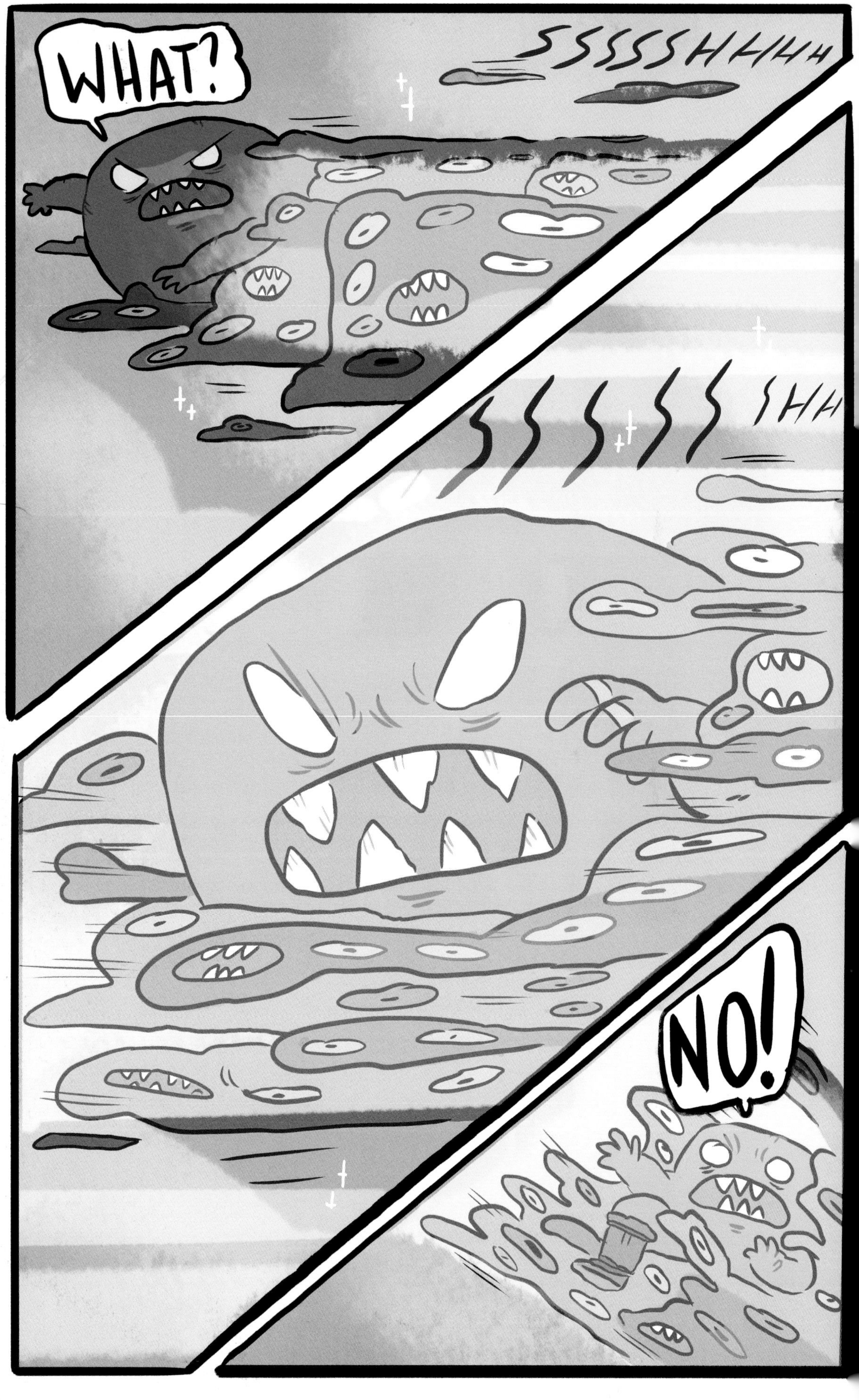
WHAT?
SSSSSHHHH
SSSSSSSHH
NO!

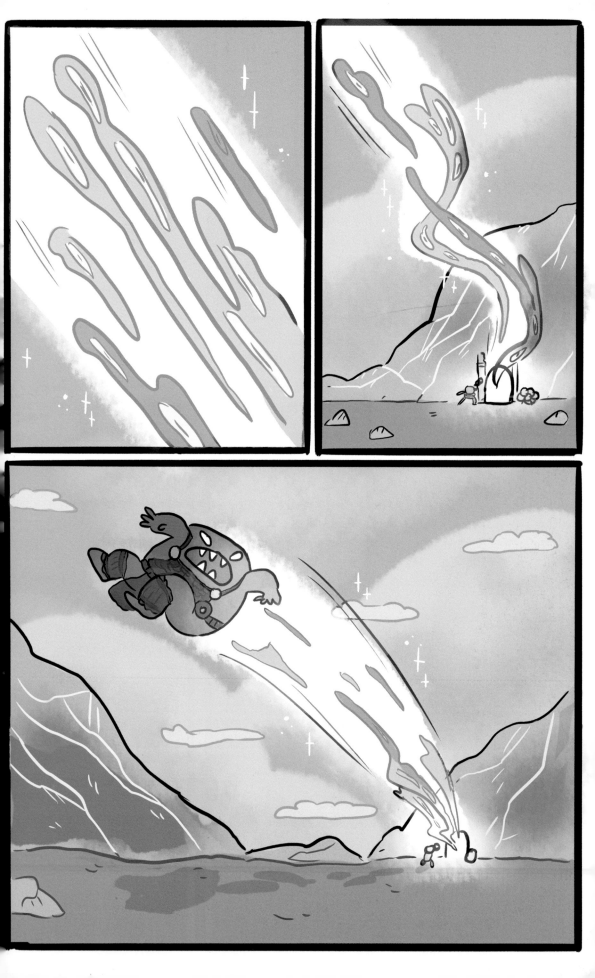

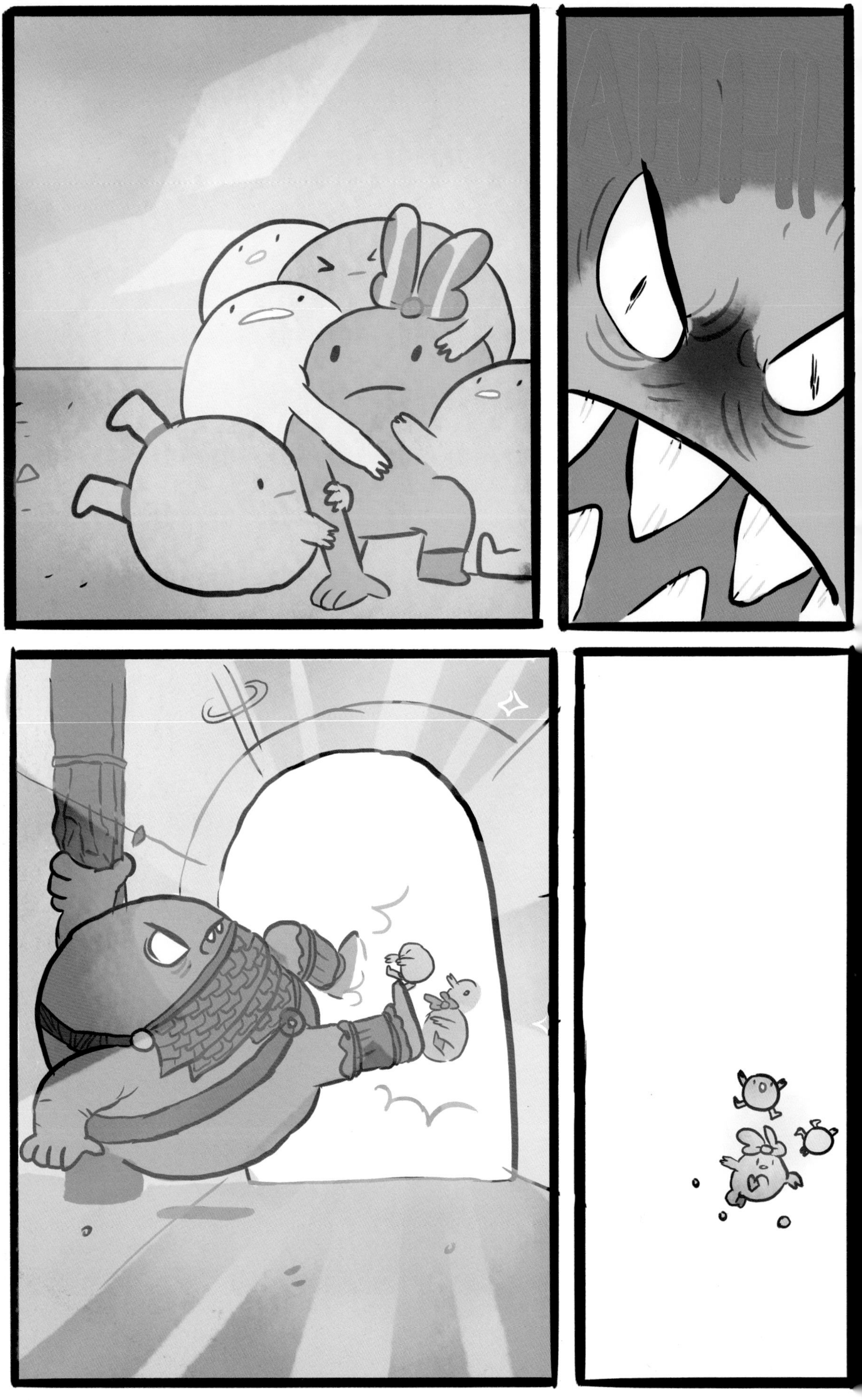

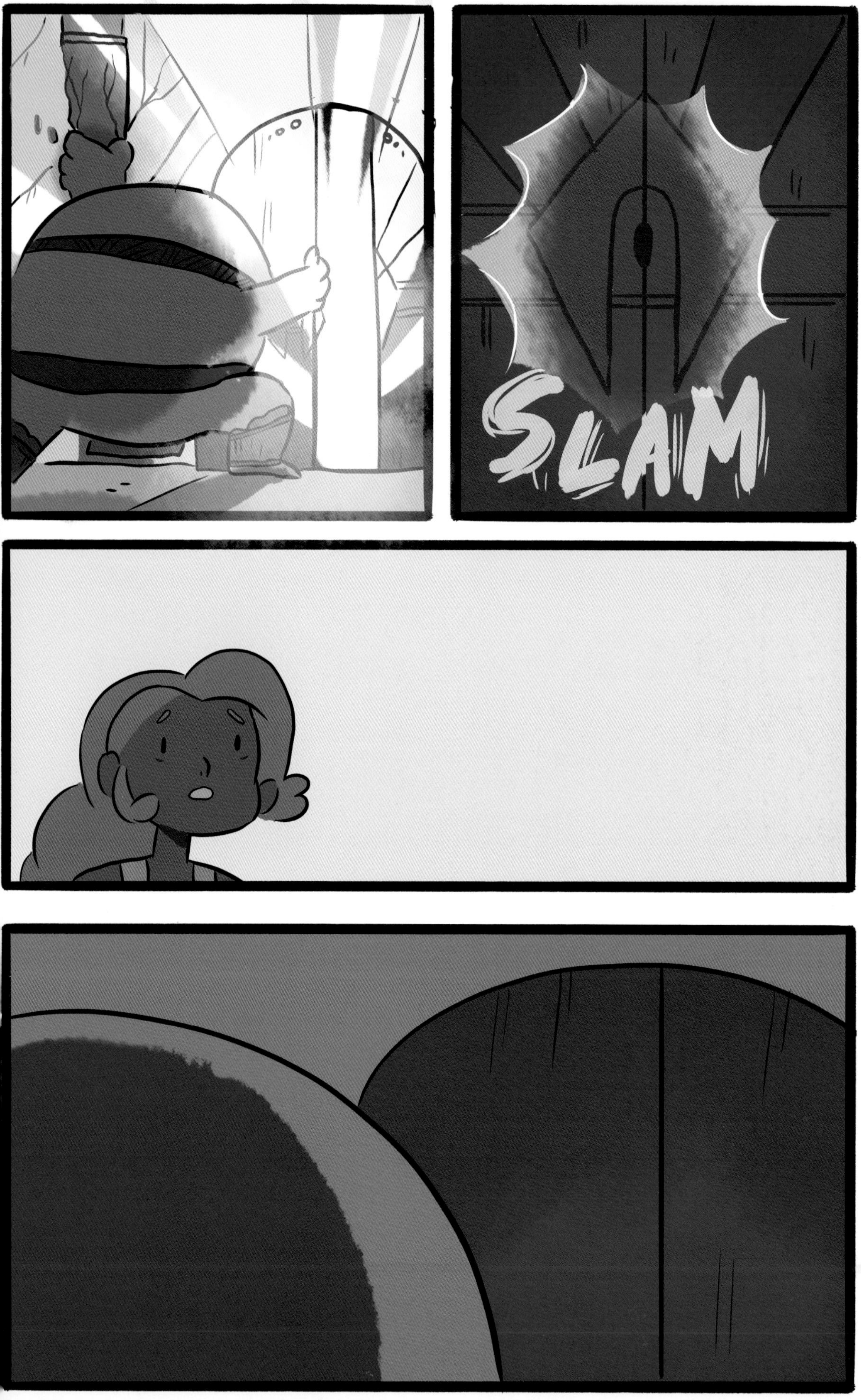
SLAM

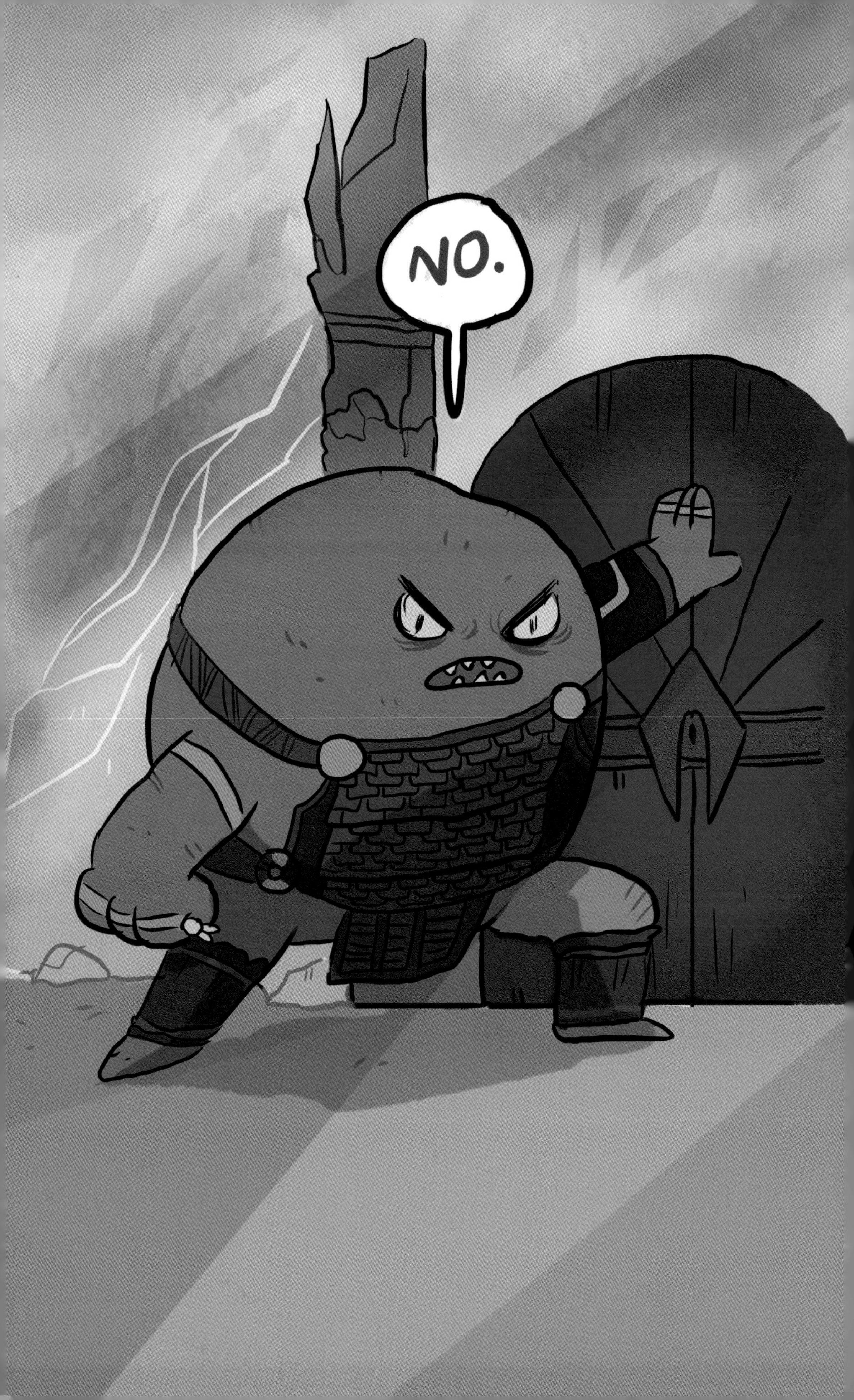
NO.

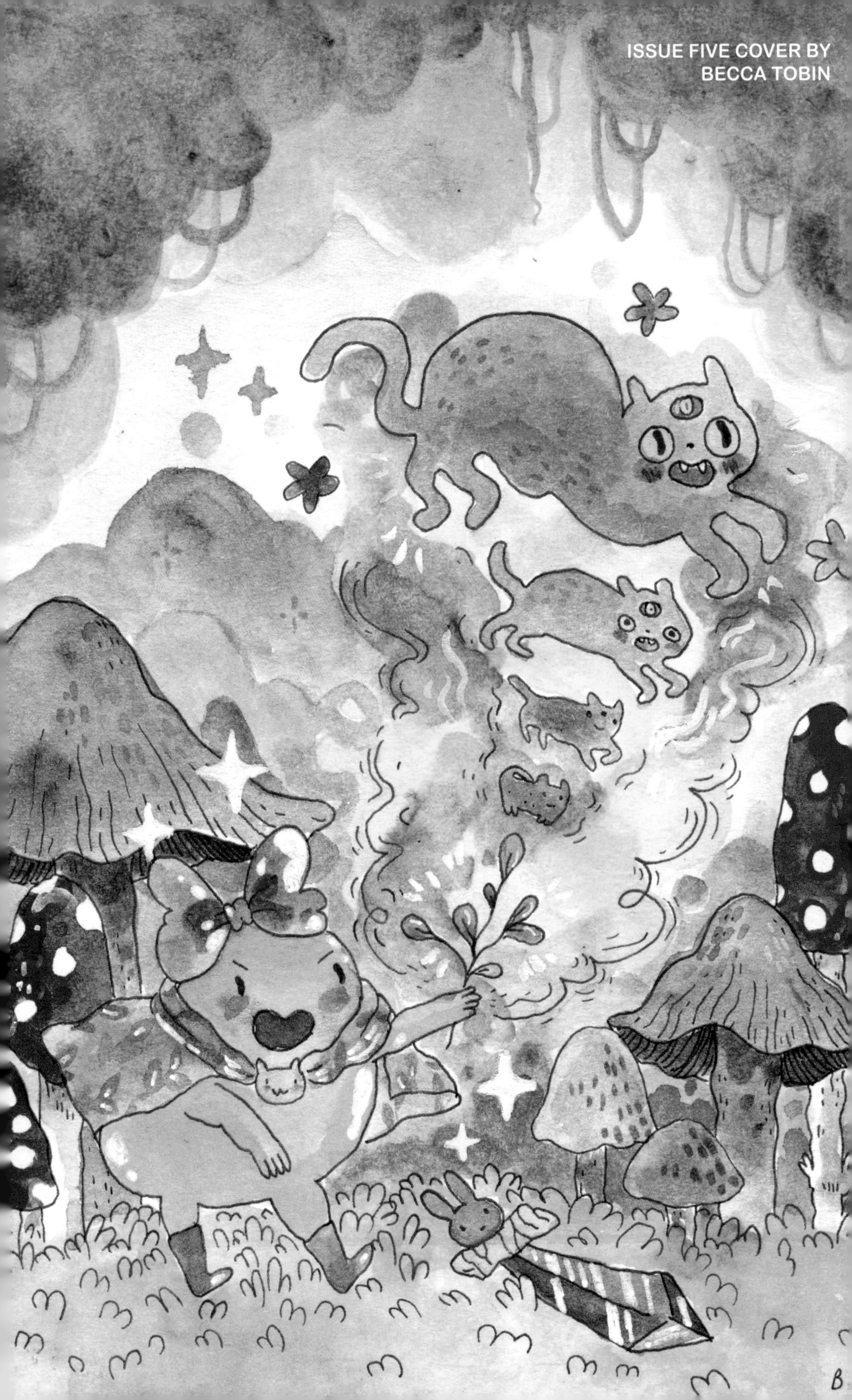

ISSUE FIVE COVER BY
BECCA TOBIN

Chapter
Six

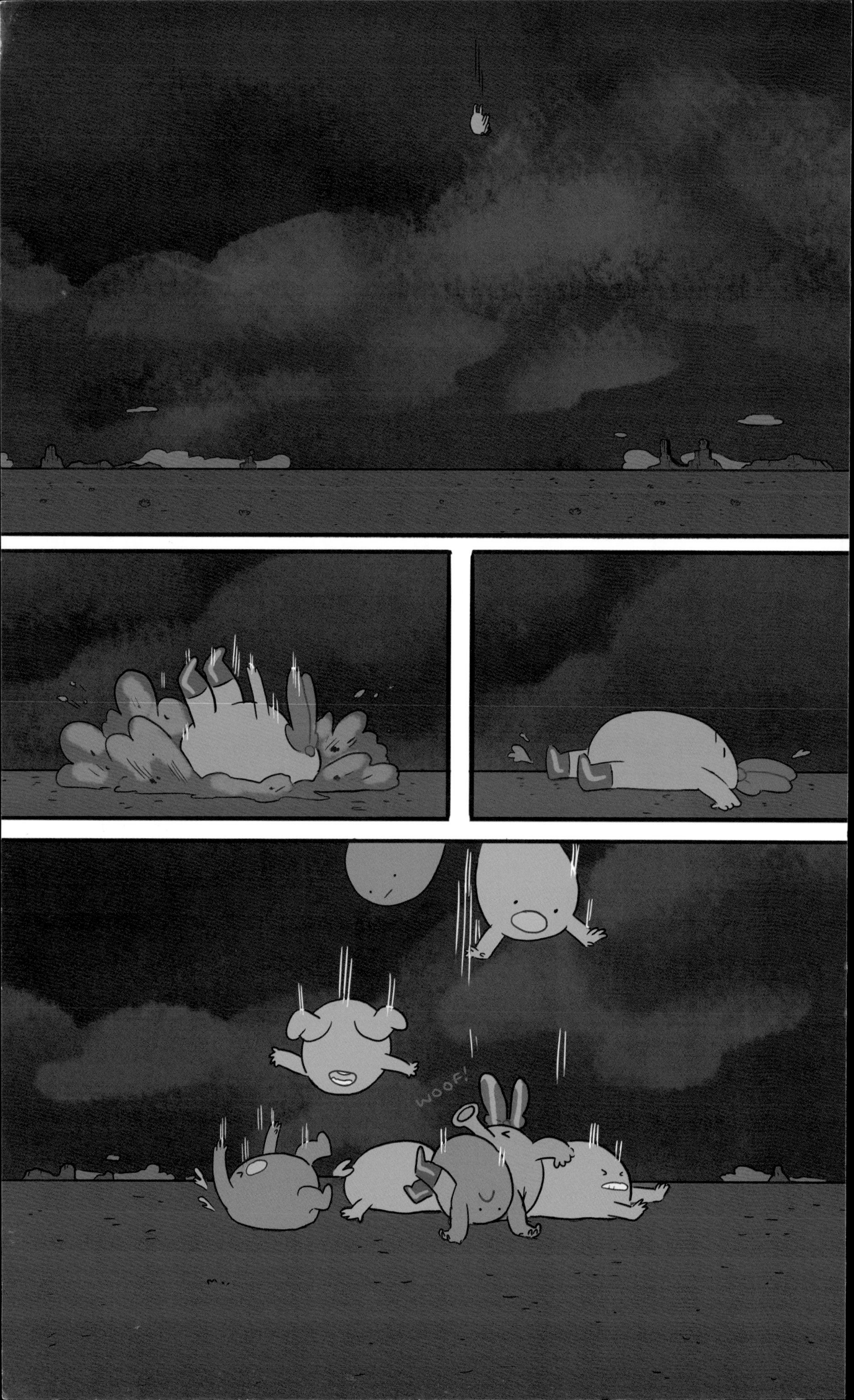
WOOF!

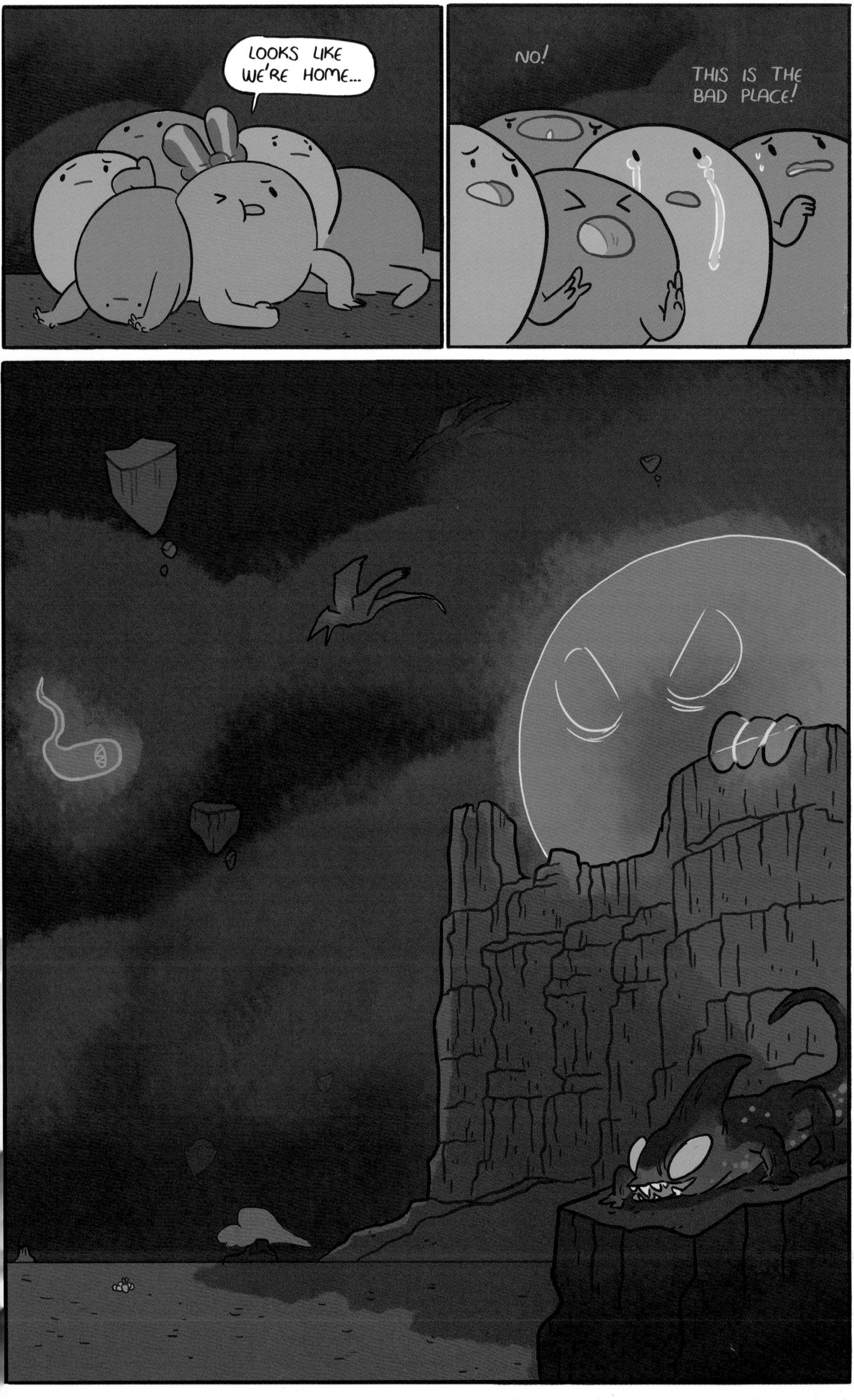
LOOKS LIKE WE'RE HOME...
NO!
THIS IS THE BAD PLACE!

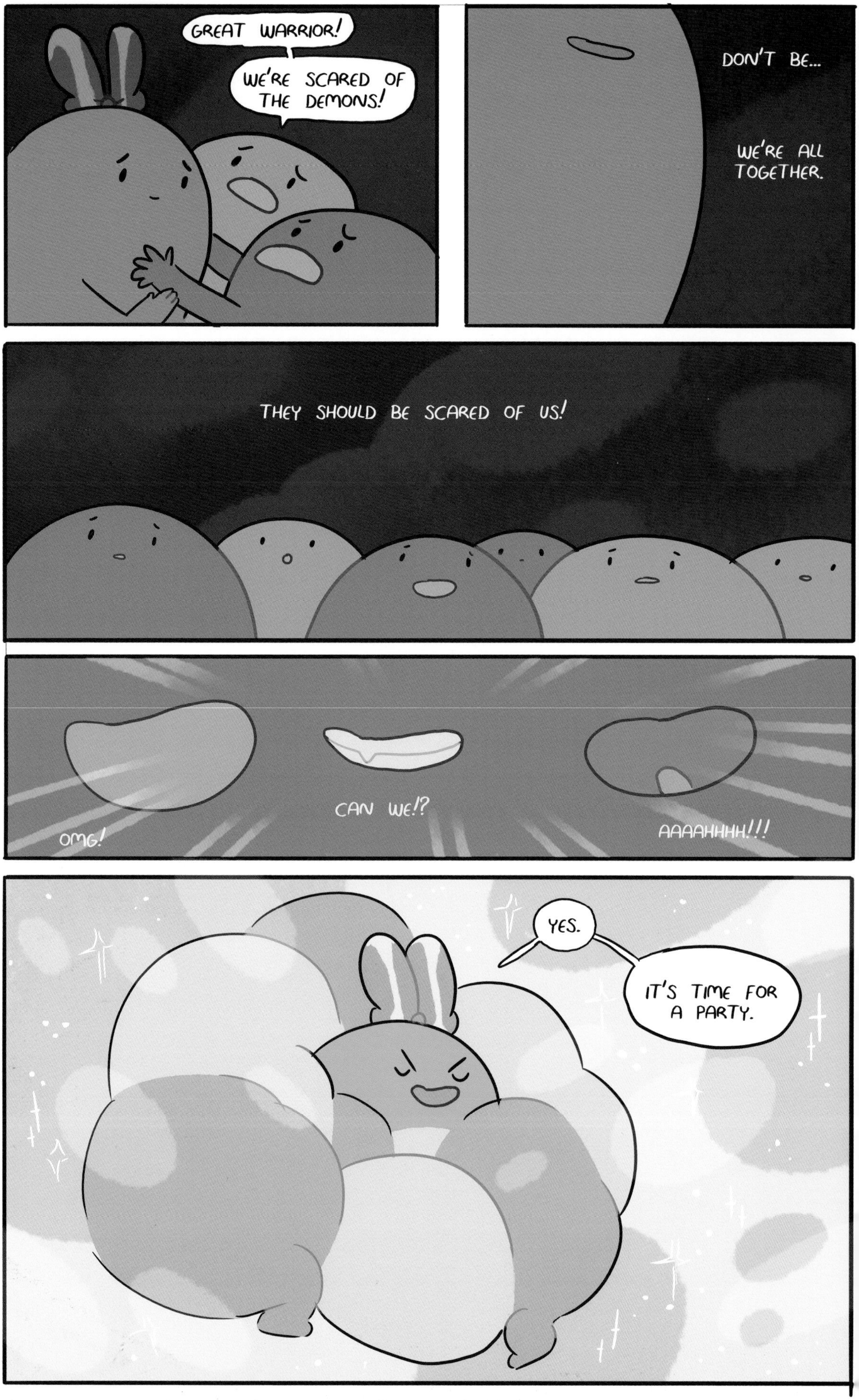
GREAT WARRIOR!
WE'RE SCARED OF THE DEMONS!
DON'T BE...
WE'RE ALL TOGETHER.
THEY SHOULD BE SCARED OF US!
OMG!
CAN WE!?
AAAAHHHH!!!
YES.
IT'S TIME FOR A PARTY.

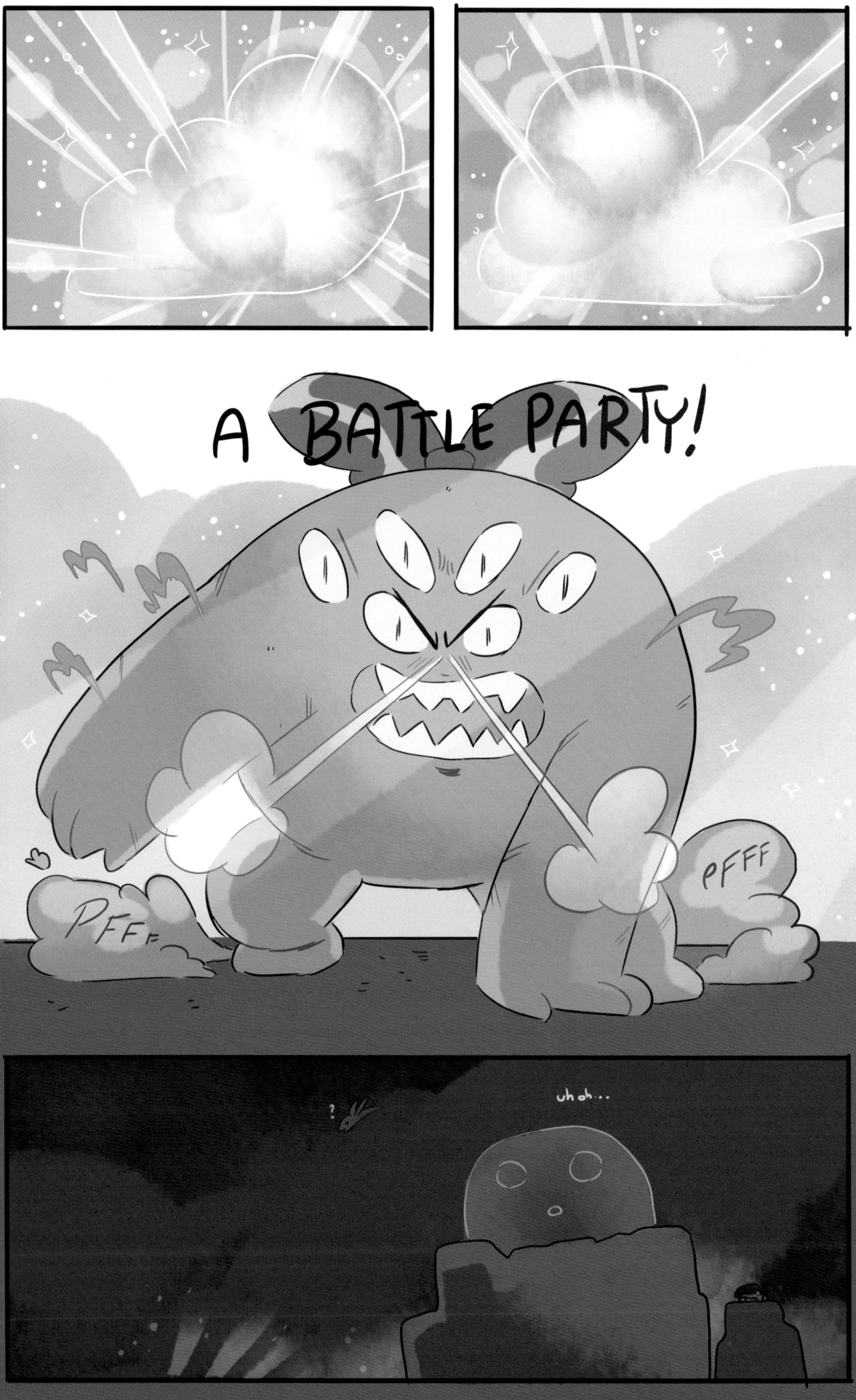
A BATTLE PARTY!
PFFF
PFFF
uh oh...

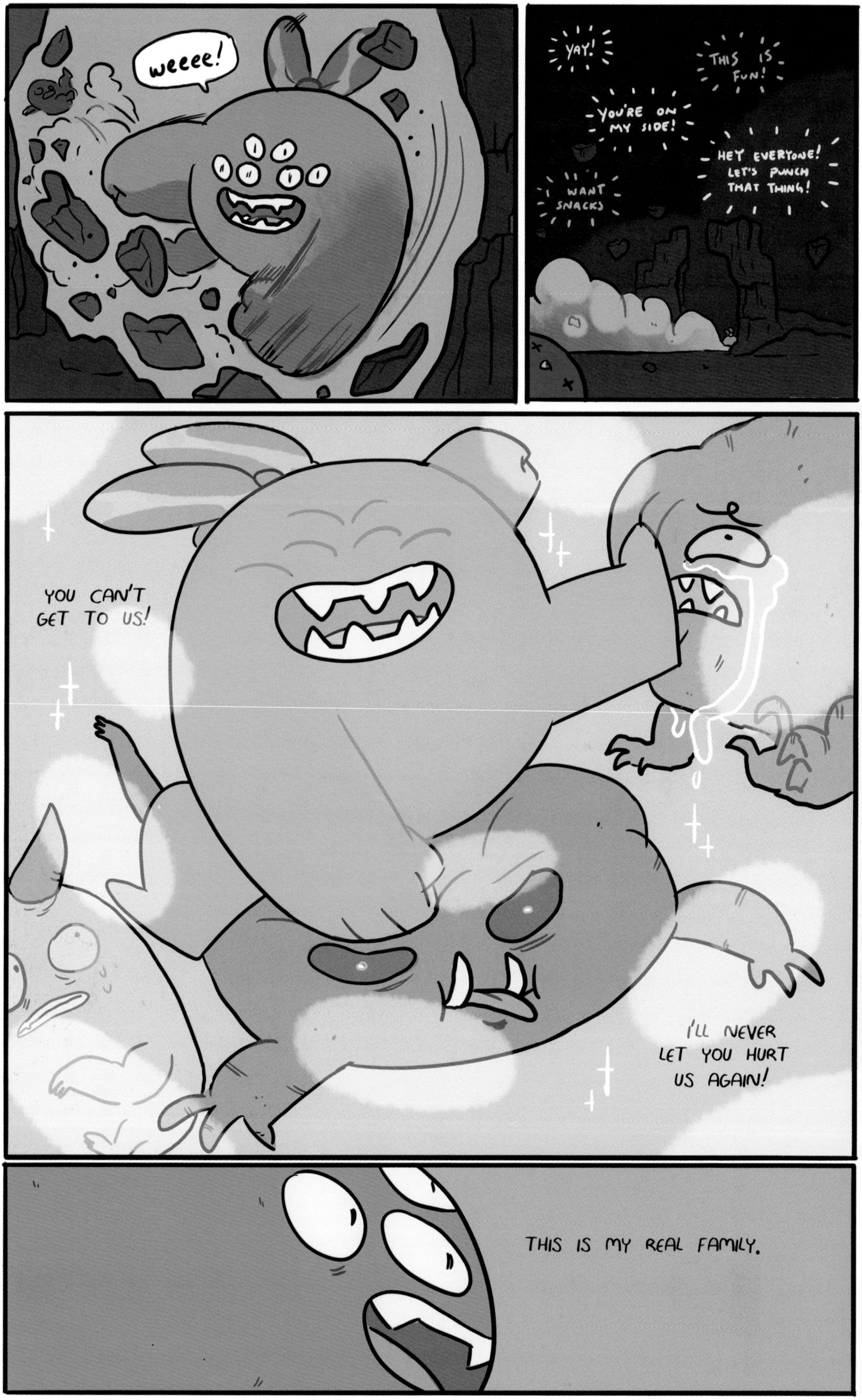
weeee!
YAY!
THIS IS FUN!
YOU'RE ON MY SIDE!
HEY EVERYONE! LET'S PUNCH THAT THING!
WANT SNACKS
YOU CAN'T GET TO US!
I'LL NEVER LET YOU HURT US AGAIN!
THIS IS MY REAL FAMILY.

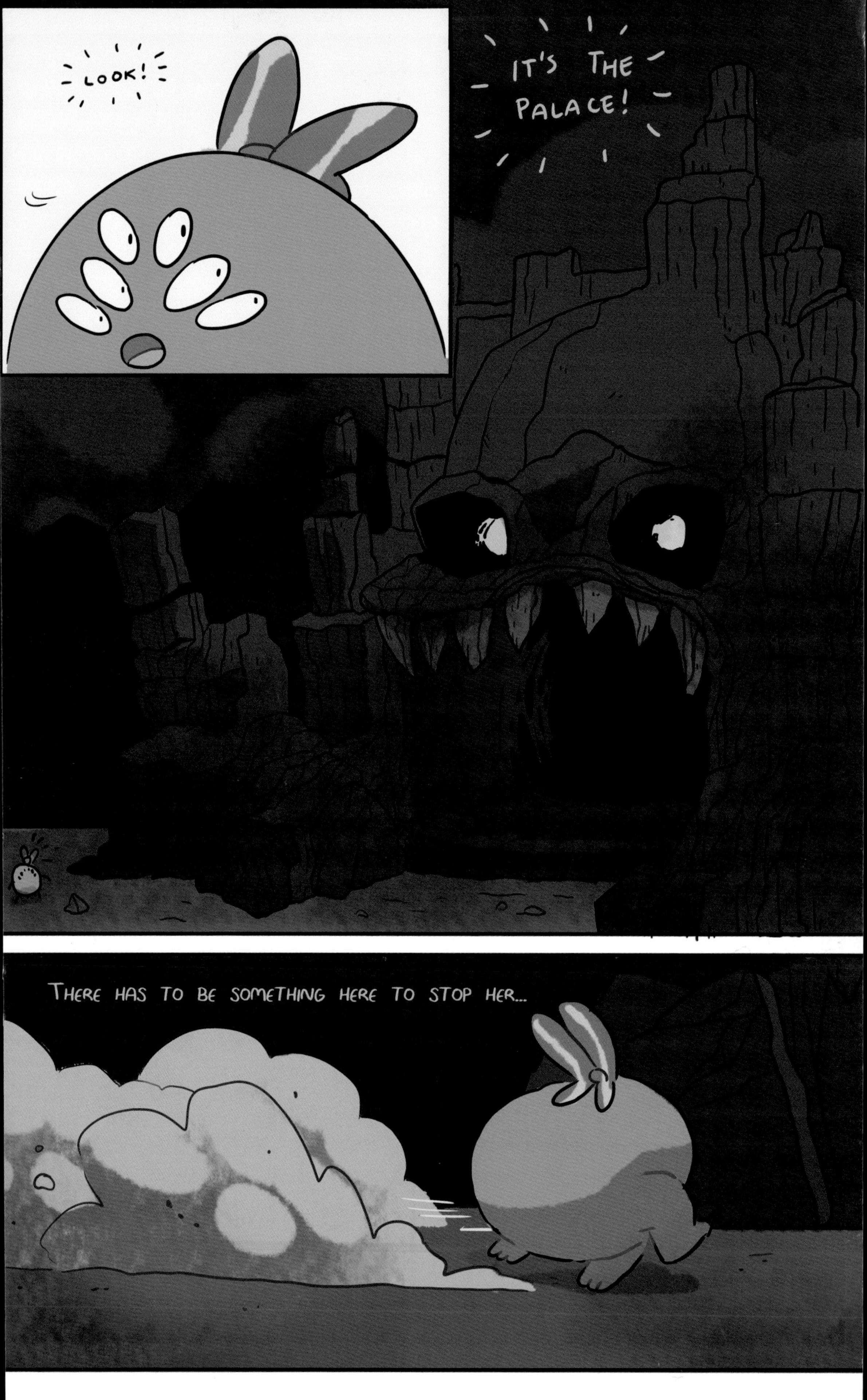
LOOK!
IT'S THE PALACE!
THERE HAS TO BE SOMETHING HERE TO STOP HER...

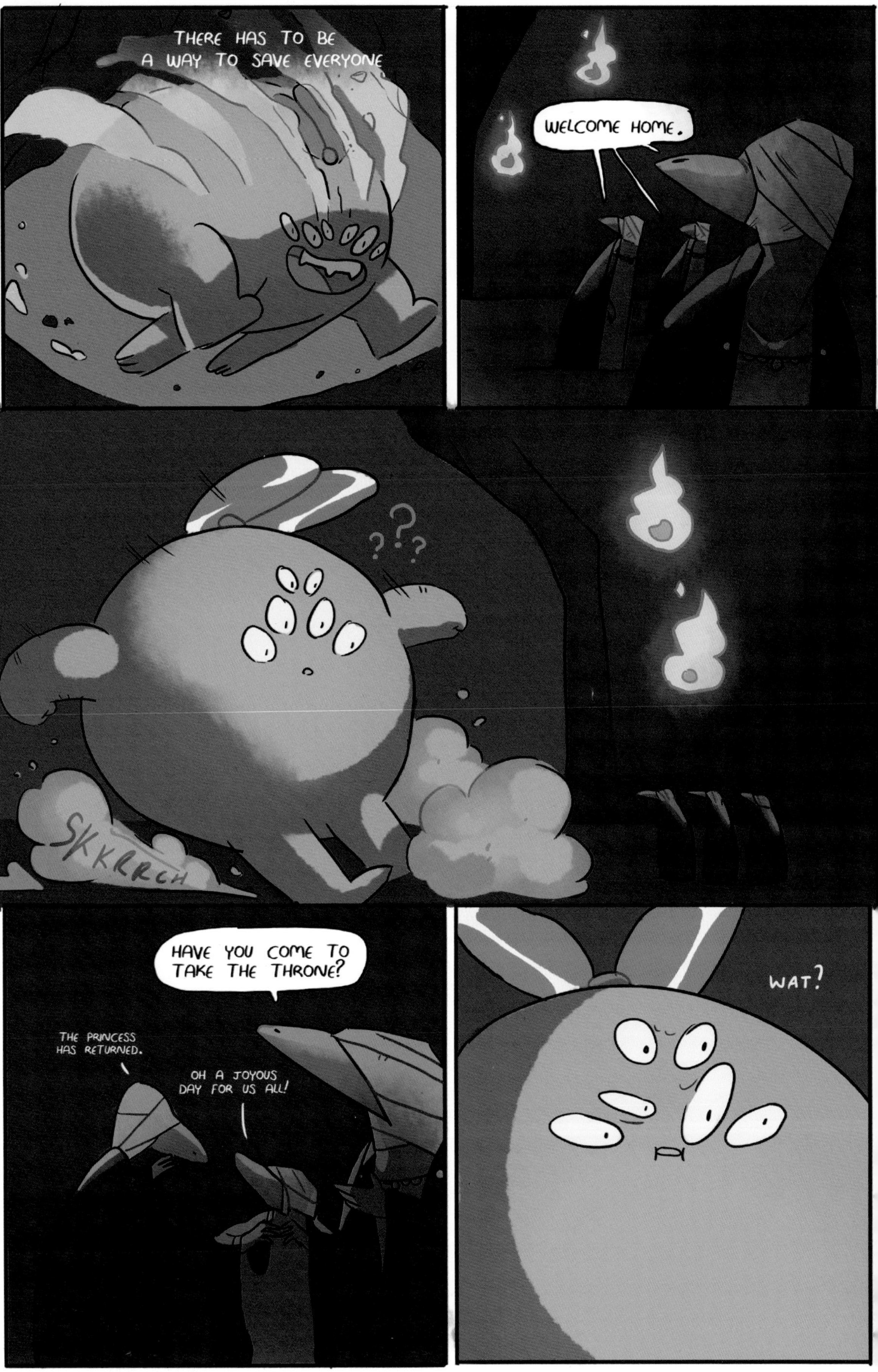
THERE HAS TO BE A WAY TO SAVE EVERYONE
WELCOME HOME.
??
SKKRRCH
HAVE YOU COME TO TAKE THE THRONE?
THE PRINCESS HAS RETURNED.
OH A JOYOUS DAY FOR US ALL!
WAT?

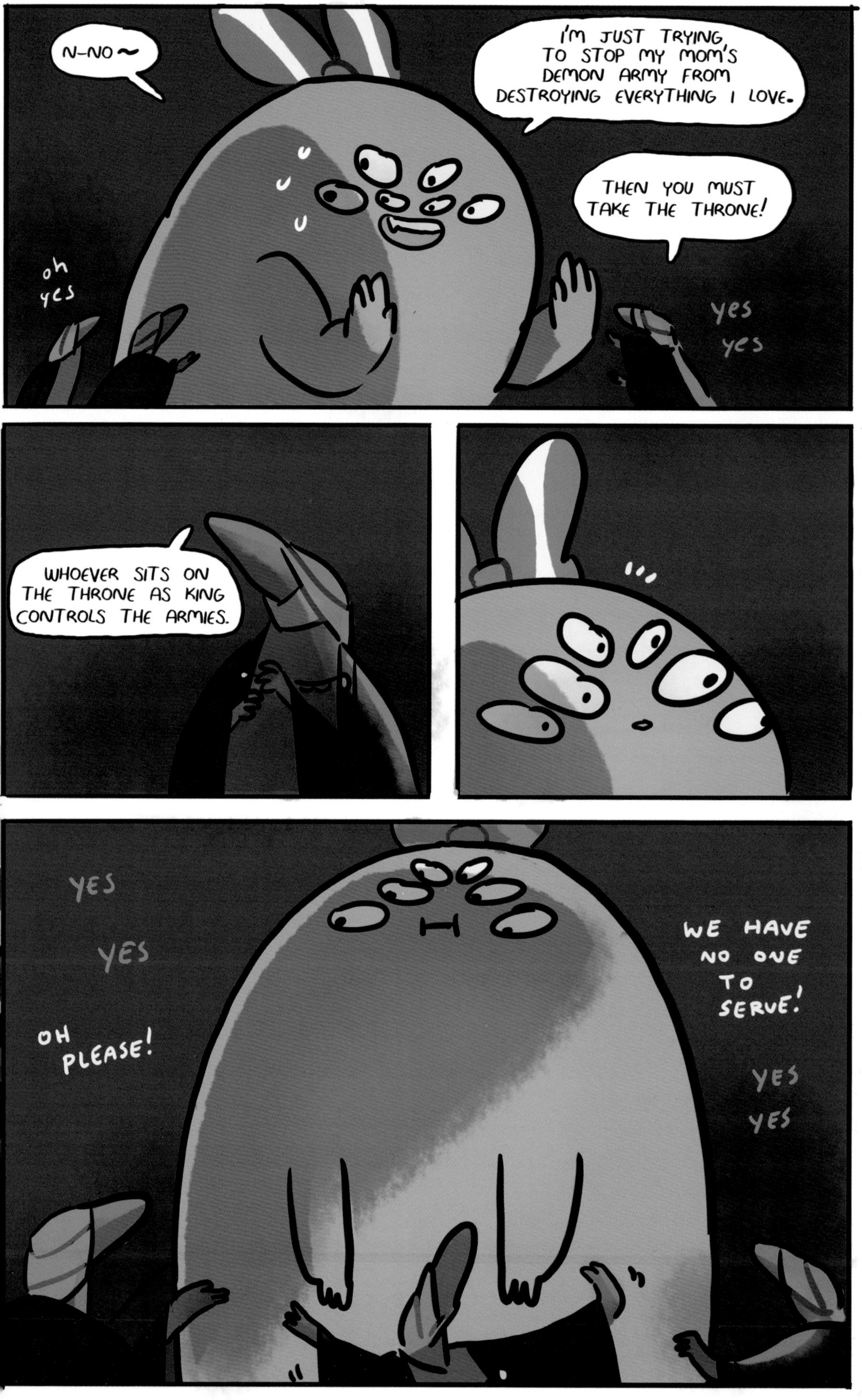
N-NO~
I'M JUST TRYING TO STOP MY MOM'S DEMON ARMY FROM DESTROYING EVERYTHING I LOVE.
THEN YOU MUST TAKE THE THRONE!
oh yes
yes yes
WHOEVER SITS ON THE THRONE AS KING CONTROLS THE ARMIES.
YES
YES
OH PLEASE!
WE HAVE NO ONE TO SERVE!
YES
YES

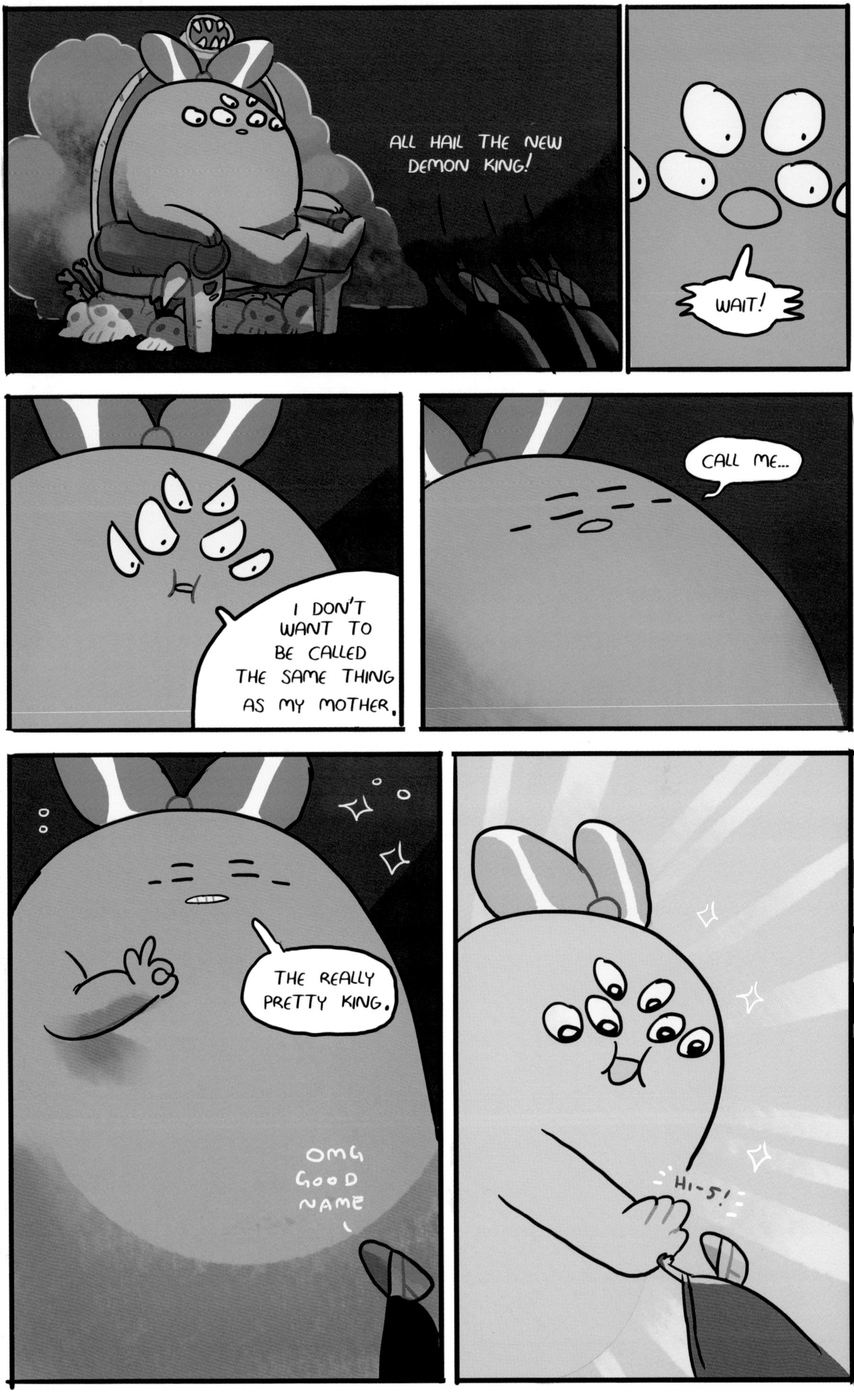
ALL HAIL THE NEW DEMON KING!
WAIT!
I DON'T WANT TO BE CALLED THE SAME THING AS MY MOTHER.
CALL ME...
THE REALLY PRETTY KING.
OMG GOOD NAME
HI-5!

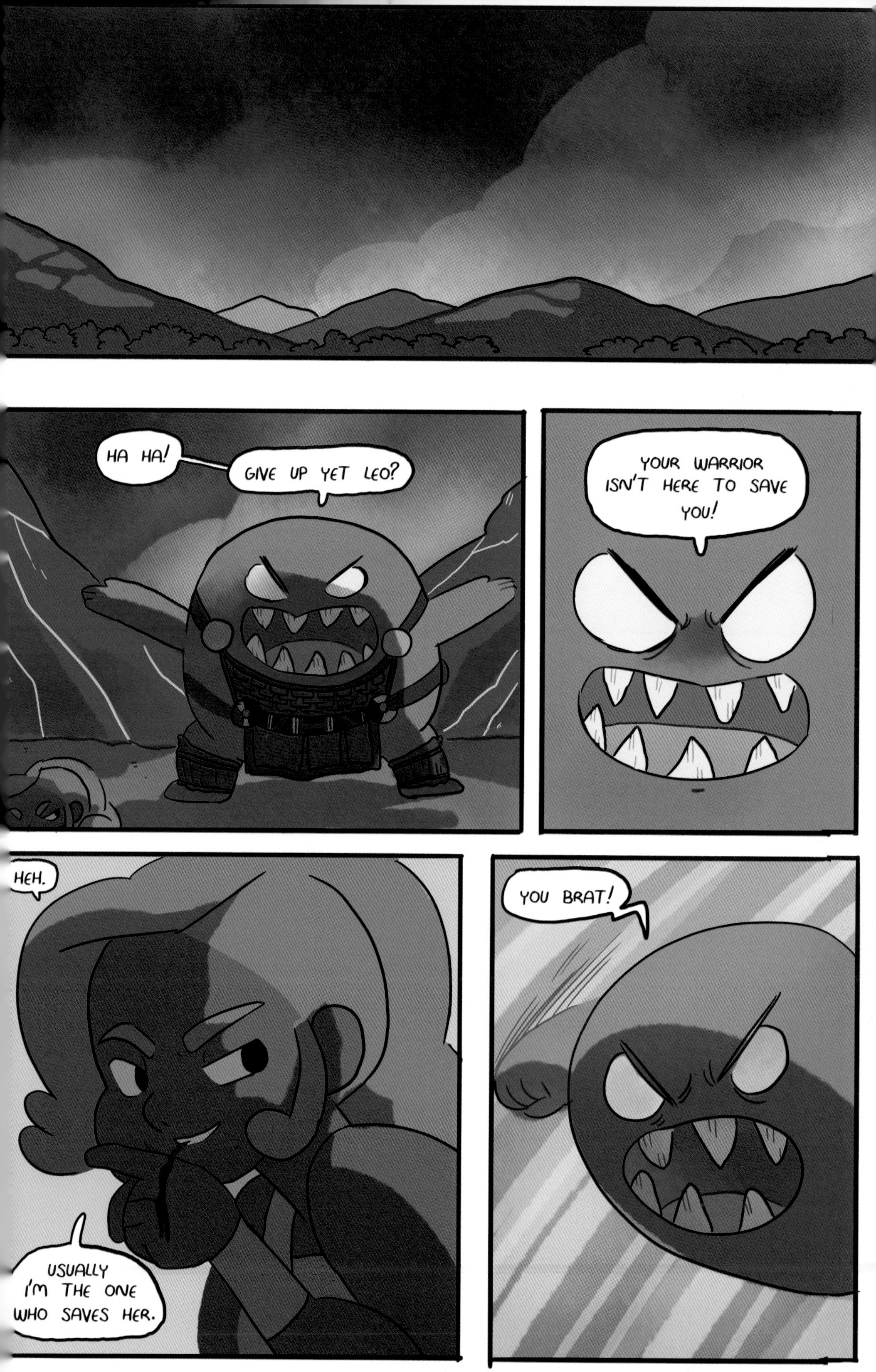
HA HA!
GIVE UP YET LEO?
YOUR WARRIOR ISN'T HERE TO SAVE YOU!
HEH.
USUALLY I'M THE ONE WHO SAVES HER.
YOU BRAT!

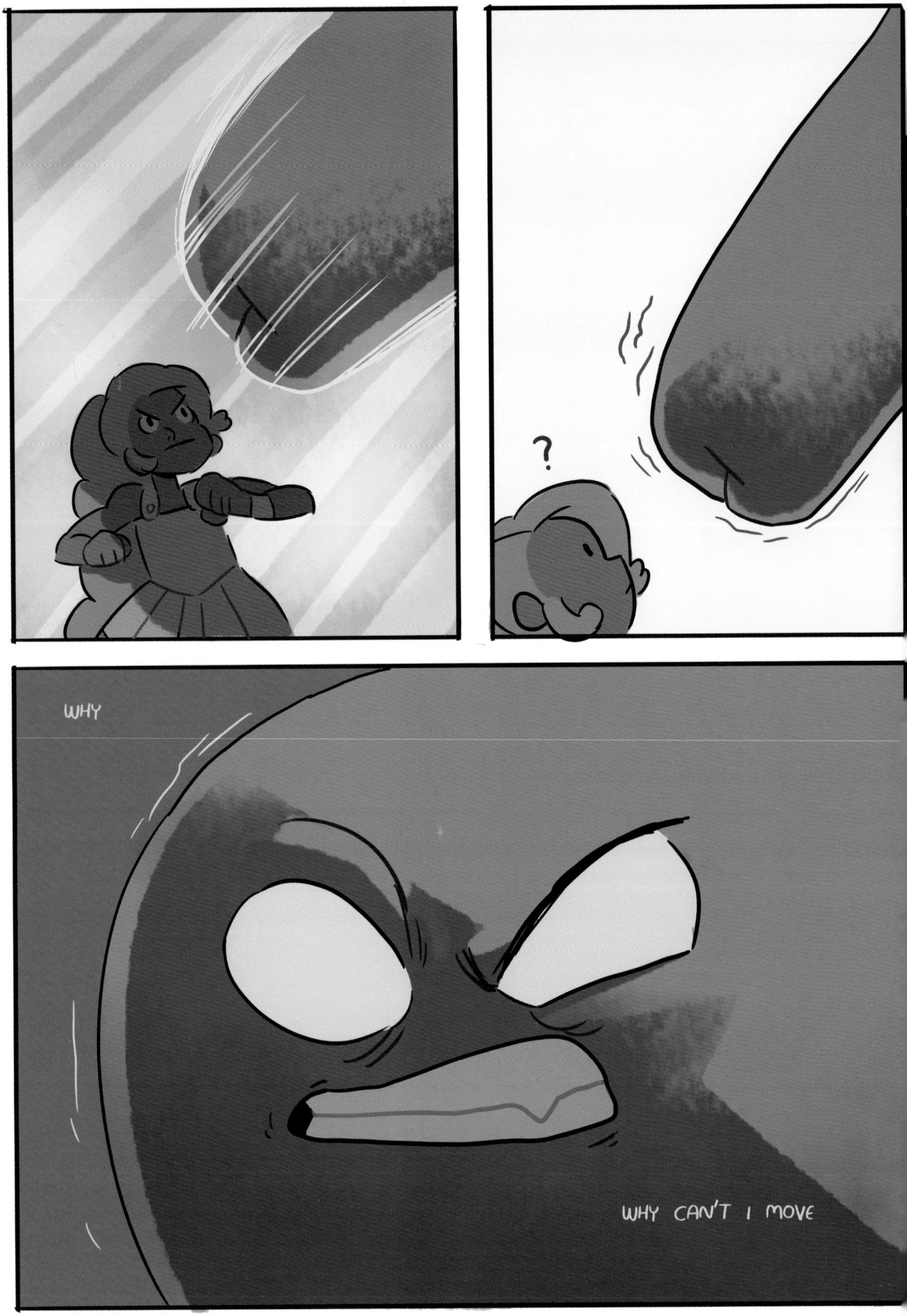
?
WHY
WHY CAN'T I MOVE

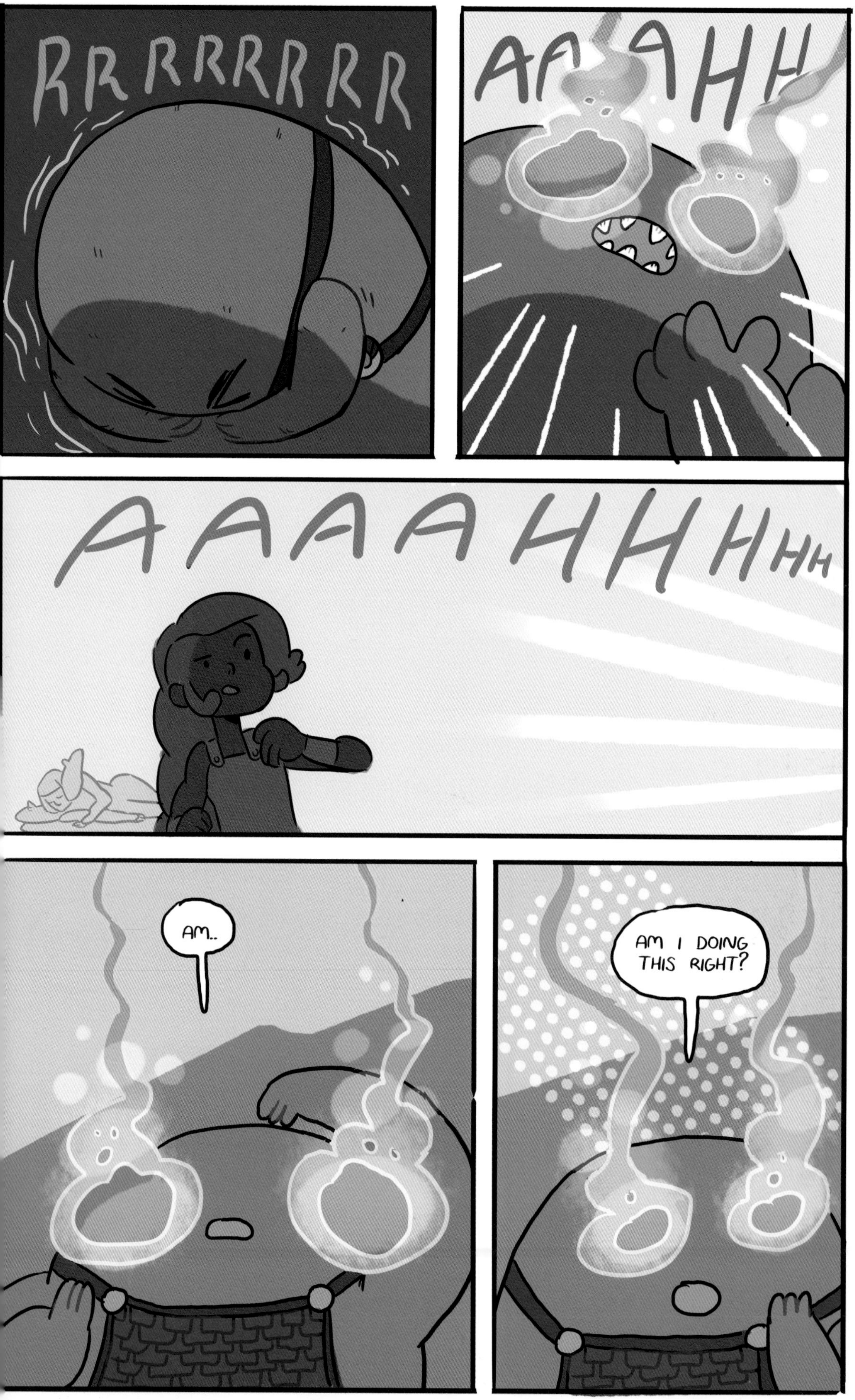
RRRRRRRRR
AAAAHH
AAAAHHHHH
AM..
AM I DOING THIS RIGHT?

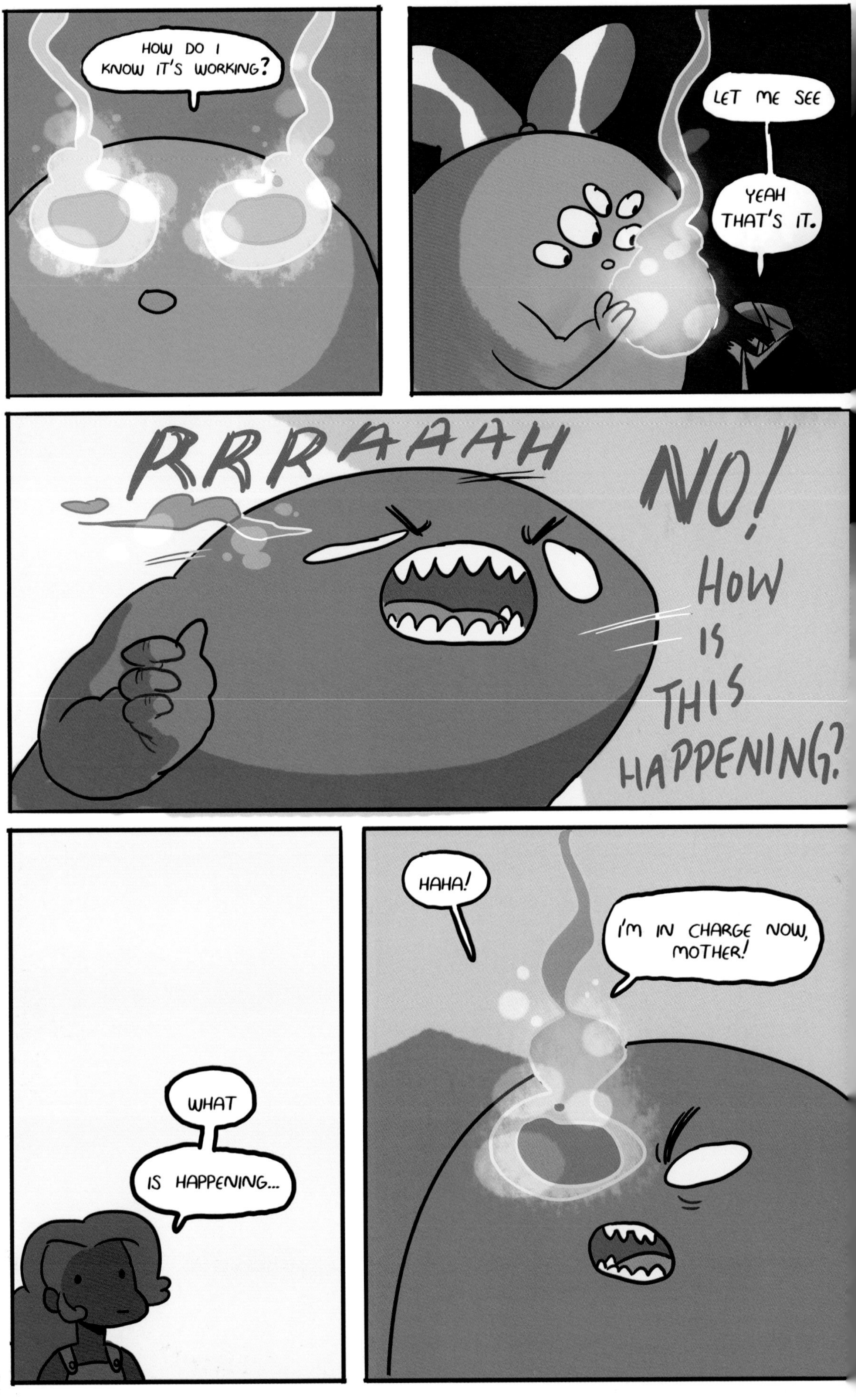
HOW DO I KNOW IT'S WORKING?
LET ME SEE
YEAH THAT'S IT.
RRRAAAH
NO!
HOW IS THIS HAPPENING?
WHAT
IS HAPPENING...
HAHA!
I'M IN CHARGE NOW, MOTHER!

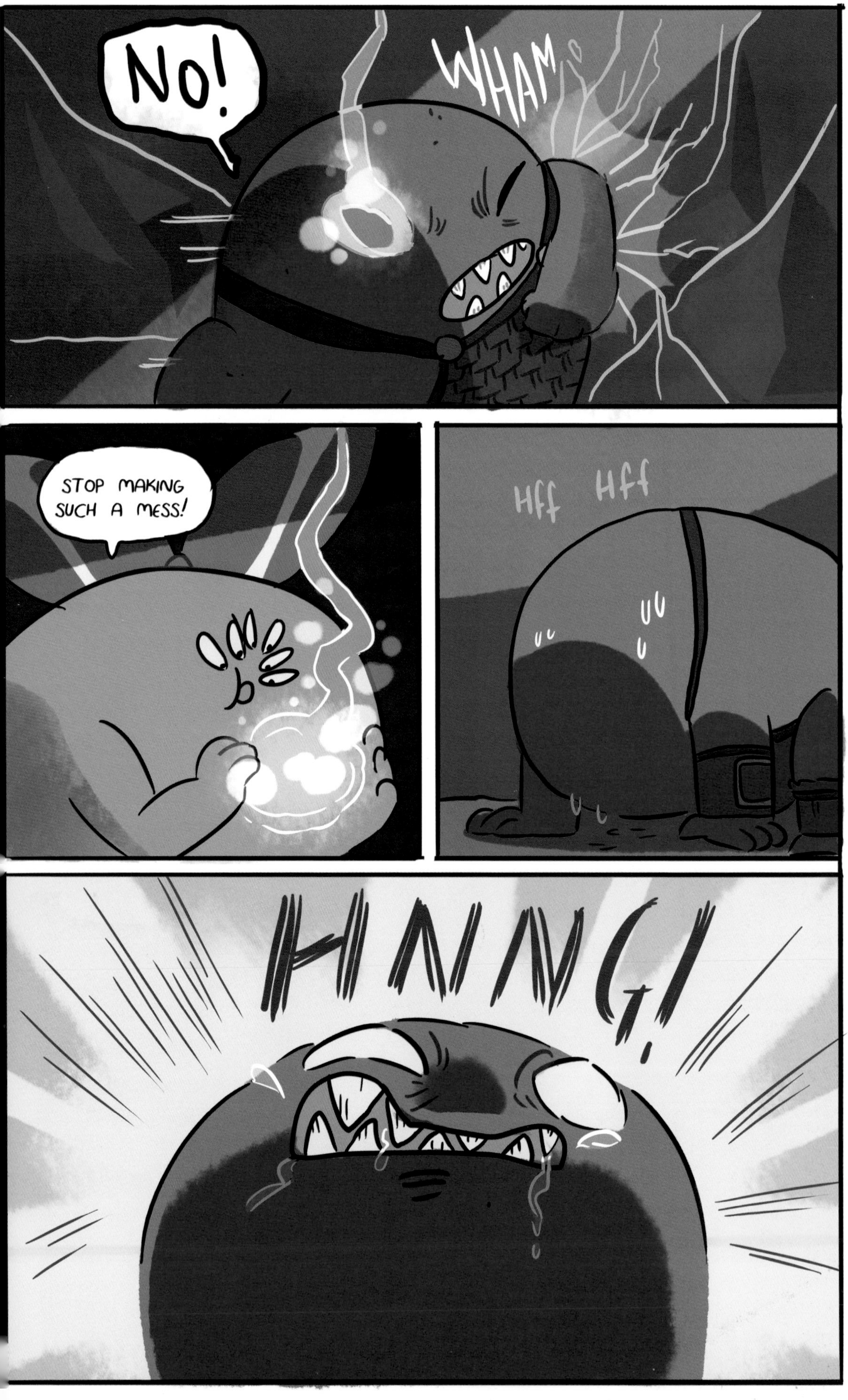
No!
WHAM
STOP MAKING SUCH A MESS!
Hff Hff
HNNG!

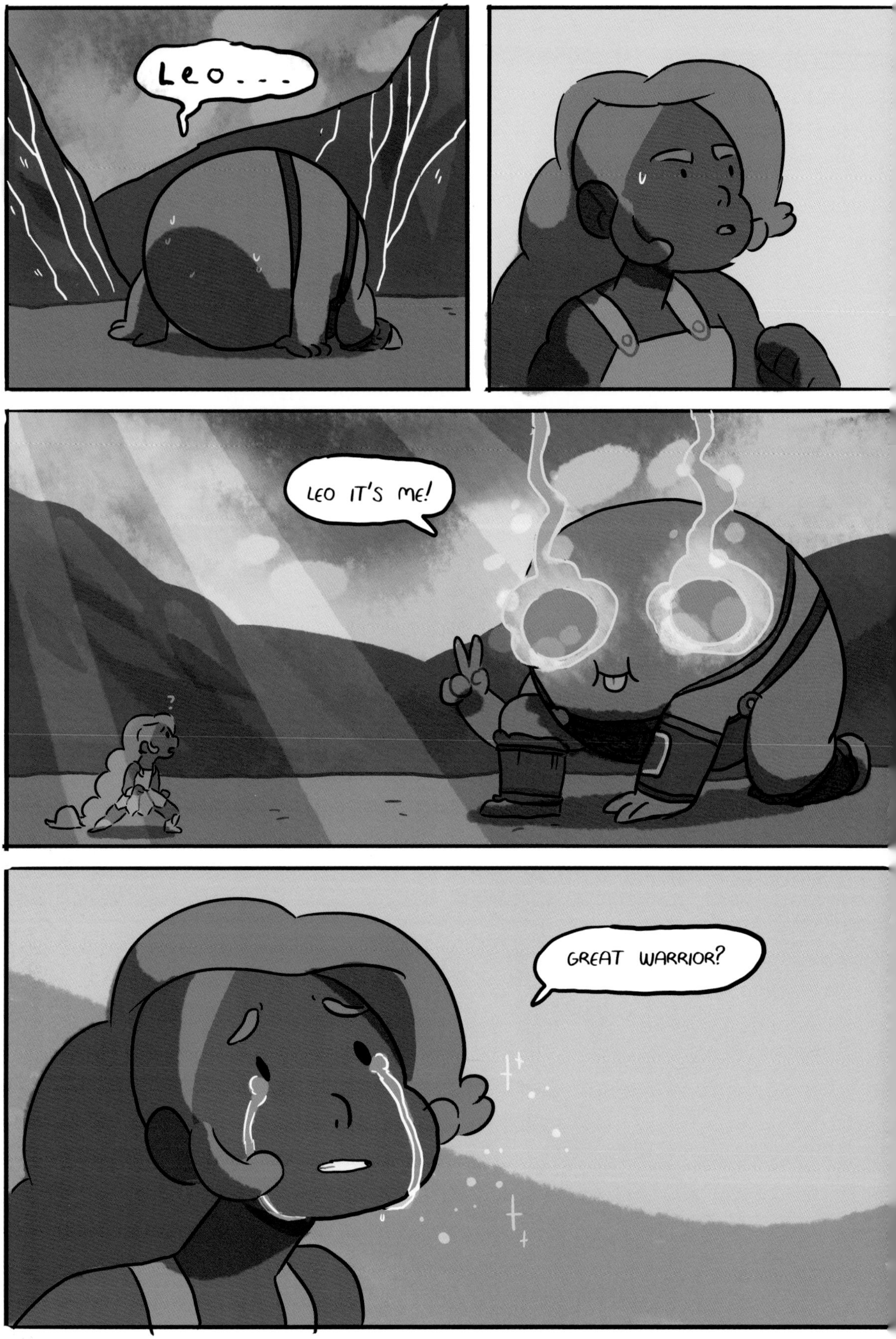
Leo...
LEO IT'S ME!
GREAT WARRIOR?

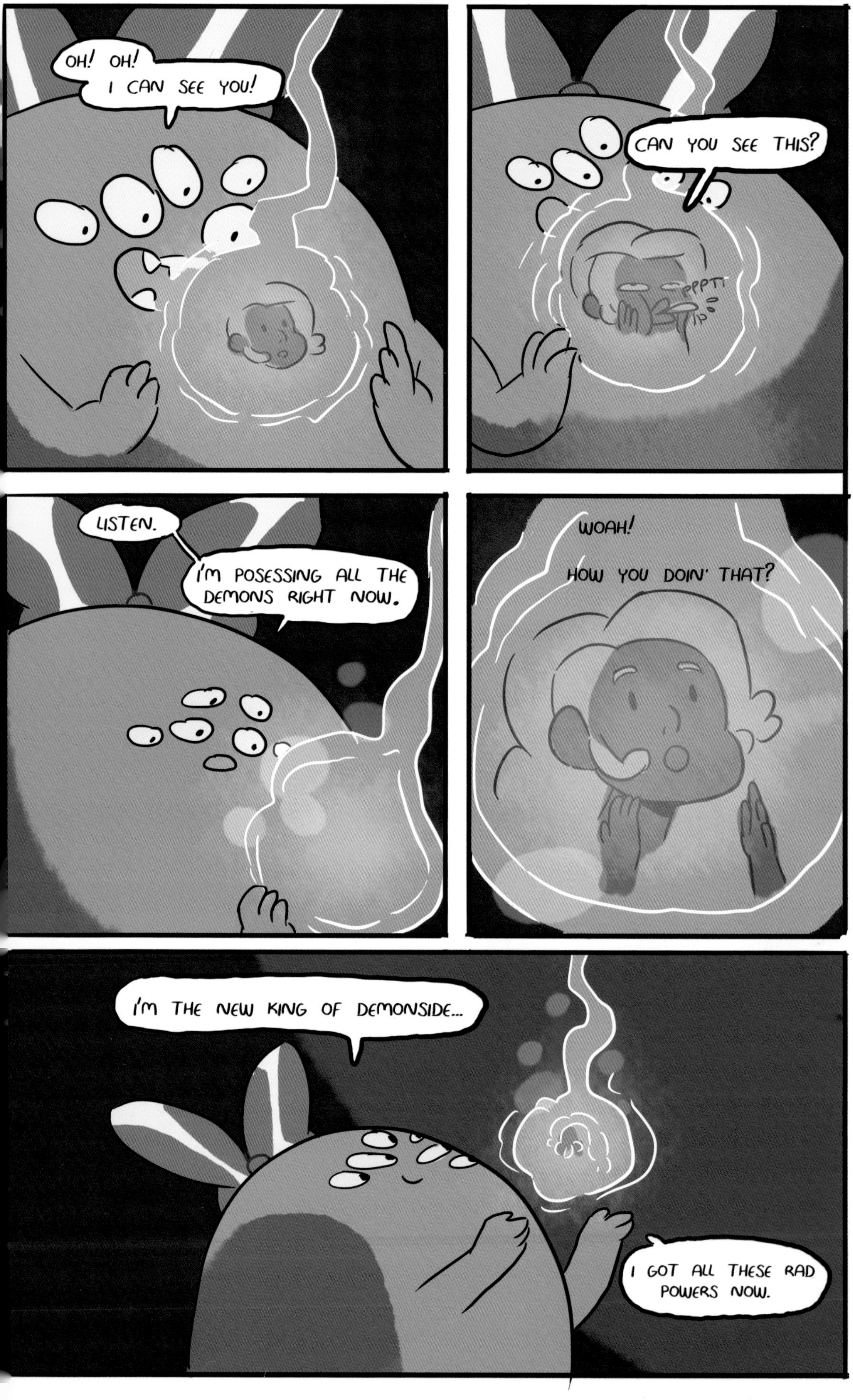
OH! OH!
I CAN SEE YOU!
CAN YOU SEE THIS?
PPPTT
LISTEN.
I'M POSESSING ALL THE DEMONS RIGHT NOW.
WOAH!
HOW YOU DOIN' THAT?
I'M THE NEW KING OF DEMONSIDE...
I GOT ALL THESE RAD POWERS NOW.

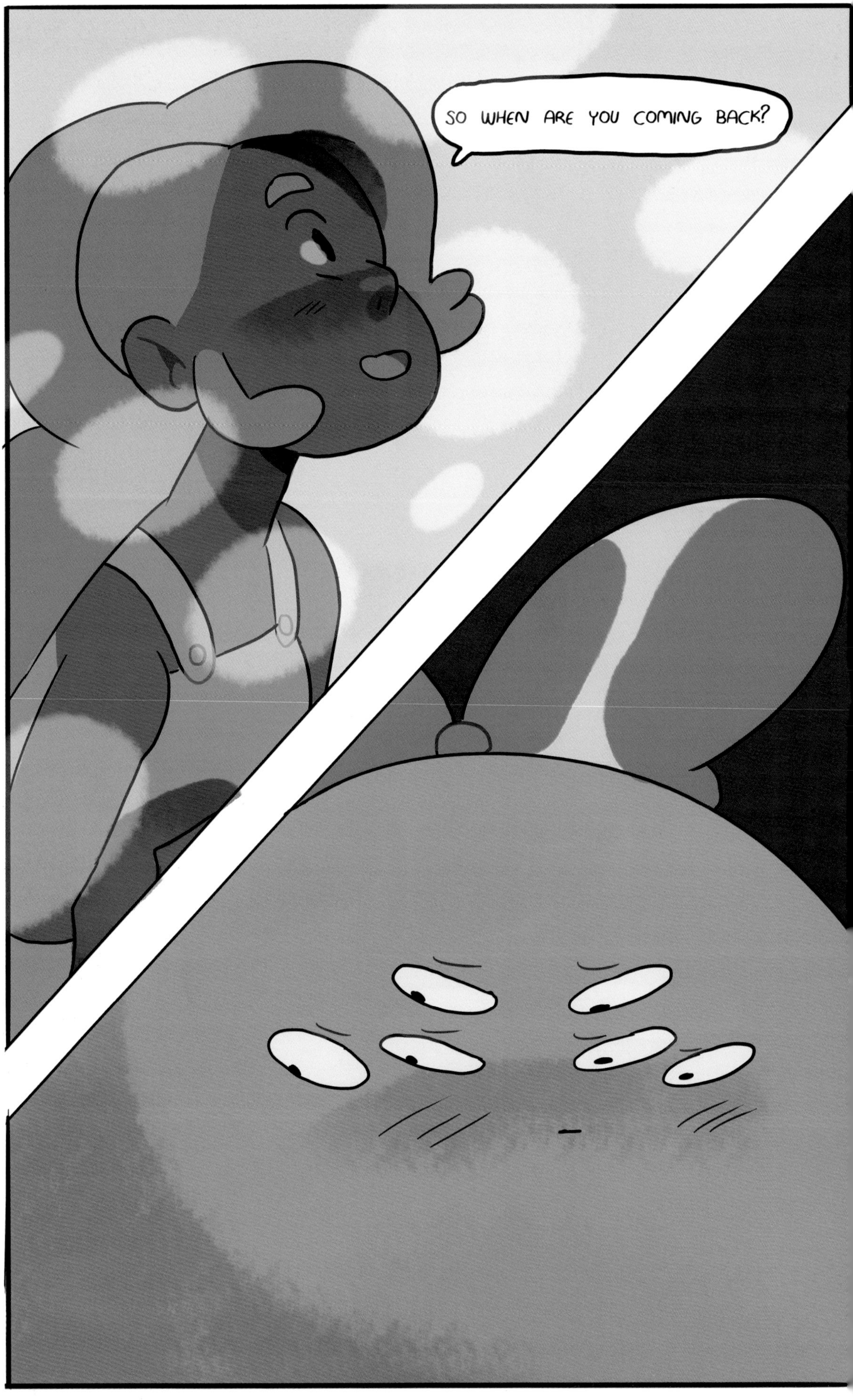
SO WHEN ARE YOU COMING BACK?

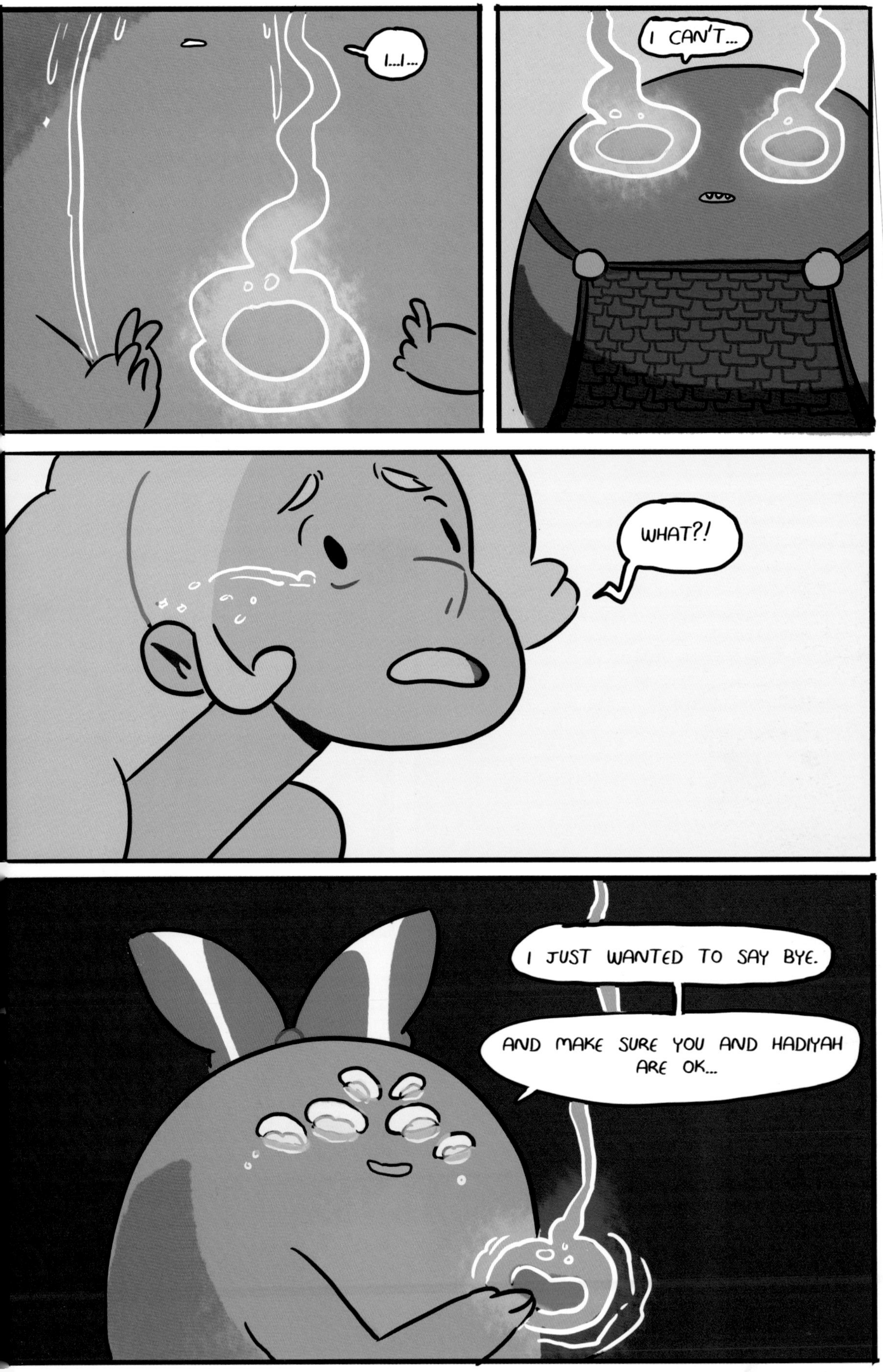
I...I...
I CAN'T...
WHAT?!
I JUST WANTED TO SAY BYE.
AND MAKE SURE YOU AND HADIYAH ARE OK...

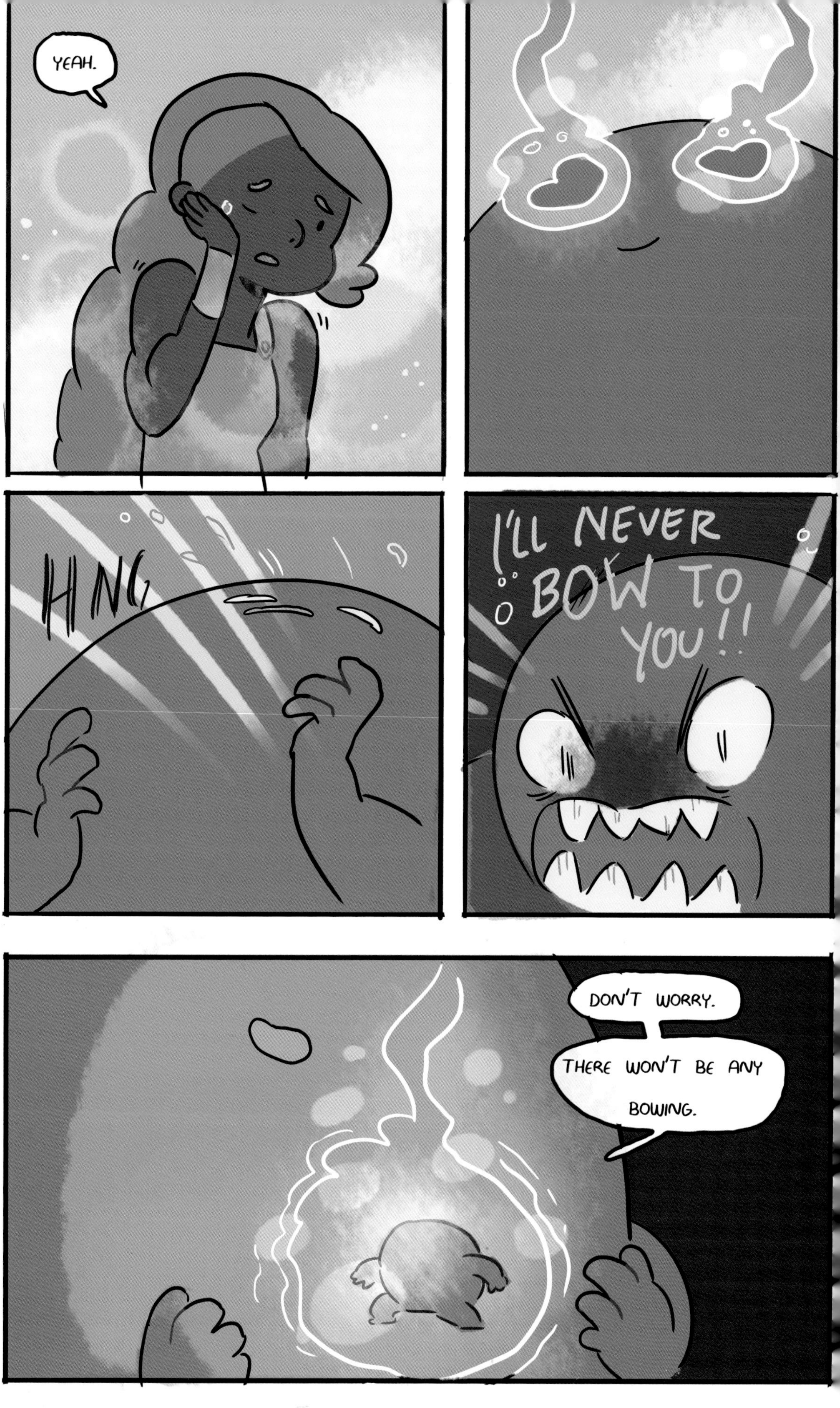
YEAH.
HNG
I'LL NEVER BOW TO YOU!!
DON'T WORRY.
THERE WON'T BE ANY BOWING.

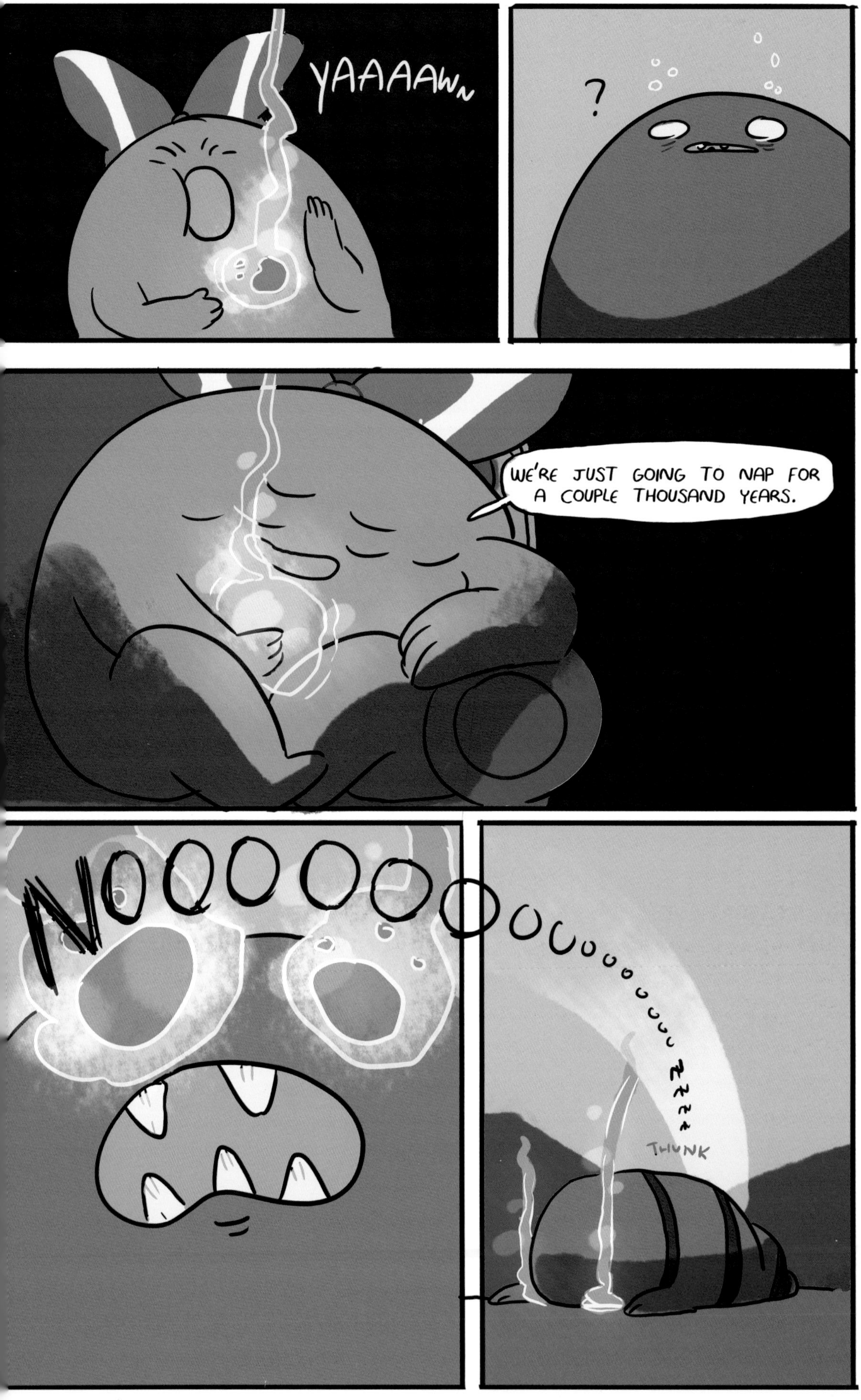
YAAAAWN
?
WE'RE JUST GOING TO NAP FOR A COUPLE THOUSAND YEARS.
NOOOOOOOOooooooooo
THUNK

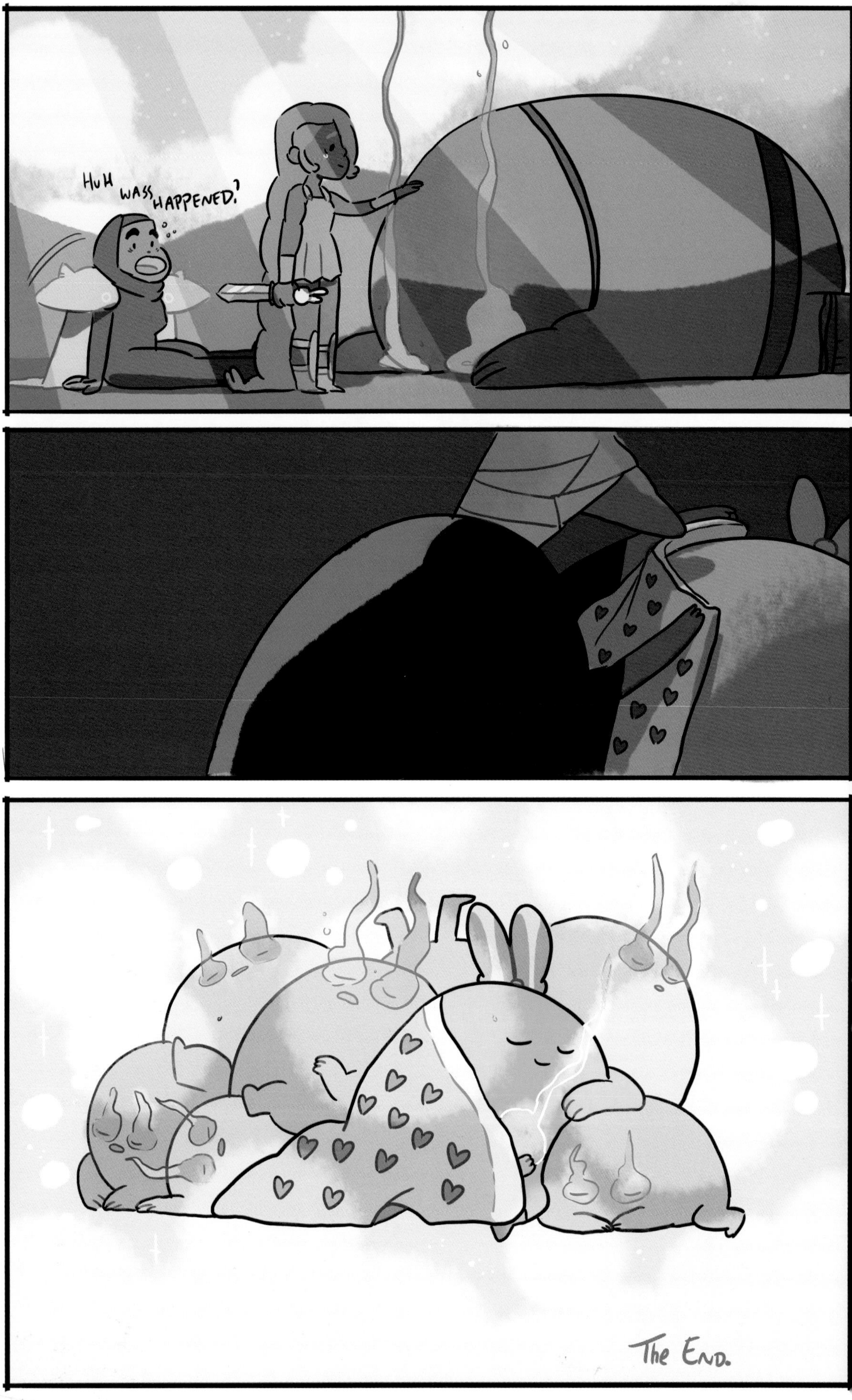
HUH WASS HAPPENED?
The End.

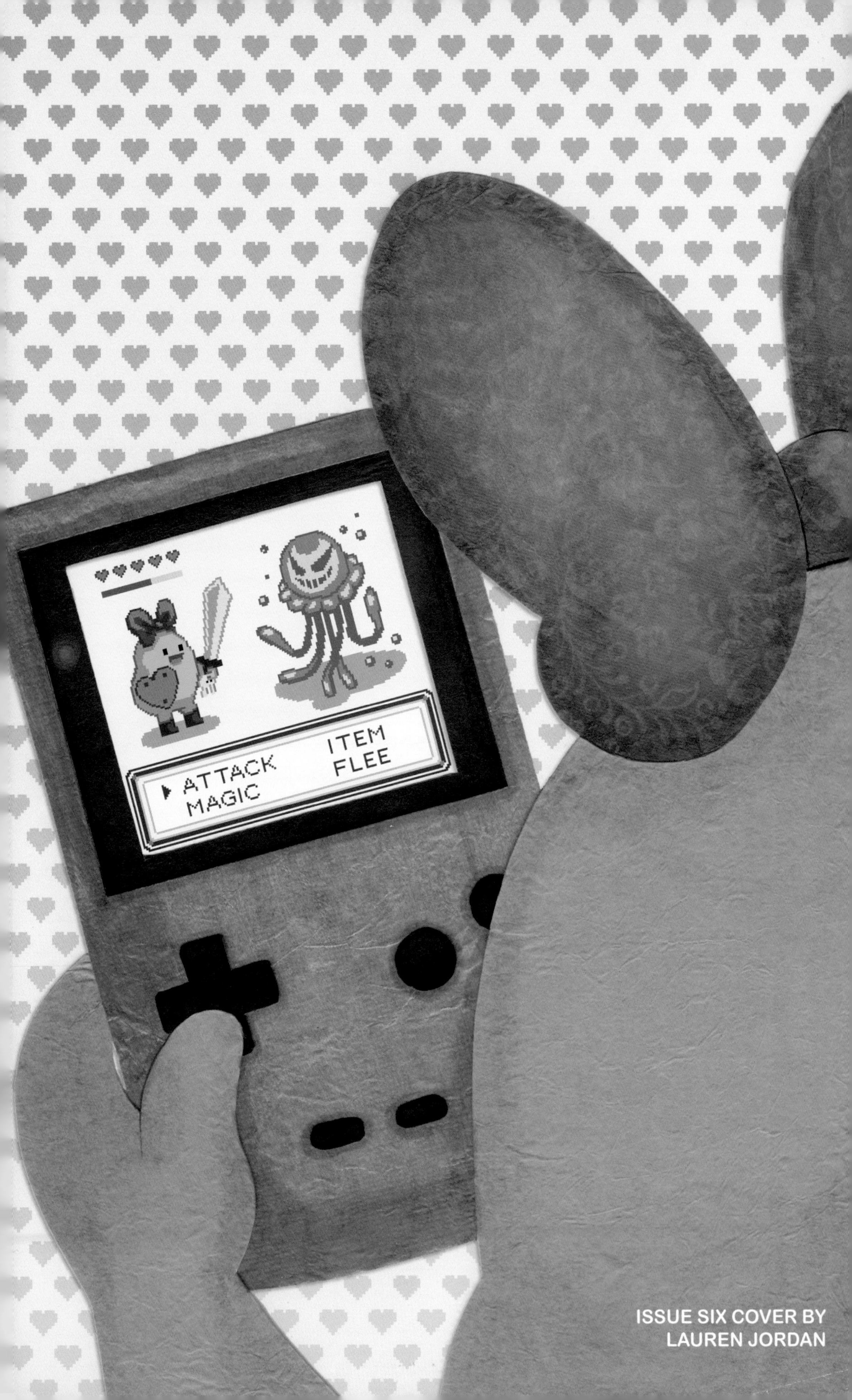
ATTACK
MAGIC
ITEM
FLEE

ISSUE SIX COVER BY
LAUREN JORDAN

ISSUE ONE BOOM! TEN YEAR COVER BY
SHELLI PAROLINE & BRADEN LAMB

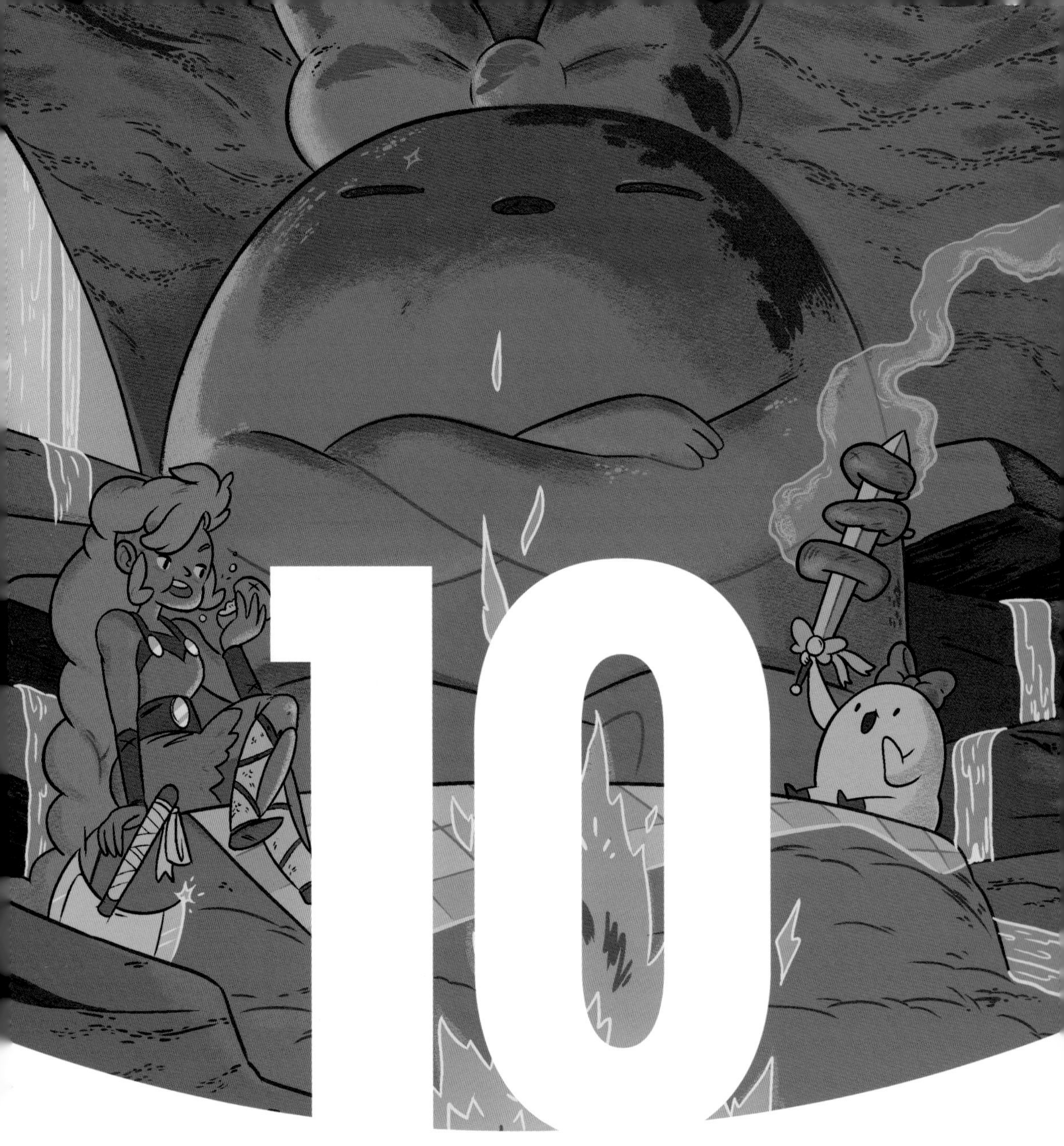

10

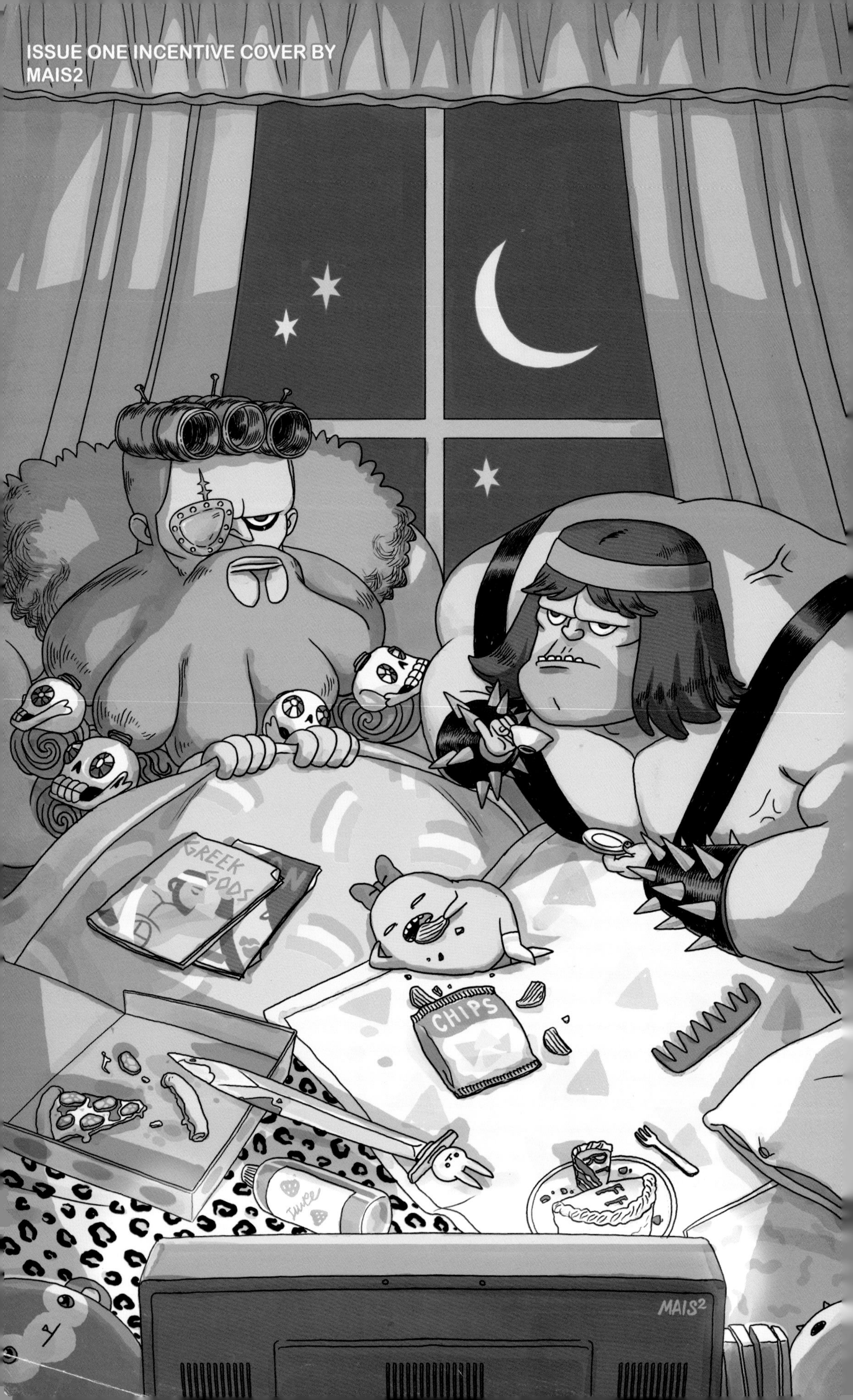
GREEK GODS
CHIPS
MAIS²

ISSUE ONE INCENTIVE COVER BY
MAIS2

Help Us! Great Warrior Classics

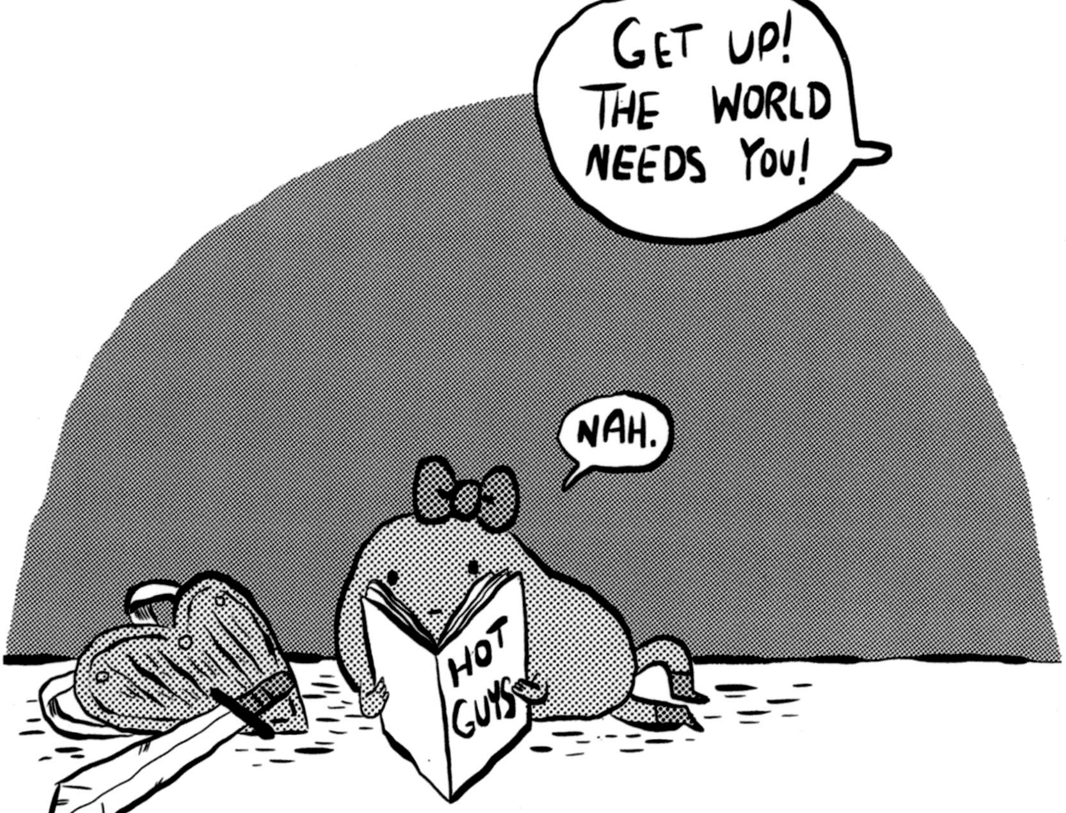
GET UP! THE WORLD NEEDS YOU!
NAH.
HOT GUYS

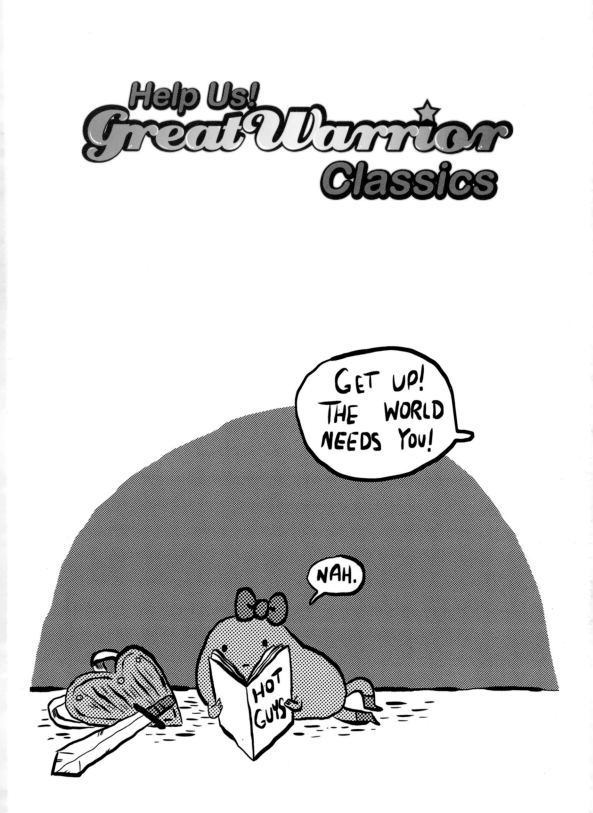

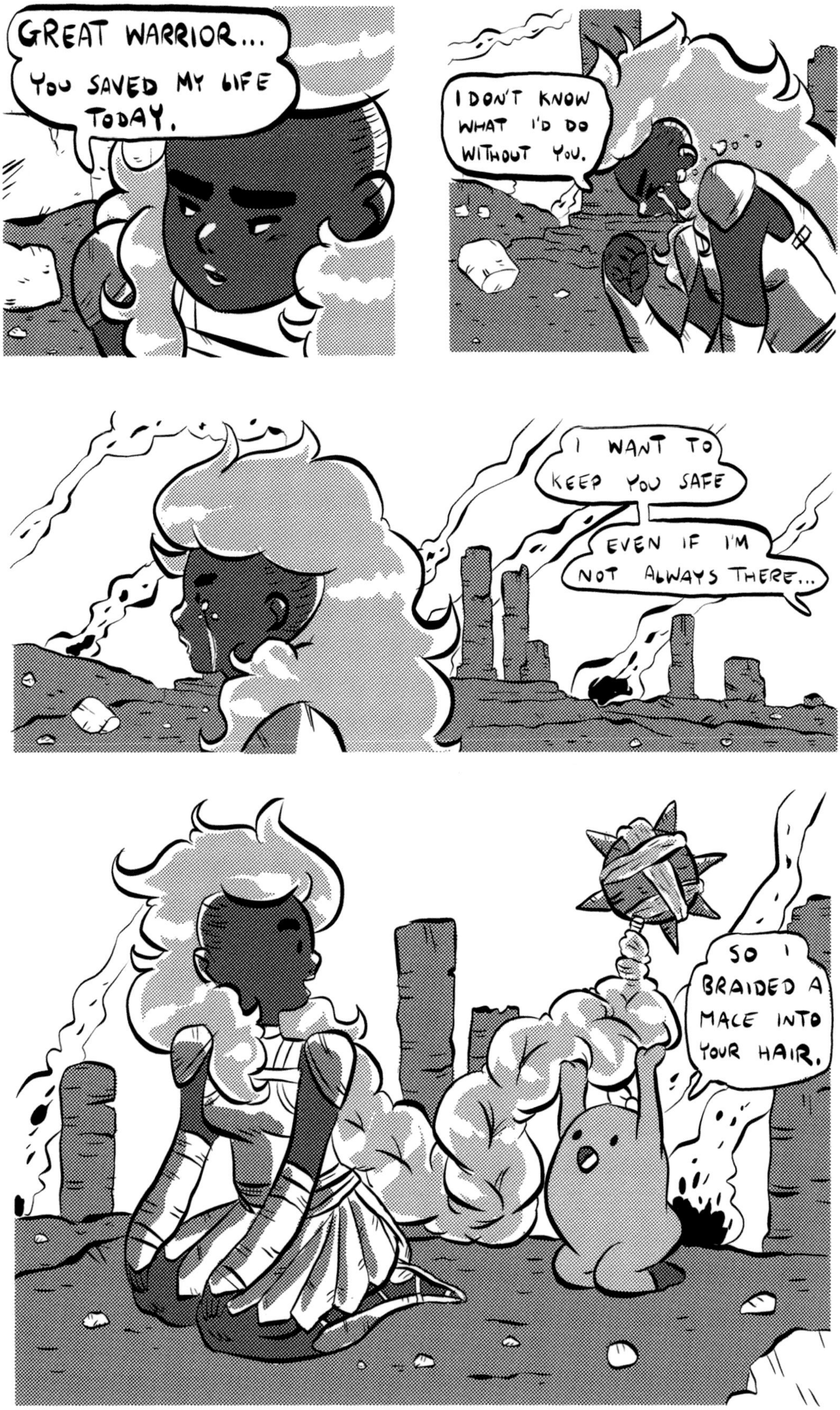
GREAT WARRIOR...
YOU SAVED MY LIFE TODAY.
I DON'T KNOW WHAT I'D DO WITHOUT YOU.
I WANT TO KEEP YOU SAFE
EVEN IF I'M NOT ALWAYS THERE...
SO I BRAIDED A MACE INTO YOUR HAIR.

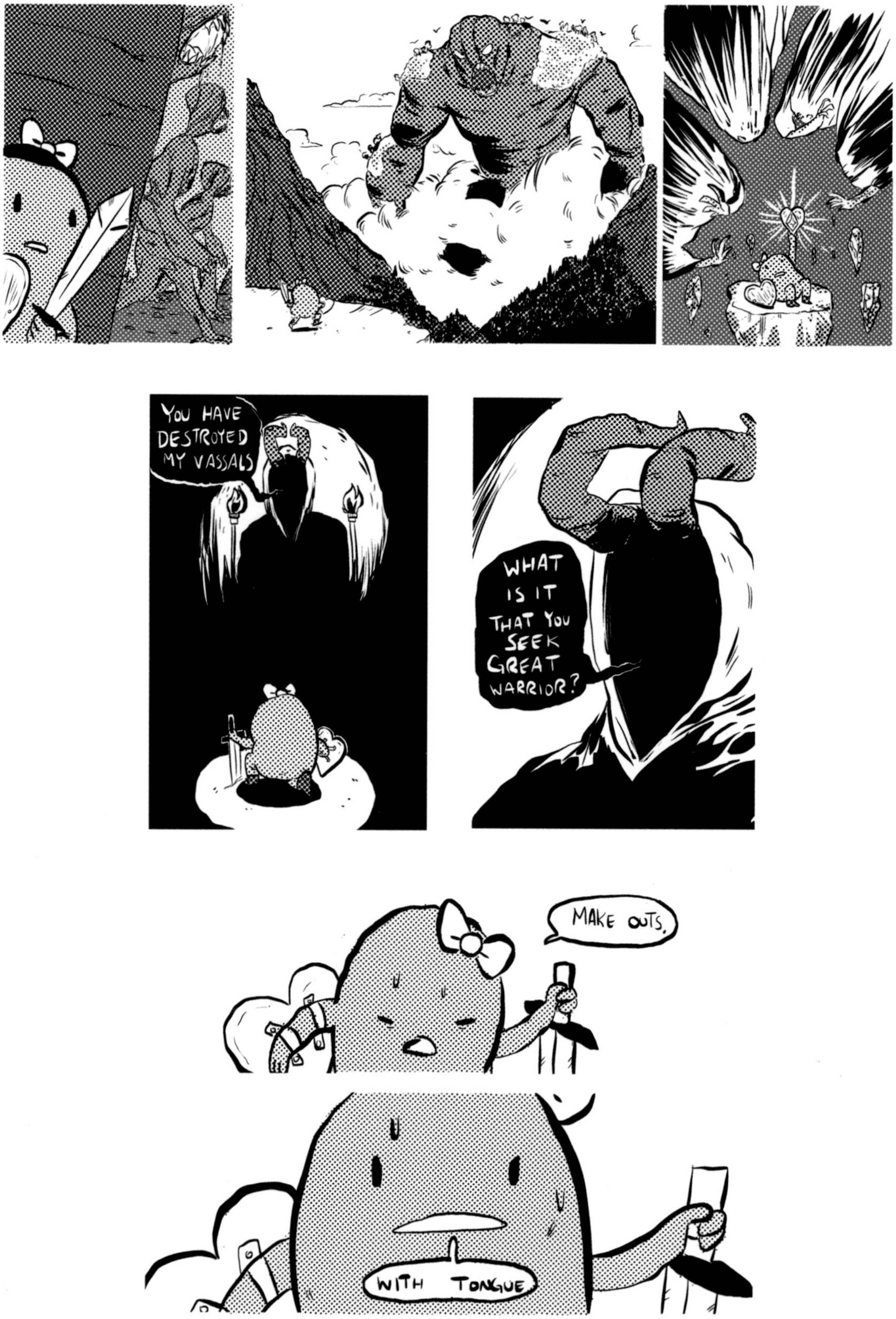

YOU HAVE DESTROYED MY VASSALS
WHAT IS IT THAT YOU SEEK GREAT WARRIOR?
MAKE OUTS.
WITH TONGUE

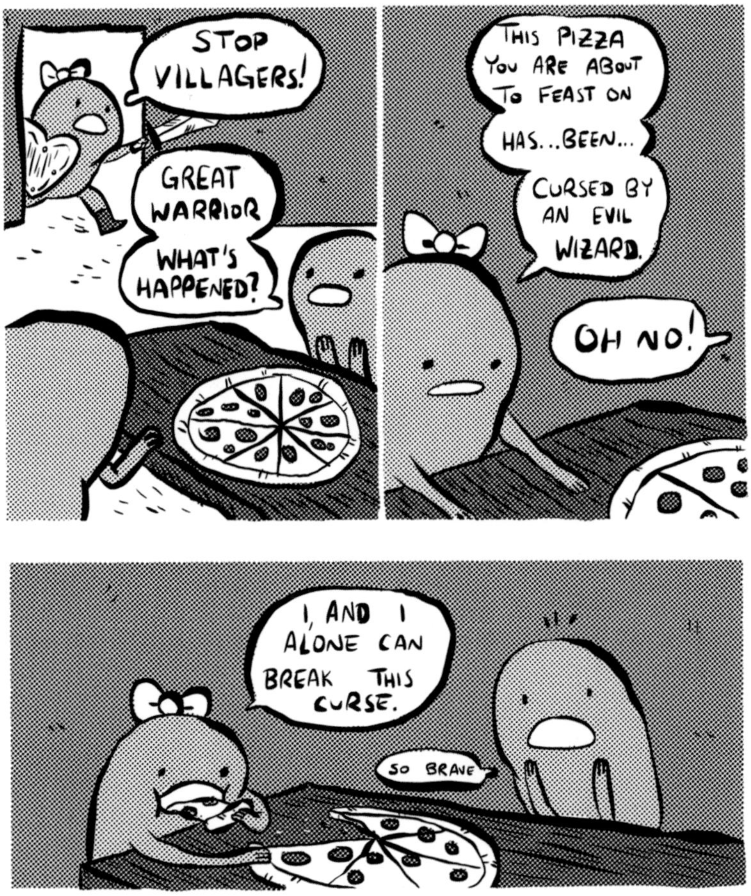
STOP VILLAGERS!
GREAT WARRIOR
WHAT'S HAPPENED?
THIS PIZZA YOU ARE ABOUT TO FEAST ON
HAS...BEEN...
CURSED BY AN EVIL WIZARD.
OH NO!
I, AND I ALONE CAN BREAK THIS CURSE.
SO BRAVE

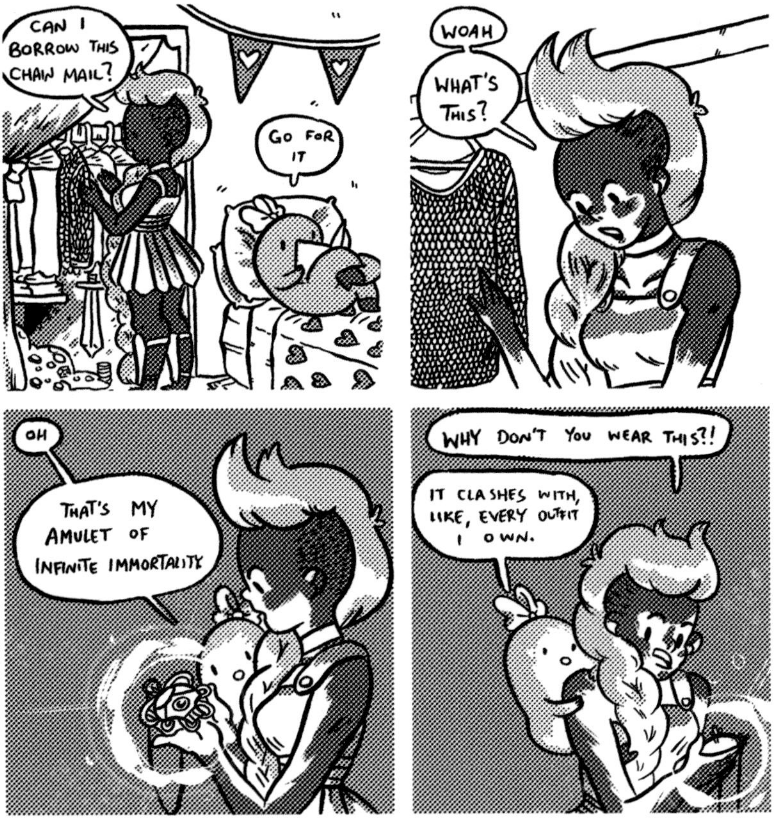
CAN I BORROW THIS CHAIN MAIL?
GO FOR IT
WOAH
WHAT'S THIS?
OH
THAT'S MY AMULET OF INFINITE IMMORTALITY.
WHY DON'T YOU WEAR THIS?!
IT CLASHES WITH, LIKE, EVERY OUTFIT I OWN.

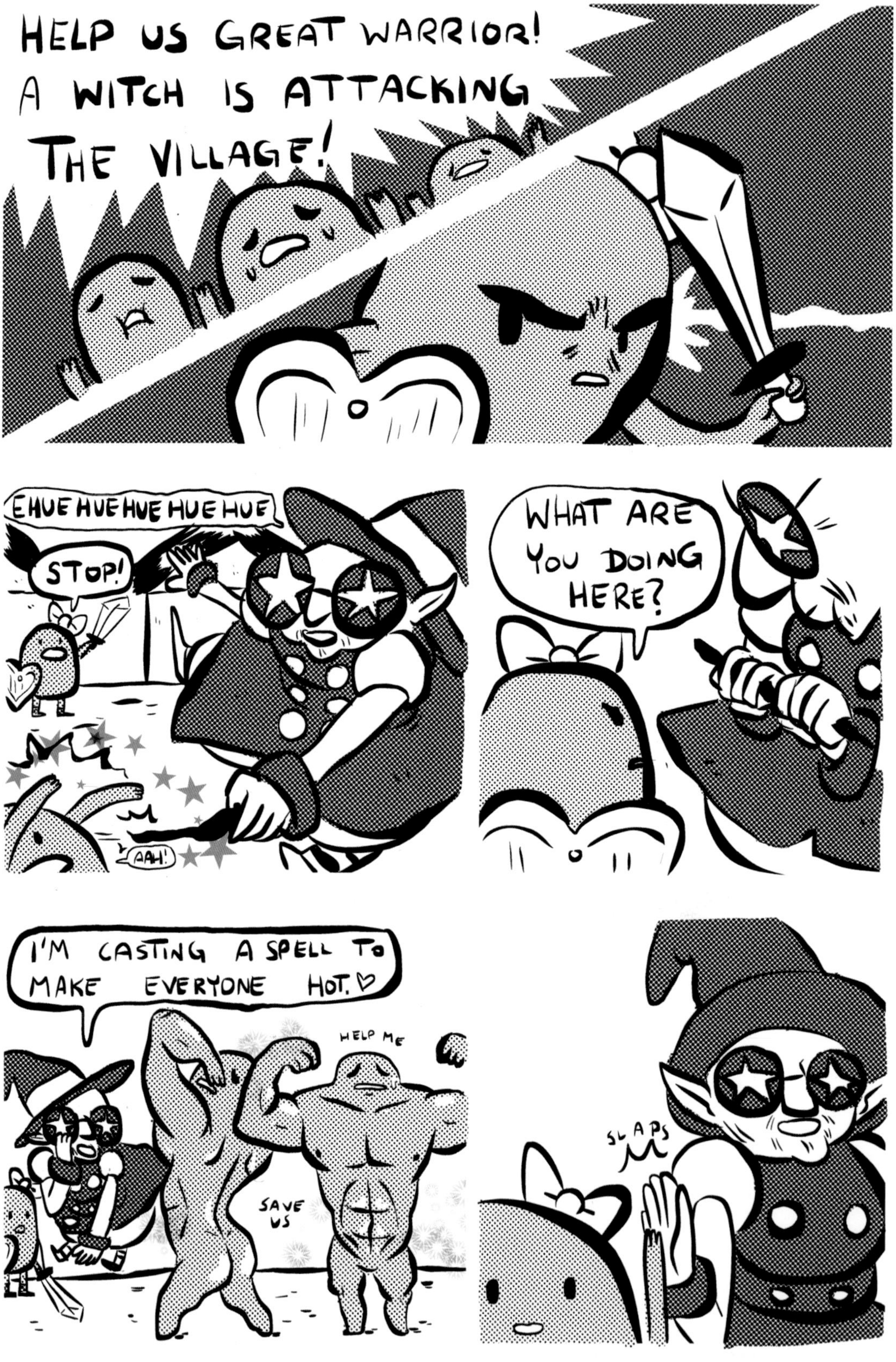
HELP US GREAT WARRIOR! A WITCH IS ATTACKING THE VILLAGE!
EHUEHUEHUEHUEHUE
STOP!
AAH!
WHAT ARE YOU DOING HERE?
I'M CASTING A SPELL TO MAKE EVERYONE HOT.♡
HELP ME
SAVE US
SLAPS

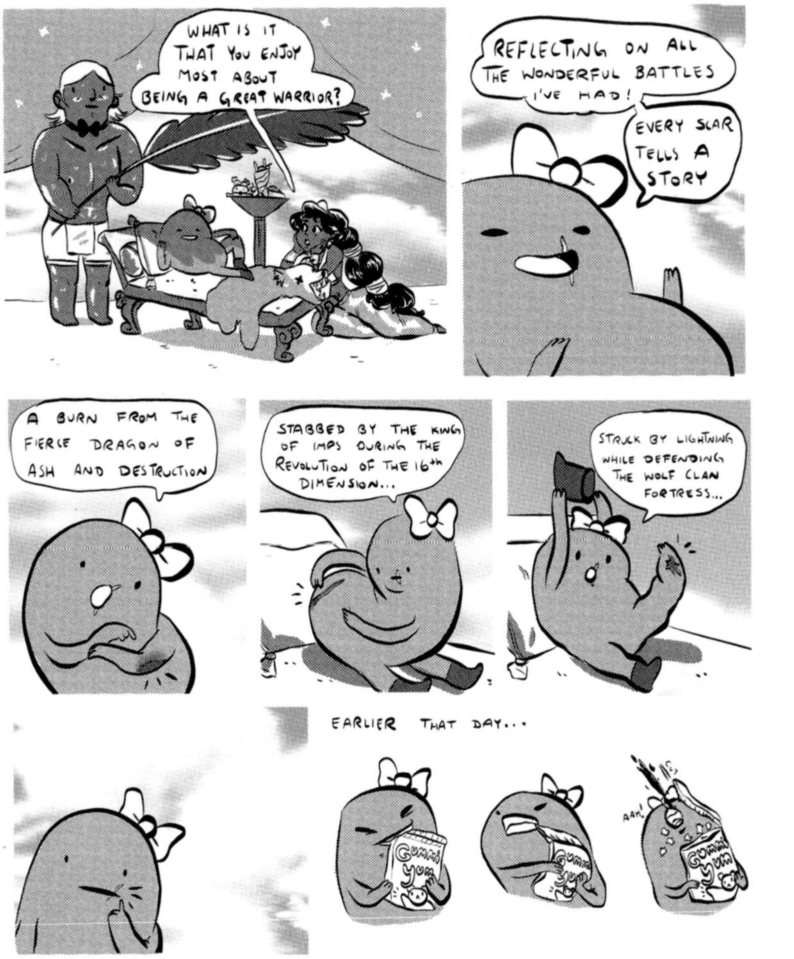
WHAT IS IT THAT YOU ENJOY MOST ABOUT BEING A GREAT WARRIOR?
REFLECTING ON ALL THE WONDERFUL BATTLES I'VE HAD!
EVERY SCAR TELLS A STORY
A BURN FROM THE FIERCE DRAGON OF ASH AND DESTRUCTION
STABBED BY THE KING OF IMPS DURING THE REVOLUTION OF THE 16th DIMENSION...
STRUCK BY LIGHTNING WHILE DEFENDING THE WOLF CLAN FORTRESS...
EARLIER THAT DAY...
GUMMI YUM
AAH!

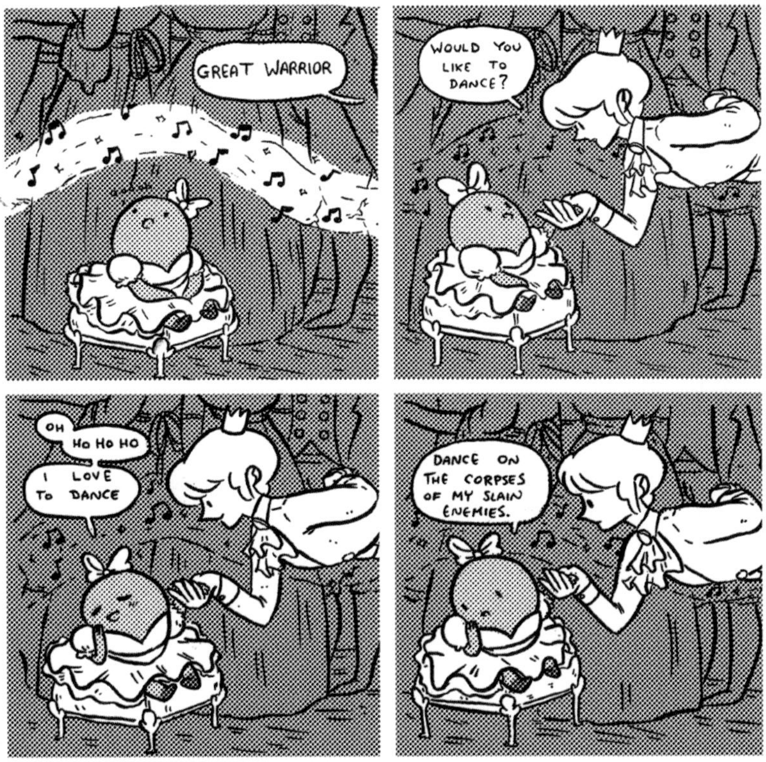
GREAT WARRIOR
WOULD YOU LIKE TO DANCE?
OH HO HO HO
I LOVE TO DANCE
DANCE ON THE CORPSES OF MY SLAIN ENEMIES.